Jo Thomas worked for many years as a reporter and producer, first for BBC Radio 5, before moving on to Radio 2's *The Steve Wright Show*. In 2013 Jo won the RNA Katie Fforde Bursary. Her debut novel, *The Oyster Catcher*, was a runaway bestseller in ebook and was awarded the 2014 RNA Joan Hessayon Award and the 2014 Festival of Romance Best Ebook Award. Her follow-up novels, *The Olive Branch*, *Late Summer in the Vineyard*, *The Honey Farm on the Hill* and *Sunset over the Cherry Orchard* are also highly acclaimed. Jo lives in the Vale of Glamorgan with her husband and three children.

You can keep in touch with Jo through her website at www.jothomasauthor.com, or via @Jo_Thomas01 on Twitter and JoThomasAuthor on Facebook.

Readers can't resist Jo Thomas's feel-good fiction:

'Warm, funny, romantic with a terrific sense of place. I loved it!' Katie Fforde

'Romantic and funny, this is a great addition to any bookshelf' *Sun*

'Warm and witty . . . Well worth a read' Carole Matthews

'A perfect pearl of a story. I loved it' Milly Johnson

'Sun, good food and romance, what more could you want?' *Heat*

'A heart-warming tale full of Celtic charm, set against a beautiful landscape. What more could you wish for?' Ali McNamara

'Perfect for those who dream of a new life in the sun!' *My Weekly*

'An utterly charming read full of rustic romance and adventure' *Woman* magazine

'Set in a beautiful landscape with lovable characters, it's a lovely story and a real page-turner' *Candis* magazine

'Best rea

'Perfect

By Jo Thomas

The Oyster Catcher
The Olive Branch
Late Summer in the Vineyard
The Honey Farm on the Hill
Sunset over the Cherry Orchard

Digital Novellas
The Chestnut Tree
The Red Sky at Night
Notes from the Northern Lights

Jo Thomas

A Winter Beneath the Stars

REVIEW

First published in paperback in 2018 by
HEADLINE PUBLISHING GROUP

1

Cataloguing in Publication Data is available from the British Library

ISBN 978 1 4722 5013 1

Typeset in Caslon by Avon DataSet Ltd, Bidford-on-Avon, Warwickshire

Printed and bound in Great Britain by Clays Ltd, Elcograf S.p.A.

HEADLINE PUBLISHING GROUP
An Hachette UK Company
Carmelite House
50 Victoria Embankment
London EC4Y 0DZ

www.headline.co.uk
www.hachette.co.uk

*This book is for Katie Fforde, for her faith and friendship
and with big thanks for the fabulous road trips.*

Because it all began with the huskies.

Dear Reader,

Welcome to my first full-length winter book! As much as I love warm and sunny Mediterranean countries, I also love the winter. I really love snow! I love the ritual; coming in from the cold, stripping off outer clothing, warming up by the fire with hot drinks, filling the house with the smell of slow-cooked foods and gathering around the kitchen table.

At college, I had a good friend from Iceland and I became fascinated with the winters she experienced back home. So much so that I had to go and see it for myself and I visited Anna and her family there a number of times. I loved the big snowfall, the dark winters and the way life adapted to it. It's there that I set my short eBook *Notes from the Northern Lights*. Once I'd written that, I knew I wanted to write another winter adventure at some point.

The spark of an idea for this book came about when I watched the final of *Masterchef*, visiting a Michelin-starred restaurant in Stockholm that cooked with just fire. Fire, smoke, heat and utterly amazing creations; going back to basics. It was captivating.

Arriving in Kiruna in the very North of Sweden, I realised that, like the sea, snow is something to be respected because Mother Nature is much bigger than us. I loved the light it gave, the sense of community it created, how life worked alongside Mother Nature and the challenges she threw up. My favourite memory of being there was when we pulled up on the roadside, the snow falling like glitter, and our Sami guide lit a fire by a frozen river having pointed out recent moose footprints and reindeer in the wild. We sat on reindeer skins, drank amazing coffee and ate homemade cakes, feeling at one with nature. Fire made it all possible . . . that and a good knife! I felt really alive and living in the now. I hope you enjoy Halley's adventure across the snowy Swedish tundra, out in the wilderness, and feel as alive as I did out there, too!

With love,
Jo
x

Never travel faster than your soul.

Sami saying

Chapter One

'*Fika*?! You want *fika*?' The voice makes me jump, catapulting me from my thoughts. I look up and see a tall, blonde young woman standing next to me with a stern look on her face. She's brandishing a long pair of tongs and snapping them, punctuating the 'f' in *fika*.

She does it again

Snap, snap!

I swallow hard. I'm used to discovering new customs. I'm a seasoned traveller. Which also means I am very wary. I mean, not everything is always quite as it sounds, like the all-over body massage in a parlour in Paris, or the moreish cupcakes in the café in Amsterdam.

I lean back, pushing my shoulders and face away from the painful-looking tongs, wondering what *fika* could possibly entail. I'm wary, but that's not to say I'm not up for new experiences. But this . . . those tongs make me think I may have misread the signs coming to sit down here. I look around at the green glass lampshades throwing soft light over the green and white tablecloths and red salt and pepper pots. I'm sitting on a soft green imitation-leather high-backed bench, looking out over the runway. It looks and smells like a restaurant. So what's with the—

'*Fika*!' she interrupts my thoughts. Her stern face suddenly breaks into a wide smile as she proudly announces, 'Coffee and cake!' and snaps her long tongs at the lines of pastries and cakes behind her on a central island.

'You can have coffee,' she points at the coffee machine whirring and steaming away, 'and cake!' She turns back and points at the row of pastries again. '*Fika*!' she repeats proudly. 'A very Swedish tradition. Everyone makes time for *fika*. Workers and bosses alike. It's where we take a minute to relax and reflect and share our thoughts.'

I glance up at the departures board and scan for my flight. 'Delayed!' I sigh.

'Where are you going?' she asks.

'Kiruna,' I tell her.

'Ah,' she nods, 'they will have big snow there. Bound to be delayed. You have time for *fika*,' she says seriously.

But I just want to get going. I only popped into this café to charge my phone, grab a bottle of water and update my journal. I like to do it as soon as I arrive somewhere new. I'm constantly on the move, and it helps me keep track of where I was and when. I look at the board again. I just want to get to Kiruna, as far north as you can fly in Sweden, find the town of Tallfors, even further north, and the hotel, and then get back here to Stockholm and the safety of the city as soon as possible. A bubble of frustration rises in me. I'm itching to be on the move. But delayed means delayed, even if it is only by forty-five minutes, and there's nothing I can do about it.

'Do you have any tea?'

'Tea?' She looks like she's been asked if she serves chopped liver. 'Um, let me see.' She rummages in a basket of tea bags.

2

'I have Earl Grey . . . or green tea, or camomile.' She gazes at me expectantly. I consider the options. No ordinary breakfast tea. Looks like coffee it is.

'In that case, *fika* would be lovely.' I smile back at her, glad that at least it didn't turn out to be some sort of Swedish massage involving tongs and hot rocks, and resigning myself to enforced grounding for the next three quarters of an hour. I'll use the time to finish my travel log entry and catch up on work emails. It's probably a useful window to do that before getting to the job in Tallfors.

I take out my travel log and place it on the table in front of me, checking for any spills on the surface first. I open it up and run my hand over the blank page near the back of the book, then I take my pen from the pen holder on the inside of the front pocket, unscrew the lid and start to write.

Date: 4 January 2018. Location: Stockholm. Destination: Lapland.

I write slowly, enjoying the feel of the nib moving over the thick cream paper. I rest my hand on the left-hand side of the open book. It's nearly full – only two pages left. I flick through the notes and photos of the places I've been since I started this job delivering precious and unusual items all over Europe, and smile, reminded of all the trips I've made over the past two years – Sicily, Sardinia, south-west France – and the things I've hand-delivered. A wedding dress, an antique violin bought in an auction, and paperwork for a businessman, for which I was treated to a seven-course meal with family, friends and colleagues before I left.

I look at the remaining blank pages again and run my thumb over their edges. Just two pages and the book will be full. I wonder if I could add some more pages in, or find another travel journal exactly the same. Maybe I'll look around the airport. It's the perfect travel companion, I think, smoothing down the cool page.

Stockholm is minus two degrees. I adjust my writing so it's smaller, using up less paper than the notes at the start of the book. *And outside the window of the airport café I'm in, snow-ploughs are clearing the runways. Maybe twenty of them. It's like watching ballet dancers performing a well-rehearsed routine. Snow is billowing up around them like icing sugar being dusted on mince pies. Who needs* Swan Lake *when I have this?!* I draw a smiley face and some snowflakes, imagining my husband Griff's face as I tell him every detail of my trip, wishing he could be here with me to see it.

I snap a picture of the snowploughs, check it and smile again. I'll print it off and stick it in when I get home, if there's room. I frown, looking at the last couple of blank pages, running my hand over the textured paper again and finding comfort in its familiarity. I love stationery, always have. My gold fountain pen was a thirtieth birthday present from my husband, with the message *Now stop talking about wanting to do it and write!* And this book – I caress the page again – this book has been my constant travelling companion for two years, since I started this job.

I put the pen to my lips and watch the snowploughs, letting the hubbub of the airport wrap itself around me like a great big hug. I love airports. The excitement, the chatter, the expectation. Everyone is going somewhere. There is such a buzz in that constant state of movement: places to go, people to see. I just love it. A contented smile spreads across my face as I watch the snowploughs swoop gracefully in circles and then file off the runway to make way for a departing aeroplane. Even the sight of the planes gives me a happy little feeling of hope, of new cities to be seen, new streets to lose myself in.

I look at the details of the town I've printed off. Tallfors, meaning 'tall pines next to a fast-flowing river'; population 523. It's about as far north as you can get before crossing over into Norway. It has a church, a grocery shop and outdoor-clothes store, a post office, a hotel and all sorts of winter activities. I give an involuntary shiver underneath my big-knit woollen scarf with pompoms around the edges, a Christmas present from my sister on hearing that this was my next assignment. No, Tallfors wouldn't suit me for a holiday. I prefer a good selection of shops, along with restaurants and museums and people.

To be honest, it's not a job I'd usually have accepted, but it was a favour for my boss, Mansel Knott, and well, let's just say Sign-Off Sybil in the office told me that if I deliver the goods safe and sound, I'm next in line for the big jobs: New Zealand, Australia, the Far East. Just perfect! Her name is actually Bev, but we call her Sign-Off Sybil because she's forever texting us with *Remember to sign the job off!* Like we'd forget. We don't get paid until it's signed off. And because she looks and sounds like Sybil in *Fawlty Towers*.

Big long-haul jobs . . . I sigh at the thought. I've been hoping for one of them since I started with Wings hand-to-hand courier service, specialists in bespoke, efficient and reliable deliveries around the world. I just had to bide my time and prove myself, and it looks as if that's exactly what I've done. My track record is impeccable – well, apart from the time I let out a pedigree Papillon dog called Lady Gaga to relieve herself at a service station on the M4 and she ended up in a romantic encounter with a Basset hound. There was some explaining to do after that. I just wanted to let her stretch her legs. Instead, I had to prise the amorous couple apart, and she lashed out with all the bitchiness of a snubbed prima donna, unhappy about having her doggy equivalent of a Tinder date interrupted. I still have the scar to prove it. I run my thumb along my chin and the indentation there. I haven't been near a dog since.

I just want to deliver the package safely, sign the job off and get back to Stockholm, where I've planned a week's sightseeing in the city. And I'm still on track to do that. In fact, despite the early start and the delay, this trip is working out so far just as I'd hoped.

I look at my schedule, complete with contact names, addresses and phone numbers, which I've printed off and have tucked in a plastic wallet into the sleeve at the back of my travel log, as well as having all the details on my phone, of course. I like to have belt and braces. I glance around at the airport once again. I can't think of a nicer, busier place to be stranded, surrounded by people making plans on their phones, dreaming of onward journeys. The hustle and bustle all around me once again fills me with contentment. *Fika* will be great. I smile and look back down at the page in front of me, and start to describe *fika* and what I thought it might entail before I discovered it was actually about gingerbread cookies and almond cake!

'*Kaffe*,' says my waitress, putting a steaming cup in front of me.

'*Tack*,' I say, having spent the flight from Heathrow studying the Swedish phrasebook I downloaded before I left home – just as I do with every new country I visit.

She smiles and hands me a plate, indicating that I should go and choose from the selection on the central island and snapping her tongs again with a naughty smile. I pick out a couple of cakes, which she puts on my plate almost ceremoniously with the tongs, and I carry them back to my table, where my small black hand-luggage case is waiting. All around me are other travellers with cases standing by their tables and chairs like obedient children joining the grown-ups at dinner.

I put down the tray, sit down and lean my case against the table leg. It feels like a trusty friend. We've been everywhere together over the past two years. My colleagues bought it for me when I left my old job in the sales office of Dionysus Travel, where I'd been working for nearly ten years.

I sip the coffee and grimace. It's strong and bitter. I pick up one of the cakes and bite into the flaky pastry, letting the sweetness sit on my tongue, reviving me from my silly o'clock start this morning. I brush off the loose crumbs that have landed in my book just as a smartly dressed man indicates to the table next to me, as if asking if it's free. I nod, a mouthful of pastry stopping me from replying. He slides into the bench seat to my right. I look at my phone and my city guide and start to make a list of the places I plan to see in Stockholm, writing even smaller than before. I love city life, just like I love airports. I love the buzz of people all around me. You know what they say: you're never alone in a crowd.

I look back out at the performing snowploughs. I know how lucky I am to have this job, seeing new places all the time. Not that I didn't like my last one, but this is a long way from the office block I used to work in; a very long way from life back then. I like my life now; a new view every day from my hotel window. New people. Never the same place or face twice. All of them documented here in my journal. I smile and run my hand over the cover. I've been to so many places, but there are still so many I haven't seen.

Just then, my phone buzzes into life. It's Sign-Off Sybil in the office. *A new job has just come in. Once you sign off on this one, I can assign you to it . . . it's a biggie. Long haul!*

I put the phone to my lips and smile, then press the book to my chest. I can't wait to write about that in here. Then I think again about how few pages I have left and vow to make my writing *really* small. I slide the book off the table and into the front pocket of my case where it lives.

I open the case and triple-check on the package I'm delivering. It's there safe and sound, packaged in a velvet-lined box with silver trim. I pull it out. I like to make sure that the goods entrusted to my care are in perfect condition. I open the stiff lid and peek in as if checking on a sleeping child. Not that I've ever had to do that other than when I've babysat for my nephews. Sara is my older sister. She thinks I need a minder, as do the rest of my family, my stepdad and brother-in-law included, but I don't. I'm fine. I'm thirty-two, for God's sake! I love them dearly but they can be a bit overprotective.

My family does everything together. And when I'm around, they have me organised too, though I've barely been there over the past two years, not since my change of career. But they understand how busy I am. I'm here, there and everywhere and very happy. We keep in touch with our family WhatsApp. Now, just for good measure, I send them all a photo of my coffee and cake and type *You want fika?!* with a smiley face. My nephews will love it!

Then I return my attention to the box. Opening the lid fully, I put it on the table and look at the two silver wedding rings, shiny and new. The work of a Swedish designer living in London, where I collected them yesterday, they have been hand-made and inscribed. Tentatively I pick one up. On the inside is written *Love you forever, my dearest Pru.* Remembering with a prickle in my eyes how it felt to make those vows and mean them, I feel an unexpected rush of joy for this couple who have found each other, just like Griff and I did.

I remember Griff proposing to me just six months after we met. He was going away on a tour of duty and took me to our favourite pizza place. After the pizzas and garlic bread, and before the ice cream and tiramisu, I heard our favourite song playing on the restaurant music system, at which point Griff dropped to one knee in between the tables and asked me to marry him. The entire restaurant cheered when I beamed and said I would. We went to see my mum on the way back from the restaurant. The whole family turned up to hear the news and share Prosecco. I loved that warm June night.

I sniff and smile and place the ring gently back in its rightful place in the box, next to its other half, then put the box in my case and zip it up.

'If you are travelling alone, perhaps I buy you some more

fika?' the man to my right says in a thick accent, maybe south of France, leaning over towards me. 'Or perhaps, when my lift arrives,' he checks his phone, 'a guided tour of the city?' It happens sometimes, but still takes me by surprise. I must have *single traveller* tattooed on my forehead. But it's not like I dress up for travelling, and certainly not on this trip, with my huge puffa coat and very sensible boots.

'Married,' I say with a forced smile and hold up my wedding finger to show him, just as my flight is called. 'But thank you for asking,' I add politely, though actually inside I feel flustered. But my wedding ring seems to have done the trick, and he nods, with regret and a gentle smile.

'He is a very lucky man,' he says politely.

Even more flustered, I run my hand over my shiny cropped hair and turn back to my case, knocking it into his. I don't know why I can't accept compliments, but they just make me blush. I grab at my case, trying not to tut at my own clumsiness, and bid an embarrassed goodbye to the smart Frenchman, who is still smiling as he watches me. I quickly turn and head towards Terminal 5 and security, pulling out my phone with my boarding card on it from my handbag. I always wear a little across-body bag with my phone, passport and purse in it, just in case, God forbid, I ever get separated from my case. But that's never going to happen. I keep a sharp eye on it at all times. It's what I do!

Chapter Two

It's cold as we walk through the tunnel to the plane entrance, and the freezing air comes as quite a shock after the warmth of the departure lounge. A dusting of snow lies on the ground and I'm glad of my big winter coat and chunky boots, my bargain buys from TKMaxx January sales.

In the cabin, all the overhead lockers are chock-a-block. It's a full flight.

'I can take that from you,' says the air hostess in a thick Swedish accent, reaching for my case.

'No, no. It's fine. Thank you. I need to be able to see my case,' I tell her firmly, not letting go of it.

'There's room further down the plane,' she insists and tugs at it, but I don't let go.

'I can make room here,' I say, and lift it up, shuffling other bags and thick coats along. I exhale with relief and peel off my padded coat, narrowly missing punching the man behind me in the eye, as we all squeeze out of the aisle and into our seats as quickly as possible. I sit down and exhale again. In amongst the tangle of limbs, coats and luggage, I can see a man pushing my case along the overhead locker in order to cram his own bag in.

I feel myself tense, watching it being moved further down the plane.

'Excuse me, I need to see my case.' I go to unbuckle my seat belt and stand, but the air hostess is beside me.

'Please remain seated and with your seat belt on,' she says firmly.

The overhead lockers are being closed and everyone is ready to leave. I give my case one last stare, imprinting its location firmly in my mind as she shuts the locker. I know exactly where it is. The man who shifted my bag to make room for his own sits down a few rows ahead of me and pulls off his grey beanie, revealing a mass of blond curls with flecks of red running through them.

I tip my head back and find myself shutting my eyes as the little plane starts to roll forward, and then, with a ping to tell the cabin crew to take their seats, suddenly shoots down the runway and flings itself into the air like a stone from a catapult. I grip the armrests, keeping my eyes shut, hoping I'm not clutching my neighbour's forearm like that time in Skiathos. This bit of the job I don't like; everything else I love, but the going up and coming down and any bumpy bits in the middle I could do without. I open my eyes briefly, catching a glimpse of the city lights we're leaving behind and the comfort they bring me, then shut them again. I keep them shut for a while, turning down the free tea and coffee. I briefly look out of the window but I can't see a thing, just cloud. The early start from just outside Cardiff for the 6.30 flight from Heathrow is suddenly catching up with me, and I feel my eyes getting heavy.

I'm dozing when I'm suddenly woken by another ping on

the tannoy. 'Welcome to Kiruna,' says the co-pilot, 'where it's a cool minus ten.' Minus ten! I shiver and make a mental note to put that in my travel log as soon as I can get to my bag.

The plane trundles to its parking place and finally comes to a halt. I look out of the window. Big snow indeed! Everything is white, from the runway to the trees in the far distance. A whole load of open empty space. I freeze, really not wanting to go out there. But the flurry of movement from other passengers pulls me back to reality. The curly-haired guy has his coat and hat on; he has already retrieved his bag from the overhead locker by the looks of it and is halfway down the aisle, practically sprinting to the exit. I jump to my feet, a little bubble of panic suddenly rising as I try and locate my bag and can't see it. Then I let out a huge sigh of relief.

'That's mine!' I call, as I spot an older man pushing it back into an overhead locker much further down the plane; it must have fallen out when the lockers were opened. 'Sorry, sorry,' I say, trying to squeeze my way towards it. But I can't. I'm stuck, other passengers in big coats blocking my path, and I just have to wait my turn.

The guy in the grey beanie is long gone by the time I reach my bag and pull it out of the locker, keeping moving all the time. At the door, I bid the air crew goodbye and am hit by a blast of arctic air, stinging my face and making me wince. 'Welcome to Kiruna,' I repeat the co-pilot's welcome. It certainly feels like minus ten as I grab the handrail and make my way carefully down the steps, clutching my bag whilst watching my feet at the same time.

Snow is falling all around me as I crunch, slip and slide my way across the tarmac to the small terminal building, wondering if my chunky boots are actually going to be substantial enough. I look around and spot a board with my name on it, held by a female taxi driver. The woman, who has very little English, smiles and takes my case from me and stows it in the boot of the car, whilst I put my passport away in my little bag, which I've hidden under my coat.

As we drive away from the airport, I see a sign: *Dog sledge parking*. They can't be serious! I think. And then I see them, a whole team of husky-type dogs attached to a sled, jumping and barking as a group of grinning tourists heads towards them. I shiver. You'd never get me on one of those. I just couldn't be that close to all those barking dogs. And I shiver again.

I feel like I've stepped into Narnia as the car pulls out onto the road, which has been cleared of snow but is banked either side with the thick white stuff. It's dark, like a winter's evening, and yet it's only two o'clock in the afternoon. The woman drives off at speed and I grip the door handle in terror and shut my eyes when another car passes us closely. Once again, heading even further north, I'm leaving the lights of civilisation behind. It feels like I'm being pushed ever deeper into the cold wilderness.

I hold my arms to my chest and let myself fall backwards onto the soft bed, allowing the thick duvet to envelop me. Wrapped in a big fluffy white towel, my skin is tingling from the hot shower. They certainly know how to do warmth and luxury here at the Tallfors Hotel. I look around at the plush purple wallpaper and silver lamps, though I'm not sure about the reindeer hide draped over the chaise longue. There's a wall of mirrors above a glass dressing table, with shelves either side of it holding beautiful crystal glasses and a small fridge below. I won't even have to leave my hotel room! Just deliver the rings to the manager to put in the safe and then hole up here for the night with room service and a drink or two from the minibar.

I stand up and walk to the window, pulling back the thick curtain a tad and looking out, wondering if I'll see the famous Northern Lights. But all I can see is falling snow, like someone shaking a pot of glitter outside my window. It's still only the middle of the afternoon.

I can just make out a glass conservatory at the back of the building. All the rooms are on the ground floor, like a big bungalow, and there are some cabins outside in rows, with bright lights over the red front doors, the little roofs thick with snow. Someone is shovelling snow with a big plastic scoop, and once again the thought of it makes me feel cold to the bone. I really am much happier inside, where it's lovely and warm.

I reach for my handbag, pull out my phone and photograph the falling snow and the icicles hanging over my window frame. Then I step away from the window, pulling my fluffy towel tighter around me, and take a picture of the room, smiling as I think about printing the photos to go in my travel log. I think about the next leg of this trip. Back to Stockholm tomorrow, to the buzz of the city and all the places and excursions I'm looking forward to: the Abba museum, the old town and the city hall; a boat trip and a night-time ghost walk.

I pick up my case and put it on the bed, the corner of my travel log protruding reassuringly from the front pocket. I notice a scuff underneath it I haven't seen before and run my finger along it. Then I realise my luggage label is missing. It came out of a Christmas cracker – no, really, it did! Griff insisted we swap and he had the puzzle instead. He wanted me to have the label as the first step towards getting to see all the places on our bucket list, just as soon as he finished in the army. It must have come off in all that chaos and my case falling to the floor. Oh, I think sadly. I'll contact the airline and complain. And I must write about this place, out in the middle of nowhere; about my taxi ride here, and the snow and the dark.

I can't imagine who'd want to holiday here, let alone have their wedding here, like the couple I'm delivering the rings for. It's as far away from my own wedding as you can get. Griff and I had the full works. Me, my sister Sara and Mum made what we could – invitations and place cards, wedding favours and the buttonholes for the men. We'd used all our money for a deposit on our four-bed house on the new housing estate near Mum and my stepdad and Sara and her family. All ready to move into after our wedding and when Griff got back off tour of duty. But it was a still a brilliant day. Griff and his mates were in uniform and we had a registry office service and then a big bash at the pub where Mum worked.

I wore Sara's dress that my mum altered. She's always been brilliant with a needle and thread; she's had to be. My dad left when I was just eight and that was that. He moved in with someone else, remarried and became Dad to her little girl. Every night I'd go to bed wishing, praying that I'd wake up and he'd be home and things would be like they used to be. But he never did come home. Very quickly contact of any kind stopped. I think it may have been the guilt. But I couldn't understand how someone you loved that much could leave you, just like that. Love is precious, and you have to hang onto it when you find it.

For a few years it was just Mum and us girls. She had two jobs, working at the school as a dinner lady and cleaner in the daytime, and behind the bar at the pub at the end of the road in the evenings, which is where she met Bryn, my stepdad. Bryn's great. He slotted into the family really well, like he'd always been there. But something inside me never lets me forget that he's not my dad. My dad left. My sister Sara lives on the same road as my mum and Bryn, with her husband and three boys.

I decide to have a drink before opening my case, to settle my thoughts before I write about my taxi ride from the airport. Don't want my tale to be full of doom and gloom. I like to keep these thoughts happy, just as if I was on the phone to Griff, telling him all about my adventures.

I turn to the minibar and look at the list, and then check and double-check the prices, my eyeballs nearly popping out of my head. Just the one drink, I think. I knew it would be expensive, but wow! I open the little fridge and take out a bottle of cold beer, expertly flip off the lid with the bottle opener and take a long draught. There's a menu there for room service as well. I read it and take a deep breath at the prices. I think the soup might be the best option. I may be relatively okay for money, but I can't afford to go around wasting it like I'm sitting on a fortune. I need to budget for the trip to Stockholm that I've added to my work visit. I love to visit new places, and as long as I'm careful with money, I can keep doing it, delivering my clients' goods and then staying on for a few days.

My phone pings with messages on the family WhatsApp, asking if I've arrived safely and when I'll be home. They always want to know when I'm due back, but usually I try and work it so I have a new job lined up pretty much as soon as I get home. If I keep to my schedule, I can get my washing done, repack and be out of the door again within twenty-four hours. It does me good to keep moving instead of moping at home when Griff's not there. I hate being in the house without him; it feels so empty, so different to his homecomings, when the place would fill with his big personality, his deep laugh bouncing off the newly painted walls.

All good, I tell them. *A quick stopover at some remote place called Tallfors, which is about as far north as you can get in Sweden. Then back to Stockholm for a few days sightseeing before I'm home. Xx* I always end with two kisses, one for my mum and one for my sister. Maybe I should start adding them for my nephews as well.

I smile and toss the phone on the bed. I'll go to reception and hand over the rings to the wedding planner in the morning. I've messaged her and she's on early shift all this week, so I'll meet her before breakfast and then be on my way back to the airport. I like to hand the goods over to the right person, not leave them to be passed on by another member of staff. Which reminds me, better safe than sorry. I must put the rings in the room safe overnight. I take another sip of beer, then, bottle in one hand, unzip my case all the way round, hoping my belongings haven't been too shaken up. The rings, I reassure myself, are in a well-padded box; they should be fine. But my dog-eared travel log may well have taken even more of a bashing, though that gives it character; the marks from the journey it's been on for the last two years.

As I'm about to flip back the lid of the case, I realise that something isn't right. It's the smell that alerts me first of all. A smell that I don't recognise. It's not unpleasant or anything. It's just . . . not my smell. Cautiously I lift the lid. The smell gets stronger. A mix of earthy eau de toilette and . . . woodsmoke. I open the lid all the way and look down at the contents of the case.

The clothes inside are all scrunched up, not folded and ironed like I was expecting to see. I don't recall packing a black hoodie, and . . . my journal? I flip the lid back and yank open the pocket where my travel log should be. It's been prodding me in the calf, reassuring me, letting me know it's there all the way from the airport. I pull it out and catch my breath. It's a book, but . . . it's not my travel journal! I shove it back, breathing in short, shallow breaths. It's not my journal! I repeat to myself, with a growing feeling of fear creeping up my neck, tightening around my throat, cutting off my air supply.

I open the lid again and look at the scrunched-up clothes in the case. If that's not my journal . . . My mind freezes and my body follows. I pick up a garment in between forefinger and thumb and hold it up. The smell of woodsmoke and men's eau de toilette is even stronger now. If that's not my journal and these aren't my clothes . . . I can barely bring myself to process the information . . . then this isn't my bag. And if this isn't my bag . . .

Freezing-cold goose bumps travel up and over my body like an invading army. Where is my bag? screams a voice in my head. And where are the rings I'm supposed to be handing over?! I reel backwards from the earthy, woody, pine-smelling clothes, and as I do, the bottle slips from my hand, landing on the tiled floor with a crack, shattering into pieces . . . just like my world.

I get dressed in the clothes I took off earlier, stumbling in my haste, putting two legs into one hole and trying to avoid the broken glass and spilt lager. I have to find my bag; whatever it takes, I have to find it.

Chapter Three

"Scuse me!' I call in the direction of the empty front desk as I launch myself out of the corridor and into the main foyer, where there is a wood-burning stove glowing merrily, big floor-to-ceiling windows, and lights outside them throwing an orange glow over the high drifts of snow. There are two seating areas either side of the reception desk, with round tables and high-backed chairs on a single silver base in yellow and red alternately. But they're empty. There's no one here and the panic that's following me is wrapping around me like a cloak.

Breathe! I tell myself. It's just a phone call to the airline. My bag is probably still at the airport. If I hadn't been so distracted by the cold of this place, I would have noticed I'd got the wrong bag earlier. I'm sure the airline will just drive it to me and pick this one up. It'll all be fine. This sort of thing happens all the time. It'll get sorted.

'Hello?' I stand at the front desk and strain to see if there is anyone in the office behind. I catch sight of my reflection in the mirror and I look like I've seen a ghost. Frankly, it feels like that.

I pick up the little silver bell on the desk, its handle the shape of a snowflake, and ring it firmly. A bit too firmly, it seems, as the bottom of the bell falls away and lands on the desk with a clatter, before spinning around and rolling off onto the floor.

'Oh no!' I drop to all fours to retrieve it, the lip of the reception desk masking the soft lighting of the foyer. All the lighting here is soft and really quite cosy, and if I wasn't quite so . . . distracted – not stressed, I try and tell myself – I'd sit here and enjoy it.

'*Hej*!' a voice says behind me, and I feel a rush of cold air around my legs and backside. I grab the bell and struggle to my feet, banging my head on the underside of the desk as I do.

'Ouch!' I stand up straight and look at the person standing in the hotel doorway.

'*Hej*!' he says again, more deliberately this time, rubbing his eyes as if wiping away tears, and then his eyes widen, slowly and fully, as if he's just seen Santa himself putting presents under the Christmas tree. 'It's you!' He is dressed in a thick padded snowsuit with the hotel logo on its chest, a woollen hat pulled down over his ears and big snow mittens.

'Um . . . yes, it's me,' I say, a little confused. He's looking at me as if he's been expecting me. Maybe he has my bag already. My heart skips happily and finally I start to breathe again. I even manage to smile, widely. 'Hi, yes, it's me!' I hold up my hand and wave, moving the two parts of the broken bell into the other hand as surreptitiously as I can.

'You're here!' he says, as if I'm the Archangel Gabriel.

'I am,' I agree, wishing he'd stop staring at me and retrieve my bag from the back office, where I presume it's waiting for me.

'You've got my bell!' He points to the broken bell in my hand.

'I have. Look, I'm sorry about that, but well, you see, I thought I'd lost my bag and was a bit . . . Sorry, I must look . . .'

'Lovely!' he smiles.

'Sorry?' I'm still a bit confused.

'You look lovely to me! And you're here!' He throws his arms wide and I'm worried he thinks I'm someone else. 'The meteor shower might not have shown itself because of the snow clouds, but still, my grandmother always told me to make a wish when the stars were shooting, and I did. And here you are, holding my lucky bell!'

Your lucky bell, I think, and squirm, feeling the two parts in my hand. I just hope it can be mended easily. I'll offer to pay, of course, or to replace it.

'Yes, my grandmother gave it to me, to bring me luck. She told me that whenever I hear it, it's a sign that my lucky stars are out there, and to keep wishing for what I want, because one day it will happen – happiness will find me somehow. And now you're here!' He beams widely and holds out his arms again.

'Yes, um, I wonder . . . Sorry, I don't know your name.'

'Lars,' he beams, dropping his arms and making his way behind the reception desk. I start to breathe a little easier, knowing my bag and I are about to be reunited. 'My name is Lars, and you are . . .' He looks down the reservations list. 'You need to check in?'

'I checked in earlier, with the other receptionist.'

'Hayley,' he confirms, and nods.

'Um, actually, it's Halley, like the comet. Halley Hopkins.'

'Beautiful,' he sighs, staring at me as if I'm some kind of

vision teleported into the hotel lobby, and I wonder if in fact he's been on the vodka already, his wide smile seemingly fixed across his face and his eyes trained on me.

'So . . . the case?' I try and jolt him out of his trance-like state and into action. I need to keep to my schedule. The rings are due to be delivered in the morning and then I'll be on my way back to Stockholm and out of this place, I look around at the deserted foyer and the possibly drunk concierge, who is still beaming like a fool.

'My grandmother told me, wish on the stars, Lars. And here you are, holding my lucky bell.'

'Ah, about that.' I slowly put my hand on the reception desk and open it. The two parts of the bell fall onto the desk and my cheeks colour with embarrassment. 'I'm sorry.'

He sniffs and puts the back of his hand to his mouth as if composing himself. I don't know if his red nose is a sign he's just cold, or if he's actually upset. Then he looks up at me with watery eyes and breaks into another big smile.

'It's perfect!' he says, a crack in his voice. 'The bell is broken. I don't need it any more! Fate has brought you to me.' He shakes his head as if trying to rid himself of a thought. 'My grandmother is never wrong. I can see that now.' He nods with conviction. I, on the other hand, have no idea what he's talking about.

'Look, I'm not sure who you think I am, or what fate has to do with any of this, but my name is Halley Hopkins and I'm looking for a man.'

Lars raises an eyebrow. 'Good, then you've found him. I'm here!' He holds out his arms again.

'No.' I blush and look at the snowflakes falling outside the huge windows around the lounge, twisting the ring on the fourth finger of my left hand. 'I mean, the man who's got my case, the one that's got mixed up with this one at the airport.' I hold up the stranger's case from beside me and point to the office behind the reception desk.

Lars frowns. 'I'm sorry? You've lost your case? Ah, a bag swap? Yes?' He beams widely again, as if this is what passes for entertainment up here in the wilderness.

'Yes,' I say, encouraged. 'This isn't my case. Someone else obviously has it and I have theirs. So, has the airline sent it on? I have the other one here if they're sending a courier.'

He looks at the computer screen. 'Sorry, there's no case here, or any message about a courier.' He shakes his head and my heart plummets again.

'But . . . I've got to find it. It's really important, it's got . . .' I stop myself. I can't tell him I've lost the rings for a wedding party that's staying here. My boss's friend's daughter's wedding. Or that I really need to find it because without my travel log . . . well, it just makes me feel safe, that's all. It's important to me. Plus, my schedule is inside it, although I do have all the details on my phone as well.

He's beaming at me again, his hazel eyes wide open like they're inviting me into his secret world.

'Look, I'm sorry,' I say. 'I don't think you understand. I really need my case, it's got . . . well, everything in it.' My voice starts to rise and I'm now beginning to panic.

'Ah, you're here for the wedding, yes?'

'Yes!'

'You've lost your clothes in your case?'

'No . . .' My voice cracks.

'Hey, don't worry, Lars is here.' He suddenly drops his smile and looks concerned. 'I'll phone the airline and find out what's happened and when they can sort it. Or if you prefer, you can speak to them yourself. Come and use the phone in the office,' he invites.

'Thank you, that's really kind.' I manage to smile and suddenly feel a little teary at his kindness.

'Tell you what, I'll get you a hot chocolate and then we will go to the office and I'll ring the airline.'

'Thank you,' I say again, and let him guide me into the back office. He slips out, returning with hot chocolate, then dials the number and begins to speak. Once again I feel a bit of control coming back into the situation. The wedding isn't until next weekend. Thank God I decided to come here first and then go to Stockholm. Forward planning is why I'm good at this job. Allowing for mishaps. This will be sorted very soon, I think confidently. I hold the hot chocolate, too hot to sip, as Lars talks.

Eventually he puts down the phone.

'So, when are they bringing my case?' I smile.

'They're not. Unfortunately, they have had a computer problem. All their systems are down. Flights are grounded. They have no information whatsoever!'

'What?' My heart thunders around inside my chest and I'm trying hard not to hyperventilate. If I don't retrieve those rings, there's no way the wedding can happen. I won't get the next big long-haul job, and I need my travel log! The world seems to spin around me, and all I can hear is the blood thundering in my ears.

Chapter Four

'Some kind of virus,' I finally hear Lars saying. 'They can't trace anything, not a thing.' I look at him, this complete stranger, realising that for once, all my forward planning and schedules are completely useless. 'What am I going to do?'

He smiles his optimistic smile. 'Well, as my grandmother always said, fate will find a way.'

'I'm really sorry, but I'm afraid I don't believe in fate. All I know is that I need to find a way to retrieve my bag. I need to find the owner of *this* bag, because if I've got his bag, he's obviously got mine.'

'Well, do you have an address?'

'I'll look . . .' I quickly put the case on the desk and start unzipping it. Suddenly there's a cacophony of sound from the foyer.

'If we hadn't had to wait for your mother to come out of the toilets at the airport, we might have made it here while it was still light! Who goes to the toilet and locks themselves in for two hours? I mean, I've heard of waiting around in departures, but never in arrivals!'

'Shh, Nan! She's upset. She's had a shock, that's all. She's just taking time to adjust.'

'Adjust? From the look on her face, I'd say it's more than adjusting. She looks like rigor mortis has set in.'

'The wedding party!' Lars beams and turns towards the door.

'Wait, Lars. I really need your help,' I say as I take a deep breath and start to rummage through the clothing in the case. 'Please, don't tell anyone I'm here.'

He cocks his head, but agrees.

'I'll be back,' he says. 'I just have to check in the wedding party and see them to their rooms. Sounds like they've had some problems. But they are here now and that's all that matters . . . just like you,' he says triumphantly.

'No, wait, Lars, I think you're mistaking me for someone . . .' But he's gone.

'*Hallå*, *välkommen* to Tallfors, and the Tallfors Hotel. Tallfors means tall pines beside a fast-flowing river' – he holds out a hand to the snowy trees outside – 'and I am Lars, your concierge and tour guide for the week.'

I sigh and stare helplessly at the bag while Lars explains the itinerary he has lined up for the guests, involving a week of outdoor activities for the families to get to know each other before the wedding at the weekend. Sounds fun, if you like outdoorsy stuff.

Slowly I extend a shaking hand to the bag and lift the lid, standing back holding a hotel biro in front of me in the other like a stick, as if expecting to find a large snake curled in amongst the clothes. I flip the lid back quickly and start to move and lift the clothing with the biro; men's clothing, I conclude, spotting the dreaded boxer shorts at the bottom of the bag and avoiding them. Once again I am enveloped in the smell of woodsmoke and pine forests – how I imagine a scene from a Christmas card would smell. Maybe how the great outdoors outside this hotel would smell, not that I want to hang around to find out. I want to find my bag and get going. Christmas-card scenes are for people who have something to celebrate, someone they want to be with. I prefer to work over Christmas and take the jobs that other people don't want. My sister wasn't very happy about that. Both she and Mum wanted me to spend the festive period with them, but I was happy to work, to keep on the move. The last thing I wanted was time to sit and reflect. Christmas to me feels a bit like life: full of promises that sometimes Santa just can't deliver.

I close the lid and look for an address label. Nothing. From the outside, the case is just the same as mine, and a sinking feeling washes over me. If I'm going through his bag and his underwear . . . is he going through mine? I shiver. He could be anyone! And if he is going through my bag, has he found the rings? If so, has he realised how valuable they are? Is he trying to get in touch? Or will he call my office and tell them what he's found, which means I'll have to own up to what has happened.

'It's no good, Gerald, I can't stay. I want to get the first flight home,' I hear a strained voice say.

'Oh no, please, Mum . . .'

'Sylvia, I really think you just need to not overreact,' a deep voice says, and I realise this must be Gerald, Mansel's friend. I freeze. I can't go out there. I can't let them see me when I don't have the rings.

'How can you expect me to stay after what I've just discovered?' Sylvia hisses. 'Did everyone else know already?

I expect they're all laughing at me. Mother of the bride, last to find out, because her daughter knew how she'd react!'

'Let me get you all checked in.' Lars is there, trying to smooth over whatever crisis has hit the wedding party.

'Please, could you book me a flight back to Stockholm, and a taxi too,' I hear Sylvia saying.

'Oh no, Mum. Why can't you just be happy for me, like Mika's family?'

'Because you should have told me!'

'And *I* knew you'd react like this!'

I look through the open door at the short, plump and very beautiful young woman with dyed deep-red hair, bosoms like plump pillows and a bottom to match. Her mother, taller than her daughter, is thin, with neat short streaked hair, her pearls sitting just above a pale-blue pashmina. The atmosphere is as frosty as the air outside. Obviously the row has been going on all the way from the airport.

'This is ridiculous! A farce!' Sylvia says in hushed but forced tones.

I look at the bride's face, etched with worry and strain. I remember the stress of getting my own wedding organised, and feel for her. And now I'm going to have to tell her I've . . . mislaid the rings! I swallow and take a deep breath.

'You had a wonderful boyfriend in Rob. He had a great job, good prospects, and you left him and broke his heart. I don't what you're thinking. It's madness. Who's going to look after you now?'

'I didn't leave Rob and break his heart. And I don't need looking after. I can look after myself! Rob and I split up. We didn't want the same things. And then . . . I just fell in love.'

Sylvia sniffs, then turns her attention back to Lars. 'Please, a flight.'

'I'm sorry,' he says, 'but all flights are cancelled. I have just contacted the airline on behalf of another guest . . .'

Please don't tell them why, Lars, I silently implore him.

'. . . but the computers are down and flights are grounded.'

'Look, let's just get to our room. You'll feel better after a gin and tonic,' Gerald says.

'Not at these prices!' Sylvia snaps, and Lars quickly books them in and hands over the keys. 'At least if she'd married Rob we'd know who was paying for what! And I'd've made sure it was somewhere cheaper than Sweden!'

I turn back to the case. There has to be some clue in here! Suddenly I feel it. The sharp corner of a book in the front pocket. The one I had assumed was my travel log. Quickly I pull it out. It's handwritten, similar to mine, but it's full of what look to be recipes. And there are newspaper cuttings too. Bingo! I breathe a sigh of relief.

I flick through the pages. The recipes are in various languages – English, Swedish and French by the looks of it. It's covered in splashes and stains and has small writing in the margins and arrows pointing at different parts of the recipes. There are sketches, too. I turn to the back of the book, where I spotted the newspaper cuttings. They're reviews of a restaurant, in Stockholm, Michelin-starred by the looks of it, and they mention a man called Daniel Nuhtte. In that moment I realise where my bag must have gone missing. At the airport café back in Stockholm, when the Frenchman tried to chat me up. He must be Daniel, and he has my bag!

Now all I have to do is work out how to get in contact with him. I try ringing the restaurant number, but there's no reply. I put the phone down in frustration, then look around for Lars. I go to wave to him but am stopped in my tracks. The short, plump bride is wiping away tears and Lars is making his way round the reception desk, handing her a tissue.

'Hey, don't worry,' he tells her. 'As my grandmother always said, fate will find a way.' I shake my head at this man's belief in fate, but also smile at his kindness.

Standing next to the bride is a taller woman, blond hair tied back, wearing a cream ski jacket that hugs her slim figure.

'Please don't cry,' she says. 'I'm sorry it was such a shock to your mother. My family have always known, but for you, well . . .'

'I just fell in love. It didn't matter whether you were a man or a woman; it's you I fell in love with. Why can't my mum see that? I'm so embarrassed by how she reacted at the airport. I thought that once she met you, she would get over the shock and be pleased for us.'

I want to step out of the office and hug the pair of them. I can't imagine how they must be feeling. My mum took to Griff straight away, like he was her own son. The taller woman hugs her fiancée.

'Don't worry. It's you I'm marrying, not your mum,' she tries to joke in her strong Swedish accent. 'It's you I love. And when we exchange those rings that we made and engraved together, we will tell the world how we feel about each other. We will be a family together and only death will part us.' She wraps her arms around the shorter woman and pulls her to her like she's never going to let her go, and I feel every bit of that hug.

Tears spring to my eyes and I quickly try and brush them away. Oh God, they made and engraved those rings themselves, and I've lost them! I have to put this right!

Lars steps forward with a smile and hands them both more tissues.

Once he has organised all the guests to rooms and chalets, including Nan and a very reluctant Sylvia, I finally step out of the office, case in hand.

'So, how are you getting on? Do you know where your bag is?' He beams. 'Can I help?' he asks, as if he has answers for all kinds of problems.

I nod. 'Lars, I think I've found my man!'

'You have no idea how long I've waited to hear those words,' he says joyfully. 'My grandmother assured me that when one door slams in your face, a window opens.'

'Not you, Lars!'

And his face actually drops.

'Living in Lapland, it's not easy to meet people. Tinder can be limiting in a population of five hundred and twenty-three. You have to first check you're not related. One site kept telling me that me and my aunt Agnes were a perfect match!' He laughs, but it quickly peters out. 'But even if you do meet someone you think is the one, it doesn't mean they'll stay with you. Tallfors isn't for everyone.' His smile slips for just a moment and there seems to be real hurt behind those eyes. But then he shakes himself and beams even wider than before.

'I need to get to Stockholm, Lars. That's where my bag is, I know it. Back where I started. I've tried to call, but there's no reply. I need to go now.'

'Stockholm?'

I nod again.

'Or you could just wait here with me until the planes move again. We could get you another wedding outfit. There's a store in the town, I could drive you.'

I can't help but smile. I need this man's help, however quirky he might be, going on about his grandmother and doors closing and windows opening. I think of the two brides, and the mother, so unhappy that her daughter just wants to celebrate being in love. I need to find that bag.

'I'm not a wedding guest, Lars. I'm delivering the rings.'

'Ah.' He nods.

'The wedding rings that were in my case, Lars.' He looks blank for a moment. 'The one that's been swapped!'

He finally gets it, and his face drops and is serious.

'I have to find my bag!' I follow up.

He nods, then tips his head. 'Well, there is another way.'

'Tell me, Lars, how can I get to Stockholm to get my bag?'

'Night train. I can take you to the station. The sooner you go, the sooner you'll come back, right?' He smiles and nods.

'Night train,' I repeat. I think about the two brides, who clearly have enough to worry about already without me losing their wedding rings, which obviously mean so much to them. 'Night train it is then. I have to do everything I can to find that bag.'

At least I have an address for the restaurant, and this time tomorrow I should have my bag and the rings back in my possession and no one will be any the wiser – not my boss, my boss's friend or the brides, no one. Tomorrow I will have delivered the rings and this job will just be a funny story to write up in my travel log. I have to go and find Daniel Nuhtte. Stockholm, here I come.

Chapter Five

Daniel bent down to greet the dog sitting patiently by the front door and rubbed the soft, furry head. His old friend looked at her owner with her mismatched eyes, one blue, one brown, and blinked against the softly falling snow, as if letting him know she was happy to see him too. Then he rubbed the second, younger dog's head. Both dogs wagged their tails as though he'd been away for a month rather than a night. Clearly they thought he'd left them again, like he had before, leaving his sister Elsá in charge.

He was pleased to be home, back in Tallfors, on the farm. There was nothing for him in Stockholm any more. That was his past now; yesterday's meeting with his solicitor had seen to that. Where he was going to go now, though, or what he was going to do, he had no idea. But he was going to have a lot of time to think over the next few days, and hopefully he'd work something out.

He pushed open the front door of the cold farmhouse and threw his black case onto the sofa, then pulled off his grey beanie hat and rubbed his curly reddish-blond curls and his much redder thick beard. It might be good to be back, but the farmhouse felt empty and unloved. His father was in the old people's home, the new purpose-built flats in town. It'd been a shock to hear from his sister that he'd been moved there after a fall. She had continued to look in on the farmhouse every day, travelling in from the apartment she shared with her boyfriend in town to look after the dog team and the other two dogs. But she was finding it hard to juggle everything, he knew that. At least he could help out while he was back.

The air was as cold inside the farmhouse as out. He looked at the empty wood-burning stove and thought about lighting it. The fire was never out in this house. It was like the heart of the home, and now it felt like that heart was missing. He looked out of the window. There was no point lighting the fire. The big full moon was too good an opportunity to miss. The snow was light, if steady. It was ideal conditions, finally. He needed to make the most of it. He needed to get going. It was time.

He went to his bedroom and pulled a big holdall down from the top of the wardrobe, filling it with clothes – thermal layers, socks, gloves – and grabbing his sleeping bag and a spare, just in case one got wet. Having somewhere warm to sleep was going to be essential on this trip. He felt butterflies of excitement. It had been a long time since he'd done a trip like this to find the herd. It felt good. Good to be putting miles between him and what he'd just left behind.

He tried the number on his phone again. It went straight to voicemail. He couldn't wait. He had to go. He took his fur-trimmed trapper-style hat from the hook by the front door, put it on and pulled it right down by the ear flaps. Then his *luhkka*, like a blue poncho, which he draped over his coat. He knew from experience how cold it could get out there, despite it being so still at the moment. He pulled on his boots and finally wrapped his belt around him and slipped his knife into the sheath. After that, he quickly went round the kitchen, gathering supplies, and piled everything on the veranda at the front of the house, where the two dogs were panting patiently in anticipation.

He took a final look around the farmhouse and at his overnight case on the settee. There was nothing in the case that he needed. He left it where it was and stepped outside, pulling the red wooden door tightly shut behind him. A flurry of snow fell from the porch roof and the icicles hanging from the gutter sparkled in the bright moonlight. He had to make the most of this light. He could get a few miles under his belt before finally pitching the tent for the night. The light would be fading by about 2:30p.m. and it wouldn't be back until around eleven tomorrow morning. At this time of year the sun barely made it above the horizon, but if the moon stayed like this he could carry on much longer, start earlier in the morning.

He called to the dogs, who were beside him in an instant. They both knew the drill, and he was going to need them today, especially if he couldn't get hold of his sister. He had no idea where she was. He just hoped she was going to meet him there. He wished his dad could be with him on this trip, but it was impossible. He was old and frail now. The memory of seeing him for the first time a couple of weeks ago after being away for so long still shocked Daniel, and the guilt twisted like a knife in his guts. He should have come back more often.

He took another look at the farmhouse. His father had built it when he'd married his mother. She'd got a job as a teacher in town, and the cabin his dad had grown up in near the summer grazing close to the mountains was too far away. Before that, there had been a cabin on the site, built by Daniel's grandparents so that they could keep an eye on the herd nearer the forests, during the winter months. And before *that*, there had just been a *lavvu*, a tepee-like tent.

Outside, the dogs in their kennels had got wind of the fact that their owner was home and a trip was in the offing. They began to bark and howl. The anticipation was growing in the snowy air. The moon was throwing out its silver light like a cape across the undulating snowy fields that surrounded the farmhouse. Daniel stood for a moment, wondering what would happen to this place now his father wasn't here. He shook away the thoughts bundling into his head: his happy childhood memories growing up here, and then the memories he had been so eager to leave behind when he left after his mother's short illness.

He walked forward through the deep snow, shuffling to make a path, the dogs' barking getting even louder, like a classroom of enthusiastic pupils waving their hands in the air, shouting, 'Pick me! Pick me!'

'*Hej, hej.*' He opened the pen door and was greeted by dogs standing on their hind legs, desperate to welcome him back. His doubts about whether they would still recognise him after all this time melted away. Having patted each and every one of them, he went to the shed and flicked on the light, the soft orange glow illuminating the rows of harnesses hanging there. He pulled on the head torch hanging on a peg, and slung his lasso across his body. Then he loaded the sled with the essentials: dog food and bowls, fishing lines, snow shoes and skis, tent and stove, as well as the provisions from the house.

It would probably take a couple of nights to get to where he was going: north across the Arctic tundra to where his reindeer herd had been grazing all summer and autumn, to bring them south – south-east to be exact – back to the forest around the farmhouse for the winter. The weather had been so bad, the annual migration was really, really late this year. None of the herders had been able to round up the reindeer because of the snow, until now.

Under normal circumstances, his sister and father would have coped. But this year, things were different and the reindeer had moved higher than before into the mountains, away from the wind farm that had been built there. In the spring they'd be going back to the mountains, but right now, he needed to bring them down to the forests behind the farmhouse. He needed to get them home and happy. Away from the wind farm. He had to make sure his females weren't put under any undue stress. An unhappy herd was never going to breed well. The sooner he moved them to the lower land of the forest and the lichen they could feed off there, the better.

He harnessed up his lead dog and attached him to the central cable. He'd been doing this since he was a boy, taught by his mother. It felt really good to be back working with the dogs again. He harnessed the rest of the team one by one, while those not being picked barked and howled into the white moonlight. He wished he could take them all, but he couldn't. He would take a big team, though, and then split them when he got to where the reindeer were being taken off the mountainside and corralled – and hopefully where he would meet his sister. Of course, the snowmobile would have been much faster, if Elsá hadn't run it into a tree and now it had gone for repairs. He couldn't wait for it to come back. The weather was too good an opportunity to miss. It had to be now. But the dog team would be fine and he might just enjoy it. Blow away the stresses of the last few weeks.

With the final dog harnessed, he did a quick check, closing up everything left behind, then attached the sled with the provisions to the leading one. It wasn't ideal, but he didn't have a choice until he could meet up with Elsá. He checked his phone one last time, while he still had signal. Finally! She'd texted to say she'd been delayed but she'd catch him up as soon as possible. Her boyfriend would drive over and look after the dogs left behind at the kennels.

The sled was bouncing as the dogs strained and pulled to get going. Daniel switched on the torches attached to the frame and watched as they lit up the undulating landscape in front of him. The dogs being left behind howled and barked. He looked out into the snow falling ahead of him, the glittery flakes dancing in the torchlight, then pulled his fur-trimmed hat further down over his ears, took a deep breath and released the sled from where it was anchored.

'*Hike, hike*!' he called to the team in front of him, and the dogs shot forward into the snowy late afternoon, the sled gliding along behind with Daniel at the helm, feeling the thrill of speed that never failed to make him come alive, the dogs' obedience at his command, and the cold against his face, raw and real. The urgency to get to his herd and bring them home filled him with a sense of purpose and drove him on, leaving the stresses of Stockholm far behind him.

Chapter Six

I find my cabin – or couchette, as they call it – which has six bunks, three down each side. Thankfully, I'm on a bottom one. I sit by the window and stare out at the cold snowy darkness, wishing I was . . . well, anywhere but here. Back in my nice hotel room would do the trick, having room-service dinner and a glass of wine. It's coming up for 6:30 in the evening but it feels like the middle of the night. Lars drove me to the station and helped me with my ticket, promising he'd say nothing to anyone about the mislaid rings!

I shut my eyes. I wish I had my travel log with me right now. I start to imagine that I'm writing in it. I'm writing about how clean Swedish trains are. I'm writing about the various types of cake, traditionally seven varieties, I was offered with my *fika* and how the custom is considered a leveller within industry here in Sweden. The workers and bosses all meet for *fika*, a chance to talk, relax and exchange ideas and news over coffee and cake – not some kind of seedy Swedish massage as was my first thought!

Then I try and remember how the pages of the book smell, closing my eyes and breathing in deeply. The aromas of the trips I've taken since I started this job two years ago.

The fragrance of herbs as you step out of the plane onto the warm tarmac in Crete, the pine trees of the south of France, the canals in Venice and the car fumes and seasickness on the cross-Channel ferry. Two years since I walked out of my old life at Dionysus Travel, picked up my case on wheels and my travel log and started on this one.

I let myself sink into the comfort of the train seat, eyes shut. I'd google the route if I wasn't trying to save my battery. Argh! How could I have let this happen? I'm so cross with myself. I'm usually so organised. What will the office say if they find out? What will Sign-Off Sybil say? And more importantly, Mansel. I'll never get that long-haul job, wherever it may be, if I make a mess of this one . . . in fact, I may not hang onto my job at all if Mansel finds out I've failed to deliver the wedding rings on time. And what if I've actually lost them? No, don't even think like that, I tell myself, taking a deep breath as I feel the train pull smoothly out of the station. It'll be fine. I just have to find this man, this Daniel Nuhtte at his restaurant in Stockholm, and return his bag and pick up mine. He's probably been trying to ring the airline too. He'll be extremely pleased I've gone to all this effort. Of course he'll want his bag back, it's got his . . . I think about the contents of his bag: a few clothes, a toothbrush, but there's that recipe book with the cuttings in it. If it's actually as personal as I think it is, he's going to be very glad to get it back.

I settle even further into my seat and look out at the passing countryside. The snow is falling like little pieces of powdered glass and the moon is throwing a strange silver-blue light from behind the snowy clouds. I resist the temptation to take out my phone and photograph it, reminding myself that with my charger in my case, I can't afford to use the phone for anything other than essentials.

I close my eyes again and finally let sleep in. By the time I wake up, I'll be in Stockholm and on my way to finding my bag and getting this trip back on schedule.

'Hey! Give me back my ears!'

I have no idea how long I've been asleep when I'm woken by someone shouting. My eyes ping open to see an elf in a pointed green hat standing in the doorway, another elf behind him, this time female, both of them balancing large rucksacks on their backs. The female elf is laughing as she brandishes a pair of plastic ears, which the male elf is trying to grab with the playfulness of a puppy.

'I want to keep these safe. I want my children to know I was one of Santa's elves in Lapland!'

I take a moment to process this information. Perhaps I'm still asleep, and dreaming. I look out of the window. We've stopped at a small, snowy station where people are boarding the train, and I realise I'm awake after all, and that we haven't gone that far. I look back at the elves, who are still bickering good-naturedly.

'Oh yes, and one day when you're being interviewed for your latest blockbuster movie on the red carpet, you can say how it all started with a Christmas job you saw advertised in *The Stage*.'

'There are worse ways to get your Equity card!'

The pair of them bundle into the carriage, followed by another girl, similarly dressed, knocking into each other with their rucksacks, which they remove awkwardly and shove under the lower bunks.

'Sorry,' says one of the girls as I have to lift my legs for her to get her bag beneath the seat.

I raise a hand, telling her it's no problem.

'Well I'm not looking for any more acting jobs. It was fun but I'm not doing another season of kids kicking my shins when they didn't get the present they wanted from Santa,' says the second young woman, taking a seat opposite me.

'And when you asked them if anyone could think of a joke when I took them on the Santa trail, you'd be amazed how many came up with totally unsuitable ones. I had to start singing "Rudolph the Red-Nosed Reindeer" to cover the punchlines!' says the man, settling in next to her. 'Now, who's for poker and vodka shots!' He pulls a bottle from his bag. 'Let's toast the end of a great holiday season. And to next year!'

I smile at them and lean my head against the window, shutting my eyes again. Not such a quiet trip after all.

'Come on, Holly, have a drink,' says one of the girls. 'You'll feel better after a few shots!'

'Oh, I don't think I'm up for it, guys. I just . . .' Her friend trails off, like something has caught in her throat, a tear or two maybe. I keep my eyes shut. 'It's just, well, y'know . . . I thought he was different, special.' She lets out a big sob, and my eyes fly open at the familiar sound. A huge, heart-stopping gulp that takes your breath away, making you judder as if expelling the loss you feel, though you never actually do.

The other two gather around her on the opposite bunk, wrapping arms around her shoulders from either side. I try to make myself as invisible as possible, not wanting to intrude. I sit still and look straight out of the window, although of course I can see the trio's reflection there in the glass.

Holly sniffs and drops her head.

'Hey!' the other young woman says. 'I know how you feel, but this is how it goes at the end of the season. You had great fun . . .'

'If it's any consolation, me and Mrs Claus have finished too,' says the young man. 'She's gone back to the States and her college studies. But we're planning to meet up again next year.'

'I don't think I'll be back. I just couldn't bear it if he'd, y'know, met someone else and moved on.' She lets out another sob.

'Have you got a tissue, Matty?' the second girl asks.

'No, but you can use my sleeve. I won't be wearing this again for a while.' The man holds out his arm, clad in a Christmas jumper.

'No, wait! I think I've got one,' I say, admiring his selflessness but not keen on a sleeve being used as a tissue. I look in my little travel handbag and find a small packet. 'Here.' I pull out a tissue and hand one over.

'Thank you,' says Holly. 'And, um, sorry,' she adds.

'Oh, don't be sorry.' I wave a hand, and as I go back to looking out of the window, I hear a reassuringly big and loud blow into the tissue.

'If you feel that way about him, why didn't you tell him?' Holly's friend asks.

'Oh, he had this thing about fate bringing him the love of his life. He said he really cared about me, but well, it was like he was too scared to commit, in case he got it wrong.'

'Pah!' says her friend. 'If you think he's the one, you should tell him.'

I think about when I first met Griff. It was him that did all the running. We met in the pub where my mum worked, on New Year's Eve. He was visiting a friend from his regiment. Midnight came and we kissed and I wanted it to last forever. But then he got dragged off to a party with his friend and I didn't think I'd see him again. But he tracked me down and came back to ask my mum to put us in touch. She checked with me first. I'll never forget her texting me, saying, *There's some bloke here says he met you on New Year's Eve*, and I knew exactly who she meant. That was ten years ago. I was probably the same age Holly is now. New Year's Eve will always be special.

'Here, keep the packet,' I tell her, handing it over. 'It's none of my business, but . . .'

Holly looks at me.

'Sorry, it really is none of my business.' I wave a hand. It's not my place to be telling people what to do.

'No, please, what?'

'Well, it's just . . . I just think that if you believe you've found love, you should grab it with both hands. It might sound silly, but love is precious, and rare. Don't miss your chance if you think he's the one,' I finish.

The elves fall silent as we gather speed and leave the snowy north behind, and Holly's heart looks as if it's slowly breaking.

'Shot?' Matty interrupts my thoughts, and I turn to see him holding the bottle in one hand and a little glass in the other, a wide smile on his face. 'We're toasting the end of our season working at Santa's grotto,' he says.

'So the ears aren't just for fancy dress then?' I say.

'A souvenir!' He beams.

'So what happens now?' I ask.

'See what's around, auditions, but for most of us it's onto the cruise liners, singing or dancing. Go on, have a drink,' he adds.

I look at the glass. Well, why not? I thank him and take it.

'Now, know any good Santa jokes?' He laughs loudly and looks at me expectantly. Even Holly is smiling, despite her red nose. It's going to be a long and interesting night, I think, and rack my brains for the best Christmas joke I can think of.

'It's not a Santa one, but here goes. What did one snowman say to the other?'

'I don't know, what did one snowman say to the other?' Matty says loudly in full pantomime voice, making me smile.

'Can you smell carrot?'

'Whoa!' He roars with laughter and the other two join in. '*Skål*!!' he says, pointing to my glass. 'Drink, drink! It's the only way to pass the *vargtimmen*!'

'The what?' I ask.

'The *vargtimmen*,' he repeats with a wicked smile. 'Wolf-time here in Sweden. The menacing hours of night before dawn,' he explains.

I look out into the blackness, and then pull down the blind and drink another shot.

After I lose count of how many shots I've had, I attempt to sleep on my bunk. I listen to Holly's quiet sobs and think about the tears I shed every time Griff went back on tour, and about the tears of joy when we married and when he finally said he was going to retire from the forces.

I wake to the sound of an announcement letting us know that we're arriving in Stockholm. Bleary, and with a banging headache, I quickly find my bag – well, Daniel Nuhtte's bag – the recipe book safely zipped into the front pocket. My travelling companions, Santa's elves, begin to wake, not half as bleary as me. That's what a ten-year age gap does, I think. I was them once! But now I need a bottle of water and a couple of painkillers. I pull up the blind and squint out of the window, hoping 'wolf time' is over. It's still not quite light, but the street lamps make me feel like I'm back in the real world.

'So, you on your way home?' Matty stretches and yawns.

'Um, actually, I'm looking for this place.' I show him the picture of the Michelin-starred restaurant from the newspaper cutting.

Matty turns to his friend – not Holly, who is looking tired but better than last night, but the other girl, Liv, who it turns out has lived in Stockholm. 'You know your way around,' he says. 'Know this place?'

'Oh yes, shouldn't be too hard,' she replies. 'It's really well known. I can show you on Google Maps,' she adds, taking charge of my phone.

As we draw into the station, Holly looks at me and then, surprisingly, hugs me. I'm not a hugging person, but somehow this hug has an awful lot of unsaid words in it and I return it, hoping she finds some comfort there. Then I bid them all goodbye and make my way off the train in the direction of the restaurant.

Everything is back on track, I think, breathing a big sigh of relief. In just a few hours I'll be back at the hotel in Tallfors, delivering the rings and signing off on this job, and that'll be the last I'll see of snow and ice for a very long time. I keep my fingers crossed that Holly finds exactly what she's looking for too.

Chapter Seven

'What? No! It can't be!' I say aloud. 'There must be some mistake.' I look down at the newspaper cutting in my hand and then back at the restaurant I'm standing in front of. I glance left and right and check the directions on my phone for the umpteenth time.

I'm in 'one of Stockholm's most affluent areas', according to the article I remember reading on the internet. There are spectacular sea views and it's the perfect place to find high-end restaurants. Certainly the street is lined with smart buildings, some cream-coloured with ornate stonework and light green finishing on the roofs, others light terracotta. There are apartment blocks with matching awnings, and rows of bicycles parked and chained all along the wide pavements, which are dotted with slim-trunked trees. Either side of the restaurant are elegant boutiques, galleries and cafés.

There is a dusting of snow over everything, much wetter than where I've just come from. More slippery too, I discovered when I crossed the road to stand in front of the restaurant and nearly skidded into the gutter. Now I stand and stare open-mouthed.

The restaurant is just the same as in the picture, its woodwork painted a trendy grey. I check the name against my cutting: *La Tir Bouchon* in curvy lettering like a well-practised, confident signature. It means The Corkscrew, I work out in my basic French; I brushed up on it when I got my first delivery job, taking a wedding dress and hat to a chateau in the south of France. From the outside, the place is discreet and almost plain. I step forward and push my face against the cold glass of the big arched window. Inside, it's quite a different story.

Opulent comes to mind, I think as I take in all the details. There are two huge glass chandeliers, art deco style; a patterned and painted tiled floor and bevel-edged mirrors around the walls, which boast ornate white cornices and surrounds. It oozes class. Tapestry-covered stools line one wall, for pre-dinner drinks. The tables are covered in starched white tablecloths, with unlit candles on each one and chairs leaning into them, as if resting until their next performance.

A menu board stands outside, in a gold surround with soft snow caught in the corners. The restaurant offers classic French dishes, some Italian ones and some I've never heard of. It looks like it's a well-established place waiting to greet its customers – except that it's quite clearly deserted.

I step forward and try the door, grabbing the handle and pushing it down. But it doesn't budge. I give it another shove to be sure, bumping my shoulder against it in case it's just stiff. But it isn't. It's locked.

I step back and stand in the banked-up snow in front of the window. As I bang on the glass, the wet snow starts to seep up the bottom of my trouser legs.

'Hello?' I bang again. 'Hello? Anyone in?' There must be

someone working in there. The place looks like it's ready to serve customers at any moment.

There's no reply to my shouts or knocks. No movement at all.

Tired tears suddenly fill my eyes and my head thumps, making me feel pathetic and ridiculous. Whoever the owner is, whoever has my bag, he's not here! No one is. And if the owner isn't here, neither is my bag, I realise in despair.

Now what? I look around, hoping for some kind of inspiration. The smell from the coffee shop opposite makes my stomach rumble. Pull yourself together, I tell myself and blink back the self-pity I can feel welling up. I just need to sit down and gather my thoughts; work out what to do. I've travelled all over Europe, I can deal with the situation. 'Yes, but you've never lost your bag before, with your travel essentials and the item you were supposed to be delivering in it!' an unkind voice in my head points out.

I take a deep breath and cross the road, avoiding the slippery kerb this time, and push open the door of the café. The smell of coffee hits me right in the nostrils, filling my head and my soul.

'You'd like *fika*?' asks the hipster man behind the counter, his hair in a tidy bun and his beard neatly shaped and trimmed.

'Yes, please.' I manage to smile. I don't even bother asking about the tea option. '*Fika* would be great.' Though I don't think I'm going to be able to taste anything. My mouth feels as if it's full of sawdust and my heart is thundering.

He hands me a plate and points to the array of biscuits and pastries. I take a couple of biscuits, and although the sweet, warm smell is comforting, I'm not sure I'll be able to eat them. I can hardly swallow, my throat is so tight with tension. I make my way to a small table in the window, overlooking the deserted restaurant across the road, and slide onto the seat there. I haven't dared check my phone for messages in case Sign-Off Sybil has been in touch, wanting to know if the goods have been delivered safely. What would I say? But I do have to say something. I take another deep breath and tentatively pull out my phone from my little bag, just as it buzzes loudly at me, flashes and goes black. Dead. And my charger in my flight bag!

'Oh bugger!' I toss it onto the table.

'Everything okay?' asks the waiter, bringing over my coffee.

'Well, it's not going quite as well as I had hoped,' I manage to say in a sort of cheery way. 'Um, tell me, that restaurant over there.' I point.

'Ah, *La Tir Bouchon*. You have heard of it?'

'Not until recently,' I confess.

'It's very well known. It has one Michelin star . . . well, it did have. But as you can see, it's closed. Overnight. No one knows what has happened, or where the owner is. You've heard of him? Daniel Nuhtte?'

'He's the chef?'

'Not just any chef. He's known all over Sweden. He's like a rock god. People came for miles to see him, eat his creations. He was, how do you say, cutting edge!' He beams at his own joke.

And it's his case that I have. Not just a chef, but a Michelin-starred chef . . . and that means that his recipe book, hand-written and hand-sketched, could be worth a fortune!

'I really need to find him. He has something of mine, and I have something of his I think he'll be really keen to get back.'

The hipster waiter shrugs. 'No one knows,' he says, still looking at the restaurant.

'No one knows?' I repeat slowly, and he shakes his head and goes to move away before suddenly turning back to the window.

'Oh, but wait!' He points across the road. 'That's Camilla, his sous chef! His second in command.'

A woman in a smart dark coat and long leather boots has opened the restaurant's grey door and is stepping inside.

'What? That woman there? She works with Daniel whatever-his-name-is?' I feel a tiny flicker of hope.

'Uh-huh! Well, she did. Until the place was closed up.'

'Sorry, I have to go.' I stand abruptly, and the coffee slops into its saucer. 'Oh, sorry again! I just have to . . . I mean, if there's a chance she knows where he is, I have to take it.' I pull out some krona and put a note on the table next to the untouched biscuits and coffee.

'I'll get your change,' says the waiter.

'Keep it,' I say, pulling on my coat and grabbing the case.

'I hope you find what you're looking for!' he calls after me as I leave.

So do I, I think.

The woman in the dark coat is coming back out of the restaurant with an armful of mail and locking the door.

'Wait!' I cry. 'Stop! I mean . . . sorry, hang on! Argh!' I try and dodge the icy kerb, fail, and skate around for a couple of seconds, flapping wildly trying to right myself.

'Excuse me!' I call again, and the woman stands and stares at me in surprise, probably wondering what on earth I'm doing. Finally I make it across the road with the little case bouncing along behind me in the slush and snow. 'Don't go,' I say. 'I really need to speak to you.'

'I'm sorry,' she replies curtly, 'but we're closed. If you're a journalist, no, I don't know when we'll reopen. And if you're an investor, I don't know if he's selling.' Then she looks at me and her tone softens. Maybe it's my tired and desperate face. 'I don't blame you,' she says. 'A place with this reputation, people are desperate to snap it up.' She looks at me with a mixture of regret and disappointment, then stuffs the post into her handbag and turns to walk away.

'No, wait! I'm not after the restaurant, although I'm sure it's lovely.' I remember the reviews in the flight bag. 'I'm looking for someone. I wonder if you can help me. The owner . . . um, Daniel.' She stops and turns back, eyes narrowed as I struggle to pronounce his surname, the tiredness and desperation getting to me. 'Daniel Nutty?'

Her look changes to one of mild amusement as she runs her eyes over me, assessing me, and it's clear she's realised I'm neither a journalist nor a professional threat if I can't even say his name.

'You're looking for Daniel?'

I nod.

'Are you a friend?' Her eyes narrow again. 'Or something else?'

My mouth opens and closes as I search for the words. I'm not a friend, I'm a something else, but not the kind she means.

'I have something of his. Something it's important I get back to him,' I tell her. And he has something of mine, I add silently, thinking about my travel log and feeling like I'm missing a part of me, as if I've forgotten something essential. Like I'm walking down the road in my slippers, or worse, with no clothes on.

'Well,' she sniffs, still looking at me suspiciously, 'I'm afraid I can't help you there. I wish I knew where he was. I have something for him too. But I've tried ringing, texting – nothing! The only thing I can think of is that he has gone to visit his family. It's just a hunch, but he was . . . well, he wanted to get away,' she finishes, and I realise she's not going to tell me why.

'Wherever he is, I have to try and get in touch with him,' I say. 'I have his bag. I think they got swapped at the airport.'

'In Stockholm airport?' She looks more interested and suddenly far less suspicious of me.

I nod.

A thought seems to strike her. 'Look,' she starts to rummage in her handbag, 'if you're going to find him . . . I mean, if you're serious about tracking him down . . .'

'I have to find out where he is,' I tell her again. I can't just give up and go home. My whole life is in that case. Without it, I have nothing to go back for.

'Could you give him something from me?' she asks, suddenly sounding very urgent.

'Oh, I don't know . . .' It's my turn to narrow my eyes. I've learnt from experience never to say yes to delivering something if you don't know what it is. The amount of offers at airports I've had! It's the first rule of the job.

'Please. I really need to find him. It's just a letter. Honestly, I wouldn't ask if it wasn't really important. If I could do it myself, I would, but what with . . . well, him disappearing like that and me having to find another job . . . I mean, I've found one. It wasn't hard. They all knew I was Daniel's right-hand man. All anyone asks about is his where-abouts and what's going on. To be honest,' she swallows, 'well, let's just say that I was really cross with him at the time. He told me he was going, that he needed the space and I wasn't to follow, and I didn't. But now, I really need to get a message to him. To tell him I'm sorry that I didn't believe him. Everything he needs to know is here.'

She holds out an envelope to me. There's a slight shake in her hand, in an otherwise cool and together appearance. A large snowflake lands on it, smudging the ink. Another falls, and another, leaving more wet blobs on the paper.

I think about what she's asked me to do. It does just look like a letter, and it's not like I'm leaving the country or anything. I'm simply going to go and look for him at his parents' place. I glance at her face, her expression imploring me. She clearly has things she needs to say to this man. Who am I to stand in the way of the course of true love? You have to grab your chance when you can, isn't that what I told Holly on the train?

'Sure,' I say with a smile, feeling like a modern-day Cupid. I take the envelope and shove it in my little handbag along with my passport, purse and now redundant phone.

'Thank you,' she says with a nod, regaining her previous composure, and turns to walk away through the snow that is now falling more heavily.

'Wait!' I call after her. 'I don't know where to go. His family. Where are they? Is it far?'

She stops and turns to me, and tilts her head. 'Didn't I say?'

'No.' I take a deep breath.

'They live up north somewhere. He never told me exactly where. Said they moved around a lot.'

'Up north?' I say, a cold chill of realisation washing over me. 'What? As in Kiruna up north?'

'Uh-huh!' She nods. 'A place called Tallfors, somewhere in Lapland. It's supposed to be beautiful up there. Sweden's snowy wilderness. Just ask around when you arrive. Someone will be able to point you in the right direction, I'm sure.'

Chapter Eight

'You're back!' Lars's eyes light up and his wide smile spreads across his face like the rising sun, something that is noticeably absent around here, although at least at the moment it is actually light. He opens his arms like I'm an old friend, or a family member returning home, welcoming me back to the Tallfors Hotel. And I can't help but smile in return. I'm exhausted, and it feels really nice to see a friendly, familiar face. 'I knew you'd come back!' he says. 'It's fate. My grandmother was right. She told me my perfect match would turn up if I wished on a star!' He beams even wider.

'Hi, Lars,' I say, too weary even to wave my wedding ring at him by way of telling him I'm unavailable.

'Did you miss me?' he asks, still holding his arms wide, and I'm wondering if he's actually expecting me to hug him. I don't take him up on the offer. If I did, I might just put my head on his chest and fall asleep there and then in the middle of reception. Instead, I turn away and lean against the desk to support my tired limbs.

'Well?' he asks, and I realise that despite his joking manner, there's a hint of seriousness there. I decide to laugh it off.

'Of course, Lars! You're the best concierge I've ever met.' I smile as I undo my coat and peel it off. He drops his arms and then looks down at my jumper.

'Interesting choice of clothing,' he says. 'I see you have fallen in love with our country.'

I look down at the souvenir sweatshirt I bought in the airport on my way through and changed into in the ladies' loos. Thankfully the computer glitch seemed to have sorted itself and I was able to get a flight. 'It was all I could find,' I admit. 'You should see the underwear.'

'I'd like that, thank you.' He grins and nods.

'No! I don't mean . . .' I wave a hand and don't bother digging myself into a deeper hole. What is it with this man? But honestly, the underwear is punishing. A bit tight and frankly rather scratchy. Like nothing I've worn in a long time.

'Sorry,' he points to my neck, 'can I . . . ?' and I wonder what he's talking about. He points again and smiles. Maybe it's some kind of Lappish custom I don't know about. I hope he's not going to try and kiss me. I lean back cautiously. He reaches forward. 'You have the tag still on,' he says quietly. He gives it a tug and it snaps off.

'Thank you, Lars.' I blush with a mixture of tiredness and embarrassment as he deposits the tag in the bin, and make a mental note to check the rest of my purchases – the T-shirt and especially the spare pants in the plastic bag swinging by my side – before putting them on. It could account for the scratchiness. 'You're very kind,' I tell him, and he is.

He lowers his voice. 'I could be kind to you forever, if you let me. It's written in the stars!'

'Lars, it's a lovely offer. But no. Thank you.' I laugh, and he does too, staring at me dreamily as if this is just part of the courtship he is convinced is going to happen.

'So, how are the wedding party doing?' I quickly change the subject when I realise I'm blushing, my cheeks glowing. His face falls.

'Not so good. I'm afraid the path of true love is not so smooth there. Let's just say, I'm not sure this idea of a getting-to-know-you holiday with the families before the ceremony was such a good one.'

'Oh, that is a shame.' I think of the two brides, obviously very much in love. 'I thought it sounded a great idea!'

'It could have been, but sadly, the bride's mother is still very unhappy about her daughter's choice of partner.'

'In other words, you think she would have preferred a groom.' I read between the lines.

'Exactly,' he confirms.

'That is sad. Love is love wherever you find it. They're lucky to have each other.'

I think about the letter in my bag from Camilla and double-check that it's still there. When I look up again, Lars is staring at me, his head slightly to one side, smiling his wide smile again. I get the feeling he is trying to send me some kind of silent signal, a declaration of his intention. He'll have a job. I'm not open to offers. This shop has long since pulled down its shutters, and nothing will get through the barriers I have around me and my heart. There's still only one person in there for me.

'Is that an ice bar out there? In an igloo!' cries a loud voice, and Lars's smile freezes.

'The bride's nan. I think she has a liking for me,' he whispers, then readjusts his expression as the older woman appears in the foyer.

'So, Lars,' she says. 'What's the plan for the rest of the day? And is that really an ice bar, with all those flashing lights?'

'We hope you will enjoy the hotel and the vantage points for stargazing later this evening, and who knows, when the snow finally stops, maybe the Northern Lights too.'

I glance outside. There doesn't seem to be any sign of a let-up in the snow, which is falling like shards of glass, layer upon layer on the ground.

'Meanwhile, lunch is ready for you in the restaurant. Hot soup and *smörgåstårta*. A Swedish sandwich cake, layered with different fillings – sliced vegetables, egg, chicken, salmon, with cream cheese.' Lars beams proudly. 'Then I hope you'll enjoy the rest of the day relaxing in the sauna and spa. And yes, our ice bar afterwards!'

'Oh, lovely. Will there be rolling in the snow?'

I shudder. I can't think of anything worse than taking off your clothes and rolling in freezing-cold snow. I pull my padded coat further around me.

I really need to speak to Lars and ask if he can help me find this Daniel bloke's family farm. The sooner I can track him down, the quicker I can deliver the rings and leave. I stand and listen as patiently as possible.

'Tomorrow will be an excursion for your whole party out into the countryside. We will go in a coach and show you the beautiful forests and frozen lakes in these parts.'

'So, jet skis?' Nan grins.

'Not tomorrow. It is a gentler day. Take a camera. Capture the wildlife. Later in the week there will be a jet-ski tour, dog sledding too, some cross-country skiing and a trip to see the Northern Lights.'

Griff and I went skiing once, with a group of friends, just after we were married. I fell over on the first day, broke my ankle and swore I'd never do it again. Give me a beach and a book any day. And that's exactly what I'm hoping my next job will be. Long-haul, somewhere hot and sunny! But first I have to make sure this one actually works out.

'Um, Lars?' I try and politely get his attention as the foyer begins to fill with members of the wedding party and before he gets absorbed with looking after his guests, which he does seem really good at.

'Yes!' He spins back round to me, seemingly delighted, with an even broader smile and widening eyes.

'Lars, I need your help.' I try and get him to focus on the matter in hand instead of what I think he might be imagining is going on here.

'Name it! Anything!'

'I need to find someone.'

'Still? I told you. I am here! It's fate!' He holds his arms out, making me laugh again, and it feels surprisingly good even if I am panicking inside about the wedding party and the missing rings.

'It's my bag. I still haven't found it,' I say.

His face drops, concerned. 'And the rings?' He looks around at the wedding party. I shake my head.

'I found the restaurant in Stockholm, but apparently the owner's disappeared. Probably visiting his family up here.

That's where the bags must have been swapped,' I add, suddenly feeling very cross with myself for wasting so much time, 'on the flight rather than at the airport like I thought. So, can you help me?'

'Of course I can help. I can get done anything in these parts. You name it, Lars can do it. What's his name?'

I pull out the envelope Camilla gave me. 'Daniel Nuhtte,' I read, and look up at him.

His eyes widen. 'What, *the* Daniel Nuhtte? The chef? The one who makes all the super-cool fancy food, like a mad scientist? The one with the Michelin star?'

I nod slowly, and a warm feeling of optimism starts to wrap itself around me. 'You know him?'

'No,' he says flatly, and my rising spirits dip again. 'I don't know him personally. He was out of school as I was starting. But I know people who will know. I know everyone. It's my job! I am a super-concierge!'

And my spirits suddenly shoot upwards like a plane taking off.

'He went to Stockholm as a kitchen apprentice. Now look at him!' I can tell Lars feels a tiny bit envious of Daniel Nuhtte's success as he looks around at his own position behind the hotel desk. 'But he was always . . . well, a bit different. He didn't really fit in at school. He didn't join in. He would spend his time with his family and the reindeer – no one knew much about him. And then suddenly, woof! He was a big chef in the city, known all over the world.'

'Except by me.' I grimace. But I can't say I'm one for high-end restaurants or cookery shows. I'm never home long enough for a night in front of the TV. And if I have got time on my hands, I've usually got my head in a travel guide or am attempting to learn a new language. I like to keep my mind busy. And talking of staying busy . . . 'What I'm hoping is that someone will know where he is now. Because he's not in Stockholm, not at his restaurant anyway. Someone said they thought he might be at his parents' place.'

'I'll ask around,' says Lars. 'In the meantime, have a seat.' He indicates the high-backed cushioned chairs in the lobby. 'The fire's lit. Sit there and watch the birds. The Siberian tits are out today,' he adds.

I don't need asking twice, and move my weary body towards the seats by the big window looking out onto the birds' feeding station.

'And Hayley?'

'It's Halley,' I correct with a friendly smile.

'Of course.' He nods. 'Hot chocolate?' he asks with a cheeky wink. I mouth thank you and he instructs one of the barmen to whip up my drink whilst he greets the wedding party and ushers them to the dining room, then steps back around the reception desk to make some calls.

The hot chocolate with thick cream and marshmallows hits the spot and, no sooner have I finished it, I sit back in the chair and watch Lars as he talks on the phone. My eyes feel heavy and I can't help but let sleep in.

'Hayley, hello?'

Slowly I open my eyes, wondering where on earth I am and who's waking me up. It takes me a while to realise that it's Lars, shaking me gently out of a dream where Griff and I are skiing again, and I'm clinging tightly to him so as not to fall.

'Oh, hi. Sorry, I dropped off.' I run the back of my hand across my dry mouth. God, I hope I wasn't snoring. Or dribbling, even!

Lars is smiling like he's been watching a baby sleep.

'Have you found him?' I ask, suddenly remembering why I'm here.

He rolls his head from side to side. 'Yes and no.'

'Yes and no? What do you mean?'

'Well, his family have a farm not far from here.'

'And Daniel?' My panic starts to rise.

'No one knows. But it's the reindeer migration. All the Sami families will be herding up their animals and moving them to winter grazing.'

'Have you got his number?'

He shakes his head. 'There will be no one at the farm. But I know where the family's reindeer are. I could take you there. Someone will be able to help you.'

'Brilliant! Thank you, Lars. You're a star!' I stand up unsteadily, still woozy from my deep nap, and gather my coat. Outside it is dark despite it being only about four o'clock.

He laughs and holds me by the elbow. 'But not tonight. Tonight I am Lars the concierge. Tomorrow I am Lars the tour guide. I'm taking the wedding party on their photography safari, and I can take you to where you'll find Daniel.'

Once again my rising spirits plummet. I give myself a shake. I only have to wait until tomorrow. Then I'll find this reindeer herd and find out where Daniel is. Someone's bound to know his whereabouts.

'Okay, Lars, thank you. That would be great. Could you find me a room for tonight? I think I need to go to bed.'

'My thoughts exactly!' he pronounces, his grin now wider than ever.

'On my own, Lars, on my own!' Clearly his skin is as thick as my protective armour, and once again I find myself laughing, despite the stressful situation I'm in.

'And Lars, remind me when exactly this wedding is?'

'Next Saturday, a week today. You have plenty of time, don't worry. And when do you leave for home?'

'Next Sunday. I was due to spend some time in Stockholm before flying back. But I have to find my bag and deliver the rings first. Looks like I may be here longer than I expected.'

'Excellent!' he says, and I'm not sure he understands my dilemma. 'We have plenty of time to get to know each other!'

I sigh. He's persistent, I'll give him that.

Chapter Nine

'Whoa!'

Daniel stood back on the brake as the dogs slowed up on the ridge of the hill, bringing the sled to an eventual stop close to the mountain where the herd had been grazing all winter. It had been a long, fast and hard trip. He took a deep breath, pulling in the cold air and filling his chest. Little crystals of snow were frozen into his beard and eyebrows.

He could see the corral where the other families had been collecting the reindeer off the mountain for the last few days. A big area in the middle and holding pens all round it, like the petals of a flower. He'd passed several of them on his way here, greeting old friends he hadn't seen in years, all wanting to know about his father's health and his sister's news. All the other families had left now, but not before gathering Daniel's reindeer for him before they went and then staggering their own departures so that the herds didn't all leave together. It wouldn't be sensible to try and move a thousand or more reindeer at one time. Only Daniel's herd was left now in the holding area. He pushed the dogs on and pulled up by the pen.

The dog team were panting contentedly, some of them even lying down in the snow. He secured them by tying a rope from the sled to a tree, and a second rope from his lead dog – stopping to pat and thank him – to another tree. The last thing he needed now was to lose the team. Once they started running, there was no getting them to come back, and with a heavily loaded sled of supplies behind them, who knows what accidents could happen.

He looked around the clearing at the foot of the mountain, scanning for any stragglers, reindeer that hadn't been herded up in the last few days, hiding behind the snow-covered trees. The cold air was making the insides of his nostrils tingle. He needed to move quickly; the weather was good and he had to make the most of it. He looked up at the big wind turbines. They weren't actually turning at the moment, as there was no wind, but they could start up again at any time. He knew they were a necessity, creating energy for the country. It was just the reindeer who didn't. All they knew was that the turbines frightened them, and that could affect their breeding.

Daniel worked quickly to split the dog team, attaching one team to the second sled. He didn't want to speak to anyone right now or explain his whereabouts or his plans. He'd just needed to get away. He couldn't stay in Stockholm after what had happened . . . or hadn't happened, as the case might be. The restaurant would be snapped up, he knew that, but he didn't want to answer any of the questions the journalists would be bound to ask. What happened? Why had it all gone wrong? Everything had gone wrong. From having it all, he'd lost it all. The eye of the perfect storm, so to speak.

But all that was behind him now. What he wasn't sure of

was what was in front of him. First, though, he needed to get the herd away from here, and safe, ready for the new calves to be born in May. Once he'd done a head count, he could get moving.

His dog Florá – different from the huskies, more like a collie dog – jumped stiffly down from the sled, followed by her son. Daniel checked his phone again, looking around the vast open space at the foot of the mountains for some sign of his sister, who was due to meet him there. Where was she? All he'd had was that brief message about being held up, and a promise that she'd try and get there as soon as she could. Should he wait a bit longer? Maybe light the fire and eat something? He breathed in again, hoping it would help blow away all thoughts of the last few weeks, and decided not to stop and cook. He wasn't hungry; everything just tasted sour. But the air out here was helping to dilute the bitter taste left by the experience of the past few weeks.

Suddenly he heard the sound of an engine, and car doors slamming shut. Thank God, she was here at last! The reindeer were milling around restlessly, ready to make a move. He turned to face the road in the distance and pulled out his binoculars, training them on the vehicle pulled up on the roadside.

Oh no! That was exactly what he didn't need right now. A bus full of Northern Lights seekers to get in his way!

Chapter Ten

'Good morning, everybody!' Lars is bright-eyed and bushy-tailed. Not a trace of the fact that he was working on reception until late into the night, and then was up early to make sure all the wedding party are gathered in reception in suitable clothing and reassure those that need it that there will be toilet stops. He hands round cameras and gives out instructions on how to use them and how to insert the memory cards everyone has been told to bring.

'Oh, a memory card?' says Nan. 'I brought a pen and paper. I find I have to write everything down if I'm going to remember it.'

Lars smiles and finds her a memory card, which she looks at suspiciously. He's working very hard to keep everyone happy. He even found me a single room for the night. Not as luxurious as my first room, but then the company paid for that one. Let's hope I'm not here for much longer. Once I track down this reindeer herd and find out where Daniel is, we could have the bags swapped back by this evening!

Pru and Mika, the two brides, are standing close together, Mika with a protective arm around Pru as her mother stands at a distance, lips pursed, chin high.

'It's no good, I'm not going. I'll just stay here. See if we can change our flights. I haven't got the right clothes anyway. No one told me this was going to be some kind of activity-themed week. I thought it was going to be a week of culture before a dignified wedding. I didn't expect to be brought here to be . . . made a mockery of!'

'Sylvia! For goodness' sake! People can hear you!' Gerald, her husband, shushes her.

'I haven't even got the right gloves. I'll stay. I can't wear my kid-leather gloves out there.'

It's still dark outside, but under the lights guiding the way to the car park I can see the mounds of snow banked up either side of the hotel entrance. Probably done by Lars before everyone got up. The hotel reception is bright and modern and full of people, which calms my anxiety about finding Daniel Nuhtte and my bag. Surely he must have realised he's got the wrong one by now.

A tall woman with a smart blond bob, an older version of Mika and presumably her mother, hands Pru's mother some big mittens.

'Here, I have spares,' she says with a kind smile. 'I hope you'll stay and enjoy the countryside,' she adds, pulling on a smart beanie hat and walking over to talk to some older members of the group.

'Just try and relax and enjoy yourself,' Gerald tells Sylvia. He's a grey-haired man, dressed head to toe in Pringle beneath the snowsuit he's zipping up. He's the same height as his wife, although with her head held so high, she seems to be looking down at him and everyone else. He rolls his eyes and turns away. I'm grateful that he's distracted and hasn't yet asked about the rings his good friend Mansel Knott has assured him will be delivered.

'You all right, Nan?' Pru asks the older lady, who's still looking at the memory card she's been handed and wondering what to do with it. She's wrapped up in a woollen hat and scarf, with just her glasses visible between the two, looking like Madame Cholet from the Wombles.

'Smashing, dear! Can't wait to get out on the jet-bike thingies! Why's your mother got a face like a smacked backside then?' Nan has a thick south London accent. Completely different from Pru's mother, who appears very Home Counties. 'Looks like she's got a poker up her—'

Pru splutters and cuts her off quickly, and Mika throws her head back and laughs.

'She's just adjusting to the idea of me and Mika, that's all. She had other ideas for me and how my life would turn out. But . . . well, I'm not sure we can go ahead if she won't give us her blessing. I want her to be happy for both of us.' Pru looks at her beautiful girlfriend, who smiles at her as if she only has eyes for her.

'She wants to get over herself,' Nan says. 'Mind you, your dad's mum was the same when she and your dad got engaged. Didn't think your mum was good enough. Stuck-up mare.'

'I just wish she could be happy for us, that's all, Nan.'

'Well, as long as you're happy, that's what counts. Now, when am I getting on one of those jet thingies, and who's riding my pillion?' She looks at Lars and gives him a wink. 'Could you show me where to put me card again?' she asks. As he slots it into the camera for her, she gazes adoringly at him. Lars's smile fades temporarily and his confident air slips a bit. He looks at me and then nervously back at Pru's nan, then refocuses on his clipboard, trying to ignore the old lady's close proximity.

'So, if I could have everyone's attention.' He raises a hand and Pru's nan shuffles in even closer under his raised arm. 'We're going to get on the coach that is waiting outside and drive out into the beautiful forests and countryside around Tallfors. And it will be cold, so make sure you have gloves and hats.'

Mika's mother looks round at Sylvia, who nods a stiff thank you but still doesn't look happy about any of this. I can't let them know the rings have gone missing. Pru's mother would probably say it was a sign that the wedding wasn't meant to be, and the brides seem to have enough obstacles to deal with. Let's just get going and find this reindeer herd! I think, stamping my feet as we shuffle out of the main doors towards the bus.

'Hayley!' Lars calls to me, cutting through the little group. I don't correct him. He takes hold of my hand. 'You can sit up front with me,' he beams.

'Dammit!' Pru's nan mutters, throwing me a dark stare, and climbs onto the waiting coach, finding herself a seat a few rows back. Lars ushers me into the seat beside the driver, where I sit and shiver, despite the heaters that are pumping out hot air. The rest of the party shuffle on and arrange themselves, Pru and Mika sitting just behind us. Once Lars has taken a head count, he pulls shut the stiff doors, finally cutting out the biting draught blowing through them.

Lars climbs into the driver's seat next to me. Thankfully, with my big coat and his, I think there's about a foot of padding and man-made fibre between us as we pull out slowly from the car park. There is a crunching of snow and ice under the wheels as we leave the hotel and turn onto a long, straight road lined with tall pine trees. Red- and yellow-painted houses nestle into clearings. Many of them have front porches with patio furniture on them, and most still have Christmas lights up, illuminating them in the dark winter morning. Snow hangs in huge clumps on the boughs of the trees, and every now and again I spot a passageway cut into the thick woods for electricity cables to run across the countryside. The road runs parallel with a frozen river, and in the distance, far off, there is a row of snow-topped mountains, like a baked Alaska.

I glance across at Lars, who is dividing his attention between me and the road, gazing at me in what looks like utter adoration, like a young Labrador waiting to be shown affection by its owner. Sadly, I know I could never look at anyone like that again. I think he thinks I'm playing hard to get. Thank goodness I'm going to be on my way back to Stockholm soon, and then on to my next job. But what if this is all a wild goose chase? What if I can't find anyone who knows where Daniel Nuhtte is? What if he hasn't come north to visit his family? What if I never see that bag again? And suddenly I feel very scared and nervous. Very scared indeed.

The journey seems to last forever. Lars has told us all stories about the local wildlife; about the moose that can be seen close to the villages with their young. He's pointed out a herd of migrating reindeer that we've spotted through the trees. He's described the wolverines that roam the woods, and if I wasn't so nervous about finding Daniel Nuhtte and my bag, I'd be fascinated. We've stopped en route at a bird feeding station and snapped pictures of the Siberian tits there as eventually, after a couple of hours, it begins to get light. But I'm desperate to move on. Eventually, as we travel on along the straight road, even further north, and I'm beginning to wonder if we'll end up at the North Pole, Lars pulls into a lay-by, a snowy clearing surrounded by trees.

'We stop for lunch and I will take you to Daniel Nuhtte's family,' he says, bringing the bus to a halt and pointing to the picnic table beside the river on the other side of the road. 'His sister usually looks after the herd these days, so I'm told.'

Beyond the trees on this side of the road, the snowy flat-land stretches away towards a large mountain. To my right there are a couple of huge windmills, but they're not turning. In fact, there's very little wind, just light snow falling.

Lars jumps down from the minibus and stands by the door to help everyone down into the soft white virgin snow. There is a silence about the place, broken only by Pru's nan, who launches herself at him, Baby in *Dirty Dancing* style, from the top step.

'Woo-hoo!' she shouts, taking a leap of faith and hoping he'll catch her.

Which he does, just. He steadies her, and himself, and eventually she lets go of him.

'Shh!' he tells her. 'You will scare off the wildlife. Have your cameras ready. You never know when you might see something hiding in these forests. Unexpected surprises round every corner.'

'Thank you, Lars. Smashing! I was quite a dancer in my day, y'know. Maybe we should try out a few moves back on the hotel dance floor this evening.'

Lars smiles widely and nods, but there's a flicker of fear in his eyes. He begins to usher everyone across the road to the clearing by the river.

'So, Lars, are we nearly there, at this family's reindeer herd?' I ask anxiously as he lays out plastic sandwich boxes on the table and tells everyone to help themselves.

'Ah, yes,' he says, smiling, and then his face seems to drop. 'But would you like some lunch first? Chef has made all sorts of sandwiches, and there's coffee too!' He holds up two big flasks.

'I'm fine, thank you. I really just need to find Daniel Nuhtte's sister and ask her,' I lower my voice, checking I'm out of earshot of the bridal party, 'where I can find my bag. I need to get the rings back. I need my . . . my life back.' Because that's how it feels. Everything that is important to me is in that bag. The rings, which are my ticket to my next job, the big one. And my travel log. All my memories. It might only be a book, but as daft as it sounds, it's everything to me.

'Are you sure you don't want to just enjoy the lunch?' Lars tries to persuade me one more time. 'We have gingerbread. Really good. And lemon cake.' He offers a box to me. But I don't have any appetite; in fact the very thought makes the knot in my stomach tighten further.

'Thank you, Lars, but I really need to crack on.' I nod my head meaningfully in the direction of the brides, who are standing close to each other, smiling and laughing, despite the freezing looks to match the snow-covered trees around them from Pru's mother.

'Of course, of course,' he says. Kind-hearted Lars knows that his guests must always come first. He puts the plastic box back on the table. 'I will show you where they are gathering the reindeer. Is that okay? Someone there will tell you what you need to know and give you a ride. There are plenty of families working over there, all neighbours. They will help you. But if you have any problems,' he looks suddenly very serious, 'any problems at all, call me. I will come and get you, whenever.'

'Now, here are skis.' He walks round to the back of the bus and pulls out a pair.

'Skis?' I think of the time Griff and I skied and I broke my ankle, feeling the pain like it was yesterday.

'Here.' He hands me the skis along with Daniel Nuhtte's bag. 'Put your bag of clothes in it,' he instructs, as though he's getting a child ready for its first day of school. I do as I'm told, folding my carrier bag of souvenir shop items and toothbrush into the case. I've brought it with me determined not to let anything out of my sight and lose anything else! Then Lars puts it on my back, as I'm hindered by my thick coat and gloves. He seems delighted to help.

'Ever done this before?' he asks.

'Er . . . yes. It was a long time ago, but I was quite good actually.' I *was* good, until the fall. I remember Griff and me pushing each other, laughing in the bright sunshine and enjoying the glow from the *vin chaud*. It seems like a lifetime ago now.

'It will be like riding a bicycle! It will hurt afterwards!' Lars laughs. 'You will need a hot bath and massage.' He beams, and I get the feeling he'd be happy to offer to help.

He leads me back across the road.

'I would come with you, but I can't leave my guests,' he says, looking round and back at me regretfully.

'It's fine.' I try and sound as if it is, but inside I'm trembling. 'How do I know where to go?' I ask, looking out at the expanse of snowy tundra.

'Daniel Nuhtte's family have grazed their herd here for years, like many other families around here.' Lars helps me on with my skis, bending down to buckle me into them, then straightens up and points. 'Go straight from here and over that little ridge towards the foot of the mountain. That's where they're gathering the reindeer. You'll find Daniel's sister there. I can't leave the party. Text me if you want me. Take my number.'

'My phone's dead,' I tell him.

'Take mine!' he offers with a wide smile. 'Oh no, wait . . . then you can't text me.'

'Tell you what,' I say. 'With any luck Daniel's sister will be able to tell me where he is, and hopefully I can get a lift with her. I'll offer to pay if I have to. If that's the case, you go on without me. If she can't, I'll be back.'

He looks unsure for a moment.

'I'll be fine. I'm good at this. If she can't help me, I'll come straight back. If she can, you go without me and I'll see you back at the hotel.'

'Hmm, okay. I'll wait for half an hour. I won't leave until

then, in case you need me. Okay? And I have my binoculars. Wave from the ridge so that I know you're okay.'

I nod. He steps back and gives me a thumbs-up, then crosses the road back to the wedding party.

'Okay, everyone!' He claps his hands. 'We will have half an hour here before making our way back to the hotel on a different route, where I will show you more of our beautiful countryside.'

I take a deep breath. Gloves on, stick in each hand, I know I have to do this. I have to do this to get my bag back.

'I will be waiting at the hotel to warm you up!' Lars calls across to me and waves.

I shake my head and give a little laugh. He really is incorrigible . . . and persistent! But I don't know what I'd do if he wasn't helping me out here.

Despite swearing that I would never strap on a pair of skis again, I have to do this now or lose everything that matters. My job, my travel log and these lovely brides' wedding rings. I pull my hat down further over my ears, then move out tentatively onto the thick snow. After a few wobbles and dips, I'm moving smoothly, but Lars is right, it already hurts. I just want a hot bath and my bed right now. The cold freezes the hairs up my nose, making it tingle, but I daren't take my hands off my sticks to rub it. In fact, I push the sticks into the ground harder. The quicker I get to the ridge, the sooner I'll be amongst people again.

In a furious flurry of flailing arms and legs, I reach the top of the rise, hot and out of breath and with a whoop of achievement look down to where the families are gathering the reindeer. I look and look again. I look from left to right.

There's a herd of reindeer, but no gathering families. In fact, there's just a single person there, standing by the reindeer's pen. That must be Daniel Nuhtte's sister.

'Excuse me!' I shout, and wave a stick. 'I'm looking for Daniel Nuhtte! I understand you can help me!'

As I tip my skis over the ridge, the figure turns away from the pen. For a moment I think their face lights up, but just as quickly it falls again to a scowl under the brim of a fur-trimmed hat and above a thick reddish beard. That's not Daniel Nuhtte's sister. In fact, it's not a woman at all. I've got the wrong person! And I'm suddenly hurtling with absolutely no control whatsoever down the gentle incline towards a herd of reindeer. I try and slow myself, slipping and sliding like a newborn foal struggling to find its feet, but I still end up careering straight into the bearded stranger.

'I'm sorry!' I catch my breath and straighten myself, pushing myself out of his steadying arms. Disappointment pulls my spirits through my boots and I can't hide it. 'You're not who I was expecting.'

'You're not who I was expecting either,' he says gruffly.

I'm in the middle of nowhere with the wrong person altogether. Now what am I going to do?

Chapter Eleven

'I'm looking for Daniel Nuhtte,' I say. 'I'm sorry, I thought you were . . . I was told his sister would be here with the herd.'

'Who are you?' He looks down at my skis. 'Don't tell me, a journalist!' He turns away from me.

'No! I'm not a journalist! I just have something of his . . . and he has something of mine. I need to get it back.'

'Really? And what could Daniel Nuhtte have of yours?'

'My bag. I think we swapped bags on the aeroplane. Well, at least, he must have, because I just took the one left behind.'

'He took your bag?' He looks at me as if I might be making it up.

'Yes, and I have his.' I drop my sticks and pull the case off my back, holding it up. He says nothing, just narrows his eyes suspiciously. 'I even have his recipe book!' I add, unzipping the front pocket enough to reveal the corner of it. His eyes widen a little, looking from the book to me.

'And he has your bag?'

'Yes! And I really need it!' I tell him.

Then his eyes narrow again.

'So why didn't the airline get in touch with . . . him. How come you're looking for him out here?'

'There was a computer glitch. Some sort of virus,' I explain, but he doesn't say anything, as if wondering whether to believe me or not.

'Look, I wouldn't be out here, doing this,' I lift one ski, 'if it wasn't really important and the only way to get my bag back. I took the night train back to Stockholm to try and track him down, and now I'm here, in the middle of bloody nowhere! Do you really think I'd be going to those lengths if I was making it up, if I was just some kind of stalker?' My voice is starting to sound hysterical and I take a few quick breaths, in, out, in, out.

He pauses. Then says, 'You've been to Stockholm? So you know who he is?'

I'm starting to get fed up now.

'Yes! I know he's some kind of big chef, Michelin-starred. And I have his recipe book.'

'Yes,' says the man, looking at the bag and back at me. I hold the bag closer to me. 'Look, do you know Daniel Nuhtte? Do you know where I might be able to find him?' My patience is running out. I have to work out how else I can track down this man. I have to get back to Lars before he leaves.

He looks at me with ice-cold blue eyes from under his big hat, practically all I can see of his face. Then slowly he says, 'Yes.'

'What?' I look at him and narrow my eyes, hardly believing I'm hearing the words. 'You know Daniel Nuhtte?'

He nods a single nod.

'And can you take me to him?' I ask cautiously, wondering whether to offer a fee for doing it or whether he'd be offended and withdraw his help. I say nothing. I don't even breathe.

'I can,' he says.

I let out a huge sigh of relief. 'That's brilliant! Are you going that way now?'

'I am.'

'Oh, thank God!' Suddenly my aching thighs, shins and buttocks seem to be worth it.

'What's your name?' he asks.

'Halley,' I tell him.

'Like the comet?'

'That's right.' I allow myself a little smile at someone getting it right first time.

'So you know about the stars? Navigation and all that?'

I shrug. 'A little,' I lie, not wanting to admit that I don't know anything about the stars. I just want to find out where my bag is.

He nods as if mildly impressed. 'And you can ski?' He looks down at my feet.

'I can, yes.' I wonder where this is going.

'That could be useful,' he says, as if warming to an idea.

'Useful?'

He nods again. 'For the trek,' he says flatly.

'Trek?'

'To Daniel's farm. To get your bag.'

'You said you were going there, you could take me,' I say, confused.

'I am, and I will, but I'm going that way,' he points towards the wild open tundra, 'with these reindeer. A hundred and fifty miles. It's going to take me the best part of a week to get there, depending on how fast I can go; maybe less. But you're pretty handy on those skis, and knowing how to navigate by the stars could help if the GPS lets us down. I need someone with me, in case there's an accident and one of us needs to go for help. My helper is,' he frowns, 'delayed. So, I'm happy for you to come along.' He smiles at me like a cat toying with a mouse.

He checks what appears to be a lasso slung over his blue cape with embroidered trim. 'I need to leave now, whilst the weather is still on my side. Are you coming?' He raises an eyebrow.

'What? I can't follow a herd of reindeer for a week!'

'Well,' he shrugs, 'that's the way I'm going.' He turns away, checking his load on his sled. 'You need your bag, you say?'

'Uh-huh,' I reply, my jaw frozen with cold and disbelief. How could I have got so far, only for this to happen?

'In that case, I can take you there.'

'But . . . isn't there anyone else who can just take me there? And what if my bag isn't there?'

'No, it's just me,' he says, tying up another lasso. 'Trust me, I'm sure you'll get your bag back.'

'How do you know?'

'I'm . . . I know the family. You'll get your bag,' he repeats flatly.

'Can't you ring him? Tell him to bring it to me?'

He shakes his head. 'No, sorry. He's not taking calls. He told me he doesn't want to speak to anyone right now. Journalists have been bugging him, so he's switched off his phone. But like I say, I can take you there, if you really need your bag.' He turns away from me. 'If not . . . I have to go.'

'No, wait!' I say, feeling panic rising. If he goes, who knows if I'll ever find my bag. This has been my only lead. 'Can't you just tell me where he lives?'

'No. I'm afraid I can't. He's a well-known person. He doesn't give out his address.'

'What about . . . what about if I go back to the hotel and wait for you there?'

'The Tallfors Hotel?' He nods, with a thoughtful look on his face. 'Sure, you can go and wait there,' and I almost get the feeling he's calling my bluff. I think about Lars, suddenly and surprisingly wishing he was here with me. But he'll be leaving any minute now. He said he'd wait for half an hour. It must be time.

All around me dogs are starting to bark and I feel myself go even colder. The man is pulling on big mittens obviously designed for the snow. The dogs are getting more and more excited. My nerves are starting to jangle and jump. My throat tightens. I stumble backwards, every bark and howl making me more and more panicked.

'I have to leave.' He goes to the gate where the reindeer are milling.

This is it! He's going and I have no other way of getting to my bag! I watch as his hand reaches for the rope around the gate and starts to lift it off.

'No, wait!' I call into the cold air.

He shrugs, still holding the rope. 'I have to leave,' he repeats. 'My help will be here soon, I'm sure. But if you want to come until she arrives, I could do with the extra pair of hands.'

'Can't you just go straight down the road, the same way I got here?'

'Take a herd of reindeer down the main road?' He throws his head back and laughs.

'Or get a truck to take them?'

'Have you seen how many reindeer there are here? This is how the Sami people have always got around with their herds. The reindeer migrate in spring to the higher ground here and then again in the winter, inland, to the forests. This is how we do things here. We work with nature.'

'But it's really important. There are . . . things in that bag that are needed for next weekend.' I don't want to tell him I have expensive rings in there that are the centrepiece of a wedding happening in just under a week's time.

'Look, I don't know who you are,' his eyes narrow again, 'but you clearly know nothing about our way of life. The Sami way of life. You see, that's the thing with reindeer. They're wild animals. Unpredictable. When they're ready to go, you have to go. And they're ready. You never know when they're going to lie down, and when they do lie down, you never know how long that's going to be for. And with just me moving the herd to their new grazing, well, obviously it's going to take longer than if there were two people. But like I say, I can meet you at the hotel when I eventually get there.'

He stares at me.

'Now, I'll bring your bag to the hotel when I . . . see Daniel.'

I glance around at the wilderness surrounding me. He can't really have been serious about me going out there with him. I look in the direction his sled is pointing.

He turns and releases the reindeer from the pen. They start to file out, ready to make a move to their new grazing.

The dogs are on their feet, barking and baying. Fear runs up and down my spine and I'm rooted to the spot.

'Give me Daniel's bag, I'll take it to him.' The man puts out a hand, but I don't move. There's no way I can lose this bag too. I have no idea who this guy is.

The reindeer are starting to run this way and that, picking up on the dogs' excitement, bouncing and raring to go. He calls to the two collie-type dogs who are racing round trying to keep tabs on them.

'Hurry, I have to leave,' he tells me, and I don't know why, but something about his tone riles me and makes me want to stand my ground. He throws up a hand and marches towards the sled.

'Wait!' My throat is tight with fear as he goes to step up behind his dog team. He turns to me and raises an eyebrow. 'And it would be quicker with two?'

'Of course.' He looks straight at me.

'How do I know I can trust you? How do I know you really do know Daniel Nuhtte?'

He looks at me. I'm gripping the bag tightly like some sort of protection between me and the dogs.

'How do you know you can trust me? Well, I suppose you don't. But I am taking this herd to my family farm.' He nods. 'And I can take you to Daniel. Tell you what, look in his bag, in the book. Read the message on the front page. I can tell you what it says. *"Kära Dánel, Kom alltid ihåg vad som finns i ditt hjärta, Jag älskar dig, Kram, Mamma."'*

I fumble with my gloves to pull out the book and open it at the first page. There is indeed an inscription there, starting with what looks like 'Dear Daniel' and ending with

'Mamma'. I wonder what it means. But right now, that's not important. I have to decide what to do. My heart is banging loudly.

I must be mad. But what else can I do? Go to the hotel and wait, wondering if the rings are going to turn up on time? And there's no way I'm just handing over this bag without getting mine in return. Once this man leaves, my trail will go dead. He is the only link I've got with Daniel and my bag . . . and my future. Because without that bag, without those rings, I don't have a job, and then what will I do? At least if I'm on the move, I'll feel I'm doing something to get my bag back. Keeping moving is always the best policy, I've found. Sitting, waiting and worrying only leads to madness. I can't just sit and wait when I could be doing something about it.

His hand is poised ready to release the brake on his sled and let his dogs run. Their barking is now at full volume and I've never been so terrified. I can't really spend a week in the frozen wilderness with a pack of dogs and a herd of reindeer, can I? But it's either that or see the wedding come and go, with no rings and no more work for me ever again.

'Okay!' I stop him. 'I'll come.'

'Well, as I say, I have help coming, but you can join me until it arrives,' he tells me.

'Fine. Wait, though. I have to let Lars, my lift, know.' I turn on my skis and sidestep up the ridge, then raise my arms and give Lars a wave. I can see him looking at me through his binoculars. He waves back and then gets into the waiting bus, which moves off slowly with a beep of its horn. I have a huge ball of trepidation and regret in my throat as I ski back down the little slope and stop. I feel like all the blood has drained from my body.

'Lars? Boyfriend?' the man says, stepping off the sled.

'No, just a friend,' I tell him, and waggle my gloved hand at him. 'I'm married,' I say firmly, setting the boundaries clearly before we set off.

'Good,' he says, nodding, and I swear he's laughing behind that beard and scarf. 'The light is good, the snow soft. We must leave as soon as possible. Can you drive one of these?' He indicates the second dog sled team, and all my fears suddenly swell up, freezing me to the spot once again.

I swallow hard. 'No.'

'Ah, shame . . . I needed someone who could run this team. Sorry, but in that case, I can't take you.'

'But I thought I would be skiing . . .' Suddenly I feel like my lottery ticket has slipped from my fingers and is fluttering about on the floor.

He shakes his head. 'Not for the distance I'm travelling. I need someone to take this second team. You'd better call your lift and get him to come back.'

I can't. Not only do I not have a phone, but I can't back out now. I need to get to my bag and this seems to be the only way.

'Well,' I say, slowly and levelly, 'you could show me.' My mouth is as dry as the powder snow settling on the reindeer's backs. They're all around me, their tall antlers swinging about dangerously.

'You've never done any mushing before?'

'No,' I say again. 'But I am a fast learner.' I glance at him.

He is looking straight at me, filling me with fear. His eyes are icy blue, light, with dark centres.

'I suppose beggars can't be choosers,' he says under his breath. 'But you will need to listen very carefully. These are my dogs and I won't have anything happen to them.'

I blanch and then bristle, but say nothing and bite my cold bottom lip. By the looks of it, he needs my help as much as I need his. Like it or not – and clearly neither of us does – we're stuck with each other for the time being. I look at the barking dog team and then back at this reindeer herder, and a feeling of dread wraps itself around me and squeezes tight. What on earth have I let myself in for?

Chapter Twelve

'This is Lucas, my lead dog, and his brother. They listen to all my commands and lead the team.' The man, who has introduced himself as Björn, rubs the dog's head affectionately and speaks to it softly. He's far friendlier to his dogs than he's been to me, that's for sure. As I watch, he pulls out something from his pocket that look like booties and starts to put them on the dogs' feet.

'Behind the lead dogs are my swing dogs; they help move the sled, following the lead dogs' path, particularly round corners. They pull the team in an arc. Then come the team dogs.' He goes down the central line to which the dogs are attached in pairs, one either side of the line, putting booties on each paw. 'Right at the back are the wheel dogs.' He points. 'They're my biggest dogs. They are strong, steady and calm, not easily startled. They take the weight when the sled moves off and up hills. Whatever happens, the dogs mustn't get caught in the line.'

He hands me a handful of booties. 'Put those on your team.' He nods towards the second sled. 'Helgá is your lead dog. She'll look after you. She's very steady and reliable.'

I look at the row of dogs and back down at the booties in my shaking hand. I step forward and try and say hello to

Helgá. She throws her head back and barks and I cross my hands across my chest, fear gripping me once more. What am I thinking of? There's no way I can do this. I'm terrified of dogs!

I turn to see if Björn has noticed. But he hasn't; he's still putting booties on his own team. I know this is the moment to say, 'Actually, I can't. Of course I can't drive a dog sled team. I'll have to go back to the hotel and wait. I'm not going to be able to get the rings there on time.' He turns to look at me. The snow is falling a little more heavily. The dogs are anxious to go. The reindeer milling around clearly want to get going too. One of them starts walking towards me, huge antlers swinging that could really take your eye out! I dart backwards and the reindeer doesn't follow me, thank God.

'Okay, ready?' Björn stands up from putting on the last bootee and tuts. 'I thought you said you were a fast learner!'

There's something in me, something obstinate that won't let this man look at me as if I'm some kind of a flake. And there is no way I'm waiting here, on my own, for Lars to come back and get me. No way at all! I have to keep moving. I think of the rings; of my travel log. I'm not on my own if I have that. I can't let Griff down by losing it. That's why I have to do this! Besides, I can just imagine that if Lars did come back for me, he'd think he was my knight in shining armour and demand my hand in marriage. The thought makes me smile, despite my desperate situation.

'The boots?' Björn barks like one of the dogs. 'Quickly! We need the light if we're to make it to our first stop tonight.'

'The boots. Of course.' I move towards Helgá again, and

start to bend down to her paws. The memory of the last time I was this close to a dog is clear in my mind. And the pain as, without warning, it launched itself at my face. But Helgá doesn't move, so I bend in a little closer, arms outstretched, my heart pounding like it's going to burst out of my chest.

Suddenly the dog throws up its head and lets out a long 'Whoo, whoo, whoo, whoooooooooo!' I stumble back, terrified, dropping doggy booties all around me. Björn tuts again, before picking up the booties and quickly fitting them onto the dogs' paws.

'And there was me thinking you were going to be a help,' he mutters. 'Helgá is Lucas's daughter. She has her father's instincts. She'll look after you. This is a steady team. You just have to stay put and they'll follow me. Now, this is your sled. You stand here . . .'

He's talking, but it's like I'm in the next room. I can't believe this is actually happening. Am I really going to be taking a dog sled team out there? I try and concentrate, but inside I'm screaming and want to run away. I look out at the snowy wilderness and shiver, a shiver that comes right from my core, and I don't know if it's cold or absolute terror. The reindeer are starting to move forward, bumping into each other, nudging each other with their long antlers – those that have them. To say this is surreal is an understatement. At least I've got something to write in my travel log when I'm finally reunited with it, and the tiniest of smiles tugs at the corner of my mouth. Soon, soon I'll be writing this down as another one of my adventures, a story filling the pages of my book. And that's how I get by, day to day, page by page.

Now the sled is really bouncing as the dogs paw at the ground, throwing their heads back, a baying mob waiting to be released.

Tears prickle my eyes. I'm scared. Terrified! I find myself wishing that Lars hadn't left, that he was still here with me. At least he would have made this seem like fun. He would have made me think it was safe.

'When I say go, you stand here and release the brake!' Björn says briskly, and I look down to where he's pointing. 'If you want to turn left, you call *haw*, and right is *gee*.' He looks at my frozen face. 'Keep your weight forward, and on corners go with the movement. But pretty much your team will follow mine. Just stay behind me and you'll be fine. The dogs will obey my commands.'

I nod, trying to remember, *haw* and *gee*. And the brake!

'Just take it steady. I don't want anything happening to my dogs – or my herd.' He nods towards the circling reindeer, a sea of antlers ahead of me. 'This isn't some holiday adventure,' he adds seriously. 'There are real dangers out there.' I notice him rest his hand on what looks very much like a gun, strapped on top of the luggage. A gun, for God's sake!

As if reading my thoughts, he speaks over the howling of dogs. 'Just listen to me and you'll be fine. We need to keep the herd together and away from the road. And whatever happens, if you fall, or tip your sled . . . do not let go of it. You understand? Only if you are faced with certain death do you let go of your team. Oh, and definitely no screaming. It scares the dogs.'

I try to nod. Understood. Certain death. No screaming. I glance in the direction of the road. Oh Lars, what I wouldn't give to see your friendly, smiling face right now!

'Okay.' Björn points to the back of the sled and I move into position. He looks me up and down. 'Haven't you got any better clothing? I have spares . . .'

'No, I'm fine,' I say. I think of the pants and sweatshirt and, thankfully, spare pair of thermals I bought at the airport and hope they're going to last me. I just want to get there as soon as possible. There's no way I want to be stuck out here longer than I have to be.

'Well, take these at least.' He passes me a pair of thick mittens and I slip them on over my thermal gloves. My hands feel like they're crying in thankful relief. 'Pull your scarf away from your face. The moisture will give you frost-bite,' he instructs. I go to argue – it's freezing without it around my face – but stop myself. 'When I give you the nod, release the brake and immediately step on the sled. Like I say, just do as I tell you, and you – and my dogs – will be fine.'

Brake. Immediately, I repeat to myself, my heart thunder-ing, my palms, despite the cold, sweating.

I see him do a final check over himself. He pulls out a small knife from a pocket on his sleeve and I catch my breath. What if he's some kind of madman? I don't even know him! Then all of a sudden, he whistles a command to the collie dogs, who leave the herd and jump onto the sled. The herd suddenly surges forward.

'Ready?' he shouts over the barking dogs.

No! I think, but I nod firmly. I'm really not ready, but there's no way I can go back to the hotel and just wait. I can't do nothing. I have to keep moving. And I have to stay with this Björn: he is the only person who knows where my bag is, and frankly, he holds my job, my future, my life in his hands.

I can't remember what I'm supposed to do with the brake. I'm terrified of falling off. I'm terrified of dogs. I'm terrified of everything that might lie ahead. My throat is tight with fear and no sound comes out.

'Then let's go!' he says, and turns away from me.

'*Hike, hike!*' He releases his brake and his dogs leap forward.

I look down at my own brake and focus everything I have on it as if my life depends on it, because quite frankly, that's how it feels. I pull it up in one swift movement and the sled leaps forward to follow the other. I quickly grab the handle, wobbling and nearly missing it, but manage to right myself and hang on for dear life as we set off into the white wilderness.

What am I doing here? I ask myself as my sled lurches across the snowy tundra. What on earth have I let myself in for? My heart is in my mouth, and I send up a silent prayer to whoever may be listening: just get me to the other end, and to my bag, in one piece!

Chapter Thirteen

The wind is biting my cheeks, hard. They hurt. I wish I could put my scarf around my face, but I can't. I can't do anything. I'm hanging on for dear life. I have my weight forward over the handle and I don't want to do anything that might unbalance me. I nearly came a cropper on the very first bend after we left the corral. Björn turned to look at me, and there was no way I was going to let him see me falling straight away and managed to throw my weight forward and right myself. Now we're moving across the soft snow, out into . . . well, nowhere, it feels like. There's nothing around, just clumps of trees, their boughs heavy with snow like they've been dipped in royal icing. The road is no longer in sight.

I grip the handle, my whole body shaking, absolutely freezing cold as the wind cuts through my clothing, and absolutely bloody terrified. Other than the wind in my ears, there is just the sound of the whooshing of the sled across the snow, and a strange clicking noise, though I have no idea where that's coming from.

'*Hike!*' I hear Björn call as we work our way up an incline in the snowy wasteland, and the dogs push forward. I have no idea how he knows where we're heading. His collie-type dogs are sitting on the sled like royalty, pink tongues lolling out in pleasure. They only jump off when instructed to keep the herd moving together.

Just when I think I might die from cold and being bent over in the same position for what seems like forever, to my utter relief Björn seems to be slowing down and bringing his sled team to a halt. Mine slows behind him, and I could cry with relief that we're nearing the end of the day's journey. The reindeer slow up too, and begin to wander around, snuffling at the snow with their big soft noses. All I want now is a hot bath, a large glass of wine, a bowl of steaming chips, and bed, where I think that for the first time in a long time I will sleep. Proper sleep. The slowly drifting off and having nice dreams sort of sleep that has evaded me for so long. Or maybe I'll just fall into an exhausted coma that I'll never wake up from.

'We're heading for that forest,' Björn shouts over his shoulder, pointing to the thick wall of snow-covered trees ahead. He slows the dogs right down and moves his sled out wide so he's beside me. 'Put on your brake!' He points to where he's standing on his own brake at the back of the sled. I try and move my frozen foot over the bar and fumble but finally step on it, wincing with the pain.

Above us, the sky is full of thick cloud and the gentle snow continues to fall like someone's dusting us with icing sugar. I take some big gulps of air. Despite it being freezing cold, I'm hot and my throat is dry. Björn puts his hand inside his coat and pulls out a bottle of water. I'm terrified about taking my hands off the handle. The dogs are straining to keep moving, and I'm standing on the brake as hard as I can, but the sled is still moving forward. But I manage to take the bottle and have a couple of gulps of the water.

'Are you okay?' he asks. 'We can stop here for a bit, take a rest. I'll light a fire and we can have coffee.' He looks at me, concerned.

I nod, despite my entire body screaming. I'm far from okay. I ache all down my legs and my lower back from balancing on the sled. My arms are stiff from the sheer tension of holding on for the hours we've been travelling across that wasteland. And my cheeks, feet and fingers feel like they're going to drop off with cold.

I wave a hand towards the forest. 'Let's keep going,' I rasp through my dry throat. I can only think about the warmth of a hotel, a fire and a bed.

'Are you sure? We've made good time.'

I shake my head.

'You want to push on? We could stop here, camp for the night.'

Camp? Is he mad? Clearly. Which makes me want to get to civilisation even faster.

'No,' I rasp again and shake my weary head. 'Keep going.' The quicker we get there, the sooner this will all be over. I survey the dogs in front of me. At least I've managed to stay on so far. Björn's lead dog turns and looks at me, one eye blue, the other yellow, and the fear runs up and down my spine all over again.

'Well, if you're sure you're up for this. We should get a couple more miles under our belt before we lose the light for the day, if we can keep up a good pace. It's a slightly trickier ride. But keep inside the sticks. See them? Markers pushed into the snow to show the way. Keep inside them and you'll be fine. It'll be colder over this bit and the dogs will want to run.'

I nod, ignoring the 'trickier ride'. How much harder can it be?

I'm so tired and numb from the cold, I don't know if I've nodded or shaken my head. My stomach roars with hunger as I realise breakfast was a long time ago, and I dream about Lars's sandwiches, regretting now that I turned them down.

'Try and stick behind the herd. That way you'll keep a steady pace. I'll move either side of them to stop them drifting.' He pauses. 'You're sure you're up for this? You don't have to. You're a beginner.'

I don't know if that's a compliment or a swipe at my lack of skills. Perhaps he thinks I'm no help at all and just a hindrance.

I nod again, more definitely this time. I pull off my gloves and run a hand over my numb face, but my fingers freeze in an instant.

'I'm fine. Let's push on,' I manage through short breaths. Big plumes of hot air billow out in front of me. Shaking more than ever from fear and exhaustion, I put my gloves back on.

He pulls out his phone, checking our location by the looks of it.

'We'll take a straight line across this way, through those poles.' He points ahead. 'Then we'll rejoin the path that will take us through the forest.' Snow is settling on the dogs' backs, on the luggage on the sled too and even on his outstretched arm. 'We have an hour or so before we lose the light, and we'll need to get the dogs and reindeer settled for the night,' he continues, and then turns to look at me, making the knot of tension in my stomach twist even tighter

'My dogs are ready. Let's go! *Hike!*' He steps off and releases his brake and commands his collie dogs to round up the herd, and I grip the handlebar and take my foot off the brake and we're off again. This time at a whole different speed. The dogs seem to be in control and I'm just clinging on, bent at the knees, hunched over the handle against the wind. The reindeer are running as a huge herd together and I don't know whether to laugh or cry. This is insane! a voice says as we plunge forward into the great white expanse. Insane!

Chapter Fourteen

'Slow down!' I hear Björn shout from the other side of the herd as his lead dog pulls out from behind the reindeer and alongside them and I begin to level with him. I try to brake, but the sled just wobbles from side to side. The dogs are pulling faster and faster.

'Easy!' he calls, and his team slow, but mine keep going faster. 'Easy!' he calls over again, but the dogs jostle and don't seem to hear him.

In front of me is a sea of white reindeer bottoms and bobbing antlers. I hear the rhythmic clicking sound again, faster this time, and I still don't know what it is. I squeeze on the brake to try and slow the dogs down, but the more I do, the more they seem to pull away. I wobble but right myself behind them, crouching lower over the handle to steady myself, but still they seem to go faster. I remember Björn's warning not to shout or scream, and bite my frozen bottom lip hard. I have no idea what's going on. The reindeer are darting away from me, moving en masse, starting to go off course. I am trying not to scream, feeling totally out of control as the dogs start to edge even further forward, faster and faster. I'm clinging on but want to just jump off.

'Help!' I finally shout, and turn to look across at Björn.

Suddenly the wheel dog lunges at the lead dog, who turns and snaps and snarls. The fear I thought I might be overcoming grips me by the throat, and squeezes. The wheel dog throws his head in the air, snarling, and lunges again, and I can't move, I'm frozen with terror, and this time I feel the sled lurch and start to tip.

'Whoa!' I shout, forgetting all warnings about scaring the dogs. I grip the handlebars and throw my weight in the opposite direction. As I do, the sled seems to steady itself and I stand upright and lean back, but no sooner have I righted it than it tips the other way, presumably having overbalanced as I tried to rectify the initial wobble.

'Nooo!' I try and push my weight forward to get the sled back on an even keel, but it just swings from side to side, the dogs stumbling and bumping into each other in front of me. *They mustn't get caught in the line!* I hear Björn's warning in my head, along with *Don't let anything happen to my dogs!* as one set of runners lifts off the ground completely. And then it happens. I hit the snow, face-planting the freezing crystals. It's like being hit full in the face by a barrage of snowballs, stinging, hurting, burning. But I cling onto the sled as I'm dragged along, even though my mouth and nose are full of snow, making it hard to breathe.

That's when I see it, a huge tree standing in our way as we near the end of the open expanse of snowy tundra and approach the forest. I wonder if the dogs will swerve. They must do. But if they do, that will mean I will most certainly hit it. I cling on, trying desperately not to let go, but the tree is now right in our path. Just as we reach it, the dogs change course and the handlebars start to slip from my fingers, but I hold on even tighter until with a thud, I come to a very sudden stop and everything goes quiet.

Chapter Fifteen

My eyes are shut tight, and I'm colder than I've ever been in my life. I'm a bit disorientated, but someone is calling my name. For one bizarre moment I think it's Griff. But then I start remembering where I am and suddenly I'm hoping it's Lars's friendly face I'll see when I open my eyes. Maybe he came looking for me? I slowly open my eyes and see a big reddish-blond beard like a lion and a fur hat with ear flaps. My heart sinks. It's not Lars.

His face is like thunder. 'You could have been killed! My dogs could have been killed!' I hear him growl. 'You should've slowed down. I knew you were too tired. It's too much for a beginner!'

'Where are the dogs?' I manage, trying to lift myself onto my elbows in the thick, powdery snow. A large dollop falls from the tree I've run into and hits me square in the face. I brush it away, leaving my lips and eyelids feeling numb.

'Actually . . . you saved my dogs,' I hear him say. 'You clung on,' and then, to my surprise, 'Well done.' He nods, and I'm suddenly wondering if this is the same Björn who has scowled at me from the moment I arrived, making me feel like some extra burden on his journey.

He heaves me to my feet, nearly pulling me over again

with his strength. 'This should be easier through the forest now. Slower. Take it easy. We're nearly at the place where we'll stop for the night.'

'Like I say, I've done tough times before. I know about clinging on to what's important.' I brush myself down, as if brushing off his compliment. I think I was more comfortable when we were a necessary obstacle and irritation in each other's lives.

'Here.' He nods towards my dog team, which he's obviously lassoed and tied to a tree. His team are similarly tied up too. 'You okay to carry on?'

I look at the team. I'm still as terrified as before. Every bit of me aches and all I really want to do is curl up in a ball under a duvet and cry. But I can't. Even if I wanted to, the tears wouldn't come. They never do.

'Just stay behind me,' Björn says. 'There's a cabin not far away from here. We'll stay there the night.'

'A cabin?'

He nods and I can't ask any of the questions I want to.

'If you'd prefer, I can hook the teams up together and you can ride on the sled.'

'No, it's fine. I'll carry on.' I've come this far. I'm determined to make it to the cabin. With shaking hands, I get back on the sled.

'Keep your brake on,' he calls to me as he unties the lasso. 'You did well back there. You remembered to hang onto your team.' He waves the lasso at me. 'Always make sure they're secured. They're not like pets. When they want to go, they'll run and run.' I nod, standing heavily on the brake, or as heavily as my shaking knees will allow.

The reindeer have stopped and are milling around, snuffling in the snow and reaching into the trees branches, tugging at them.

'They're looking for lichen,' Björn tells me. 'It grows on the ground and the trees here.' He points to a clump that two reindeer are both reaching for. 'This is why they come down from the mountains in the winter, for the lichen. He unties his own team. 'Ready?'

I nod.

'Sure?' he checks again, dipping his head. I nod again, more firmly, despite my shaking body. I just want to get to the cabin. The stubbornness in me won't let me give up, despite desperately wanting to admit that I'm terrified. But I can't do it. I can't give in and ask for help.

'It's not far,' he says, as if reading my mind. 'Let's go. *Hike, hike!*' he calls to his team, at the same time instructing his collies to round up the reindeer and move them on.

I follow right behind him on a path leading through the forest. It's quieter here, less windy. It's like a blanket has been wrapped around us. The dogs are travelling more slowly, and I suspect that Björn is doing this deliberately. The two collies work hard to keep the herd moving and together, darting around them.

'We call these dogs Lapp dogs,' Björn says over his shoulder, his words reaching me through the swoosh of sleds over the snow and the clicking sound, which is much louder here in the forest. It takes me a while to understand the joke, my brain fuddled by cold and exhaustion. But finally I get it – because we're in Lapland . . . Lapp dogs! And a tiny smile tugs at the corner of my mouth.

It's getting darker.

'Here!' Björn finally points to a little wooden cabin in amongst the trees. I'm torn between utter relief and unbelievable disappointment. It really is just a cabin. But I'm so happy to be at the end of our day's journey, I don't care any more. He pulls up his dogs, jumps off, puts a stake in the ground behind him and then goes to the front of the team and ties a rope from the central line to a tree. My team pull up alongside his. I step on the brake hard, ecstatic and exhausted all at the same time.

'You did it!' He turns to me, and if I'm not mistaken, he's actually smiling – well, not frowning anyway. And to my surprise, I find myself smiling back, though even that takes effort.

'I did it,' I agree quietly. I look up at the darkening sky and say louder, 'I did it!' and find myself jumping off the sled with a sudden rush of adrenalin and triumphantly punching the air with utter exhilaration. We're here! The day has finally come to an end. I've made it. Shutting my eyes, I revel in the moment, until I hear Björn shouting too.

'*Nej*! *Sluta*! Whoa!'

I turn quickly to see my team leaping forward, picking up pace and shooting off down the forest path . . . without me! Arms flailing, I try and launch myself through the thick snow towards the disappearing sled, but it's no good. I can't catch them. They're gone. All triumphant feelings completely dissolved and utter devastation setting in, I turn slowly to see Björn's glowering face. I didn't think today could get any worse, but it just did. Now what am I going to do?

Chapter Sixteen

'Gone.' I hear his voice behind me as I stand and stare at the tracks in the snow where the dogs were just seconds ago. There's a pause. Then, 'Once huskies start running, there's no stopping them.'

'Can't you call them, get them back?' I say through my dry throat. I'm speaking quietly, but you can hear every word, every noise here in the woods with the snow on the trees acting as soundproofing.

There's an even longer pause, during which I think I can still hear the dogs' pounding feet in the distance, and then, in a very measured voice, which is obviously taking a huge amount of restraint, he says wearily, 'They're not like pets you can get to come back on command.'

'So what now?' I turn quickly, in complete despair and feeling like an utter idiot, and look directly into his ice-blue eyes, but he stares straight through me.

'Look, there's the cabin. You go in. Get the fire going.' He pauses. 'You can light a fire, can't you?'

'Of course,' I say automatically, whilst a voice in my head disagrees, panics and repeats, 'No idea, no idea!'

'Well, you go in,' he repeats with a deep sigh. 'The key will be under the log by the door.'

'Just go in?' I look at the dark cabin, then back at him.

He nods. 'It's fine.'

'What is this place?'

He sighs again, clearly wanting to get on his way. The reindeer are all standing around, snuffling in the soft, powdery snow.

'It's my family's cabin,' he says. 'But lots of families use it now. Sami families.'

I don't say anything, so he explains.

'I'm from a Sami family. We are reindeer herders. Only the Sami people can keep reindeer here. Our whole way of life is linked to the reindeer. Without them, we would never have survived out here. This was my father's family cabin when he was growing up, and his father's before that. They would stay here in the summer and then travel with the reindeer. But when he met my mother, she was a teacher, so they built a house nearer the town and the winter grazing. Now this place is used by other families when they are checking on their reindeer or following the migration. We all help each other out here. It's the only way to survive.' He looks at me as if to check that he's explained enough. 'Now go on in, light the fire, and when I get back . . . with my dogs, hopefully,' he raises an eyebrow, 'we'll feed them and the reindeer and bed them down for the night.'

My teeth start chattering loudly, the sound echoing around the branches and the dark shadows beneath them. Björn goes to untie his dog team, who immediately jump into action, barking and straining to get going. I, on the other hand, want to fall down where I am with exhaustion. Every bit of me aches. But despite that, I look around at the dark forest and the reindeer contentedly munching and say, 'Actually, no.'

'Sorry?' He looks at me in disbelief, then waves a hand – 'It's fine. I'll be quicker on my own' – and goes to release the sled again.

'No, wait! Please!' I say. 'I want to come. I want to help.'

'It's fine. My dogs will help.'

'No!' I say, more sharply than I intended. 'I need to come. I . . .' I can't tell him that the last thing I want is to be left here on my own, just me and my thoughts. 'I lost the dogs. I have to come and help find them.' I may be terrified of them, but I wouldn't want anything to happen to them. This is all my fault.

He shakes his head. 'Infuriating,' he mutters. 'I pity your husband.'

I catch my breath, the insult hitting me like a punch in the stomach. I feel like saying that it's no wonder he's out here on his own; he's so bad-tempered probably no one would come with him. But I don't. Instead, we glare at each other. Then he marches to his sled, rummages in a bag and pulls something out.

'Here. Put these on. They will be warmer than the clothes you are wearing.' He hands me a pair of trousers and a poncho, the same as his. I say nothing, but take them and slide them on. The trousers are way too big, but I just roll them up at the bottom, feeling the extra warmth they're bringing me already. The poncho is not something I'd usually wear, but right now, I really don't care. It's surprisingly warm and my hands are free at the same time.

'The reindeer should be okay for a little while feeding. I'll leave Florá with them.' Björn calls to the Lapp dogs. The older of the two is there in an instant, followed by the younger one – her son, he tells me as he instructs them to stay. The old dog sits immediately and the young one just a split second or two behind her, both staring obediently at their master. He touches them both on the head and says something quiet that I don't hear and probably wouldn't understand anyway. Then he turns back to the sled and makes a space in front of the luggage. He pulls out what looks like a reindeer hide and places it there, and then points for me to sit on it.

'Keep your feet and hands in when we're going through the forest,' he instructs. 'The light is fading. We don't have long.'

Behind me is a pile of supplies covered with a waterproof sheet. In the short time we have been standing here, a layer of snow has coated it. Tentatively I lower myself onto the fur, feeling squeamish. I mean, this is the skin of one of the animals around us! But its warmth draws me in.

'Okay, let's go and find these dogs. Here, you'll need this,' and he hands me a head torch. He puts on his own and turns it on. I try and do the same, but have to pull off the big mittens I'm wearing, and even then it's a job with my hands shaking, still furious over his quip about Griff. But I know we have to find the dogs. I couldn't bear it if I'd lost them.

Björn stands behind the sled, releases the brake. '*Hike, hike!*' he calls to the dogs, but they need little encouragement.

I grip the lip of the sled just in front of me as we set off across the snow under the darkening sky. Björn says nothing; there's just the sound of whooshing as the dogs pant and their feet pound, and I can finally look at the countryside around me instead of focusing on the fear I've felt for the last few hours. The reindeer hide wraps around me like a great big hug.

We follow what looks to be the line of a frozen river. It's getting darker, and I'm getting more anxious. Björn is looking around for the dogs all the time. He switches on the lanterns on the sled and hands me a big torch, which I use to scan in between the trees. I find myself talking nervously non-stop, but I can't seem to shut up.

'Is there a chance they could have gone back the way they came, to the cabin? And you're Sami, you say? How many Sami are there? Is reindeer herding still big business? I expect you get asked questions like that all the time.' My mouth just keeps motoring as the sled keeps on moving.

'Shh!' he says finally, pulling the sled to a halt. 'Out here, we respect the forest and everything in it. We don't disturb it and hopefully they won't disturb us.'

'Wh-what kind of things don't we disturb?' I say in a dry whisper, the silence more nerve-racking than any loud city I've been in. Way more scary than New York, with its sirens wailing and alarms going off all night. I was only there for a night, but I found the constant noise and bustle of people a comfort in a way. This, though, this is a long way from comforting! I shine the light around the trees, their branches thick with snow.

'Moose mostly,' Björn says, looking about him. 'They can be dangerous if they have young ones. And of course wolverines. They're the worst. They're a real danger to the reindeer.'

I think briefly about the *vargtimmen*, the wolf time that Matty told me about on the train. The hours of darkness before dawn. The hours I hate the most. I shiver.

'And sometimes golden eagles . . . they can take a whole deer.'

'A whole—'

'Shh!' He cuts me off abruptly, and I stop mid sentence, my mind whirring about what might be lurking in the shadows of the trees.

He jumps down, pulls off his lasso and secures the sled to a tree. The dogs are more passive now. Even they must be getting tired. Björn grabs a lantern and looks down at the snow, bending over. Then he steps into the woods, following something on the ground.

'This way.' He holds up the lantern. 'The dogs have been through here, but there have been moose here too, earlier today, heading that way.' He points over his shoulder in the direction we've just come; to where we've left the reindeer, with only his dogs to guard them. 'Let's go quickly.'

He unties the sled. '*Hike, hike*,' he calls to the dogs. '*Haw! Haw!*' and the team veers off the path to the left between the trees, Björn ducking down as the snow falls from the branches around us, landing in big plops on my lap and head.

It's not long before we find them, standing by a tree, the sled on its side and caught against the trunk. He pulls up, jumps off and secures his team, then runs over and checks each of the dogs. I follow, feeling useless and frankly a complete liability.

'Dammit!' he says, throwing his hat down on the snow, revealing a head of curly reddish-blond hair.

'Look, I'm sorry. I . . . I shouldn't have jumped around like that. I should have tied the dogs up and not got so over-excited.'

'No, you shouldn't.' He pulls his knife from his coat pocket. 'Do you have a knife?' he asks.

'A knife? No.'

'You're nothing out here without a good knife,' he says, cutting at the tangled line, unwrapping it from a tree and the huskies, checking out each dog as he does so.

'Dammit!' he repeats, and I feel the same fear I felt when the dogs started barking and baying. He runs his hands over the lead dog, the bitch, and is suddenly talking and soothing her.

'Shh, shh,' he says, and then something in Swedish that sounds a lot like 'good girl'.

'Is she okay?' I ask, clenching my fists, squeezing them hard. He looks up at me.

'She's on heat, by the looks of it. I should've realised. I was so keen to get going whilst the weather was good and when I thought that you'd be able to help . . . I should've taken more time. Thought it through. Checked each dog again before leaving. I shouldn't have agreed to let you come. It's my fault. Some things can't be rushed.'

'No, it was my fault. I said I could drive the team. I shouldn't have agreed to push on.'

'It's my team. My mistake,' he says, shutting down the conversation, clearly furious with himself. 'She's on heat and this boy obviously made a lunge for her, tried his luck. That's what made them so lively . . . apart from the fact that some idiot didn't tie them up.'

I bristle, but I know he's right. I was an idiot. Too busy celebrating the fact that I'd done what he didn't think I could do; that I'd proved him wrong.

He rights the sled and hands me the supplies that have fallen from it, and I stack everything onto the one sled, grateful to be helping out with something. Then he goes to work, clipping the dogs to a new line until they are all one team and then attaching the damaged sled behind the one we're riding.

'Let's get them back before anything else happens. I need to be with the herd. There are all kinds of dangers for them in the forests.' He nods back in the direction of the cabin in the clearing on the other side of the trees.

'What about Helgá? I mean, will she be okay?' I may be terrified of the dogs, but I really don't want her to suffer because of my silly mistake.

'She'll be fine. She just needs to be kept away from the boys. Given some space. We'll put her in between a couple of other bitches until she's ready to mix again.'

Finally, with the dogs reunited as one team and the damaged sled ready to be pulled home, we set off across the snow back to the cabin. If I wasn't so terrified and cold, it could almost be a magical trip through the forest with the snow falling, being pulled by a team of dogs. But it's not magical. I'm freezing and worried we're going to be eaten alive. I try and remember all the details to write in my journal when I'm reunited with it, though.

When we pull up in the clearing, Björn looks relieved to

have all his charges safely back together. He checks on each and every one of the dogs again before making a fuss of Florá and her son, presumably thanking them for doing such a good job.

'Right, let's get the supplies inside,' he says. 'We don't want to be leaving food out here to attract wildlife. Then we'll feed and bed down the dogs.'

I nod and realise that feeding ourselves is right at the bottom of the list for Björn. His animals come first. And that can't make him all bad, can it? He may care about his animals, but he clearly doesn't feel the same about me. In fact, I think I'm more of a hindrance to him than a help, slowing him up. Let's hope his real helper turns up soon. The sooner the better for both our sakes.

Chapter Seventeen

He locates the key to the cabin under the big log with an axe wedged in it outside the door. Finally, I think, standing holding a plastic box of food, we're getting to go inside. Every part of my body aches. I long for a hot bath and bed. I long to write up my adventures in my travel log and keep trying to replay everything that's happened so I don't forget. If only I had something to write on. He unlocks the wooden door and pushes it open, and I could cry with relief at the prospect of finally being warm. He steps in and I follow. But instead of it being warm inside, it's as cold as it is outside, maybe more so. It's just a bare cabin, dark and freezing.

I stand and shiver, feeling more alone and miserable than I have for a long time. It's no good. I can't go on. There's no way I can stay here tonight, no way at all. I need to get in touch with Lars to tell him to come and pick me up. I put my hand on my phone, and then remember it's dead. My spirits plunge even lower, if such a thing is possible. All hope of being rescued from this hell is gone. Now what am I going to do?

'Put the box down there and we'll get the fire going,' Björn says.

But still I just stand there. I don't know if it's exhaustion, fear of all the predators out in the woods, or if I am quite literally frozen to the spot. But I don't move. How on earth did I get myself into this mess? How do I know this man is actually taking me to Daniel Nuhtte's farm? Although we must be heading somewhere. It's not like he's in the forest with a herd of reindeer for no reason.

I watch him as he walks past me from outside, carrying a bundle of small sticks and logs, and over to what looks like a little wood-burning stove in the corner of the cabin. He opens the door, which squeaks, and puts down his armful of wood. As he herds it into a neat pile with his feet, I notice he's wearing boots made from what appears to be reindeer hide. On anyone else they would have looked like little pixie boots. But somehow on him they don't look out of place.

He pulls a knife from the sheath around his waist, then bends over and runs the blade down the edge of one of the logs, creating little curls, like the ribbon you get on gift wrapping in smart shops in France. Except I'm as far as I could be from some Mediterranean hilltop town and its lovely gift shops and cobbled streets with the sun on my face. I'm in the middle of nowhere, freezing. Freezing to death it feels like. Why would anyone choose to live like this? Why would you choose to be a reindeer herder?

I watch as he strips some more bark from the birch branches and arranges them in the stove, then pulls out a flint from the zip-up pocket on his arm. In no time at all a flame appears around the curls of dry wood, burning brighter and bigger as it travels along the branch. Just seeing the flame ignites a tiny spark of hope in me that I'm not about to die out here in the Lapland wilderness.

'You need a hot drink,' he says. 'I'll put the kettle on.' He pulls out a little cast-iron kettle from the plastic box he's carried in and takes it outside, letting in a blast of cold air. The fire seems to respond by roaring back big orange flames. When he returns, he shuts the door firmly and puts the kettle on top of the stove.

I stand near the fire while he busies himself in the bare little cabin and look at my surroundings. There are just two beds, bunk beds. And no en suite, I'm pretty sure.

'Here.' He hands me a plastic cup. But I can't move. He reaches out and slides off my mittens, and I don't complain. I can't. I can't do anything. Then he places the cup in my hands.

'Thank you,' I manage to say, feeling its warmth. I wrap my hands around it like a comforting hot-water bottle, and hold it to my chest. Its smell suddenly hits me, reaching right up into my nostrils and down into my chest. My stomach roars loudly, and Björn, I think, sort of laughs.

'Wow! What is this?' I look down at the cup.

'I guessed you were more of a tea drinker, what with you being British. So, this is tea. Pine tea.' He nods, this time with a real smile. 'From the trees. It is the best sort of tea. It will warm you whilst I cook.'

I slowly lift the cup to my freezing lips and let the steam start to thaw my frozen nose hair, tickling as it does. I rub my nose before it makes me sneeze, then take a sip of the tea. It's surprisingly good.

'I'll check on the herd,' Björn says. 'When you've thawed out, come and help me. We'll feed them and the dogs, and bed them down for the night.' He makes for the door.

'Um . . .' I finally manage to say. He stops. 'What do you do for, you know?' I look around at the single-room cabin. He raises an eyebrow, and I'm not sure but I think under that beard he may be smiling. He doesn't help me out, waiting for me to ask the question. 'The bathroom,' I finish.

He points. 'Outside. And if needs be, take the shovel by the back door.' He opens the door, letting in another fresh blast of cold air, and this time I know he's laughing at me. Outside! This is even worse than my worst nightmare! Well, nearly . . .

I drink the tea in tiny sips, hoping that will mean I won't need to go to the loo any time soon. Then, because I know I have to put some of the mess I've made right, I pull on my mittens and go back outside to meet Björn.

'You can help me feed the dogs and settle them in for the night,' he tells me, handing me a shovel. 'Each dog needs a hole dug in the snow for it to sleep in.'

I listen and follow his instructions, despite my freezing nose and cheeks. Muscles aching, I dig, toss the snow and do it again. When he's satisfied I'm doing it right, he moves away and collects up snow in a big pan, which he takes inside to put on the fire to boil, to pour over the dogs' frozen food. 'The water also helps them take in fluid, which they can be reluctant to do,' he explains. As I carry on digging, the wind whips up, the dark night wrapping itself around me. At least I will be indoors with a fire tonight, I think as I look at the dogs' snow holes.

'Will they be okay out here?' I ask.

'They'll be fine. They have thick fur. This is what they're bred for. Not to be kept as pets in centrally heated houses. If the weather worsens, we'll dig deeper holes. But,' he looks up at the sky, 'the weather's still good. Gentle snow. They'll be happy.'

'And the reindeer?'

'Their fur has hollow fibres. The cold is no problem to them. As long as they have enough lichen, they're happy.'

No sooner has he fed the dogs than they curl up and settle into their snow holes. I look at Helgá, who looks back at me with her one eye amber, one eye blue. I wish I could go over, pat her, and say sorry, but I just can't get that close.

'Time for us to eat,' Björn says, and I feel like I am finally being allowed onto the next level of an exhausting computer game, ecstatic that one level has finished but with no idea what to expect from the next. I put my hand to the cabin's wooden door, push up the latch and let the heat from the fire draw me in.

'Take off your outer clothes,' Björn instructs, peeling off his. Despite the fire doing its best, now pumping out an orange glow, there are holes and draughts all around the old wooden cabin. 'I'll get more water boiling for drinks and to wash with. Keep a bottle of water in your sleeping bag so it doesn't freeze.' He hands me one.

I just want to keel over on the spot from exhaustion.

'Here, sit.' He nods to a simple wooden chair by the fire, pulling off his hat to reveal his curly hair, and unwinding his scarf. Then he takes a bag of tea lights from the plastic box, lighting them and placing them around the cabin. The little flames dance and light up the wooden walls and the place feels a whole lot less inhospitable.

'I always carry tea lights,' he tells me. 'You can make

anywhere feel like home with a bit of light; my mother taught me that.'

I look at the flickering flames as he busies himself in front of the fire, and suddenly there's a glimpse once again of someone entirely different from the grumpy, frustrated reindeer herder who'd rather have anyone but me as a travel companion.

I sit, letting the heat penetrate my face and hands, feeling it sting and burn as it does. Björn abruptly stands and disappears outside again, and I turn anxiously as the door slams shut behind him and I'm on my own in the sparse cabin. I can feel my heart start to bang in my chest and my breathing quicken. It's so silent here. Even the dogs outside aren't making a noise.

My heart picks up its canter again and I look around for something to distract myself. Björn has brought in Daniel Nuhtte's case from the sled. Maybe there are some clues in his recipe book as to where his family farm is. I pull it out and flick through it but can't see anything obvious. Outside there is a banging sound, making me jump. It sounds like wood being chopped. I wish I had my travel log. I look down at the recipe book. There are a few blank pages at the back. I wonder if I could just tear out a couple and make a little notebook to keep me going.

I grab two and then go back and gather up a third and send up a silent message of apology to Daniel Nuhtte, wherever he might be, for what I am about to do to his book. But needs must. I'm halfway down the page, carefully making tiny tears in the thick paper so it comes out as neatly as possible, when the door opens. A blast of vicious cold air rolls in, but I feel strangely relieved that I'm not on my own any longer.

'Everything okay?' Björn asks, his arms full of freshly cut logs. He looks from the open case to the book I'm holding in my hand.

'I'm . . . I'm just borrowing some paper,' I say.

'From Daniel's book?' The armful of logs he's holding wobbles.

'Yes. I'm hoping he won't mind. It's just he has my book and I need to put some thoughts down and my phone is dead.'

He sniffs and looks at the book again. 'Tear away.' He waves his free hand dismissively and drops the logs noisily by the fire, then feeds a couple more into the belly of the stove.

I go and sit back down by the fire and fold the three pages into a little book, using the recipe book to lean on. 'I just needed to write some notes,' I tell Björn as he grabs a frying pan, puts it on top of the stove and drops a lump of yellow butter into it. It froths and bubbles almost instantly and my mouth waters. 'My travel log is in my other bag and I want to remember where I've been, what I've done. I like to keep track of things.'

'What, like a travel reporter?' He snaps his head round to me and looks at the book again.

'No, no, nothing like that. It's just for me . . . and my husband. I sort of write this up to tell him where I've been. Letters to him. He's away. British forces,' I offer by way of explanation. 'But I never show anyone else my writing.'

He seems to breathe a sigh of relief and then pulls out his knife again and slits open a plastic bag of meat, like mince, dropping half of it into the pan. It hisses and spits and then the meat begins to cook and caramelise and my mouth waters like it's sprung a leak.

'Hungry?'

I nod.

'Good. You must eat. Keep up your strength. We have a long day tomorrow,' he says, and I wonder if I've heard him right. Tomorrow? He wants me to do it again tomorrow?

'Didn't you hear from your helper?' I ask hesitantly.

He shakes his head. 'Not yet.'

I think about going back on the sled and my hands shake violently all of a sudden.

'You made a mistake,' he says quietly and firmly. 'It happens. Tomorrow will be different. You were scared, so you pushed on so you wouldn't have to feel the fear.' He's sitting on his haunches, moving the meat around the big pan with a wooden spoon. Now he stops and looks at me. His hair covers his neck and practically touches his shoulders and his beard obscures the bottom of his face, but his eyes sparkle like snow in the moonlight. 'Sometimes you need to feel the fear in order to get over it.'

He holds my gaze and I feel myself swallowing hard. Then he turns back to his cooking. He's wrong, of course. My eyes sting and I put it down to the smoke from the stove. The way to deal with fear is to keep going, keep moving on, don't let the fear catch up with you.

In no time at all, the draughty little cabin is full of the most wonderful smells, reminding me of going to my mum's on a Friday when the family used to meet for a fry-up, or for a roast on Sundays. There was always room for all of us and enough to go around, no matter how many of us turned up. Family is what matters to my mum. Being there for each other through thick and thin. That's why she messages me all the time and why my sister keeps sending me job adverts closer to home. They want things back the way they were, Friday fry-ups and Sunday roasts. But I haven't done that for at least two years now. I blink in the smoke again.

My stomach roars again and I hold my hand to it, and I swear Björn smiles. Finally I peel off my coat and scarf and the waterproof trousers that were way too long and let the warmth of the fire do its job. My mouth waters as Björn warms flatbreads from a Tupperware box on the stove, then holds one in his hand and piles in some sort of red jelly and then the browned meat he's been frying in the golden butter. Finally he puts it on a paper plate and hands it to me.

'Here, eat!' he instructs.

I take the plate from him and breathe in the smell of the caramelised meat and sweet sauce. I wrap the flatbread into a parcel, then hold it to my mouth and bite. Just like my dead phone needing to be brought back to life, I feel like I've been plugged in and my battery is being recharged at a rate of knots. My flagging spirits revive with every mouthful.

'This is amazing,' I finally say through a mouthful of bread and meat. 'Thank you. What is it?'

'*Suovas*. Reindeer, smoked and salted,' he says matter-of-factly, and I suddenly stop chewing.

'What? As in . . . ?' I point outside.

'Of course! What did you think? That we keep them for fun, for when Santa needs more helpers?' He shakes his head, laughing lightly at my naivety.

'No, but . . .' I bristle. 'I just didn't expect to be eating one of the herd!'

'Out here, we rely on the reindeer as much as they do on us. We work together to survive. We also respect each other. We respect everything in the forest. If we kill an animal to eat, we use the whole of it, everything. For the boots I'm wearing, for rugs, everything. That way, a life has not been wasted. The animal has died for a reason and we're grateful to it. It is like having pigs or cows, except these animals are where they belong, out here in the forest, not in sheds or barns.'

I say nothing more as I put down my plate, though not before popping in the last bit of bread and leaving only a mouthful of meat.

'Now, we wash up, wash and sleep!' Björn instructs, picking up the plates. Once again he goes outside and brings in a billycan full of snow to boil up on the stove, stoking the fire to keep it blazing. I never imagined that eating and washing could be such hard work. I think of my practically unused kitchen back home. The slimline dishwasher. The fan-assisted oven. The fancy coffee maker. The combi boiler for hot water. I will never take those things for granted again. I just hope I don't need the loo in the middle of the night!

Chapter Eighteen

After a night on the bottom bunk, lying on top of a reindeer rug in a thick sleeping bag that Björn has given me, listening to the snores of a strange man on the bunk above, the sounds of the reindeer moving around outside and the occasional barks and bays from the dogs, I feel like I've been hit with a shovel.

And then I smell something I wasn't expecting . . . coffee.

I sit up stiffly. Björn is outside, feeding the dogs by the looks of it in the still-dark morning, the silvery moon throwing long fingers of light across the snow, which appears to have had another gentle layer added to it overnight, like filo pastry, thin layers on top of each other to make a thick, soft casing hiding what lies within. I can't put it off any longer. I'm going to have to go and use the bathroom, so to speak!

I'm just pulling on my thick leggings over a clean pair of souvenir shop knickers when Björn comes in with his usual blast of cold air and goes straight to the stove. I whip them up quickly, blushing, hoping he didn't get a glimpse of my nylon-clad bottom.

'How's Helgá?' I ask, worried that she might still be traumatised by yesterday's accident.

He nods. 'She's fine. I'll put her back in the pack today, in between a couple of other bitches.'

'Oh good,' I say, pulling on the too-long waterproofs and rolling them up at the bottom, practically suffocating in my scarf, which I've already wound around my neck to stop the draughts, before venturing outside to find a nearby tree.

I wasn't quite as prepared as I thought. Squatting in the dark, with many layers of clothing, to piddle in the snow is definitely an art form I have no desire to perfect.

On my return, Björn hands me a mug. 'Here,' he says, looking at my shocked face, and I swear once again there's a hint of a smile or maybe a smirk at the corner of his mouth. I want to say that it isn't funny, and actually, it's easy for him just peeing against a tree, but he should try getting out of waterproofs, leggings and cheap pants whilst hundreds of reindeer eyes stare at you, but he stops me before I start. 'Let's eat and then we'll set off. And don't worry about the dogs, I have a different form of transport for you today,' and that smile is still there. He holds out a plate to me. This time there's a flatbread with mushrooms, and one with jam, possibly the same lingonberry jam as last night, as well as hot, strong coffee.

'This is delicious,' I find myself saying.

He stops eating briefly to say, 'It's all from the forest. If you know what you're looking for, well, like I say, the forest is where we Sami people survive. It is our friend. We collect the food in season and store it for when we need it, like now.'

We pack away the sleeping bags and the plates, cups and pots into the plastic boxes and Björn secures them on the sled then teaches me how to chop wood so that we can leave fresh kindling and logs by the fire.

I am determined not to let him think I'm a complete city dweller. I stare at the log. 'Good, and again!' he instructs. I pull back the axe, feeling the ache in my arms from yesterday, but swing anyway.

'Where do you want these?' I ask, holding an armful of logs and puffing a little, my head torch lighting up the cabin as I stand in the doorway.

'By the fire, for next time,' he says. But as he gazes around the cabin, I wonder when next time will be. It's as if he's giving the place one last look, saying goodbye with a certain amount of melancholy. Standing aside, he lets me out, then pulls the door shut firmly and puts the key back under the log. And there, outside, beside the dogs, stands my new form of transport.

'This is Rocky. He'll look after you very well He's a castrated male. His job is to pull a sled. Slow and steady. You bring up the rear. I will run the dogs and keep the herd together. You keep the stragglers moving forward.'

I stare at the big reindeer harnessed up to a wooden sled, then take a step towards his head and pat him tentatively. 'Hello, Rocky!'

He turns to look at me and lowers his antlers in my direction. I take a step back. They are so long!

Björn laughs. 'You have to make friends with your reindeer, bond with him, work as a team.'

'Bond,' I repeat. Rocky is looking at me as if we are never even going to be acquaintances, let alone bond and become lifelong friends.

'So, you hold this orange rope here.' Björn hands it to me. 'It's attached to the halter around his neck. You can use your voice, like with the dogs, to get him moving on.'

I take the rope and Rocky gives me another derisory look. Björn smiles.

'We'll keep to the forest path rather than going out on the tundra. It may take longer but I think it's safer. We'll stop when we get to the frozen lake. Catch some fish for supper.'

The reindeer are milling around in amongst the trees looking for lichen and once again, I can still hear the clicking. 'What is that noise? That clicking?' I ask.

'It's the reindeer's ankle joints. It's a form of communication. So when there's a storm, a whiteout, for example, they can hear each other and stay as a herd.'

'Safety in numbers, eh?' I smile. 'Just how I like things too.' I find myself attempting conversation.

'Not converted to the great outdoors then?' he laughs.

'No, I'm still more of a city girl . . . but then you've probably guessed that.'

'Here.' He holds something out to me, his head torch casting rays around the dogs and reindeer.

'What's this?

'A walkie-talkie. In case we need to be in touch.'

I take it and put it in my pocket, thinking how much my nephews would love these.

'Okay?' asks Björn, doing a final check of the sled. 'Ready?' The dogs are barking and jumping as he moves to stand, tall and proud, behind them. I have no idea how he can control such a big pack. I couldn't even manage four, but then he looks like he's been doing this all his life.

'You keep the reindeer moving forward from behind,' he repeats. 'It'll slow us down a bit, but it's better that we get there in one piece.' He looks at me with his ice-blue eyes and I catch my breath as he pulls on his fur-trimmed hat, tugging the ear flaps down firmly. 'We have a Sami expression that says, "However the journey starts, so it will continue!" I'm hoping to prove that theory wrong!' He slaps his hands together. 'So let's get moving, and take it steady this time!'

The dogs start their usual baying and barking in anticipation of the trip ahead, and the sled swoops forward and past me, much to Rocky's chagrin.

Chapter Nineteen

'Twenty-two, twenty-three, twenty-four,' I count under my breath. 'No, dammit!' I say out loud, but no one hears me. Björn is way in front of me, directing the Lapp dogs and reindeer. I've counted the one with only one antler before, I think. And that one with the really big antlers that he swings around. The one next to him, or her with no antlers and a white bottom, I haven't counted. I'll start again from there and try and count in sections this time. I'm trying to keep my mind busy as we move slowly through the snowy forest. I have to keep an eye on the reindeer. I don't want to be responsible for losing anyone today.

The snow has a crisp layer to it, like a crème brûlée, that crunches as we travel over it. I think Rocky could be sulking. He's moving in fits and starts, one minute shooting off so fast I nearly fall off the back of the sled, and the next slowing right down to practically a standstill so that I have to cajole and coax him on.

It's still cold, but there's less wind. It's so quiet, as if a soft duvet has been wrapped around my world. You can just hear the clicking of the reindeer's ankles and the clattering of antlers when occasionally there's a falling-out. It's beginning to get lighter, and I start to relax a little, because the darkest hour is always just before dawn. The *vargtimmen*.

I begin my counting again, just to stop my thoughts from wandering to the closed box at the back of my mind. I see if I can do it in Swedish. '*Ett*, *två*, *tre* . . .' My 'Learn Swedish' app on the plane journey to Stockholm suddenly seems like a very long time ago! I count the reindeer in blocks of ten in Swedish and give each of the blocks a name connected to something I've seen, so that I remember to write it in my improvised notebook, which is zipped into my coat pocket.

'I'll call you Night Train!' I say to my first group of ten, to remind me of my train journey with the elves. 'And you ten Husky Ride!' The next lot will be Snow, then Pee Tree!

We pass through a clearing. The trees are thinner here, and to my left there is a shaft of pink, purple and then orange light on what I think is the horizon. The reindeer spread out and Björn works the dogs to keep them together. I do the same at the back of the herd.

'No, no, keep moving,' I say, and wave an arm at a practically white reindeer with fawn patches on its side. I nearly miss a little one that nips back into the forest. 'Hey, you! Robbie the Reindeer!' I call after him. That reminds me of watching films with my nephews back home at Christmas, and I quickly push the memory of us squished up on the sofa out of my mind. I have to jump off the sled and shoo him back to the herd, waving my arms and sinking into the deep snow. He swerves round me like a tearaway youngster, and then dashes up to a large fawn reindeer with darker fur on her belly and nestles into her: running back to Mum after a telling-off.

When Björn pulls up and tells me we're stopping for lunch, I'm relieved, but at least this time I don't feel as terrified or out of control as yesterday. I think I've counted nearly three hundred reindeer, but I'll recount after lunch because I'm not actually sure; I think I counted quite a few twice, and maybe missed some too!

He ties the dogs to a nearby tree, and then the sled. I go to do the same with Rocky, who I swear dips his head and takes a swipe at me with an antler as I grab the orange lead rope, so that I have to jump sideways.

Björn smiles and shakes his head. 'I see you and Rocky have yet to become friends!'

'He's so . . . prickly. And stubborn!' I say, thinking about the couple of times he's just stopped, and I've had to pull and then cajole him and the sled forward through the snow. 'And then when I do get him to move, he suddenly shoots forward and I can't stop him.'

Björn raises both his eyebrows. 'Maybe,' he says slowly, 'his stubbornness is his way of saying he's scared and needs help. If he keeps running, he doesn't have to see or hear the things that scare him. It's how he deals with things he doesn't want to face.' He looks at me, and I feel like I'm in one of those bad dreams when you're walking down the high street naked. I go to change the subject quickly.

'So . . . how many reindeer have you actually got here?'

He stands up tall and looks at me. 'Asking a Sami person how many reindeer they have is like asking them how much money they have. So, how much money do you have in your bank account?'

For a moment I try and think of how to answer.

'Well, it's . . . I . . .' I'm not going to tell him about my bank account! 'Look, sorry, I didn't . . .' I realise I've made a faux pas and am worried I'm about to put our new-found tentative working relationship back three steps.

Suddenly he throws his head back and laughs. Glints of red in his beard catch the light through the snow-dipped branches, making them look like flashes of fire.

'It's okay. Just this once I'll let you off. You didn't know. But you will for the future. It's very bad manners to ask.' He smiles, clearly enjoying his own joke, and I find myself letting out a sigh of relief but also smiling too. 'Let's find some wood,' he says as the reindeer mill contentedly around in the trees, the Lapp dogs sitting watching and occasionally rounding up one that strays too far. I notice it's the younger dog that is doing more of the work. Björn walks into the woods, gazing silently down at the ground.

'What are you looking for?' I ask in a loud whisper as I follow him.

'Tracks,' he answers flatly. 'You never know what might be about.'

'What, moose and wolverine?'

He turns to look at me. 'Or maybe dinner.'

'Dinner?'

'Shh,' he tells me, then points to tracks in the snow. Not little feet marks, but like something has been dragged through it. 'Ptarmigan,' he says. 'Very tasty if we can catch one.'

I grimace, though I know I shouldn't. He looks at me.

'We take only what we need from the forest, no more. *Lagom*,' he says, then stops and glances around as if searching for something.

'*Lagon*?'

'*Lagom*,' he corrects. 'It means . . . well, it's about our way of life: not too much, not too little, just enough. A balance. We take no more than we need, but we take enough to live.'

I nod. That makes sense. I think again of my house back home and all my appliances, mostly wedding presents that have never come out of their packaging or seen the light of day. Way more than I need. Maybe I'll have a bit of a sort-out when I get back, give away some of the stuff I never use.

'Here, this tree is dead. We'll use that.' He holds the axe out to me. 'Let's see if you can remember how to do it.'

He instructs me where to cut, and I listen and focus and put all my effort and the frustration I didn't know I had in me into bringing down the little dead tree. Then he goes back to the sled for a saw and between us we pull and push and cut up the tree into little logs and stack them on my sled, putting some aside for the fire.

Björn uses some tiny bits of moss and bark to light the fire in the big wok-like fire bowl as I get my breath back. At least I'm warm now. Slowly he feeds the little flames with twigs and then bigger sticks from our fallen tree, using every bit of our haul. He stands back as the smoke curls up from the fire bowl, looking into it as if lost in his own thoughts. He seems very different from the stressed herder of yesterday.

'You love it out here, don't you?' I venture.

He sighs. 'Out here . . .' he pauses and looks around, 'I can think better, clearer. It's all about the silence.' He breathes in deeply and the smoke billows upwards. 'Out here, it feels like freedom, no constraints.'

He starts pulling out pots from the plastic box. 'We'll get this going, then have some lunch. Here, grab some snow. We'll make coffee. And if you want to make a friend,' he nods at Rocky, who is standing with his back to me, 'collect up some of the lichen from the trees for him. He'll have pellets later, but he'll love you if you find him some lichen.' He reaches up into the tree and pulls out a handful. 'Show him you want to be his friend. Work with him. Get his trust . . . let yourself trust him. The Sami and the reindeer have relied on each other for generations.

I take a moment to think what life must be like out here and thank my lucky stars I'm going back to a life of modern technology. But in the meantime, I do need this reindeer's cooperation.

I look around and follow Björn's instructions, picking lichen from the trees, getting showered with snow every time I disturb a branch. Then I offer it to Rocky. At first, he swings his antlers about and eyes it suspiciously. Then he takes a tiny nibble, just to see if I am offering him the real thing. When he realises I am, he stops swinging his head around and eats from my hand, even allowing me to stroke his head whilst he chews. I go to find more and put it on the floor in front of him, and he snuffles at it hungrily. I pat his hindquarters, but he swings round quickly, and I take it we still have a little way to go in our relationship.

'How's it going?'

'We're getting there. Baby steps.' I sit down on a log that Björn has covered with a reindeer hide next to the fire bowl.

'We'll eat,' he says, 'then go and lay some nets. See if we

can catch something for supper.' He's adding what look to be dried mushrooms to the pot on the fire, cut up on a board on his lap whilst sitting on another log. He pulls the coffee pot from the fire with a stick, then, using a thick glove, pours and hands me a mug. I take it and let the aroma fill my senses, then sip it. I used to find coffee bitter and way too strong, but this, this is different; smooth, not too intense.

'This is delicious!' I say, feeling surprised.

He laughs. 'It is the way we make it. We crush the beans, not grind them. And then the water must be heated three times in the fire. It's how my father taught me and, well . . .' I wonder if he has anyone to pass the skills on to but don't ask. 'It's the best coffee,' he finally says. 'And drinking it out here of course adds to the flavour.' He waves an arm around at the clearing and the open space beyond the line of trees.

'Mushroom soup okay?' he asks.

'Lovely,' I reply.

'We gather what we need from the forest and then dry and pickle it for the winter, when there is nothing. Mushrooms, blueberries, lingonberries, cloudberries.' He points around with the spoon he's holding. 'Cloudberries are delicious.'

We fall back into silence, and I pull out my little notebook and begin to write about my journey and my relationship with Rocky. I describe the ride, the dryness in the air despite the snowfall, the trees, the snow like layer upon layer of dustings of icing sugar. I explain how I counted the reindeer and nearly caused offence by asking how many reindeer are in the herd. I write about the fire, which seems a constant comfort in this snowy landscape, like a warming hug pulling us in, and I wonder, just wonder, if I might see the Northern Lights, but I know I'm not here as a tourist. I'm here to find my bag and get those rings to that hotel. I wonder whether my mum and sister are worrying about me, having not been able to message them. I have lots to tell them all when I get back.

I can feel Björn looking at me as I write. He's cooking, but when he's not, he pulls out a small piece of antler he picked up earlier in the day, lost by one of the young, small males, and starts working it with his knife, whittling it, scraping off the mottled fur that has been mostly rubbed away against the trees.

As ever, I begin each entry with *Dearest Griff,* and write as if I'm reading it to him. I'm just describing the reindeer foraging and snuffling at the lower branches of the trees, making the snow fall in isolated showers on their soft fur, big black noses and mottled antlers, when Björn interrupts my thoughts with a plastic bowl and spoon and the most amazing-smelling soup, earthy, nutty and garlicky. My stomach roars its appreciation. 'And here . . .' He hands me a square of the Sami bread, toasted on the fire with cheese on top. I take it and bite into the hot, soft bread and melting cheese. Suddenly I'm in heaven!

'This is delicious!' I say again.

'Thank you.' He smiles, pouring out his own soup. 'I've had practice.'

'Really? You cook a lot?'

He suddenly clams up, then slowly says, 'This sort of cooking was part of my growing up. Days off from school always involved a fire and cooking. It's in here, part of who I am.' He holds his hand to his chest and then tastes the soup and gives a little nod of approval to himself.

We eat in silence, just the snuffling of the reindeer around us and the occasional bickering between the resting huskies. Other than that, all I can hear is . . . well, nothing. Just the falling of snow from branches, and the clicking of the reindeer's ankles as they move around the trees, pulling at the lichen, shuffling in the snow

It's getting harder for them. The weather is warming, and that means that some of the snow melts in the day then freezes again at night, turning to ice. It's much harder for them to get through ice to reach their food. That's why they're looking up to the trees. And in turn, we are happy. I glance around at the herd, with their amazingly thick coats and big dark eyes.

'How come some of them don't have antlers?' I ask, finishing my soup and accepting seconds.

'They lose their antlers every year, the males first at about this time. The females later so they can protect their young once they're born. The antlers come back in the same shape every year. That one over there only has one antler and it grows back the same every year . . . just like her son.' He points to another with only one antler.

We finish our soup and cheese on toast, the best I've ever eaten, then tidy up. I wash up with water we've boiled in the embers of the fire.

'Okay, let's lay some nets,' Björn says. 'Get some fish for supper.'

'Lay nets? Where?' I look around.

'Over there.' He nods towards the tundra beyond the trees. Just a big flat open space. 'In the lake.'

'That's a lake?'

'Uh-huh,' he confirms.

'And you want me to walk across it?'

'Uh-huh.' He smiles broadly for the first time since we've started our trip, and I'm not sure it feels like a good thing.

Chapter Twenty

He's holding out snow shoes to me.

'You want me to walk across a frozen lake,' I repeat. And still he seems to find this amusing.

'You only have to worry if the ice has melted a bit,' he says.

'Melted?'

'It will freeze again. It's all fine,' he says as if this is an everyday occurrence, and I think out here it is. 'Look, you can stay here if you prefer. I'll go and lay the nets.'

'Do lots of people come and lay nets out here?' I try and gauge how normal an activity this is as I put on the snow shoes.

'Only the Sami are allowed to lay nets under the water.' He pulls a big orange corkscrew off his sled. 'Others can just drop a line and fish. We will leave the nets down there for a few hours while we take the reindeer on to our next stop, then I'll come back for the fish.' He smiles, the sort of smile that says he's buzzing. He loves being out here, catching and cooking his food.

'And you're going out there now?'

'Yes, how else do you think we can lay these?' he says as he gathers nets from his sled, and, if I'm not mistaken, picks up a gun in a case and straps it across himself, checking his lasso is firmly in place too. 'What are you planning to eat tonight? Chinese takeaway? I'm not sure they deliver out this far!' he teases me.

I look out at the expanse of white.

'That's the ice road,' he tells me, pointing at poles stuck in the snow. 'We'll take the reindeer that way later.'

'Couldn't we just have more mushroom soup for supper? I'm really not that hungry.'

'You will be. We still have another couple of hours to go. You're no good to me or the reindeer if you can't pull your weight because you're exhausted. You have to feed yourself as well as the animals.'

He starts to walk across the soft, powdery snow, holding two poles. The dogs, seeing him go, suddenly start to bark, chilling my already frozen body. There's no way I can stay here on my own.

'Björn! Wait!' If he's going out on that lake, it must be safe, mustn't it? He's been doing this his whole life, I keep telling myself. He turns, and with my heart in my mouth, I follow.

We set out across the frozen lake, and all the time I'm thinking, oh my God! This is a frozen lake! The ice could crack, we could be swallowed up by dark, freezing water at any time! But the reality is that it doesn't feel any different from the snow we came over this morning through the forest.

Björn doesn't seem to share my concerns. In fact, he looks positively content. He stops suddenly and I'm so busy looking down, I nearly career into the back of him. He glances around and then at me.

'You know, you are going to miss a lot of life if you never look up and see what's around you,' he says.

It's all right for him, he thinks this is all perfectly safe, but it can't be, can it? We're walking on ice, frozen water, and beneath it . . . I shudder. Keeping your eyes on where you're going rather than just standing and looking around is a much better approach to life in my opinion. That way you can watch out for the pitfalls.

'Here will be fine. We will lay nets in four holes,' he instructs. He takes the huge corkscrew from off his shoulder and dumps it in the snow with a thud, and again I panic that we're going to go crashing through into the freezing depths below us. Oblivious, or just ignoring my concerns, he carries on matter-of-factly. 'First we clear the snow.' He uses a shovel to dig down, revealing the thick, glassy ice beneath. 'Now we make the hole,' and he begins turning the corkscrew into the ice, grinning, showing his white teeth and high cheekbones above his thick beard with the reddish streaks, like highlights being picked out in the bright winter daylight.

He twists and twists the corkscrew through the ice, and I take a step back, just in case it cracks. Then he pulls it out and asks me to hand him the nets, which I do, reaching out as far as I can so as not to have to stand right next to the hole. It makes sense, right? He feeds the net into the hole and secures it with a stick in the snow.

'So we know where it is!' he announces proudly. 'And now the next.' He straightens up, picks up his shovel and giant screw and marches away whistling.

I follow. It's much windier out here than in the protected

forest. I pull my hat over my ears, then look at Björn's and wish I had one like it.

'And then we'll do one over there, and one over there.' He points. 'In a square, so we remember where they are!' He smiles and nods. I'm clinging to the edges of my hat. Maybe if I do something, like the log-splitting, I'll warm up a bit.

'Here, Björn, let me!' I nod to the shovel, peeling an arm from around myself and holding it out to him, shivering. He nods back approvingly and passes the shovel across. I want to show him I'm not as useless as I was yesterday, when I lost the dogs. Once I've finished digging the hole in the snow, he nods again and hands me the giant corkscrew. By the time I've screwed it in, my muscles are aching but at least I'm warmer. Then, like before, he feeds in the net and puts in a stick to remind us where it is.

We're just walking to our third hole, me using the shovel as a walking stick, when there's a shout behind us. We turn and see two men waving to us, and if I'm not mistaken, it's not a friendly wave. Some forms of communication are just universal. They're on a snowmobile and are scooting towards us at speed. They too have a shovel and a giant corkscrew, and a gun across the handlebars by the looks of it. Björn stops and turns to them, sighing as he does so.

'What's the matter?' I ask. 'Have we done something wrong? Is this their land?'

'In Sweden, everyone has a right to roam,' he tells me. 'You can go almost anywhere in the countryside as long as you do not disturb, and do not destroy. They even put the whole country up on Airbnb because you can camp out in most places.' But his smile slips as the men call to get his attention again, and I don't think they look happy as they pull up, get off the snowmobile and march towards us, one carrying the gun.

Björn stands and waits for them. They seem to be asking him who he is and what he's doing, pointing at the nets. He pulls himself up to his full height of over six foot and lifts his chin, and the men, both much shorter than him, take a step back. He is clearly not about to be intimidated.

The men seem to be questioning him again. Björn looks at the nets and then slowly turns back to the men and looks at them hard. I can feel myself shrinking on their behalf. One of them goes to speak again, stepping forward and pointing to the huskies at the edge of the lake. The other man puts his hand on the heel of his gun, slung over his shoulder, as if expecting trouble. I look between Björn and the two men and suddenly wonder how serious this is going to get. I'm out here on a frozen lake, with no phone and only a shovel for protection. And if I'm not very much mistaken, this is turning ugly.

Chapter Twenty-one

Finally, after a long, tense pause, Björn speaks, in a low and measured tone. I don't understand what he's saying. I'm not even sure it's Swedish; in fact, I'm sure it isn't. I hear the word Sami and then I'm sure I hear the name Nuhtte, and then I do hear it: Daniel Nuhtte. He points to the dogs and back towards the hills behind us, the direction we've come from over the past day and a half.

I'm listening and trying to pick out words I might understand, but none of it is making any sense to me. Instead, I turn and look at the two men and attempt to read their faces. They're giving nothing away. I look between them and Björn and wonder what on earth is going to happen next. Their eyes narrow, but the aggression seems to be seeping away. They nod at me, questioning him. He looks at me, then back at the two men. I'm so frustrated; I have no idea what's going on. He keeps his head held high, and continues to speak in a slow, measured voice. Suddenly he slings his arm around my shoulder and to my shock and surprise hugs me to him. I hold my breath. I can smell the woodsmoke on him from the fire.

The two men look at each other and say, 'Ah!' then smile widely. They reach forward and pat Björn on the back and point to the nets, and I think they're now wishing him luck with his fishing, before bidding us farewell. Björn keeps one arm around me, only releasing me to take the fish they offer him with a smile and good-natured nods. I glance at him. This guy can obviously charm the fish out of the water . . .

The men climb back on their snowmobile and wave to us before driving off. Without a backward glance, Björn sets about digging out the next snow hole, clearly unfazed by the encounter.

'Björn? Those men! What was that all about?' I say, tripping over my snow shoes.

'It's fine. It happens. Don't worry about it.' He goes back to digging and I think he's just told me to mind my own business.

'But they had guns and everything. What did you say to them?'

He sighs, as if wondering whether to explain. 'It happens,' he says. 'Like I said, only Sami people are allowed to lay nets for fishing out here.'

'And?' I shake my head, not understanding.

'I don't look Sami. I don't know if you've noticed, but I have fair skin and am a foot taller than most of the Sami people. I look like I came over on the first Viking ship.'

I blush. I have actually noticed he is very . . . Nordic-looking. Classic fair skin and steel-blue eyes that seem to terrify me as much as his lead dog's do! I drop my gaze, suddenly unable to look at him for fear of blushing again. He blows out air, his cheeks filling like two big gobstoppers, then looks me up and down. 'And you clearly aren't Sami. I'm with a . . . tourist!'

I go to object, but he's right. I still have my 'Welcome to Stockholm' sweatshirt on.

'Like I say, it happens all the time. They spotted the dogs, thought I was a musher and challenged me.'

'But you are a . . . musher, right?' I find the word odd to say, but that is what someone who runs huskies is called.

'My mother was a musher, before she met my father and became a teacher. A lot of the Sami don't like the mushers. They come here for the snow, for the good terrain to run their dogs. But whatever people think, I am Sami through and through,' he holds his hand over his heart, 'even if the dogs and my appearance say otherwise! The Sami people are a close-knit community, helping each other out. Those men didn't recognise me; I haven't been around for a while. When I told them . . . Well, it was fine. They wished us good fishing.'

'And me?' I think about him pulling me to his chest, and find it strangely unsettling.

'Oh, I said we were together. Engaged. It made it simpler.'

'What?!'

'They wished us luck and a big family!' He laughs, and starts digging again.

We finish the fourth and final hole and then make our way back to the herd in silence, both lost in our own thoughts. I think about Björn, his life out here as a reindeer herder and what kind of a father he would make if we really were together. We'd probably have at least four children, I think, and he'd have them all out learning to mush and herd reindeer from an early age. He'd take them fishing and teach them to look after the dogs and use a lasso. I find myself smiling, then suddenly, as though I've been punched, I remember Griff and the family at home and feel a wave of guilt wash over me. My cheeks are no longer freezing, but burning with shame instead.

The dogs greet Björn and I rejoin Rocky, who looks at me warily but at least doesn't try and swing his antlers at me as I untie him, which could be considered progress. We set off again, this time moving the herd out onto the frozen lake, and even though we've just come from there and nothing bad happened, my heart is still in my mouth. What if the extra weight of three hundred reindeer causes a crack? Who knows where the danger might be; we could easily step in the wrong place. This ice road clearly doesn't come with a map. I like a map. I like to know where I'm going.

The sled sways as we move across the lake, but despite my fears, I feel much more in control. Rocky seems to be getting used to me; the lichen must have helped in some way. And much as I would like to be moving faster, I've accepted that I'm just going to have to take this journey one leg at a time. Slower but safer, and we should still make it.

Finally we reach the other side of the lake and move back onto uneven ground, the sled bumping and lurching.

'We'll keep going for a bit,' Björn calls out to me, 'whilst we have the light.'

'What about the fish?' I nod back in the direction of the lake as we start up an uneven incline.

'I'll go back for it when we get to our next stop!' he calls. 'Over this hill and then on to the forest. We'll stay there the night. Switch on your head torch when it gets darker!' The light is turning to early-evening dusk, and I realise it hasn't snowed all day . . . so far.

As we reach the brow of the hill, the sky seems to open up and show itself to me. A huge expanse of different blues, dark navy through to light, soft grey, with wisps of clouds like silhouettes against the big blanket before me and a tiny line of yellow spreading out into orange along the horizon from the sun that never came up and has already disappeared for the day. Björn turns and smiles at me, acknowledging my appreciation of this beautiful sight. Then before we know it, the streak of yellow and orange has disappeared and the sky has turned a dark inky blue, like someone's tipped over the ink pot. The moon comes up, white and bright, throwing out an eerie blue iridescent light across the snowy path towards the trees down the other side of the incline, and there are some tiny dots of stars across the sky, like someone's thrown a handful of glitter on a thick velvet scarf.

Together we switch on our head torches, lighting up the furry behinds in front of us, and head down the hill. It's much faster than I'm expecting, but this time I hold on tight and find myself smiling as we go, and actually enjoying the ride. I can't wait to see the cabin. I'm exhausted but also feeling a little elated from that downhill run. I sniff. It's getting colder as night falls. The hairs up my nose freeze and tickle. I can't wait for the warmth of my sleeping bag and bed. I don't even mind if it's a bunk again. I know my sleep will be fitful, it always is, but just being in a comfy bed is such an inviting thought.

'Not far now,' Björn calls to me as we move into the shelter of the trees, which wrap their branches around us as if welcoming us in out of the wind. A few minutes later, he pulls up and so do I. The reindeer stop and start foraging amongst the trees. I look around for the cabin but can't see it. There is no cabin. Björn has tied the dogs up next to what looks like a bundle of long sticks leaning against a tree.

'Our home for tonight,' he announces proudly. 'Out here, each Sami leaves the poles for a *lavvu* against a tree for the next traveller to use.' He takes one of the poles and lays it in the clearing.

'Sorry, *lavvu*?' I tie up Rocky and grab a handful of lichen, putting it on the ground in front of him.

'Uh-huh.' Björn takes another pole. 'A traditional *lavvu*, in which Sami have lived for hundreds of years. We are nomads, following the herd. When the herd choose to migrate, we follow, and we need portable accommodation.' He stands holding a third long pole.

'Portable accommodation?'

'Uh-huh. A *lavvu*, like a tepee. A tent.'

'A tent? We're camping tonight?!' And my slightly lifted spirits hit the floor once more.

Chapter Twenty-two

'We put the poles together at the top,' he says, looking up at the point at which the three poles meet. He glances at me and instructs me to bring some more of the poles. I do as I'm told but inside I'm glowering, simmering, furious and sulking. A tent, in winter, in the Arctic! He puts the other poles in place, forming a tepee shape, and then gives it a good shake to test it.

'Solid! Good! Now for the covering.' He smiles and goes to the sled. 'Here, take the other side,' he says, and we pull out a tarpaulin-like sheet, which he wraps around the poles. 'There!' he stands back proudly, and I have to admit, it's a pretty impressive instant shelter. It even has a doorway, a flap that he pulls back.

Next he gathers some rocks and arranges them in a circle inside the *lavvu*, right under the point where the poles meet. Then, like last time, he gathers moss and bark and puts it in the middle of the circle of rocks. When he lights it, the smoke curls up and out of the hole in the top of the *lavvu*. There is no way that's going to keep us warm tonight. I could freeze to death out here. Camping, in January, in Lapland!

He looks up at me. 'Take the saw and your knife and cut down some birch branches; we'll use them as flooring.'

'I don't have a knife,' I remind him.

'Oh no, of course. Here, take mine.' He hands me the knife from the sheath around his waist and I take it carefully, avoiding the blade.

I march out into the trees and cut some branches, shaking off the snow and feeding Rocky the lichen that I pull off. Once I've got a big armful, I head back into the *lavvu*, dipping my head and suddenly meeting a wall of warmth.

'Great, put them down here and then get me some more,' he instructs. I turn around and step back out into the cold, still very grumpy. By the time I return, he has spread the branches across half the *lavvu* floor and laid reindeer skins over them. The fire is roaring, and a pan of water is balanced on two sticks over the flames and beginning to boil. Together we lay out the rest of the branches and in the heat of the fire they quickly dry off. He fetches more reindeer hides from the sled and lays them over the top of the branches beside the fire.

'Take off your clothes,' he says.

'Pardon?!'

He laughs, soft and full. 'I meant take off your coat and outside layers. That way you'll get warm.' He gets up from beside the fire. 'There's pine tea in the pan. I'll go and get the fish. Keep the fire going; I'll be back with supper.'

'I'll come!' I say quickly, staggering to my feet.

'No, I'll be quicker on my own.' He pulls his lasso on over his long body and turns away without waiting for a response. 'Chop wood. Keep the fire going. Florá and Erik will stay with you.'

I stand in the doorway of the *lavvu*, the smoke drawing

up and out through the hole where the poles meet at the top, as he marches, arms swinging, over to the dog team, who start up their usual baying and barking, though this time I know they're just happy to be going on a run and my terrified goose bumps don't appear.

'*Hike, hike!*' he calls. He raises a hand to me, then releases the brake and he's off, as eager as his dog team.

'No, wait!' I call after him. 'Björn!' but it's too late: he and the dog team are zipping back along the track through the trees and I'm left standing here, surrounded by reindeer. I can't stay on my own, I want to shout. I don't . . . I can't . . . I can't be on my own. But he's gone, cutting through the snow at speed, the dogs running faster than they have all day, still with plenty of power in the tank, Björn standing tall at the back of the sled, head torch throwing out its icy blue glow, following the moonlit path.

I can feel the panic starting to rise in me. God! I wish more than ever that Griff was with me, that I wasn't doing this alone. My heart twists and my throat tightens. I hate it! I hate being on my own! I hate being left! I begin to feel the familiar itch over my whole body as I start to stress. I look around, see the axe and grab it. I swing it angrily a few times and then walk a little way into the trees, my head torch lighting up the branches and the reindeer. They turn from their contented munching to look at me, the rustling and snuffling making me jump as they appear around every tree, their big brown eyes looking green in the torchlight.

I remember Björn's warning about the dangers lurking in the forest, and my heart starts racing. But I notice the dogs have followed me, obviously seeing me as one of the herd now and not wanting me to stray too far, and I feel strangely grateful to them.

I see a branch sticking out from a tree and tap it like Björn did, checking to be sure it's dead, then swing the axe, putting all my anger and frustration into it. I chop, and chop, then step back as the branch comes down with a swish and a thud into the snow, making both me and the reindeer jump.

'Shh, it's okay,' I say, trying to calm them.

I drag the branch back to the *lavvu*. 'Take just enough. Respect the forest.' I hear Björn's words and realise with a sense of satisfaction that the branch is *lagom* – just enough.

I brush off the snow, rub my cold nose with the back of my mittened hand and sniff, then start swinging the axe, bringing it down onto the branch with force. The rhythm of the swing echoes the loud beating of my own anxious heart, reminding me I'm alive. By the time I stop and stand back, out of breath, the anxiety still there but quieter, I have a fair scattering of logs around me. I pick up an armful and step into the *lavvu*, which is surprisingly warm. Kneeling by the fire as I've seen Björn do, I start to feed it with the logs. They spit a little and smoke, but then start to burn. I stack the rest by the fire and dust off my hands.

Next I grab a billycan, the pot with the handle, and dip out through the *lavvu* door, checking left and right for noises, signs of wolves or bears. I fill the pot by scooping it in the thick snow, and go back inside thinking I'll never take my coffee maker for granted again. Or central heating. Or hot running water. Or moan about takeaway deliveries being late. I will never complain about anything else again, ever, just so long as I get out of here in one piece! I look up at the dark, star-scattered sky and wonder if anyone can hear me, or whether I really am on my own.

I shoot back inside the *lavvu* and pull the door flap shut. Silence falls again, leaving me alone with my thoughts . . . where I don't want to be. I strip off my poncho and coat like Björn has told me to do, and then wrestle my way out of my waterproof trousers, feeling like Barbarella as I thrash around on the reindeer rug. Then I pull out my little makeshift travel log from my coat pocket. It's got bent, and I try and smooth it out, but the corners just curl.

I decide to use Daniel Nuhtte's recipe book to lean on while I write. I take it out of his bag and run my hand over its worn, dog-eared cardboard cover, mottled with splashes and stains, drops and doodles. It's like an old school book that bears the scars of being both well used and well loved. Slowly I lift the corner. I've flicked through it before, when I was trying to find out the owner of the bag. I know now that it's this Daniel Nuhtte, the one I heard Björn mention to those men yesterday, the only thing I understood. The Michelin-starred chef with a partner back in Stockholm trying to get in touch with him.

So why would he just disappear? Why was he on that plane to Stockholm with a few belongings and this book? What sort of a man is he? I look at the newspaper cutting tucked in between the cover and the first page. It's in Swedish, and all I can work out is that it's about his restaurant. The first page in the book is a recipe, the title written in pencil, underlined but fading. I focus hard on trying to work out what it says, to keep my thoughts from straying and wondering about any little noise outside. If only

I had my phone, I could translate the whole lot!

Throughout the book there are little pictures, more doodles and notes down the side in pen that seem to have been added later. I study the handwriting to see if that tells me anything about the man. But there are no swirls or flamboyant flourishes; just bold lettering pushed firmly by the pen into the page, leaving its mark. As I turn the pages, the writing becomes more confident, growing in size and boldness. I'm guessing this is a determined person who knows what they want. I see a word I think I recognise and run my finger under it, getting a strange feeling of connection from where he's put his thoughts and clearly his inspiration on the page.

I wonder with a jolt if he is reading my thoughts too, in my travel log. And I suddenly feel like I'm standing in a room full of strangers, totally starkers again. Lost in my own embarrassment, thinking about the feelings I've put down on the page, feelings I would only share with Griff. My cheeks burn. I feel sick. I clutch Daniel Nuhtte's book to my chest, as if to protect my modesty.

'*Hej*!' The flap of the *lavvu* falls open.

I let out a little shriek as a blast of cold air engulfs me. There, towering above me, is Björn, holding a handful of fish and beaming.

'I didn't hear you!' I manage to say through my tight throat. Reading Daniel Nuhtte's book certainly managed to block out any noises and sounds.

'Everything okay?' he asks, looking at me and then at the recipe book I'm clutching to my chest.

'Fine!' I lie.

He looks at the little wood pile and the glowing fire.

'Impressive!' He nods, and I find myself swelling a little with pride. I'm pleased he doesn't think I'm a total waste of space out here. I'm glad I proved him wrong, I realise, after my disaster with the dogs.

'Reading?' He nods down to the book still held to my chest.

'Just interested.'

We both stay silent for a moment. Then I say, 'I was just wondering if it would give me any clues to Daniel Nuhtte, what he's like really.'

He shuts the *lavvu* flap, banishing the cold air.

'And did it?'

'Well . . .' I think about the question. What had I found out by looking through Daniel Nuhtte's private thoughts? 'He obviously loves what he does. And he has favourite recipes, where the page is more worn than others. There are some recipes that look to be home-cooked food, and then later, recipes from all over the world, like he's written his food memories as some people might write . . . a travel log. Food seems to be his life. And he's funny, too, he does little drawings.' I go to show him, but Björn bites his bottom lip and looks away.

'And what would he find in that notebook you always seem to be writing in if he went snooping?' he asks.

'I wasn't snooping! Just . . . looking!' I feel aggrieved. 'And if he was going through my bag, he'd find the wedding rings I need to deliver to the couple getting married at the weekend and would probably realise they were really important.' Suddenly we're back to how we were when we first met.

'Weddings! People shouldn't need to tell the outside world how much they love someone. Weddings are all for show.'

'Not at all!' Suddenly all the anxiety I felt earlier is bubbling up and over. 'These two people want to show the world how much they mean to each other. And those rings are a big part of that.'

'How much you love someone should be all that matters, not how much the world needs to see it. That way, the world can't judge you when the love isn't there any more.' He puts the fish down on a birch branch, takes off his coat and pulls out his knife.

I think about my travel log, and the love that is very much still there in its pages, my love for Griff.

'You're obviously a cynic and don't know what it means to really love!' I run my hand over the book. 'This Daniel Nuhtte clearly knows about love and passion; it's here in his book, in his food.'

'So go on then, tell me, what would Daniel Nuhtte find out about you, other than the rings you've misplaced?' He begins to gut the fish on a little wooden board with swift, precise movements. 'What is it that means most to you in that bag?'

I pause, watching as he pulls off his hat, revealing a head of blond curls shot through with red, and for a moment I wonder if I've seen hair like that before. Was it somewhere on my journey here? Or maybe, it was in the recipe book I'm holding. I look down at a little doodle of a face with big curly hair in the margin of one of the pages that makes me think about it. Next to it is another doodle, a bottle and some berries and a little scribbled recipe, lingonberry vodka I think it says. I'm about to tell him about my travel log, but suddenly I stop. Why would I confide in this man about what's most important to me? As far as he's concerned, I'm only interested in finding the rings and delivering them safely. And that's all he needs to know.

'Nothing. There's just the rings, and my travel schedule,' I say. I slam the book shut, and for some reason it makes him flinch. He looks away quickly and back at the fish.

God, I think, I wish I wasn't here. I wish I was anywhere but here!

'Hungry?' he asks after a few minutes.

'A little,' I say, my pride preventing me from telling him how starving I actually am, but my treacherous stomach letting him know otherwise and roaring loudly. He laughs and shakes his head, then opens the plastic box and sprinkles something over the fish – maybe salt, maybe something else, I'm not sure. Then he threads the fillets onto a long stick and rests it over the fire, the flames gently toasting them. The smell is amazing. He serves them with a dollop of cloudberry sauce and some sour cream he's brought with him. The fish melts in my mouth as soon as it hits my tongue, and I shut my eyes. Paired with the tart, creamy cloudberry sauce, it is actually divine. We eat in silence, both lost in our thoughts.

After we've finished eating, and I've returned from the horror of visiting the pee tree, something I will never get used to, he says 'Get some sleep. We've got a long day tomorrow. We need to cover a lot of miles if we're to make it to the river in time.'

'The what?'

He stops putting away the pan and plates he's washed with boiled snow.

'The river. The weather is warming. It's a problem for reindeer herders. The rivers used to be frozen all winter, but now they are thawing much sooner. The weather is good for moving the herd, but we need to get to the river before it starts to melt.'

I swallow. 'Why?'

'To cross it, of course.'

I stare at him in horror.

'Cross it?'

'Yes, what's the matter? Suddenly not the package holiday you were hoping for?'

We seem to have gone one step forward in our working relationship and two steps back!

'We have to cross the river to get to the farm . . . where your bag will be, I'm sure, and whatever it is that's so important to you, your rings and your schedule.'

'Fine! Across the river it is then!' I say, but I can't help an involuntary shudder at the thought of it.

'If you're cold, come and sleep by me,' he tells me matter-of-factly.

'I'll be fine,' I say, laying out my sleeping bag as far away from him as possible.

He knows nothing about me and I know nothing about him, and frankly I'm happy for it to stay that way, I think as I lie fully clothed inside my sleeping bag, teeth chattering, on a bed of birch branches and reindeer hide, which is surprisingly comfortable.

I stare out through the tiny hole at the point of the *lavvu*, catching a glimpse of stars through the smoke and thinking how Griff would have enjoyed this, ever the adventurer, loving the unknown. I think about Lars back at the hotel, waiting for news of my return. I picture his smiling face and his wide-open arms and wish I could turn back the clock and be at the hotel now, with the rings I need to deliver. I wonder if my boss has worked out that they haven't actually made it there yet!

Then I suddenly think about Daniel Nuhtte again and wonder if he needs that recipe book badly. I think about the hours of love that must have been poured into it; recipes he's gathered over the years, possibly from all around the world. He's a Michelin-starred chef, for God's sake! It's probably worth a lot of money! Then another thought strikes me. If I'm looking for him, is he looking for me, for his book? But I've got no way of contacting him and only Björn to help me find him, and he doesn't seem to understand the urgency. He's just worried about the herd. Let's hope his helper gets here before we reach the river, because the tundra has been bad enough; there is no way I'm going over a frozen river!

I curl up into a tight ball, pull my sleeping bag hood over my head in an attempt to blot out the sound of snoring, and try and suppress the urge to actually kill him.

Chapter Twenty-three

Stepping outside the *lavvu* the next morning is how I'd imagine it would feel to step into an industrial freezer and shut the door, then have a hairdryer set to cold blow in your face. My cheeks and nose are instantly freezing. Even my teeth are cold!

'Come on, we have a long way to go today,' Björn says, handing me the dog bowls to hold as he puts the frozen feed into them and pours on boiling water. Once they have cooled, we hand them out to the excited dogs – me at arm's length – who jump about in excitement at the prospect of a new day and a new adventure.

Back in the *lavvu*, he takes out a pan and begins to fry up leftover fish from last night. My taste buds immediately start watering. Then he toasts bread on the glowing orange and white embers of the fire, and its comforting smell fills the air.

I pull off my poncho and coat and sit down. The heat from the fire immediately warms me, but the atmosphere between us is still frosty, and we eat in silence. I savour the flavours of the smoky fish, my heart in my boots about the prospect of going outside again.

'Okay, let's get moving,' he says when we have finished.

'We'll load up, take down the *lavvu* and then get the dogs ready.'

I nod and do as instructed.

I look out at the sea of antlers. Okay. Get your reindeer, he says. But which one is he?

Björn looks at me with an air of disappointment, like a teacher who's told a pupil to do something and then sighs when it doesn't happen. He stands and marches towards me in the deep snow.

'There, that one.' He points to a reindeer standing patiently by a tree, reaching for lichen.

Now that I see him, of course it's Rocky. I pull the lichen down and put it on the ground for him, and he seems to sense my low spirits, standing still while I harness him up.

'Now let's get moving.'

'Of course,' I say through chattering teeth.

Despite Rocky doing all the walking, my legs are numb with cold and feel like jelly standing on the back of the sleigh. Ice is forming on my lashes, and even my eyeballs feel frozen. It's eerily quiet. Just the clicking of the reindeer's ankles.

We stop for a break. *Fika*! Björn makes coffee and hands me home-made cake from a Tupperware box. It's sweet and syrupy.

'You need to keep your strength up out here,' he says.

'Is your helper on their way yet?' I ask as I eat the cake and drink the coffee.

He shrugs. 'I hope so. The more hands we have, the quicker we'll get there.'

And the quicker I can get to the farm and collect the

rings. Or, maybe as soon as the help turns up, and we see a town, I'll make my excuses and go and find a phone and ring Lars to come and get me and wait at the hotel after all.

Björn checks the dogs, giving extra attention as usual to his lead dog, speaking to him in soft, hushed tones. It's amazing that he has such a way with animals but not with humans – well, not me at any rate.

He stands, listens, then looks around at the trees.

'Do you hear something?' I ask, seeing the look on his face. He scans the trees again, then turns back to me.

'Out here, we respect the forest. We don't disturb what is living here and in turn they will respect us and leave us alone.'

'When you say what's living here, what do you mean? What is it?'

He looks at me as if wondering whether to say more. Then he points.

'You see there, those tracks?' and I do see them.

'Wolverine,' he says, and my blood runs even colder, if that is possible. 'We have to keep moving.' I don't need telling twice.

There's a noise behind us and we both turn to look. There's nothing there. It comes again, but it's just snow falling from the branches of a tree in big clumps with a thud. Not a wolverine, thank God.

'We must push on.' Björn's face is set. 'The mild weather means the snow is softening. The ice on the river will be starting to melt in places. We need to get there and get over it by the time the light goes, or we'll never make it.'

He checks that we have left nothing behind, then calls to Florá and Erik to start rounding up the herd. And despite the coffee, my mouth is as dry as the desert. I'm terrified of what's hiding behind us in the woods, and terrified of the melting river ahead.

'Björn?' I call to him.

He turns to me.

'What if the river is starting to thaw? What happens?'

'We will have to change our route. It could put days on the journey.'

'But I . . .' I don't have days to spare. 'The wedding is on Saturday! I know you might not think it's important, but it is to the people getting married, and to me, for my job, my life really. I have to get there.'

He nods, checking that I'm ready to go, and I nod back. However much my legs ache, I know we have to make it to the river, and across it, today.

Chapter Twenty-four

'We can go round, the long route.' Björn looks this way and that along the river. 'Or I can look for the safest place to cross,' he says as if asking me the question.

'See if you can find somewhere safe, please,' I practically beg. There's no way I can afford to be here for longer. He nods, and the sled disappears out of sight down into the valley.

My anxiety starts to ramp up once again, my heart quickening as I wait. Suddenly there's a bang, like a gunshot. I shriek, and the herd jumps and scatters a little. I bite down hard on my lip to stop any more sounds coming out.

'Björn!' I can't help myself: I call out and spin, stumbling and falling in the snow, righting myself to see where the sound is coming from. Oh God, what if he's been shot, wounded? What if I'm here on my own with an injured man, or worse, and a herd of reindeer? Suddenly I see the dogs reappearing around the corner. What if he's not with them, and it's just the dogs on their own? Then I see him, standing upright at the back of the sled. He hasn't been shot, and I find myself letting out a long, slow sigh of relief and finally breathing again.

'What was it?' I ask as soon as I think he can hear me. 'Are you okay? I mean . . . what . . .' I stop myself.

A slow smile pulls at his mouth. 'For a moment there I thought you were worried about me.'

'Just wondering what I'd do with a herd of reindeer and a dog team in the middle of nowhere,' I bite back. The relief has gone and irritation replaces it. He laughs.

'Really? Sounded like you were—'

Bang! Another shot. I jump. It echoes around the valley, bouncing off the snowy banks, making the herd jump again. Björn's laughter disappears, as does my irritation. My heart is thundering. His focus is back on the snowy terrain around us.

'It's the ice. It's melting in places,' he says economically, his eyes darting around, clearly assessing things. 'Maybe we *should* take the long route,' he says finally. 'This way could be dangerous.'

'But the other way means days longer. I don't have days.'

He listens, putting his gloved finger to his lips, waiting for any more signs and sounds. Then he looks at me, staring hard, as if trying to see what I'm really made of.

'Are you sure you're up for this?' He nods his head towards the river.

'Crossing here? I'd prefer to be airlifted out, but if this is the quickest way to get where we're going, then . . . let's do it.'

'Okay. But if any of the herd turn back, the rest will follow and we'll never make it across. We've got just one shot at getting over before the ice starts to give. Do you understand?'

I can barely nod, but I must have done because he turns the dogs.

'I think the ice is thickest just down here, though it's not the shortest crossing,' he says. My teeth chatter loudly, and I can't stop them.

He calls to his Lapp dogs, who start moving the herd.

'You bring up the rear on one side like before, I'll be on the other. Just keep them moving forward,' he calls back, 'and don't stray. I can't afford for them to turn back once we start.'

Forward, yes, forward, my frozen brain repeats. I nod once in understanding.

'Scared?'

I nod again, imperceptibly this time.

'Being scared is always part of the journey,' he says quietly, and then he turns back to his lead dog and calls his name. 'Lucas!' The dog looks up, as if sensing the importance of what is facing us. Then he slowly turns to his master, dipping his big furry head, and Björn nods back. It's as if they're showing each other mutual respect, owner and dog, like they have a bond all of their own.

Björn looks up and calls, '*Hike, hike,*' and we're off! Moving the herd forward down the snowy descent to the icy river. My heart is pounding like it's trying to burst from my chest. There's a whooshing in my ears that I think might be my blood crashing around my body. The reindeer's ankles click loudly as they jostle across the icy waste, slipping occasionally as we head down the steep incline and then out onto the frozen, snow-covered river. My sled feels like it's got a life of its own, swaying this way and that, but Rocky keeps a steady, sure-footed pace and I know, right now, that my life is in his hands. One false move and that could be it.

In the distance I hear another bang. I swing round to look at Björn, but he is focused forward. Slowly I look left and right and realise we've reached about halfway, right in the middle of the river. For a moment the herd seems to jostle, and my heart leaps into my mouth as I wonder if one of them is about to turn and head back.

'*Heja*, *heja!*' Björn urges them, waving, driving them forward, and it seems to be working. I join in, and the herd on my side keeps moving. We are beyond the halfway point now. He turns and gives me an encouraging nod. 'Keep them going, don't give them time to think too much, that way they can't get scared and try to bolt,' he calls over.

'*Heja*, *heja!*' I call again and wave my arm. My heart is still pounding like the hooves of a hundred reindeer, and I'm practically holding my breath. The riverbank, covered in snow-laden pine trees, is now in our sights. I turn briefly and glance back the way we've come. The far bank is a long way behind us now. But as I look forward once more, I see that little Robbie, the reindeer I had to round up the other day and send back to his mum, has followed my gaze. Suddenly he starts to turn.

'Stop him! Don't let him go back!' Björn shouts.

'*Heja*, *heja!*' I shout urgently, but he's facing the other way now. The reindeer either side of him glance at him, and by the looks of it, they're thinking about turning too. Oh no! He's moving back through the herd! I can't let him! I have to stop him!

'Grab him! Turn him round!' Björn shouts. But the little reindeer isn't listening to our shouts, and now another one's coming out of the pack.

'Lasso him!' Björn shouts, but I have no idea how to do that. There's only one thing I can do, and I know I only have one shot at doing it. I let go of the sled with one hand and then, holding on with the other, reach over as far as I can. I reach and then reach even further, praying I don't tip the sled, and then I grab, feeling the antler in the palm of my hand.

'Pull him round,' Björn shouts, and I tug with all my strength. I know that Rocky won't let me down and shoot off this time, and slowly I turn the little reindeer back round the other way to join the rest of the herd. The others are thankfully moving forward again, and he seems to be following. I think I may have done it; I think he's back with the herd, and I can feel myself breathing for the first time in I don't know how long and look up at Björn, who is actually smiling, nodding and giving me a big thumbs-up. I did it!

And then, as if I've been shot in the back, I hear the crack again, and the *zoosh*, *zoosh*, *zoosh* as the crack splits and opens up just behind the herd. The rear corner of my sled suddenly dips, unbalancing me, and we start to slide backwards, only juddering to a halt as Rocky takes the strain. The little reindeer, Robbie, turns to make another run for it, but instinct makes me grab his antler again and cling on, despite finding myself up to my knees in freezing water on the precipice of a crack in the ice.

'Hold on! Don't move!' Björn calls. I really don't intend to! I think as the freezing cold starts to seep up my trouser legs.

The lasso is off him and flying through the air and around my body in what feels like seconds.

'Grab it and hold on! And don't let go of the reindeer!'

I do exactly as I'm told. Björn and Rocky will need to pull together to get me, the sled and Robbie out. I only hope they can!

Chapter Twenty-five

Finally the reindeer start to filter up the riverbank and spread out through the thick snow in amongst the trees. Is this it? The other side? Can we really have done it? I wonder with a mix of elation and incredulity. I'm shivering with cold and relief as I glance back at the far side of the river where we've just come from and hear another shot of cracking ice. I look at the herd. They're all over safe and sound, every single one of them – including little Robbie.

At the top of the snowy bank, the land plateaus out and we stop. Björn ties up Rocky and turns to me. His chest is heaving, and I wonder if he's going to be furious that I nearly landed us all in the water. Then his face breaks into a huge smile.

'We did it!' he beams, throwing out his arms. 'We did it!'

Excited goose bumps run up and down my spine.

'We did it!' he repeats. Then he says, 'You were fantastic!' and taking me completely by surprise, he envelops me in a huge bear hug, pulling me into the fabric of his big poncho, where I find myself breathing in the familiar smell of wood-smoke. 'You were completely brilliant out there! You saved my herd! Thank you!' he says, and hugs me tighter, this time actually lifting me off my feet. For a moment I wonder if he's going to kiss me. He looks into my face, his eyes dotting to and fro between mine and my lips, then his smile drops and he becomes serious again.

'Let's get you some dry trousers and boots,' he says, putting me back down quickly, but still clearly buoyed up. 'It'll have to be snow boots like mine. We'll stuff them with hay for extra warmth.'

In the wooded clearing, he lights a fire and gathers pine branches for tea, whilst I slide out of my trousers as quickly as possible and into some others he hands me, which are actually just about the right size.

'My sister's,' he tells me. 'I thought she'd be here by now and would need them. But she won't mind. You just saved our herd!' And now I know one more thing about him: he has a sister. 'These too,' and he produces some hand-stitched snow boots, made from reindeer hide. I put them on, and he pulls out some hay from a small bag and stuffs it into them, feeding the remnants to Rocky and Robbie.

'Stand still!' he says, laughing as he pushes the hay around my ankles.

'It tickles,' I squeal. But it is also, I realise, very warm.

We are both buzzing, adrenalin coursing through us, warming us as we share the story over and over of how I thought I'd been shot and how I saved the herd from turning back.

He builds a bigger fire than usual and hangs my wet clothes from the branches around us, including, to my embarrassment, my souvenir shop knickers.

'You have the wrong day on!' he says, smiling.

'Sorry?'

'The pants. They say Saturday across the bottom in Swedish. It's not Saturday.'

I blush and we both laugh.

'You know,' he says, handing me a mug of hot pine tea, 'I bet your husband would be very proud of you. When we first met, what I said about pitying your husband, I was just being an idiot. I bet you can't wait to tell him how well you did today.'

Our fingers touch as I take the tea and I feel a leap of something go through my body, like a tiny electric shock, and then I freeze, the cup in my hand, feeling like all the blood has drained from my face. I didn't think about Griff in all that adventure. I didn't even think about reaching for my notebook to write to him. Suddenly panicked, I pat my coat, looking for the pad. I pull it out. It's wet, and some of the ink has run.

'Oh no!' My mood does a nose dive from euphoria to desperation. 'All the notes I've made, ruined!' I hold up the little home-made book.

'Don't worry! We can dry them out. You and that book,' he laughs, teasing me, and then he stops very suddenly and I hear him say softly, 'Hey, are those . . . tears?'

He stands from his usual position looking after the fire and moves towards me. My vision is blurred and I can't see his face, but I know he's standing right in front of me – I can smell the woodsmoke and feel him there. I can hear the reindeer snuffling and munching in the trees and the dogs panting as they lie resting nearby.

I sniff, put the back of my hand to my nose. It can't be. I shake my head. It can't happen, not now. Not after all this time. I hold my breath and hope any tears that have formed will evaporate in the cold air. But no! Instead of going away, they seem to be multiplying, my vision even more blurry. This never happens to me! I don't cry! Why now?

'Look, I meant it! Honestly.' Björn takes hold of my arms, just above the elbows, which only seems to make things worse. 'I was really rude back when I met you. If it's any excuse, I was stressed and worried about moving the herd and . . . well, other stuff. It doesn't matter.' He waves a hand. 'Your husband would be really proud of what you did out there today. You were amazing! I have to admit I didn't think you'd manage it, but what can I say, I don't think anyone could have done better!'

As he's talking, my head drops, the top of it practically touching his chest. It's no good, I can't fight the tears, no matter how hard I try. All my usual techniques to stop this happening, that I have worked so hard to develop over the past two years, have completely left me. Maybe it's elation at getting the herd over the river. Maybe it's the near-death experience, thinking that I could have drowned back there had Björn not been so quick with that lasso, that has brought it all to the fore. Or maybe just exhaustion. Exhaustion from being out here. Exhaustion from hiding from what's really in my heart.

Slowly, really slowly at first, I shake my head.

'Oh dammit!' he says with despair, as if this is one obstacle he wasn't expecting today. An over-tired and emotional woman. He lets go of my arms and I feel disappointment now stir itself into the mix of everything else I'm feeling. I can hear him scrabbling around as I stand there feeling pathetic. Tears slide down my cheeks and are frozen by the time they're wiped away by my gloves.

'Here, use this. It's a T-shirt. It's all I could find.' He waves it at me. I'd like to say thank you but there's a lump in my throat the size of a golf ball, and I mop my cheeks in silence, then blow my nose.

'Now look, borrow my phone, and let your husband know you're safe and we're on track to be at the hotel in good time for the wedding on Saturday.'

He pushes a phone into my hand. A link to my life in the outside world. If only it were. I look down at it, then slowly push it back towards him.

'It's fine,' I say with a crack in my voice. 'I'm fine. Thank you.'

'Are you sure?'

I nod and slowly lift my head. 'You're right. He'd be proud. But I'll just write it all up and tell him when I'm back.'

He looks at me and then slowly says, 'And . . . where exactly is he, your husband? You didn't say.'

'He works away.' I swallow hard, slipping back into my usual routine. 'He's forces. Goes away a lot. Impossible to get hold of him, so I write it all down.'

Björn looks at the book. 'Well, we'd better get this dried by the fire and see what you can save from it.' He gives me a soft smile and takes the pathetic pages from me.

'Thank you,' I croak again. 'Just tiredness, y'know, bit overwrought after all that . . .' I attempt to gather myself, but as I turn away, I can still feel Björn's eyes on me, as though he is trying to read between the tightly written lines of my lies as I attempt, as ever, to carry on as normal and hope I've got away with it.

He makes a little spit to go over the fire and drapes my soggy pages over it one by one, spreading them out gently to dry. As he watches them to make sure they don't catch light, he pulls out the piece of antler again and whittles at it with his knife whilst the coffee pot comes to a boil. When it does, he takes it out of the flames, lets it cool and then puts it back in. He does this three times, I notice.

'Just the way my father taught me,' he tells me with a smile, whittling contentedly at the piece of antler, enjoying the moment. When was the last time I enjoyed the moment? I wonder. I'm always thinking about where I'm going next. I pull the reindeer hide he's wrapped around my shoulders even tighter.

'Here,' he says as we pack up, handing me the dry pages, some with inky smudges where words used to be, the paper warped and crisp but intact.

'Thank you,' I whisper. He doesn't know what it means to me. I look at him and see the kindness in those blue eyes. Or maybe he does.

Dry and warmer, we move on, over the snowy plateau with the river behind and below us. Onwards towards the much lower hills, rather than the mountain range we've come from.

'We'll follow the line of the river, in between it and the main road over there,' Björn says. 'It'll be quicker if we stay out of the forest for this bit, and we don't want the reindeer straying anywhere need the road, either. We're heading over that way, to Tallfors.'

'Is that where you'll take me to find Daniel?'

He is riding beside me, the dogs travelling at a steady pace.

'To his farm . . . to get your bag. Yes.'

'How do you know Daniel? Are you his brother? Are you related? I heard you talking about him when we met the men fishing.'

He looks sideways at me as if to consider the question.

'No. I'm not his brother.' He looks straight ahead. The dogs are working their way through thick snow, and every now and again he scoots with his foot to help them along. 'I just grew up with him. Spent my twenties and thirties with him,' he adds, looking straight ahead at the herd and beyond as the light starts to fade.

'What's he like?'

He keeps his gaze fixed ahead.

'A bit arrogant. A bit naive. I think he's spent too much time thinking about where he is going and not enough about where he's come from.' He gives me a quick glance. 'And now . . . now I think he's lost.'

He looks around at the snowy tundra, with the forest to our right. I feel almost nervous about meeting Daniel now. If I am going to meet him, that is.

'Are we heading back towards the hotel?'

'Yes, the farm is just beyond it. Over the hill on the other side.'

'Have you lived here all your life?'

I can hear the clicking of the reindeer's ankles and the sleds' runners sliding over the snow.

'Well . . .' he begins slowly, 'I grew up here. In the town

183

we're heading for. Like I said, my father is Sami, a reindeer herder, one of seven children. And my mother, an only child, was a teacher who loved working with huskies. They married. She got a job at the local school and had me and my sister.'

'And do you still live at your family farm?'

'What is it with all the questions today?' He laughs good-naturedly.

I say nothing, but somehow asking Björn about his life means I'm not having to talk about my own, and it beats counting reindeer's bottoms! He moves the dogs out to round up a straying reindeer and I think the conversation is over, but he comes back.

'No,' he sighs. 'I don't live in the farmhouse. No one does at the moment. I've been working away. My mother died when I was eighteen. But recently old age has caught up with my father, and after a stroke, he was moved into a retirement flat in the town.' He shakes his head. 'I should have been here. I should have visited more. Helped out,' he says, as if talking to himself, his voice full of regret. Then he glances at me again, as if remembering he's talking out loud. 'But now at least I can move the herd from the summer grazing, and he will know they are safe and will be able to visit them. I have seen most of them born. Like Robbie's mum over there. She was born on my birthday! The same day my mother gave me my first husky. Lucas is his son.'

And I swear the dog lifts his head at the sound of his master speaking his name. Björn smiles and laughs and so do I. The boy and now the man and his dog.

'What about you?' He asks the question I dread, and suddenly my smile disappears. 'What's life like for you?'

I slip into my well-rehearsed routine.

'Well . . . of course I'm a courier, so on the road most of the time, or plane or bus!' I try and joke but can't help but feel his eyes on me again, inquisitive as if reading between the lines once more.

'And your husband?' he says cautiously.

I swallow hard, and this time it's me that looks forward, straight ahead, focused.

'Like I say, he's away. We barely see each other.'

'And when you do?'

'Well . . . it's like he's never been away. But he's with me all the time. That's why I write my book.'

'Your travel log? The one in your case? The one you're making notes to put in.'

'Uh-huh,' I manage to say. 'My . . . husband gave it to me.'

I'm still looking ahead. I remember it as if it was yesterday.

'On my birthday, just befo—' I stop myself and bite my cold lower lip, hard. I never tell anyone that he gave it to me just before he was due to come out of the army, before he went on his last tour of duty. Afterwards, we planned to settle down, have a normal life, go travelling, see the world. I never tell anyone.

'And you miss him?'

'What is it with you and all the questions today?' I try and laugh as I echo his words, but he just falls quiet. Then, when I think the conversation is over, he says:

'Maybe you travel so you don't have to think about missing him.'

I grip the handle of my sled. I can hear the whoosh of the snow under the runners, or maybe it's my own blood, rushing around my body again.

'Maybe you don't really know anything about me!' I snap, and I'm cross with myself for doing so. 'Maybe it's better if we forget the small talk and stick to counting reindeer's bottoms!' I try and speak lightly, hoping that the hot tears that are burning my eyes and have been absent for so long don't spill, and that he hasn't heard the crack in my voice. Staying silent is best for both of us, I think. And he appears to agree, lost in his own thoughts as we fall back into listening to the click of the reindeer's ankles and the sliding of the sleds over the snow. Snow begins to fall once more all around us, like confetti, and the light starts to slide from the darkening sky.

'If we push on,' he says after what seems like miles of silence, 'we may reach the next village.'

'Won't that be a problem, travelling in the dark?'

'Lucas will lead us. It's a flat, straight run. I trust him. There's a Sami village coming up; not many people know about it. It's quiet. We should be able to stay somewhere more comfortable tonight. It won't be like your fancy hotel in Tallfors, but it should be warm and comfortable.'

Well, that's something, I think, and my aching back and legs practically dance for joy. A bed! A bath! Heating!

'See that star over there, that bright one?' He points in amongst the wisps of cloud.

I nod.

'That's where we're heading. That's home.'

I feel a warm glow wash over me.

'It's always the brightest and the first to shine,' he says with a smile, and knowing we have an end goal in sight makes me smile too.

But then I hear a buzzing, a noise cutting through the silence of the snowy wilderness. It's not wildlife, it's not a natural sound. We both turn to look in the direction of the forest. It sounds like . . . like a snowmobile. It *is* a snowmobile, emerging from the trees. Could it finally be his helping hand? Could I finally be getting out of here? I could be in the hotel tonight, waiting for Björn to meet me there with the bag, if I can ring Lars from this Sami village! And my heart does a weird leap and a twist at the same time.

Chapter Twenty-six

Björn slows the dogs down, bringing them to a standstill, then pulls out his binoculars and looks through them at the two headlights bobbing at speed towards us.

'Who is it?' I ask.

He says nothing, just keeps looking into the binoculars.

A second snowmobile emerges from the trees. Oh joy! Maybe I could even get a lift back to the hotel. Wait for Björn to reach the farm and then meet him there. Much as I have come to like these reindeer, Rocky in particular, the thought of my comfortable hotel room, with hot water and a proper bed as I wait for Björn to finish the trek and meet me at the farm is just . . . well, heaven! To be out of this constant cold, which has obviously affected my mood, bringing me down. No wonder people out here struggle, with so little daylight. It would utterly depress me. I mean, I nearly told him about Griff! I cried! I never cry. Thank God I'm not needed here any more. And it's not like I'm leaving without my head held high. He told me how well I did getting across the river, getting the herd over there. He told me how proud Griff would be. The tears that have eluded me for so long suddenly spring up again.

I watch as the dark blue snowmobiles, their yellow headlights shining across the snow, come towards us like knights in shining armour, followed at a distance by a whole army of snowmobiles. It feels like the cavalry has arrived. Hooray! I beam, watching the little swarm heading in our direction. I feel the tension in my shoulders seep away, already imagining myself in that hot bath, and turn to Björn, but he's not smiling; in fact he's scowling.

'Oh Jeez! That's all I need!' he growls.

The lead snowmobile is travelling at speed straight towards us.

'Slow down! *Sakta ner*! Slow down, idiot!' Björn calls. But frankly, the sooner they get to us, the better as far as I'm concerned.

'Over here!' I call, waving my arms. Even the reindeer seem to be getting excited by the arrival of the rescue party, starting to jostle and run around.

'It's going too fast!' Björn shouts. 'It'll scare the reindeer!' Suddenly my euphoria melts away like snow in the pan on the fire. I look at the reindeer. He's right. They're not excited. They're scared. Ready to run, by the looks of it.

'Shh, shh . . .' I try and settle them, but the snowmobile keeps coming, its lights getting brighter and brighter across the white snow.

'I'll head them off,' Björn tells me. 'Stay with the herd.' And with that he shouts, '*Hike, hike*!' and his dog sled team set off at pace towards the snowmobile.

'Shh, shh,' I repeat to the agitated herd. 'They've come to take you home,' I tell Robbie, who is running around anxiously but thankfully staying with the herd. 'And me too,

I hope!' but for some reason, the smile I should feel doesn't meet my lips.

Björn is careering towards the snowmobile and for a moment my heart misses a beat as I think there's going to be a collision. But he stops, and so does the snowmobile, just in time. The rest of the snowmobiles are some way behind, still catching up. I watch as Björn tears a strip off the lead rider, no doubt berating him for his stupidity and for not respecting nature. Then he turns the dogs, and the snowmobile follows him back towards me and the herd, at a much more leisurely pace.

'So, you must be the missing helper! Boy, am I glad to see you,' I say, stepping off the sled and walking in the thick snow towards the snowmobile. Björn still looks furious, though. His face, under his big fur hat and beard, is as dark as can be.

'Looks like your knight in shining armour has arrived,' he growls.

The snowmobile rider takes off his helmet and beams.

'Lars!' I say with a mix of delight and disappointment.

'I came to find you!' He beams even wider. Soft snowflakes in the air settle on his short blond hair.

'Did you ask him to come?' Björn turns to me.

'No. I mean, it's not that I haven't wished it. But my phone died ages ago.'

'I came with a message.' Lars's smile is a mile wide. 'A Mrs Valerie Bevan rang. She was worried she hadn't heard from you.'

'My mum!' Those tears that have eluded me for so long suddenly spring into my eyes.

'She said she just wants to know you're safe and well.'

I nod a lot and smile and sniff. 'Thank you. Yes. Fine. Sort of. Thank you.'

'And another message.' He pulls out his phone. 'From a Mr Mansel Knott,' he reads from the screen, and my spirits, which seemed so lifted by hearing from my lovely mum, suddenly plummet. 'He says he hasn't heard from you and the job hasn't been signed off. As this is a very important job for his good friend, he'd like to know that the goods have been delivered, otherwise,' he continues, and my mouth goes dry, 'he will have to give the new long-haul assignment to another courier.'

Suddenly it feels like the light has disappeared altogether, like someone has taken the sun and I'm left cold and shivering.

'I can get you back to the hotel to return the calls,' Lars says.

'Well then, looks like you have a lift out of here!' Björn turns away furiously and goes to check the dogs.

'But the herd?' I say, looking around at the familiar faces.

He turns back and shrugs. 'I'll manage. We've done the worst of it. The river. We're over halfway. It should be a fairly straightforward run from here. There are more villages now along the way. I can get help if I need it.'

'But—'

'I'll get your bag for you, drop it at the hotel.' He looks at me with his piercing blue eyes and I wonder if he's going to say something else. What else could he have to say to me? That I wasn't a total waste of space, that actually I was good . . . Maybe, don't go, stay?

I nod slowly, and he suddenly looks away.

'I'll text you as soon as I reach Daniel's place,' he says.

I swallow a large lump in my throat. When I say nothing, he turns back to me and we stand and stare at each other for a moment. A whole load of unsaid words seem to be in the air.

It's Lars who finally breaks the moment between us.

'I have a helmet for you!' he says joyously. 'Climb aboard. We're going to try and see the Northern Lights this evening.'

'How did you know where to find me?' I ask politely, my mouth dry, trying to shake off the moment that just seems to have happened.

'The old postal route is well known with snowmobile tours. There's a vantage point for the Northern Lights up there.' He points to a snowy plateau. 'Sorry. I was going too fast. I was just so impatient to see you, once I got your mum's message. I was worried too. I wanted to make sure you were all right. I mean, she could be my future mother-in-law!'

I go to tell him that she's not his future mother-in-law and that I'm already married, but Björn is giving me a strange look. I want to tell Lars that his wish on the shooting star might not be his fate, but then I hear the buzz of the other snowmobiles getting louder.

'Come on.' Lars beckons. 'It's the wedding party!'

'Yes, go on,' says Björn, and for someone who's so keen to get rid of me, he's being really grumpy about me going.

'I . . . I could stay,' I say very quickly, and just as quickly he shakes his head.

'I'll cope. Maybe my help will arrive soon.' He waves his phone. 'Besides, you snore.'

'I do not!'

I realise he's attempting a joke because he can see I'm torn. I feel bad leaving him and the herd out here with the rest of the journey still to go. But he is already unharnessing Rocky and attaching my sled to the back of his.

I walk slowly to Lars, who hands me the helmet as if it's a crown.

'Thank you,' I say. Unsure why I feel so reluctant to leave when this is what I've wanted from the moment we set off.

'Are you sure?' I suddenly turn and ask Björn.

'Quite sure. You've been a great help. But I can go on alone from here. The river was the hardest part.' He looks at me and I feel a sudden rush of sadness. Then he says slowly, 'I'm sure you have your own journey to make too.'

And I realise he's not talking about my trip home. He means me, me and my life. I freeze. Lars looks between us, his ever-present smile slipping just for a second, then raises a hopeful eyebrow.

'Me?' His smile returns. 'You have a journey to take with me? Definitely.'

Björn raises both eyebrows. 'Maybe it is time you moved on,' he says, and again, I know he's not talking about getting on the snowmobile. I know that he knows. He's guessed. Maybe it is right for me to get out of here. Once again this man makes me feel like all my defences have been stripped from me, like I'm out in the cold with nothing to protect my shattered heart.

'Yes, hop on. Let's go!' Lars starts the engine.

I put the helmet on, and pull the visor over my face so Björn can't see my eyes, can't see into my soul any more, suddenly furious that he has reached in and snuck a peek at my secrets. How dare he?!

'Fine! This is me moving on!' I say.

Björn backs away from the snowmobile. Lars pulls on his big gloves. I have no idea how I'll feel about having to wrap my arms around him for the journey home, but right now, getting as far away as possible from Björn seems like a good idea. He's come too close to the truth. I have to leave.

Just as Lars is about to climb aboard, there is the squeal of an engine being thrashed. We turn and see a snowmobile careering at speed towards us.

'Get your snowmobile safari away from my herd!' Björn shouts. 'Now!'

Lars turns and runs towards them, waving. 'Stop! Slow down!' he calls. I join in, but the snowmobile has already reached us at speed.

'Wheeeee!' cries the unmistakable figure of Pru's nan as she whizzes past, and the herd splits, separating like the Red Sea parting, and then bolts in two different directions.

'Shit!' says Björn.

'Oh no!' I cry.

He jumps on the back of the dog sled and glances in an agony of indecision between the separated herd, half of them heading across the virgin snowy wasteland towards the melting river, the other half to the forest and the road, their fluffy bottoms held high.

'You go that way!' I shout, indicating the road. 'I'll go after the others!'

He doesn't need telling twice. '*Hike, hike!*' he shouts to the dogs, and they set off towards the trees separating the tundra from the road.

'Sorry, Lars, I need this,' I say, shuffling forward into the driver's seat and pulling back on the accelerator. 'How does it work?'

But he doesn't need to show me: within a split second I've worked it out and turn the throttle. The snowmobile leaps forward, sending Lars stumbling back.

'Press the big red button if you need to stop!' he shouts after me.

I ease up on the throttle and steady the vehicle, pointing it in the right direction, already gaining on the galloping herd. I go wide, so as not to panic them and make them go faster, and then attempt to pull the snowmobile round and circle in front of them to slow them down. I'm heading towards the river at speed, downhill. The ice has thawed here and the water is running and tumbling fast and furious, like my heart.

Just as the herd are about to meet the row of high trees lining the water's edge, I manage to swerve the snowmobile in front of them, in between them and the tree trunks, and slew across the snow, pulling on the brake. Then, on instinct, I put my thumb on the horn and sound it long and hard. Rocky is at the front of the herd. He looks at me.

'Rocky! Stop!' I shout, the cold air hurting my lungs. He scutters to a standstill, and the herd finally slow down, skidding and stumbling, backing off from the snowmobile horn and finally grinding to a halt. Now all I have to do is get them to go back the other way to join Björn and the rest of the herd.

'*Heja, heja!*' I call. I don't have a plan here; this is something I'm going to have to do without a map or a schedule. I'm just acting on instinct, following my heart, and it feels surprisingly good.

Chapter Twenty-seven

'I'm sorry, Lars. I have to stay. I can't leave.' Much as I want a hot bath and a gin and tonic, I think. 'It's only a few more nights and we'll have the herd home, then I'll travel on to the hotel with the rings.'

'You're sure?'

'Absolutely!' I say, not sure at all, trying to plaster a smile onto my face. Every part of my body aches. I'm so tired I could lie down here and now and sleep in the snow and wouldn't care if no one found me. But I can't just go. What if something like that happened again? If I had left with Lars and the herd had gone in separate directions, there's no way Björn would have been able to get them back together. I look over at him as he hand-feeds the reindeer with pellets to settle them again, moving through the herd, talking quietly and soothing them.

'Can I do anything for you?'

'Actually, Lars, could I borrow your phone to let my mum and sister know that I'm okay?'

'Of course.' He pulls out his phone and hands it to me.

'Just okay?' He looks at me and then at Björn. I follow his gaze.

'More than okay; I'm actually really good,' I say, and start to type, telling Mum and Sara that I'm fine, happy and actually having the journey of my life and promising to tell them all about it in a few days' time.

They both reply within seconds, and my sister attaches a job advert for a holiday sales team leader with experience in travel and adventure. Well, I've certainly got that, I think. Could I do it? Could I stop travelling and settle into life back home, spend more time with my family? The closing date is just after I'm due back. The job looks amazing. Everything I could hope for really. I text back telling her I'll give it some serious thought – and I will – but that first I have three hundred reindeer to get to their bed and breakfast for the night. She texts again checking that I really am okay and not taking drugs or having some kind of breakdown, and telling me that she and Mum have already polished up my CV and put in an application for the job on my behalf. And I wonder again what it would be like to finally stop moving on, and find myself warming to the idea as I hand the phone back to Lars.

'I'm sorry about my guests,' Lars says, loud enough for Björn to hear, but he doesn't respond. 'I think they were a little overexcited and very irresponsible. But I should have been more thoughtful too. I was just so pleased I'd found you.'

'Lars, I'm really grateful you came. Thank you. But—'

'No need for thanks.' He starts putting his helmet back on. 'I came because I wanted to see you were safe. I'm here for you, you know that.' He reaches out a hand and puts it on my forearm.

'About that, Lars . . .' I don't want to give him any false hope.

'Oh, looks like I need to round up a herd of my own.' He looks back at the wedding party scattered across the tundra, zigzagging this way and that.

'How are they?' I ask.

He shrugs and shakes his head. 'Sadly, they are not the happiest wedding party I have ever looked after.'

'When you find love, you should hang onto it as tightly as you can and make the most of every day,' I say as I watch the snowmobiles' headlights darting to and fro across the white plain like fireflies.

'You should.' Lars breaks into my thoughts and I quickly turn to find him watching me with a look of . . . well, longing in his eyes. Now would be a good time to tell him about my husband, about Griff, like I always do when I meet new people. Explain that he works away. But somehow I can't find the words. Suddenly it feels like lying, whereas before, before I made that river crossing today, it felt like the truth – that he *was* working away – and that's how I managed to operate, to keep going. I'm not sure what's happened, what's different. How has the river crossing changed all that?

'Thank you again, Lars, for coming to find me.'

'No problem. Remember, just phone. I'm there for you. I'll be waiting for you.' He throws me one of his huge smiles, then starts up the engine on the snowmobile and slowly rides off in the direction of the unruly wedding party. I watch as he goes, and smile. He's a good man, I think, with a kind heart; just desperate to love someone and for her to love him back. I hope he finds her, but I know it isn't me.

'Thank God he's gone!' says Björn, dusting off his hands and moving out from the middle of the herd. 'Bloody snowmobile tours! I could have lost my herd,' he seethes.

'Well, they're all here, thank goodness. They *are* all here, aren't they?' I look around, concerned, doing a check of all the antlers I recognise, then try and use my counting method, putting them into named groups of ten.

He nods. 'You could have left with the snowmobile tour,' he says. 'I know that. I would have been in trouble. Looks like I owe you.'

'A large white wine would go down well,' I say. I think about the Sami village we're heading towards.

'It's a deal. But I don't think we're going to make the village tonight now. I'm sorry. We'll have to camp in the forest again.'

My spirits practically fall through the floor. A tiny bit of me imagines the other me back at the hotel, stepping into a hot bubble bath and sipping a cold wine. I shake it off.

'But I will cook you something special, and maybe a vodka or two?' He lifts his eyebrows over his ice-blue eyes.

'Okay!' I find myself smiling back. 'Will we still make it back to the hotel in time for the wedding?'

'Providing we don't come across any more idiots like your boyfriend!'

'Lars? He's not my boyfriend. I'm marr—'

I stop myself as he tilts his head and looks at me kindly.

'Lars is just a friend,' I finish, my mouth going dry as I feel a shift inside me.

Chapter Twenty-eight

This time I know what to expect. We make the *lavvu* with the poles, fetch firewood and birch branches, light the fire and get the water on to boil. Then we feed the dogs and scatter pellets on the ground for the reindeer, which are milling in amongst the trees, pulling at branches and snuffling for lichen. I find Rocky an extra big lump of lichen and feed it to him, thanking him for today and for stopping before the herd leapt into the river.

As Björn feeds the fire, kneeling beside it, watching the flames build and grow in character and confidence, I sit on a log, pull out my little notebook and start to record today's adventures, my writing as tiny as I can make it, using every spare bit of the page, even up the edges and in the little margin.

'Thanks for today. I know you could have left.' He hands me a cup into which he's poured a clear liquid.

I stop writing, take the cup and sip. It burns as it slips down.

'Lingonberry vodka,' he tells me.

It gets all my taste buds standing to attention.

'It's fine. I need to get my bag, remember. The rings.'

'And the travel log,' he adds.

'Yes,' I agree. 'And my travel log.'

'To write up your journeys,' he says, the flames softly lighting his face. 'To save them to show your husband.'

I swallow and grip my little notebook, then take a deep breath and look up at him in the firelight.

'Yes,' I say steadily, almost steely, because that's what I've learnt to do: protect my shattered heart with a steel casing.

He holds my stare and for a moment I wobble; then, just as I feel the final thick layer of my protective casing about to crack, he pulls out the piece of antler from his pocket and starts whittling it again.

'And what have you got to tell him about this trip, your husband, in your journal? What will you say?'

'How I'm stuck with this really annoying man and lost and nearly killed his husky team. I'll tell him about the fish I ate straight from the snow hole, which tasted so delicate and melted on my tongue. The pine tea I thought was like grass to start with that I now find myself craving. My lovely reindeer Rocky, how I've come to trust him. And how I can be around the dogs now without breaking into a cold sweat and wanting to run for the hills every time they bark.'

'And the river crossing. Don't forget the river crossing!' He waves his knife at me but doesn't look up from what he's doing.

'And the river crossing.' I find myself smiling.

'The way you saved little Robbie and stopped the rest of the herd going back. And you didn't scream, which would've scared the dogs.'

'And I didn't scream,' I agree, and nod.

'And my impromptu snowmobile ride!'

I smile at the thought of bringing the herd back together

and the euphoria I felt after we'd crossed the river safely and know that's a memory that will stay with me forever. It's in my head, imprinted. A happy memory. And it's been a while since I've had any of those. It feels like an old friend returning to reacquaint itself with me. I smile wider.

'And those ridiculous pants you bought from the souvenir shop. I bet he'd laugh at those.'

'He would've done.' I smile and blush. 'He always thought I had great taste in underwear. He'd definitely have laughed at these ones!' and suddenly I stop, and try to recover. 'I mean, he thinks I have, always, he tells me.'

Björn looks up from the antler in his hand. The candles he's put round the fire and in lanterns hanging from the temporary washing line light up the contours of his face, which, if I'm not mistaken, is actually really good-looking underneath all that hair. The orange glow illuminates his features, creating golden highlights, and the cream canvas of the *lavvu* behind him makes him look really soft, like there's someone very kind beneath that bad-tempered exterior. Like a Kinder egg, hard on the outside with a surprise in the middle.

He just looks at me, patiently. It's as if he's waiting for me to take the first step.

I open my mouth and close it again. The words just won't come out.

'Say it,' he encourages quietly.

I look down, my vision blurred by the tears filling my eyes and falling in big heavy plops into the notebook in my lap.

'I can't,' I whisper.

'He's not working away, is he?' Björn says in the same low

voice. I turn my head to the left and then very slowly to the right, and find that I am shaking it. 'When did he die?'

'Two . . .' I manage to get out before my throat tightens so much it threatens to strangle me.

'Two years ago?' he helps.

This time I lift my head and slowly drop it to my chin. 'In Afghanistan. Landmine,' I manage. 'Night patrol.'

He nods slowly. 'And you don't tell people?'

I shake my head and then manage to say in one big breath through my tight and painful chest, 'They don't need to know. It's no one's business but mine.'

He says nothing. Outside I can hear the reindeer moving around, the clicking and snuffling that have come to be familiar sounds out here now, and I seem to actually be drawing some comfort from them.

'And that's why the book is so important to you, this travel log?'

I just nod, without looking at him, like his voice isn't actually part of a real person sitting just a few feet away from me. If I don't look at him, this conversation isn't really happening.

'It's why you keep travelling, doing this job, so you don't have to stand still and live in the real world.'

My head snaps up. 'I picked up my passport and haven't looked back. I have a great life right now!'

He lets out a long blow of air and then says with his usual directness, 'Looks to me like you've learnt how to survive . . .'

'I have,' I agree.

'. . . but not how to live,' he finishes, and once again, I'm lost for words. Then suddenly the dogs bark, making me jump, and Björn's eyes release mine. I'm relieved, yet feel I'm in free fall, terrified of what might be outside.

'I'll check.' He picks up the gun that has been lying by his side and pushes back the flap of the *lavvu*, letting in a freezing-cold blast of air, giving me a reality check, letting me know that I am very much living in the real world. I pull the shutters back down on my memories whilst Björn checks the herd.

'Something's out there, but it's gone now,' he says, ducking back inside. 'The dogs'll let us know if anything happens. I think you'd feel better if we went to bed. No point trying to fight it.' He starts undoing his trousers.

'What?!' Suddenly all sorts of thoughts are crashing about in my mind. I'm not looking for a new relationship, or even a brief encounter. I've kept every man at arm's length for the last couple of years. I'm just . . . not ready. 'Look, Björn. It's very flattering and I realise that underneath that grumpy exterior you're really quite nice, but just because you've found out I'm widowed doesn't mean I'm going to—'

Björn suddenly stands up very tall, holding onto his trousers, which are halfway down, revealing thermal long johns over tightly muscled thighs.

'I meant we should get into bed, our own beds!' he says with the ferocity of an injured dog fighting its corner against a hostile pack. He's so fierce it makes my eyes smart. 'Just . . . just go to bed and get some sleep.' Suddenly he sounds like an exhausted parent. 'Here's your sleeping bag.' He tosses it in my direction and I catch it, embarrassed by my mistake.

'Do you need to go outside before I turn off this lamp?' he

adds with a sigh, pointing to the final lantern. 'I promise not to look, just in case you think I'm trying to make a pass at you.'

'I just thought—' I want to put things right between us, but he cuts me off.

'I know exactly what you thought. So let's get this straight. I'm sorry you've lost your husband, I really am. But I am not about to turn into some sex-starved beast. I wasn't attracted to you before I knew you were . . .' he falters just for a split second and then recovers, 'a widow. And I'm not attracted to you now. Are we clear?'

'Perfectly!' I say, tight-lipped and feeling very, very stupid. I've spent so long trying to make sure no man comes within a mile of me, being loyal to the memory of Griff, that I've convinced myself every eligible male is going to jump on me. I mean, why would they? I think about how long it is since I've actually had a proper shower or change of clothes. What was I thinking? That every man who finds out I'm alone is going to want to sleep with me?

'I can go alone,' I say, and rush outside into the bitter air, holding the lantern high and finding the biggest tree without batting an eyelid. Anything that might be lurking in these woods can't be half as terrifying as the angry reindeer herder inside the tent.

When I return to the *lavvu*, Björn is stoking the fire. It's roaring, pumping out yellow and orange flames. I head straight for my sleeping bag, pull up the covers and turn my back to him, facing the tent wall. Then I curl up into a ball, like a hedgehog making sure its spikes stick out to deter anyone who tries to get too close.

* * *

Björn looked up at the clothes hanging along the string inside the tent. The jeans, totally unsuitable for these conditions, and still damp from their soaking in the river, despite being by the fire earlier. The floral socks and the *I ♥ Sweden* knickers! What was it about her? he thought, one hand behind his head. She'd been amazing out there on the river today. Really. He couldn't have hoped for a better helper. How had it come to this? Just like back in Stockholm, he had shown someone some kindness and they had misread the signals and got it all wrong. It was why he and Camilla had split up; why he'd left. It was why everything had fallen apart.

Life had been good. He had won awards for best international cuisine. He'd had a Michelin star, for God's sake. He and Camilla had had a solid relationship; they'd worked well together as well as being bedfellows. They'd been a team. He'd been at the top of his game, an internationally renowned chef, everything his mother would have been proud of. And he had been proud of it too. But then it had started going wrong. People began to copy his dishes, pulling them apart, deconstructing them, second-guessing what he was going to do next. He had to keep upping his game. Everyone was a critic, judging his food, judging him, to the point where, in the end, he doubted his own instincts, he didn't know what he was making, who he was any more, what was in his heart. And then, that night, his house of cards had come tumbling down, and now he had absolutely no idea what he was doing or where he was going once the reindeer were delivered home.

Seeing Halley looking through his book, hearing about the recipes in there, had just transported him back. Back to the confusion and doubt he had begun to feel about his signature dishes and to the night when he'd lost everything he'd worked for. He never wanted to see that book again. He couldn't bear to think about the restaurant and what people must be saying about him now, how he had let down everyone who had believed in him.

And now, even out here, he had hurt someone he was coming to really admire and respect, and, if he was honest, find very attractive.

He looked at the Mickey Mouse socks hanging overhead, and found a little smile waiting there as he listened to the sound of gentle snoring. At least she was asleep. He didn't think she'd slept since she got here. Her face looked haunted. He had known early on that there was something she was running from. It was in her eyes. He could tell there was hurt in there that went deep. He'd known that hurt when his mother had died, and he had run too. Her guard was permanently up, making sure no one knew the hurt that she was really feeling. He'd felt the same. Abandoned. Deserted. But in turn he had deserted the people who needed him, his dad and his sister. He hadn't been there when they'd needed him. He should have visited more often, helped more.

He'd all but turned his back on his home and his family over the years. He couldn't believe how much his father had aged when he'd finally visited him in the retirement flat, just before his trip back to Stockholm to see the solicitor and agree the sale of the restaurant only a few days ago. He'd hated seeing his father in the flat, cooped up like that. His dad had lived out here all his life, outdoors with his reindeer. At least now that he was on the mend, he should be able to move back into the farmhouse and look out on the herd every day.

Björn berated himself again. He should have come sooner, but he'd been too busy thinking up fancy recipes for fancy critics to pass judgement on. His sister had kept him up to date after the stroke, but he'd had no idea how quickly his dad had aged. He hadn't been there and he should have been. He'd been busy launching a new menu, to the great excitement of the press, trying to win back that Michelin star, thinking he was making his family proud when he should have just been with them instead. He realised that now. The awards and reviews didn't mean anything, not even the bloody star. He'd realised that the night after the launch of the new menu, and the staff party to thank them all for their support and loyalty and reassure them that they were hopefully over the bumpy patch and would be claiming that star back with this new, highly intricate menu, to which they'd all raised their glasses and applauded.

But what a difference a few days could make. He might have had it all in Stockholm, but what he recognised most clearly when he met Halley was the loneliness in her. Appearing to have it all, and actually having nothing on the inside. Being back here had filled that vacuum. He could be out here in the wilderness on his own and never feel as lonely as he felt back in the city surrounded by the wolves, people waiting to bring him down, tip him off his throne. Well, they'd nearly managed it, but he'd walked first, just like when he'd left here after his mother had died. Could you really keep walking, though, or running for that matter?

He let his eyes drift across to the sleeping mound beside

him, huddled and hunched up. One thing he knew for sure: he mustn't do anything to make her think he liked her – not that he did, of course: she was infuriating. Infuriating, but fascinating, and very attractive. But she mustn't know he felt that way, or she'd take the first chance to run again.

He sat up and placed another log on the fire as quietly as he could. She murmured in her sleep and suddenly turned over towards him, her face screwed up into a frown. He knew where her dreams were. He hoped that one day she'd be able to dream carefree dreams again. Wasn't that what had happened to him when he had arrived back here? Maybe if she let herself fall in love again . . . But he couldn't be that person. Maybe this Lars would be. He himself didn't need to be with anyone right now. He couldn't make someone else happy until he could work out what he was doing, what he needed to do. A new adventure, a new challenge? He felt like he was standing at a crossroads, not knowing which road to take, but once he got the reindeer to the farm, he was going to have to make a decision. He had to go somewhere. London? Paris? Not back to Stockholm. He thought about his notebook, containing recipes from all over the world. He could go anywhere he liked. Why, then, didn't that make him feel good?

He shut his eyes and finally drifted into sleep, and dreamt of being out on the tundra, him, his dogs and the reindeer, the ice cracking beneath them like his roots were falling away from under his feet, but every time, she had saved him. No matter how much he tried to shake her from his dreams, she kept creeping in and rescuing the herd, his livelihood, his roots . . . him.

Chapter Twenty-nine

The next morning, I'm awake and first up, ready to push on and get out of here. I begin pulling my clothes off the washing line hanging over us.

'What the . . . ?' Björn sits up groggily in his sleeping bag.

'Just getting dressed. We should crack on before the bad weather comes,' I jabber, yanking at the clothes with gusto. The line wobbles and bounces and my jumper lands on Björn's head. I grab the knickers before they can join it.

'Oh great.' I hear his muffled groan before scooping the jumper off his still sleepy face.

'We should get going,' I say to him.

'Yes,' he sighs. 'But not before we and the dogs have eaten. We need some more wood to boil water, then we can start packing up the tent.'

'I'll get wood,' I say quickly, keen to get out of close proximity. 'Just turn away whilst I dress. And shut your eyes. Tight.'

He tuts but does what he's told.

The morning is much the same as the other mornings have been. We start out wearing head torches, him guiding the herd from the dog sled with his Lapp dogs and me bringing up the rear with Rocky and the sled loaded with supplies. As we trek through the ancient forest, the walkie-talkie crackles into life.

'We're coming out of the forest and it should be open tundra on the other side,' Björn says. 'We need to make sure the herd stays together, over.'

'Received,' I say, and sigh and sniff, my nose as cold as ever, and the walkie-talkie crackles again and falls silent. That's the most he's spoken to me since we set off this morning. I'm alone with my thoughts and it's not a place I like being. The day I got the news that Griff had died keeps replaying in my head. The letter that his best friend and best man at our wedding handed me, which Griff had written in case anything were to happen. The promise he made me make that I would go and see the world, travel, keep on living. Then I think of Björn's comment, 'You've learnt how to survive, but not how to live.' What does he know about me or my life?!

The herd attempt to speed up as we move out of the forest and onto the tundra, snaking across the virgin snow like a pencil squiggle on a clean page. I have come to recognise the characters of lots of the reindeer, individual in colouring and antler shape as well as personality. But of course young Robbie is still one of my favourites. The hills in the distance now seem so much closer. My journey's end is almost in sight, I think with a strange mix of longing and loneliness.

Our first sight of the Sami village is like a mirage, a wonderful optical illusion in the middle of the endless snowy wasteland. As we move off the tundra, through some trees and onto a wide track leading into a clearing, there is a cluster of wooden huts, cabins made from thick tree trunks, all lit up by lights carefully positioned in the trees and on poles guiding us down the path towards them. There's one big round cabin and several smaller ones dotted in amongst the trees with lights over their front doors, plus another large hut on the edge of what looks to be a frozen lake. The snow is banked up around them and smoke chugs cheerfully from their chimneys.

'You wait here. I'll go in and organise us some rooms. Don't,' Björn looks around, 'lose anything: dogs, reindeer . . .' I bristle. I haven't lost anything since the first day! 'Just stay put.'

'On my own? With the dogs?'

'Yes, on your own. I'll only be a few minutes. You'll be okay?'

'Fine.'

'Fine,' he confirms with a nod and turns to walk towards the round hut.

I watch him go and then pull out my little home-made notebook, crisp and curling at the edges: battle scars, I think, and smile. I begin to write, standing in the pool of light from a nearby lamp, describing the starry sky above me and the Sami village, just like the photo in one of the travel brochures from my old job. My thoughts turn to the new job my sister has sent me, back in the travel market, selling holidays again, settling into family life.

'Hello there!' A voice makes me jump and drop my little book. I pick it up quickly before it gets wet again in the snow and shove it in my pocket, then spin round.

'Hi, it's, erm . . . Pru, isn't it?'

'Yes. Lars said you're the courier who brought our wedding rings, aren't you?' she asks.

I swallow and nod, a lot. 'I am,' I say with all the confidence I can muster.

'It's amazing here, isn't it?' She looks around at the big dark sky. The moon is just starting to spread its iridescent light over the snowy ground, which throws up a silvery glow of its own. 'Can I say hello?'

'Sorry?' I ask, confused.

'To the reindeer and the dogs?'

'Oh, I see! Yes, of course. They're very gentle.' I encourage her to move amongst the herd and not to worry about the antlers. Behind her I can see a snowmobile parked up on its own.

'Not with the rest of the wedding party?' And I wonder if they're nearby.

She attempts a smile, then drops her head. 'Taking a break from my mother, to be honest.'

'Ah,' I say, understanding. 'Family can be great, but sometimes their best of intentions are the worst of ideas!' We both laugh. I think about my mother and sister's attempts to get me to join in with family occasions while my life fell apart. But being with them reminded me of everything I'd lost; highlighted the one person who wasn't there. They meant well, but it was the last thing I wanted to do. Could I think about taking a job back there now? Somehow, I feel different since I've been out here.

Pru is rubbing the reindeer's noses. I pull some lichen out of my pocket.

'Here, put some of this in your hand, and then hold out your palm flat, like this.' I show her how. 'This is Rocky, and this little one is Robbie.'

'They all have names?'

'No.' I smile and shake my head. 'Only a chosen few. They're a herd, wild animals living in their natural environment, where they should be. But some have special jobs, like Rocky here. He's a castrated male; his job is to pull the sled. And Robbie, he's my favourite. I named him after Robbie the Reindeer from the film.' He nuzzles into my cupped hand, eating greedily. I rub his head. 'He's cute, but naughty. They all have different markings and characteristics; some are more dominant than others.'

'How do you tell them apart?'

'Well, I started by learning their antler shapes.' I think of the hours I have spent staring at a sea of bottoms and antlers. One bottom is much like the next, but antlers are more distinctive.

'How are the plans going for the weekend?' I ask tentatively.

'Apart from my mother still not coming around to the idea and refusing to attend the actual service, we're all sorted. And we're really grateful to you. The rings are just such an important part of it; thank you for bringing them. We had them hand-made, even helped make them and put in our own inscriptions. That's what's really important to us. Thank you.'

'Well,' my voice cracks, 'it is my job.'

'And the dogs?' She turns to the huskies, who stand up from their resting position as she starts to fuss them.

'Well,' I say tentatively, 'this is Björn's lead dog.'

'Björn? He's the guy with the beard, the reindeer herder?'

'Yes, that's him!' I step forward without thinking and place my hand on Lucas's head.

'And how did you two get together?' Pru asks, smiling whilst fussing the dogs.

'Oh, we're not together.'

'Oh, really? Sorry, I thought . . .'

'No, we're just . . .' I can't even say we're friends. 'I'm helping him out for a friend.' I think of Daniel and realise that I'm looking forward to meeting him. I feel I know so much about him already from his book. I'm intrigued by him, fascinated by his passion for cooking and his dedication to his art. Who knows, in a different time, it could have been fate! I think about Lars, his grandmother, his wishing on a shooting star, and smile.

I move down the pack of dogs and stop when I get to Helgá, bending down and stroking her head. She seems to like it and so I carry on and realise how far I've come since the first day I met the dogs, when I was terrified. Now . . . well, I can do this at least.

'He's the one who was so cross about Nan,' Pru says, referring to Björn. 'Sorry about that.'

'Can't your nan talk your mum round?' I ask. I'm thinking back to that first day in the hotel foyer, when her nan seemed so pleased for her.

Pru shakes her head. 'They don't get on. She's a bit of a wild one, is my nan. I don't think my mum has ever forgiven her for leaving her dad. But she says she found love and had to follow her heart. It was really sad – her new husband died not long after they married. But she says she's never regretted the time she had with him. He made her find herself. Gave her the wings to fly, so to speak.'

I feel tears spring to my eyes.

'She's lived life to the full ever since, never wasted a moment. She's living for now because you never know when it's going to be taken away. She's the reason I went for it with Mika. She told me to follow my heart, wherever it took me. If only my mum could be as pleased for me.' She rubs the next dog's head. 'Please say sorry to your . . . to Björn. Nan's just a bit overexcited.'

'Don't worry. We got all the reindeer back.' I'm kneeling next to Pru as she rubs each dog in turn and I stick to making a fuss of Helgá. 'Björn's not known for his way with people, but when it comes to animals, well, he's quite a different person. Kind, sensitive. You should see the relationship he has with his lead dog. It's like they work as a team, they can read each other. It's amazing.'

'Almost fanciable by the sounds of it, if I was that way inclined.' Pru laughs and so do I.

'*Almost* fanciable,' I agree. The laughter hangs in the air as she fusses over the dogs, and I'm actually not feeling scared at all right now. If anything, I'm feeling safer than I have in a long time, like I'm where I'm supposed to be. I laugh again. 'Maybe if he didn't have that big beard—'

'Well it seems your friend Lars has had the same idea as me.' A deep voice behind me makes me jump, my heart banging and the blood rushing in my ears.

'Björn!' I stumble slightly in the snow as I stand, blushing. Pru remains crouched down over the dogs and puts the back of her hand over her mouth, presumably to hide a smile, and I don't know whether to laugh or be mortified. I seem to be doing a mixture of the two, a sort of slightly hysterical embarrassed giggle, as I look at Pru and roll my lips together to stop it turning into a full-blown uncontrollable laughing fit, which it is in danger of becoming.

I have absolutely no idea if he heard me or not. The last thing I want is for him to think I am in any way attracted to him. Because I'm absolutely not and never will be. Definitely not!

Björn sighs again, and I don't know if he's trying to cover up what he's just heard or if he's really very irritated. Either way, at least we get our own rooms tonight and some space away from each other. I can write up my little book in peace. I might even admit to my Björn faux pas. It's how I keep everyone at arm's length.

'So, your friend Lars,' Björn continues like a weary teacher as Pru and I try to smother our giggles and straighten ourselves out, like we've been on the vodka. 'He's booked in here for the night with his wedding party. He obviously has his eye on the ball. It's a great location, especially for a tour like this, people wanting to see the Northern Lights and experience the "real" Lapland.' He uses his fingers for inverted commas.

'But that's exactly what this is, right?' I look around, and then he does the same.

'Yes, that's exactly what this is. These people have lived here for generations. It's just a shame that they are struggling to make a living. Reindeer herding isn't exactly lucrative. Tourism, on the other hand, is. They just need more people to know they're here. If people hear about it, they'll come.'

'And have they got room for us?'

'They have, but . . . just the one. We'll have to share.'

'What? Oh, but hang on.' Camping out together in a

makeshift hut is one thing. 'I can't share a room with you.'

He shrugs. 'You could always take the tent again,' he says, and starts pulling his bag off the sled. 'There's a corral we can put the reindeer in and a sauna if you want to strip off and take the plunge before dinner.'

'Take a what?'

'Have a sauna, a shower and the plunge into the snow.' He points. 'Helps you relax.'

I look over at where he's indicating. Next to a small wooden cabin is a big bank of snow, lit up by candle torches, and beyond that a jetty leading onto the frozen lake.

'So, what's it to be, the room or the tent?' He nods to the loaded sled.

I sigh. There's no way I'm doing another night in the tent, no way, especially not on my own.

'I'll see you later,' I tell Pru.

'Good luck!' she says and winks at me. I blush all over again.

I stand and look around, taking it all in. There is a small wood-burning stove pumping out plenty of heat, and tea lights in holders flickering on every surface. A table and two chairs stand in front of the window looking out on the sauna, and on the far side of the room there is a wooden-framed double bed.

'You've got to be joking!' I look at the bed, covered in a thick duvet and soft reindeer hide. There are cushions there too, and I just want to throw myself into them, face down, and stay there forever. But not with Björn! Somehow, sleeping under canvas and in the cabins felt acceptable. This feels different. Weird. Like I'm going to be sharing a bed with a man . . . which is exactly what I am going to be doing.

'You need to not be so buttoned up,' he says, peeling off his outer layers. He points out of the cabin window to the big wooden hut with steam coming out of a chimney, the pathway cleared of snow and well lit. 'The sauna's just over there. You can get cleaned up there too; there are showers and sinks.'

And a big snow bank for plunging into, I think with a shiver.

'The sauna really cleanses you, body and soul. It will help you relax.'

I look out at the hut and the jetty beside it. There are tiny flakes of glittery snow dancing in the air. It looks beautiful.

'I'll let you go first while I write up my notebook,' I say, pulling out the battered little booklet. He looks at it and then at me.

'You can't hide behind that forever,' he says softly. 'You need to live it, not write about it.'

I go to answer but can't find the words. Instead I sit down at the table by the window and gaze outside, focusing on how I'm going to describe the scene. I'm going to have to write really small, I only have a page and a half left. I look at the book, then back to Björn to tell him I'm living life perfectly well, thank you, when the words catch in my throat. He's pulling off his tight-fitting long-sleeved top, the last layer, to reveal his broad chest and muscular arms. On the inside of his forearm is a tattoo, of a reindeer's head, neck and antlers. There is something very sexy about it, I realise, and I catch my breath and quickly turn back to looking out of the window, but not before I see a little laugh in the corner of his mouth.

'Are you worried about me changing here? I can go to the sauna if you like.'

'No, it's fine,' I tell him in a strangely high-pitched voice.

'Good, because nudity is a part of life here in Sweden. It's nothing to be embarrassed about,' he says. 'It is not done to be sexy most of the time. We do it because it feels natural.'

I go to tell him that where I come from, we don't just get undressed in front of total strangers, it's not natural, but as I turn, this time he's stepping out of his long johns. A muscular thigh covered in light hair is now on show. He's laughing gently to himself and shaking his head.

Oh for goodness' sake! I snap my head round to look back out of the window, my heart doing some strange thundering. I hope he's going to wear something to bed!

'You're uncomfortable with nudity,' he says. 'But it's just being ourselves, like nature intended. Not hiding behind anything. Showing the world who we are.'

'I'm not used to sitting in a room with a total stranger taking his clothes off, if that's what you mean.' I sound like a prude and I feel like one too. 'I'm—'

'Married?' he finishes for me, and I swallow hard and fall silent. 'Even married people get naked out here.' He tries to break the uncomfortable silence between us with a bit of humour, and although I'm grateful he's trying to help, I carry on staring out of the window. The treetops are covered in snow, like thick double cream on a delicious dessert, and my stomach rumbles.

'We'll be eating in a while,' I hear Björn say. 'I'm going to help the owners prepare dinner. They have a lot of people to feed tonight.' He leaves the cabin and I hear the door close behind him. Naked? Did he just go outside naked?

I hear the rumble of engines, signalling the wedding party arriving back at the hotel on their snowmobiles. Just then Björn comes into sight around the side of the building. He's wearing a white towel wrapped around his waist, and towelling flip-flops, but other than that, nothing. The snow is settling on his broad shoulders and mass of curly blond hair with its little red strands. Well, at least he has the towel on, I think, trying to refocus on my booklet but finding it strangely hard to pull my eyes away from him out in the snow, the lights outside the sauna throwing a yellow glow around the little building. At least he'll be inside before the wedding party get off their snowmobiles. I glance up to see him approaching the hut, opening the door and disappearing into the sauna.

Moments later, he reappears and runs up the jetty, his towel still round his waist. At the end I can see a large dark square of water, a hole cut into the snow and ice, surrounded by candles in lanterns. He's not going to do what I think he's going to do, is he? Just as the wedding party, led by Lars, comes around the corner in front of the cabin, Björn reaches the end of the jetty and whips off his towel, revealing curvaceous, muscular cream buttocks, like a marble statue. Oh God! He's actually naked! I'm feeling slightly panicked, and I'm not sure if it's because I'm not used to seeing men naked, or because the wedding party is just about to walk this way, or because the sight of his naked buttocks is actually making my cheeks burn and my stomach stir with something

I haven't felt in a very long time but that feels a lot like desire. I experience a mixture of fury at myself and at him for doing this to me. I don't fancy him, not at all. I haven't fancied anyone since Griff died. Why has my body suddenly woken up now?

With a shout and another flash of his backside, he jumps from the edge of the jetty into the freezing water. There's a huge splash, an excited shriek from Pru's nan and a round of applause from the party – everyone except Lars, that is.

I try and look away, but Björn emerges almost immediately from the swimming hole, pulling himself up the wooden ladder and onto the jetty, water dripping from his curly hair. He rubs his face, grabs his towel with a smile, slings it over his shoulder, then opens the door to the sauna and disappears inside. Well, really! That man is such an exhibitionist! I'll write about him, tell Griff how infuriating he is. But somehow the words won't come, and I can't seem to connect with Griff through my little booklet, as though the line is breaking up on a long-distance phone call.

Björn opened a beer the owner had left for him at the sauna door, with the bottle opener on a piece of string. He placed his towel on the bench, poured a scoop of water from the bucket over the coals and listened as they spat and hissed. Steam rose, creating instant heat, and he sat on the towel and leant back, inhaling it. It felt good, really good. Cleansing and relaxing. He breathed in deeply and then took a long swig from the cold bottle of beer, his thoughts turning to Halley. She'd done a great job so far, getting over the river and rounding the herd up when they'd scattered. She was a herd animal herself, he thought. She liked to stay in the pack, preferring crowds and cities. She thought she was safer in a pack and couldn't get hurt again.

He took another swig of beer. Was that how he felt being up here, away from the city? Safer? Away from the pack that wanted to attack him? Was he just as bad as her? She needed to loosen up, try new things. Not just write what she saw in her little book. But it wasn't his problem, he knew that. Very soon she'd be gone. Back to her own life, moving on to somewhere new. They just had another night or so and they'd be at the winter grazing site. He hoped his father would be able to come home now. He knew he should have been a better son. Instead, he'd been building his career. And for what? To have it pulled from under him in one swift move. His reputation, his career, his confidence. He'd been about to lose the lot. It was far better that he'd gone before it hit the news. After all, had it really meant that much to him? Hadn't he felt more alive being back here with the herd than he had for months, maybe years, running the restaurant and creating the 'perfect plate', drawing on his travels and experiences from all over Europe, looking for inspiration everywhere except in his own heart, ignoring what was in there all along?

Just then, the sauna door opened. For a moment he wondered if it might be her, taking a leap of faith, and his heart did a flip.

I watch the wedding party disperse, then sit and look out onto the snowy night. I need more paper, so I pull Daniel's recipe book from his bag, hoping he won't mind if I take another page. I flick through it again, looking at the notes in the margins and running my hand over the splashes and stains, marks from the past. As I turn the pages, I find myself more and more intrigued by the man who wrote these words and cooked and perfected the recipes with such passion and precision, judging from the crossings-out and rewrites.

A movement catches my eye from outside. I look up and see Pru's nan tiptoeing through the snow in a floral swimming costume and matching hat, heading for the sauna. She opens the door, slides in and shuts it behind her with a cheeky smile, making me smile too. Some time later, Björn reappears with his towel tied firmly around his waist, holding the door open for Pru's nan and pointing. I wonder if he's asking her if she'd like to try a dip in the swimming hole, but instead he leads her to a snowy mound, where they stand side by side and on his count fall backwards into the snow, making snow angels with their arms and legs. Pru's nan is laughing with joy and exhilaration, making me smile even more, and once again, those tears that have stayed away so long creep into the corners of my eyes. So, he's kind to old ladies as well as animals. Maybe it's not all humans he has an appalling way with. Looking at him now, creating snow angels like a child, I want to be there doing it too.

Have I been buttoned up since Griff died? Would it hurt to undo a button or two? But just as I think what fun it might be to join them, the moment has gone. Björn is helping Pru's nan out of the snow and waving goodbye as he heads back to the cabin. I turn my attention back to my little booklet and go to write about the infuriating man I am travelling with, but once again, I find I'm lost for words.

Chapter Thirty

'I'm going to help the owner and his son,' Björn tells me.
'They are slaughtering a reindeer. Do you want to come
too?'

'What?'

'I said,' he repeats whilst rubbing his hair dry with a towel,
'I'm going to help with the reindeer slaughtering.' He stops
rubbing and looks at me. 'Do you want to come?'

'No!' I say, and then remember that these are not pets.
Without the reindeer, people out here wouldn't survive. I
realise the family have included us in their way of life, and
add, 'Thank you.'

He tosses the towel to one side. I look at it, damp from
the hot shower he's just had. I suddenly realise there's
something very different about Björn. He's shaved his beard
off! His clean chin shows off his high, wide cheekbones, and
his eyes look even bluer than before. I stare at him. 'But
you'd like to eat tonight, right?' And I have to focus really
hard on his words. He has a glow about him, clean and fresh,
that frankly I envy. And his face is so different. So . . .
attractive.

'You'd like to eat tonight?' he repeats.

'Yes, please.'

'The animal has to have lived for a reason, and we respect it by using every part of it after its death.'

'Every part,' I repeat.

'Every part,' he confirms, pulling on his boots and lacing them up. He looks at me as though trying to gauge my reaction. 'It starts with the slaughter. We all help. It is our way of thanking and respecting the animal.' He puts down his now tied boot with a thump on the wooden floor.

I nod. I understand everything he's saying, but there is no way I can go and help slaughter a reindeer. I just can't.

'I . . . I'm going to use the sauna,' I reply. 'While it's quiet.'

'And the dipping hole?' He smiles.

'No, not the dipping hole.' I shake my head, then stand up and pick up his towel and put it back on the wooden towel rail by the fire.

'Everything has a place, doesn't it?' he says. 'Everything has to be in order, like living by a schedule. What would happen if you just took life as it comes?'

'I'm here, aren't I?' I retort.

'But still keeping to a schedule. We have to have the reindeer home and have your bag back by Saturday to keep things on schedule.'

'Yes, because otherwise . . .'

He looks at me, and I hesitate.

'Well, otherwise nothing would make any sense, would it?'

'Maybe that's exactly what it would do. You need to let go of your schedules and routines . . . unbutton a bit. You might find you like it. You might find someone you want to get unbuttoned with.'

I spin away from him and look out of the window.

There's Lars, with the rest of the wedding party, and from the looks of it they're all wearing swimming costumes, thank goodness. Maybe I will unbutton a bit. Use the sauna. I'll keep my pants on and wear a towel.

After the sauna, I dry off, shivering but feeling strangely invigorated. I look at the double bed that I'll have to share with Björn tonight and have an idea. I roll up my clothes and some spare towels and arrange them in a line down the middle of the bed. That should make things a little more comfortable. Then I leave the cabin, with newly washed hair and feeling cleaner than if I'd been put through the dishwasher, and make my way to the dining room that Lars has pointed out to me.

Outside it, under a snow-covered gazebo, there is a fire pit. Björn is there with two men I assume are the owner and his son, all with bottles of beer in their hands. As I get nearer, I can see there is a grille over the fire and a big pot bubbling away, giving off the most delicious smells.

'Dinner's nearly ready,' says the owner. 'Thanks to your man here, we have got quite a feast for you.'

I go to point out that he's not my partner, but they have already moved on to a different subject and the moment passes. But we'll be gone tomorrow and I won't see these people again.

Björn gives me a small smile as the men stand around chatting, and I'm not sure what the look means, but something inside me flips over and back again. *Almost fanciable . . . if he didn't have that big beard . . .* Isn't that what I said to

Pru? The very last thing I want to do is start fancying Björn, but my treacherous heart and delighted insides seem to be thinking otherwise. I must stay as far away from him as possible, keep my distance, keep him at arm's length. There is no way I can be attracted to this man!

I make my way into the dining room, tapping the toes of my boots against the door frame to shake off any excess snow. There is a big stone fire pit in the middle, surrounded by wooden tables with benches. Flickering tea lights make it feel cosy. There's the earthy fragrance of wood burning on the fire, and wonderful cooking smells welcoming me in. At the back wall stands a round-faced woman wearing traditional Sami dress, blue with bright red and green edging at the cuffs and the bottom of the skirt. She has an embroidered belt with red tassels, a red and green scarf and a hat to match. She turns, her face as cheerful as her traditional dress.

'Hello. Welcome. I am Álvá. I run this place with my husband and son. Björn has been very helpful this evening.' She holds out a hand to a long table piled with plates of food. All sorts of different dishes. 'I hope you enjoy the smorgasbord,' she says. 'There is gravlax with mustard and dill sauce to start.' I look at the folds of beautiful pink salmon and its yellow sauce on the side with flecks of green. 'Pickled herring and beetroot salad,' she points to a deep purple bowl of salad, 'and soup. Then sliced potatoes in cream to go with our main dishes.' She hands me a shot glass of clear spirit. 'Aquavit,' she tells me. 'Help yourself to starters and take a seat.'

I take a little of everything and she places a cup of soup on my plate too.

The wedding party filters in. Lars makes a beeline to sit next to me, but the Sami woman moves him to my other side, telling him the seat to my left is for Björn. Lars keeps smiling but looks a little miffed.

The family all take their seats. Pru and Mika are beaming and glowing after their plunge in the dipping hole, and everyone has stories to tell about their snowmobiling day. They are all wondering whether they will get to see the Northern Lights later tonight from the vantage point higher up the mountainside. Lars is taking them on a lantern-lit walk.

'Come and join us,' he beams. 'It will be very romantic!'

I tell him I have to stay and keep an eye on the reindeer. But he doesn't seem deterred. I am going to have to explain to him that there can't be any romance between us. But I'm dreading letting him down.

I pick up my cup of soup and breathe in its restorative, earthy aroma. It's mushroom soup! Just like Björn made in the forest. And it reminds me that my time out here is coming to an end. I feel a surge of relief, then I taste the soup, its creamy, hot, pungent flavour, and I feel a sense of regret wash over me too.

The fire is roaring in the wooden cabin, the candles are flickering and everyone seems in high spirits, particularly Pru's nan, who's having the time of her life. Only Pru's mother isn't enjoying herself; she still hasn't thawed by the looks of it and certainly didn't take part in the plunge pool. Nan, on the other hand, is positively glowing and keeps giving Björn longing looks over the top of her steaming soup as he strides across the room, beaming and nodding to everyone, and takes his place next to me. I can't look at him.

I can't meet his eye. Clean-shaven he is a different man, and my silly heart has started to beat at double time while my stomach feels like a shooting star has just gone off in it. I look down at my soup and keep my eyes there.

The soup cups are cleared away and people are invited to come and enjoy the rest of the smorgasbord. Álvá is handing round plates. Water jugs are passed up and down the table and glasses filled, and I decide to wait until there is more room at the long table. I sip my water and watch Pru and Mika, who are laughing and smiling and hugging each other. Lars is helping hand out plates and serve up.

'This reminds me of Christmas,' I suddenly say to Björn and look up. Catching a glimpse of his piercing blue eyes looking straight at me, I wish I hadn't. I look back at my empty soup cup and plate.

'And what would you eat at Christmas?' he asks, picking up his fork. Lars is still at the smorgasbord table but keeps glancing over.

'Roast turkey. The smell of that on Christmas morning always makes me feel good. Or on a Sunday, roast chicken. We'd get the papers when Griff was home. Go for a pub lunch and then have roast chicken.'

Björn nods. 'And when you have roast chicken now?'

I nod and look at him. He understands, I think. This brash, rough, irritating man understands.

'I always think of those Sundays with Griff.' I swallow down a piece of flat Sami bread, like I ate on that first day. 'I burnt the first one I ever cooked. Couldn't work out the oven. But Griff ate it anyway and told me it was delicious.'

'Sometimes it takes a few attempts to get things right.

But those memories make us who we are today. No one can take that away. I remember fishing with my dad, like we did the other day, and cooking over the fire. All our days out here ended with a fire.' He smiles.

'And where's your dad now?'

'He's . . . in a retirement flat in the town, where your hotel is. He had a stroke and . . . well, I wasn't around to organise things, so the hospital and my sister thought it would be better if he went there.'

'And you don't agree that that's the best place for him?'

Björn shakes his head. 'He lives and breathes his reindeer. That's why I'm taking them to him. Hopefully when the herd is home for the winter he'll improve.' He wipes his mouth with a paper napkin and places it back on the table. 'I should have been here more, before it came to this. These reindeer are his life. I can't let anything happen to them. It's the least I can do. After my mother died, he was always there for us, me and my sister, but I wasn't an easy person to help.' I can feel his eyes on me and snatch a glance at him, and another shooting star whizzes through my stomach. 'The least I can do is bring his herd home for him.'

'Have you been away, then?'

He looks at me. 'Yes,' he says flatly. 'More than I should have.' His expression changes. 'Wait! I have something for you.'

'For me?'

He comes back to the table with a small piece of white meat in a light gravy-like sauce with creamy sliced potatoes.

'Here! Roast chicken, or nearly.'

I taste it. It takes me right back there, to when life was happy and settled.

'It's really good.'

'It's ptarmigan. Its plumage is white in the winter and then when the snow leaves, it is a mix of grey, brown and black. It's like a grouse. But reminds you of chicken?'

I nod and smile. 'It does, thank you.' It reminds me of chicken and happy times.

'Okay, I have something else for you to try, the other dish.' He swings his leg over the bench and returns to the smorgasbord, where Lars seems to have lost his smile and is beginning to glower. I really must explain to him that I'm not with Björn; I'm not with anyone. I'm here on my own and will be leaving that way. And I suddenly realise what I've just admitted to myself. I'm on my own and, well, I feel okay.

Björn puts another plate in front of me.

'What's this?'

'Roast loin of reindeer with lingonberries,' he says proudly.

'From . . .' I look at the plate, 'from the reindeer . . . today?'

'Yes.' He picks up his knife and fork. 'Like I said, here we respect the whole animal. We eat everything, use everything so its life has not been wasted.'

I swallow hard.

'It's an honour that we live with the animals and survive here because of them,' he says in a low voice. 'Here, try.' He takes a forkful of the food and holds it to my mouth, his eyes again meeting mine and my insides feeling like they are melting.

'I don't think I can,' I whisper.

'Just close your eyes and think of something lovely,' he whispers back. 'Remember how the roast chicken made you think of happy times. Think of something in the forest on the journey that has made you smile.' He moves closer. 'It's my special sauce,' he says. 'Try it.'

Tentatively I shut my eyes and remember the euphoria I felt at getting the herd across the river safely, and the thrill of it as we climbed the riverbank on the other side. I taste the loin and sauce. At first, I'm silent. I can't speak.

'Like it?' I hear him say, and I can feel his breath on my neck.

'It's absolutely delicious,' I say finally, slowly opening my eyes.

'Sometimes you have to be brave and try new things to discover you love them,' he says. 'The chicken was part of the journey. It was familiar, and it helped you try the ptarmigan, which was new and different. And even though you were scared to try the reindeer, thinking you wouldn't like it, you let yourself be brave.' He smiles, and a whole meteor shower goes off in my stomach.

Álvá and her husband are watching us, nodding and smiling, big, beautiful smiles.

'What's in that sauce?' I say, taking the fork and helping myself to a second mouthful.

'It's a secret . . . from the forest.' Björn raises his eyebrows, teasing. 'Remember the lingonberry vodka we had?' And suddenly it reminds me of something. Something I've seen or read somewhere.

'And this?' I point to something on my plate I don't recognise.

'Fried lichen,' he tells me, as if it is the most natural accompaniment to my meal.

Lars returns to the table with his plate and I turn away

from Björn, who starts to eat his own food.

'This place is amazing,' I say.

'The guests love coming here,' Lars tells me, swinging his leg over the bench. 'Well, most of them!' We look at Pru's mum, who is barely eating, pushing her food around her plate.

'She needs to stop looking back at what might have been and realise there's a lot of happiness to be had in the here and now,' I tell Lars, who nods in agreement.

Björn, on the other side of me, stops eating for a moment. The words hang in the air between us. 'The owners were lucky you were here to help them out with the food,' I say, changing the subject quickly. He nods and wipes the corners of his mouth again, putting his knife and fork down.

'If only they could get more people to come and stay,' he says. 'These days Sami people can't just rely on the reindeer to make their living. They need tourists. This has been a big party for them, but they're few and far between so they can't afford full-time help. No one knows they're here. Lars has done well to find them and bring his guests here.'

Lars's beam returns.

'It is such a shame more people don't come.' I take another mouthful of food, this time with the creamy potatoes soaking up the sauce, and look round at the warm, inviting cabin.

After dinner, the owners put out tea and coffee and pour little shot glasses of vodka.

'A toast!' the owner calls. 'To health and happiness.' We all raise our glasses – 'Skål!' – and down the shots in one, then the glasses are refilled and the owner calls on Lars for a toast.

'To fate and finding your one true love!' he says, looking

longingly at me, and I down my shot for courage. I have to tell him!

Björn is asked to make the final toast.

'We have an old Sami saying, may you never travel faster than your soul.' He raises his glass but doesn't look at me. '*Skål!*' and we all drink.

The owners thank Björn as the rest of the party get ready, pulling on coats, hats and gloves ready for the lantern walk to search out the Northern Lights. I make a jotting on the back of my paper napkin about the food we've eaten and the flavours that are still lingering on my tongue and writing themselves into my food memory bank, next to roast chicken.

'You still making notes for your travel log?' Björn asks as the wedding party prepares to head off. Lanterns have been lit and everyone is holding one, illuminating the room like the Christmas lights in town. Everyone is feeling excited about what they might see.

'Come with us!' Lars calls over to me. 'You can share my lantern,' he adds, smiling broadly and then glowering a little at Björn.

'I can't. I have something I want to do,' I call back across the excited room.

'Are you sure you don't want to go?' Björn is close to me again and I feel his breath on my neck. 'Maybe Lars is the reindeer loin; something new.'

I turn to look at him, knowing that it's not Lars who is the reindeer loin. My mouth is tingling with its new taste sensation and I'm wondering if it's the delicious dish I've just eaten or the way Björn is looking at me that's making me feel like that.

* * *

After everything has been cleared away, I ask Björn if I can borrow his phone. I'd borrow his charger, but we have different phones. I know he's looking at me wondering who I'm phoning and whether home is on my mind. When I've finished, I join the owner's family around the fire pit. They give me a reindeer throw to wrap round myself. There's light snow in the air, but no one seems to mind. It's a clear night and it's warm by the fire.

'Can I show you something?' I ask Björn after a while.

'Sure, let's walk to the jetty,' he says. I stand and he insists I keep the throw around me.

The dipping pool is still lit up by the candles surrounding it. In front of us I can see the wedding party making their way across the lake, like fireflies in the night, to the tree-covered bank on the other side.

'They may not be interested,' I say, feeling shy as I hand Björn his phone, 'but I've set up a Facebook page for this place. The signal is good here. I took some pictures, and added them with a brief description of the village and what people can expect if they come here.' I show him the screen.

Björn looks closely, the glow from the candles lighting up his face, his Lapp dogs at his feet.

'This looks fantastic! And it reads well, really well. Is that something you do? Were you a journalist?'

'No.' I laugh at the idea. 'I just worked for a travel company, in reservations . . . and sometimes when it was busy, in complaints. On the phones. But I used to love it when the new brochures came in. The pictures, the words describing them, selling people their dreams. I would have loved to have worked on those brochures.'

'Then why don't you?'

I shrug and shake my head.

'I think you're scared,' he says. 'Scared to try.'

'It's not . . .' but I stop myself.

'Look at what you've done this week, the obstacles you've overcome, facing your fears. You shouldn't be scared of what's in your heart.'

We look up at the dark blue sky scattered with stars, which are getting brighter all the time, and the snow easing up, fluttering around us.

'I just never thought I could write well enough, but if it helps these people . . .'

'But this is brilliant. You could sell snow to the Sami with stuff like this!'

'Well, I suppose I've had a lot of practice since . . .'

He doesn't help me this time.

'Since Griff died,' I finally say, feeling as exposed as if I had taken off all my clothes and run into the plunge pool totally naked.

He nods, and puts a hand on my shoulder. 'You've been writing for all this time, not showing anyone, keeping what's in your heart locked in there.'

I nod.

'And now you've done this. Welcome back to the real world!'

As Björn returns to the fire pit to show the owners what I've done, I look up at the star-studded sky again. I have tears in my eyes and I have no idea if they're tears for what has happened in the past, or for what's to come . . .

I join him showing them the Facebook page and the pictures I've put up there of the cabin with the candles glowing and the candlelit plunge pool. He translates what I've written, and they are delighted. I tell them to keep it updated so people can see what's happening, and show them how to do it on their phones. If they need any help with the English words, they can always use Google Translate. It's amazing that somewhere as remote as this has such good wifi! Then I show them TripAdvisor and the review I've posted there.

They thank me profusely, then hand us more beers and retire to bed, leaving Björn and me sitting by the fire, wrapped in throws, looking up at the big dark sky and the stars shining brightly.

'The stars are always there, familiar and reassuring, ready to guide you if you look up,' he says.

I nod. 'I wonder if the others saw the Northern Lights.'

'That's the thing when you go looking for something like the Northern Lights,' he says. 'You're so busy chasing what you'd like to have, you miss what's right under your nose.'

I'm about to ask him what he means when we're interrupted by someone coming out of the sauna cabin. It's Pru's mother, Sylvia, carrying a towel and wash bag.

'Hi!' I say, surprised. 'Back so soon?'

'Didn't go in the end,' she says, but not like she's sucking a lemon this time. This time there's a sadness about her. 'I'm still . . . taking it all in.'

'Shame. But come and see these stars. They're amazing!'

Obviously the beer and the thrill of writing my first ever copy has given me a confidence boost.

She comes and joins us by the fire. Björn offers her a beer, and she hesitates before accepting it with a smile. We sit and look up at the stars. Björn gives her a reindeer hide to wrap around herself, and she thanks him politely. A very different woman from the one I've seen so far.

'Björn was just telling me that we shouldn't go in search of something that might not be out there . . . we should enjoy what's in front of us here and now,' I say, taking another sip of beer – not that I need any more, clearly.

'Björn may well be right.' She looks from me to him and back again. 'She had a fiancé, you know. Rob. I could see her future laid out in front of her. A life together. A good life. Children. And then they finished, just like that, and the next thing we knew, she'd met someone else. Mika. But she never told me . . .' She swigs from the bottle and then looks down. 'She didn't tell me that Mika was a woman. I wasn't expecting it. I mean, everything changes. What about grandchildren?'

'They could still have children,' Björn says, looking up at the sky again.

'But would they still be my grandchildren? How will I feel? How will I feel about them as a couple? Will I love Mika like I would a son-in-law?'

Suddenly feeling bold, I say, 'We don't know when we're going to find love or lose it. But I do know that if we find it, we should make the most of it while we can.'

She looks at me and back at Björn again.

'It might not be what we went looking for, or what's familiar.' I think of the roast chicken, and then of the reindeer loin. 'But it might be just as heavenly. I think they're very lucky to have found each other. Isn't that what we all want, to love and be loved?'

She says nothing; just looks up at the stars in silence, as do we, all lost in our own thoughts. Finally she says quietly, 'I suppose it is.' Then she drains her beer and bids us both goodnight.

Björn tips back his head and sticks out his tongue, letting the snowflakes land there and dissolve. I laugh and do the same. After a while, we stand and blow out the candles, and as I do, I suddenly feel something hit me on the back of the head. I turn to see Björn rolling another snowball in his hands and aiming it at me, a big smile across his face.

'Like I said, you need some loosening up!'

'Right!' I bend and make a snowball of my own, then lob it, but it falls short. I roll another one quickly as he sends his into the air. I dodge and it lands in the snow behind me. This time I focus and land one right on his chest. 'Yes!'

He picks up another handful of snow, this time running towards me. I turn to escape, and he's chasing me. I bend and grab some snow as I run, just as he catches up with me, slipping his arm around my waist, and we're rubbing snow in each other's face, laughing, tumbling and suddenly falling together into the mound by the sauna where Björn made snow angels earlier with Pru's nan. He's lying on top of me heavily, his breath hard and fast, his thick curly hair falling around his face and neck, and I remember the tattoo up his forearm and the image of his buttocks as he leapt into the lake.

We hold each other's gaze, locked there, wondering if

either of us dares to take the next step and move in closer. A yearning starts to burn in me and I feel my arms reach around him to pull him towards me, when all of a sudden his breath tickles my nose, making me shake my head and lift my hand, breaking the moment. He pulls away, moving his weight off me, and I don't want him to, I want that moment back. I want to go forward, go further, suddenly craving his body on mine, his breath on my face and neck, his lips touching mine.

He stands up and reaches a hand out to me, still smiling a lazy, sexy smile, then pulls me to my feet before letting me go again, to my shriek of delight, and we make snow angels of our own, knowing that by the morning they'll have disappeared, but the memory won't.

We're still laughing as we tumble in through the door of our cabin, and I suddenly see the line of clothes rolled up down the middle of the bed like a wall. It brings me up short, remembering we're not going to fall into bed and have a night of lovemaking, even if I wanted to back on the snowy mound. All my confidence is slipping away at the reality of what I contemplated doing, the line of clothes reminding me that I'm not quite there. I haven't quite let Griff go; he's just holding on by his fingertips. I can't say goodbye for good. I have to stop it happening.

'No snoring or you're out with the dogs!' I joke, the beer and vodka having found their voice.

'And that goes for you too.'

'I don't snore!' I retort with fake huffiness.

We both try and get ready for bed without the other looking, but eventually I give up, dump my inhibitions and strip down to my undies before sliding under the covers. I mean, it's not like we haven't spent the week living with each other, even if I can't let it go any further.

The light from the stars and the silvery moon throws a path across the bed. I lie there listening to the breathing of the man next to me. There is no way I can let myself get close to anyone. I have lost all the men I have loved, my dad first, and then Griff. I can't let myself care about anyone else.

'Thank you for doing the Facebook page for Álvá and her husband. It will help.'

'Build it and people will come,' I say tipsily.

'But you were the one to put the words out there and tell people. Thank you.'

We lapse into silence.

'And thank you for getting me to try reindeer and that delicious sauce,' I say sleepily.

'Respect the animal. Make it a life that was worth living,' he says.

Just for a moment I wonder what it would be like to turn to him and see his face in the moonlight. What if I were to reach out and touch his hand and remember that I'm alive; to stop surviving and start living again? I chew my bottom lip. What if . . . what if I could let someone back in again? Could it really be this infuriating man lying next to me? I stretch out my hand and my little finger meets the wall I have built between us, knowing he's still on the other side.

Björn lay there listening to her breathing, just a few centimetres from him. He wished he could turn and look at her, see her face in the starlight. But he knew he couldn't.

How had this happened? How had she got in? He'd been determined not to fall for her. But somehow, in between losing his dog team and saving his reindeer herd, she had got right under his skin and into his heart.

He knew that only she could decide where she wanted to go from here. He had no idea where he himself was going, but he'd love her to go along for the ride with him, even though he knew she wouldn't. She'd move on, like she always did. She didn't even know who he really was. Even if he wanted to tell her, he couldn't. He should have told her right at the start. If he owned up now, what would she think? Maybe he should just tell her. Get things out in the open. At least he wouldn't feel as guilty as he did now. But for now, he reached out his hand and his little finger met the wall of clothes between them, and he knew she was just the other side.

Chapter Thirty-one

When I wake from the deepest sleep I've had in ages, I realise something is different. I'm warm! Actually warm! There is balmy air on the back of my neck and I feel like I'm wrapped up safe and sound in a kangaroo's pouch. As warm as toast, hot buttered toast. I take a moment to enjoy just being here, stuck halfway in that drowsy place between vivid dreams and reality. Slowly I start to remember where I am: in a cabin in the middle of snowy Sweden. But if I am in a cabin in the middle of winter in Sweden . . . why am I so warm and cosy, like a giant hot-water bottle?

Then I realise why. Body heat! My eyes ping open like they're about to pop out from their sockets. It's Björn! He has his arm wrapped right over me and is curled around me like a slumbering bear.

I freeze and try and put my fuzzy brain into gear, and finally, with relief, I realise that nothing has happened. I didn't sleep with him, not in that way. The relief is followed by a tiny bit of desire, like I'm remembering last night's dinner all over again. I turn slowly and try and move his arm. He doesn't wake. I look at his soft, smooth, closely shaven face and have the urge to run my finger down the side of his cheek. Almost fanciable! His expression is relaxed. I wonder what he dreams about. I wonder where he's been away to. Where does a reindeer herder go?

I remember him holding the fork to my lips last night in the candlelight and can taste the reindeer and its sauce all over again, wrapping me in its warmth and reminding me of my trek through the forest. We have come so far. Something feels different about today, and I don't know what it is. Is it because we're nearly at the end of our trip? Or maybe it's that I know what to expect from the trek today and am looking forward to saying good morning to the reindeer. Perhaps it's just that I feel refreshed after the sauna, the lovely meal and the stargazing. Or is it that something inside me has woken up from its long winter hibernation? Whatever it is, I know this man has something to do with it.

Suddenly Björn's eyes snap open, like he's just been resting them, ever alert for predators. How long has he been like that? Did he know I was staring at him? I throw myself to the far side of the bed and roll quickly out from under the covers. Then, realising that I'm just in my underwear, I drop to the floor and make it to my clothes and bag on all fours.

'Probably good if we get going,' I say, dressing as quickly as I can in the dark to hide my blushes and shuffling into clean pants and trousers. I manage to bump into every piece of furniture in the room as I jump around pulling on my boots, trying to keep moving to avoid any awkwardness and blot out the fact that Björn has just woken to find me studying his face like a map, wondering where the lines have come from and where they go from here. But isn't that the same as any of us? We have lines and scars telling the story of our past, but none of us really knows the way forward, no matter how hard we plot and plan it.

As I pull on my *I ♥ Sweden* hoodie, I feel something in the pocket. It's my little home-made notebook. And that's when I realise what was different about this morning. For the first time in two years, I didn't wake up thinking about Griff, and what I had planned that could get me through the day. I feel . . . How do I feel? I feel guilty not thinking about him; thinking about someone else. Like I've cheated on him. Even though nothing happened, I've cheated on his memory.

'What's up?' Björn says, pulling on his thick jumper over his broad chest. I can just see his outline in the moonlight. Stop looking at him! I tell myself. I have to do anything rather than fall for someone else. I'm not ready! I can't leave the past behind yet. Because if I'm not that person any more, I have no idea who I am.

I hold my hands over my face. Björn comes to crouch by me.

'Hey! What's up? You don't think you can do it today?'

I shake my head.

'Come on, just one footstep in front of the other. That's the only way to go. We all get days like this. You've come so far. You've done brilliantly.'

'I just don't think I can . . . I need to go back.'

'You can't go back! We're over the river now. More than halfway there. The only way is forward,' he tells me. 'You know that. Come on. I'll be there.'

And that, I think, is exactly what I don't need.

'Let's get moving,' I say. Keeping moving is the best thing. The last thing I want is to have to admit that time has moved on; that life has moved on while I've stood still. I'm not going to do that. If I keep busy, I have something to write in my travel log and my life is still as it was. *And you'll still be living in the past*, says a voice in my head that I try and brush away.

Björn is still kneeling beside me. He looks at me with his ice-blue eyes, just like those of his husky dog. 'Are you sure? We could wait here a while until you're ready.'

'No, I'm sure. Let's get moving . . .'

And we pack our bags silently and step out into the newly fallen snow, like turning to a fresh page in my travel log.

Chapter Thirty-two

Onwards we go, like Groundhog Day. We move the reindeer out of the corral before the rest of the wedding party has even woken up. The dogs, as ever, are barking and leaping, raring to go. Is that what Björn thinks I do? Keep moving, excited about the next journey, never really reaching a destination? Maybe he's right. I just don't know where my destination is supposed to be, and maybe I have to keep moving until I find it.

And now, I smile, these guys. I look round at the herd and pat Rocky. Björn glances over at me without a word and smiles encouragingly. 'Ready for the homeward stretch?'

I nod, and a stray shooting star from last night erupts in my stomach, leaving me excited and exhilarated and a little nervous about what lies ahead.

Just as I step onto the sled, I turn back and look at the cabins scattered amongst the trees, where Álvá and her husband and their children live with their families. Smoke is coming out of the chimneys. Maybe, just for a while, it did feel like I'd stopped moving; like I'd taken a break from my journey for one magical evening. There's only one way to reach the end of a journey, I've realised, and that's to just carry on until you get there, and when you do, there may be a whole new beginning for you. But right now, all I can do is keep going.

I turn back and look at the reindeer, already starting to make a move. There's a wide stretch of virgin snow-covered tundra in front of us, and a line of orange, pinks and lilacs where the earth meets the huge sky. Handfuls of wind-bent trees are scattered across the incline leading up to the forest, with its snow-laden treetops. As the sky begins to lighten, and the wind swirls around my face and ears, there's an ethereal feel to being out here. It's peaceful but exhilarating at the same time. I watch the herd in front of me moving forward against the building wind, and sway with the motion of the sled as we travel across the freshly fallen thick snow. It's almost like time has stood still out here, like I've been in a dream.

I wonder what life will be like when I get back to the real world, to the buzz of the city. Maybe things will never become easier, simpler or better; maybe I just need to enjoy being here now. I look at Björn, standing on the back of the sled, the ear flaps on his hat fluttering in the wind as he keeps an ever-vigilant eye on the herd. Suddenly he turns, looks at me and smiles, and I wonder why I feel as if everything inside me has shifted, like the ever-changing landscape around me, one minute in darkness and the next in light. Maybe here, in the middle of this mad dream, caught in the no-man's-land before I have to return to real life, is the happiest I've been for a long time. I haven't had to make anything up, hide behind a lie. I've just been me. And now, we're nearly there. We've nearly done it. One more night and we'll be where we've be trying to get to.

* * *

As we reach the forest, Björn brings the herd to a standstill and stands up tall on the back of his sled. The wind is whipping up more strongly here. The snow is like icing sugar dusting the top of a huge Christmas cake.

'See that? Over there?' He points towards the distant mountains, like meringue peaks. There, beyond the trees, is a town. Not a big one, but a town all the same, with roads and two-storey buildings. 'That's Tallfors,' he tells me.

'That's it? We're home? I mean . . . where the hotel is?' I correct myself quickly.

He nods. 'And on the other side of it,' his chest seems to swell, and he lifts his head, 'is the winter grazing for the reindeer.'

'So we're nearly there?'

He nods again slowly. 'Not far now.'

'Will we make it by this evening?'

He laughs. 'Still rushing.'

'I need to get the rings for Saturday, remember? I need to find my bag!'

'Your bag will be there, don't worry.'

'How do you know?'

'Have faith. I know. We'll get there. You'll get your bag.'

He fixes me with a stare, the corners of those blue eyes lined by the weather. Something in his expression tells me it's all going to be fine. Maybe I should just enjoy my last night out here with the reindeer and the dogs . . . and Björn, I find myself thinking.

'Come on, we just have to work our way through the forest. I have a friend who lives there. I've texted him. His family have a smallholding not far from the town. They make charcoal and keep reindeer. I grew up with them. We'll stay there tonight before going on to the farm tomorrow. Then you will be free to carry on travelling, wherever it may take you next.'

Still he holds my gaze, and I feel everything inside me shifting all over again. Australia, that's where life's going to take me next. Just as soon as I deliver the rings and get back to the airport. But where are the butterflies? The excitement that I feel every time I get a new job sheet? It must be the cold affecting me, I tell myself firmly.

I think about the job my sister sent me and wonder whether finally putting down some roots is actually what I want. I'm tired. Maybe I'm tired because I've been out here, but I'm tired of running away from everything back home, too.

'Best we keep going.' Björn interrupts my musings. 'You never know when this weather is going to break.'

'*Hike, hike!*' I hear his familiar shout to his dogs as they move off. My sled creaks into action too. I'll be gone from his life by tomorrow, when I finally meet Daniel Nuhtte and get my belongings back. I look at Björn and wonder if Daniel will be anything like him.

Finally, around lunchtime, we stop for a break just inside the forest, in a clearing by the river. Björn ties the dogs to a tree and then takes out the fire bowl and lights it as I've seen him do so many times before.

'Look,' he says as he starts to make coffee, 'about Daniel . . .'

'Yes?' I'm suddenly keen to find out about this Michelin-starred chef who has travelled all over the world and put his heart and soul into his recipes and his restaurant. 'He seems to have such a passion for what he does,' I say. 'All I do is travel.' Is that what *my* passion is? I wonder. 'It's what's kept me sane these last two years.'

'I think it's your writing that's done that,' Björn says. 'Not the places you've been to, but the way you describe them. I haven't really read much, just what you did on Facebook, but I don't think you know how good you are. I think the book is more than just a link with your husband. He may not be here, but he's helped you find your passion. It's your words that have taken you on your journey, not aeroplanes, buses and trains. It was in you all the time. We all think we can run from how we're feeling, but the feelings come with you wherever you go, no matter how far you travel. Eventually they catch up with you. You can't ignore them; you can't leave them behind.'

And for a moment, I wonder if he's talking about how I felt about losing Griff, or how I'm feeling right now, here in the forest with him: like something inside me has woken up after two years of lying dormant.

I stare into the flames.

'Look,' he says, 'it's all very well me telling you this, but you're not the only one running away from how you were feeling—'

'I wouldn't call it running away,' I interrupt, and I know as soon as the words have left my mouth that he's right and I'm wrong. It's what everyone else has been trying to tell me for the last two years, but I've ignored them. I think of all the messages from my sister and my mum. The articles my mum has sent me from the paper on finding new love, and the job adverts and houses on Rightmove Sara has emailed me so that I can be close to the family. I've ignored them all.

'As I say, you're not the only one. You see . . .' He stands up and pokes the fire with a stick. It's something I've seen him do now, a lot. When he's stressed, when he's relaxing, he pokes the fire. Or stokes the fire. Or chops wood for the fire.

'You love fires, don't you?' I say, realising I still know very little about this man, despite having been closer to him than I have been to anyone else for two years.

'Out here, fire is our best friend. Everything I did as a kid here,' he nods towards the direction of the town, 'days out, fishing, following animal tracks, it always ended with a fire. It's in here,' he bangs his chest. 'It's always in here,' he adds quietly, then drops his hand and prods the fire once more, deep in thought as he stares at the flames.

'Look, about your bag and Daniel,' he says suddenly, his face contorted and troubled.

'Yes?'

'Oh, before I forget. Here, I finished this for you last night.' He pulls something from his pocket, wrapped in cloth.

'For me?' I hold out my hand and take it from him.

'It's just a . . . well, a thank you. Before we get . . . well, before you get your bag . . .' He trails off.

I unwrap the cloth and there is the piece of antler he's been whittling.

'It's a knife handle. We'll put the blade in it when we get to my friend's house. He's a blacksmith as well as a charcoal maker.'

'A knife of my own! From reindeer antler!' I look at it in awe, at the intricate carving on it of the river, a *lavvu*, a reindeer who I just know is Rocky. 'I love it, thank you.'

'It's to keep you out of trouble. Because let's face it, I think you will get yourself into it wherever you go!' We both laugh.

I study the handle again, and the detailed engraving on it that he has done by hand.

'It's beautiful. Thank you.'

'Like I said, it's my way of saying thank you. I have to admit, I didn't think you'd be much help when you agreed to come. And then you lost the dogs and that Lars turned up, who I thought was your boyfriend . . .'

'Lars isn't my boyfriend,' I correct. 'I'm . . .' He raises a questioning eyebrow. 'I'm single, remember?' I finally say. 'Not with anyone.' And it feels like such a big moment, a huge leap forward. I'm single. Widowed too, yes. But not married . . . not any more. Griff will always be part of my life, but I have to move forward now, on my own. And yes, I'm still scared, but it's the only way I can go. I have to start living again.

I turn the handle over in my hand.

'Respecting the whole animal . . .' I say, understanding.

'Respecting the whole animal,' he repeats.

'And Daniel? What were you going to tell me about him?' I have the feeling there's something he needs to get off his chest.

'Ah, yes. It's just that . . . well, maybe I misled you a bit, about me and him growing up together . . .'

'Go on,' I encourage. And then I hear a noise: '*Hike, hike!*'

just like Björn calls. The dogs hear it too and prick up their ears, lifting their heads from between their paws and barking and lunging as a two-dog sled team appears on the forest path, coming towards us.

'Oh no! Not again! How did he know where we were?' This time, even I'm not that thrilled to see Lars and the wedding party on their husky safari. What was it Björn was about to tell me?

'Hey!' Lars beams, slowing his dog team and bringing the other teams behind him to a halt at a respectful distance.

'Oh, great fun!' says Pru's nan, jumping off her own sled as it comes to a standstill, and her two dogs taking off again down the forest track towards us, just like mine on the first day. This time, both Björn and I are ready and split up across the track. The herd shift uneasily but we soothe them. Björn goes to step in front of the dogs, but they dip from his reach and skirt around him, off the path, heading towards the jostling reindeer. I'm not losing the herd, though. No way, not when we're nearly there.

'Whoa! Whoa!' I call to the dogs, and eventually, with me running after them just a little way, they do come to a panting stop, like excited kids on a sugar rush giving the grown-ups the runaround and finally accepting it's time for bed.

'Hey!' Björn takes the dogs from me with a smile whilst Lars catches up.

'Sorry, sorry,' he pants.

'No worries. It's easily done,' I say. 'Rookie error!' I laugh, then suddenly stop and find myself looking back over my shoulder towards where we've travelled from, as if realising how far I've come. I'd never have been able to do that at the start of this trip. So many things, actually, I've come to appreciate in the last few days: lighting fires, chopping wood, fishing, drinking vodka, learning about the stars and about myself as well. That it's okay not to keep to a schedule. To go with what nature throws at you. And nothing bad happened.

'This is a coincidence,' I smile.

'Not really.' Lars beams back. 'This is the route we always take with the dogs.'

Björn is scowling again. 'There are other routes!' he snaps. 'Keep those dogs under control. The last thing you want is for them to get caught in their lines and end up breaking a leg or strangling themselves.' He's scolding Lars just like he did me on that first day, and I realise that he too has a barrier he puts up against the outside world. It's not just me. We're both hiding behind our own armour. I just wonder what Björn is hiding from and why he dislikes Lars so much.

I turn to watch him. He's taking himself off into the trees, swinging his axe, looking for firewood no doubt. Either that or he's planning something far more murderous. He couldn't actually . . . like me like that, could he? Wouldn't he have kissed me in the snow mound back at the Sami village? Is that why he doesn't like Lars? Because he thinks I might get together with him? I have no idea what is going on in this man's head.

I try and think back to last night. He didn't touch me in bed. He didn't make a move at all. I thought it was because he didn't fancy me, that the near kiss was just an accident, that it was in my head. But could it be that he doesn't think I'm ready to be with someone else, or maybe . . . maybe he isn't either? I remember crossing the river, how proud he was of me. I recall how he told me to think of a particular food when I wanted to remember the one I loved, and I find myself thinking of reindeer and sauce, no matter how hard I try and taste roast chicken.

'I came to find you,' says Lars. 'You left early, and what with you having to share a room . . .'

'Ha! I've shared smaller spaces with Björn!' I watch his big shoulders swinging the axe at an overhanging branch. He steps back as it falls into the clearing and glances at me briefly, and I blush and look away, then take a huge breath. 'It's not like that,' I say, feeling awkward and very embarrassed. 'I'm not with anyone. I'm widowed, Lars. I don't have a husband working away. He died two years ago, nearly to the day.'

'Excellent!' he beams, then lets his face drop and says, 'Sorry, I mean . . .'

'It's okay, I know what you meant. Look, I don't know if it's fate or whatever that brought me here. But I do know that I don't know where I'm going from here and the thought of that is very scary. I may never fall in love again, but at least I know I have loved . . . and lost. I also know . . .' I swallow, 'that I'm not in love with you. You have been a great friend to me and I wish it could be you. But I know it's not. Fate has someone else lined up for you, I'm sure.' I feel bad hurting him. But better to let him know that even though I might have finally realised that I am single and there might be life for me after Griff, it's not with him. I just don't feel it.

He looks at the ground and nods. 'I hope you're right,' he says. 'There was someone I thought was right for me, but she left. I should have gone after her, but then I got thinking

257

about my grandmother's words and how she said to wish on a star and my lucky bell and fate would come. And then you turned up and I thought it was you!' He drops his head. 'But I think the one I love may actually have been and gone. Fate has passed me by.'

'Oh Lars!' I say, and I can't help but hug him.

'We should get back.' He steps away from me and snaps back into tour guide mode. 'We have fancy dress night in the restaurant.'

'Goodbye, Lars,' I say. 'Thank you for coming to find me.' He may have come to find me, but I think I may have found myself already.

'Goodbye, Halley,' he says sadly.

'I'll always be your friend,' I tell him.

'And I yours,' he says, but right now, it isn't a friend he needs. And I know how it feels to be in love with the thought of someone who isn't there at all.

'I'll see you at the hotel,' I tell him, 'for the wedding,' and he puts his cheerful host face back on and guides the team around and back through the forest towards the hotel, which feels within touching distance now.

I glance at Björn, who is walking towards me through the deep snow, axe over his shoulder, a pile of logs in the other arm.

'Has he gone? Your friend?'

'Yes, he's gone. And yes, he's a friend. But not a boyfriend. I . . . I . . .' This is all so new to me, as new as virgin snow. The irony of that isn't lost on me. I'm not a virgin. I'm a thirty-two-year-old woman who never thought she'd ever look at another man, let alone think about what it would be like to sleep with one. I blush like a teenager at the thought of it, at the thought of Björn walking to the sauna and then letting his towel drop, and I swallow, hard. But my cheeks carry on burning.

'Okay,' he says, his face lifting from its scowl but still not smiling. 'Let's get going.' He checks the dogs, but turns to look at me as if wondering himself what on earth could be going on here.

'Scared?' I remember him saying as we crossed the river. Then, 'Being scared is always part of the journey.' It certainly is, I think to myself. And my cheeks blush and burn despite the cold wind and the snow starting to fall, heavier than before.

Through the big fat flakes we set off again, my heart racing. Part of me wants to turn around and run back, safe in the story that my husband is working away. And part of me wants to move on and see if there is a new life ahead of me. Björn was right. I had learnt how to survive, just not how to live. As we come out of the forest and start down a hill, the animals and sleds pick up speed again and suddenly I feel alive, very alive. I look at him and smile and he smiles back broadly. Suddenly what's in front of me seems very exciting indeed.

Chapter Thirty-three

'*Hej!*'

We pull in down a snowy driveway towards a yellow two-storey house, and on the front porch is a man in his late thirties who runs down the couple of steps to meet Björn, arms outstretched. They hug each other hard, like they haven't seen each other for a long time. On the veranda behind him is an older man and a woman, also ready to hug him.

'This is my old school friend Egel and his family.' They come down the steps towards us. 'This is Halley,' he introduces me. 'She's been my travelling companion and herder. If I say so myself, a pretty good one at that!' And I feel myself swell with pride.

'Put the reindeer in the corral. Help yourself to saunas. Then help me with dinner, will you, Björn?'

'I will.'

'And we have a surprise for you.' Egel's father points towards the house, and I realise it's been a long time since I've actually been inside a house, someone's home. 'Someone to see you!'

Björn frowns, intrigued, and ties up the dog sled and team. I do the same with Rocky, and the two men herd the reindeer into a corral for the night. I wonder who it is who's waiting inside. Could it be a girlfriend? I mean, I know nothing about this man. Perhaps a wife and kids! My head suddenly starts spinning.

Björn closes the gate on the wire and wood enclosure and then walks with purpose back towards the farmhouse, pulling off his mittens. He looks at a snowmobile parked out front, then picks up the pace and starts running.

Suddenly there is a shout, and a woman appears on the veranda. I feel sick. He was spoken for all along! She is blonde like him and, I notice, curvaceous. She hugs him and kisses one cheek, then the other, like a mother to a child, hugging him again.

'This is Halley,' he says from her embrace. 'She's travelled all the way with me.'

'What? The river crossing too?'

'Uh-huh!' He smiles at me.

The woman still has her arm around him. 'Hi! Nice to meet you! That's impressive. The river crossing is the worst part. Thank you so much for helping him out. I hope he wasn't too much of a grump.'

But all I can do is shake my head. My tongue is tied.

'Come in, all of you,' says Egel's mother. 'There's someone else here.' She opens the door, and Björn and the woman go inside arm in arm. I follow behind, wishing I was anywhere but here right now. There was me thinking I was finally ready to move out of the woods and into the open tundra of life, and all the time he was spoken for! I thought I was the one who wasn't free to fall in love, when all along it was him.

There in a chair by the fire is a small, frail man wrapped in a big blanket, which he throws off when he sees Björn. He stands unsteadily, holding his arms out. 'Pappa!' cries Björn. The old man says something, and from the way Björn hugs him as if his life depends on it, I think it was 'Welcome home, son.' The blonde woman steps forward and hugs them both, and for some unknown reason I find myself with tears in my eyes at the joy of this meeting. I blame it on the smoke from the fire and rub my eyes, feeling the sting.

Finally the three of them let each other go. They are beaming and talking in Swedish, or at least I think that's what it is, but it sounds different . . . and then I realise it's Sami. And this, obviously, is Björn's dad.

At last Björn turns to me, and it looks like the smoke got into his eyes too. He blinks and rubs them.

'Pappa, this is Halley.' He beams as he introduces me. 'Halley, this is my sister Elsá . . . the one who was supposed to be helping me! Where have you been?' he scolds.

His sister! This isn't a partner or wife . . . it's his sister!

'Pleased to meet you!' she says in perfect English. 'I can't tell you how grateful I am to you for helping out and bringing the herd this far.'

Björn puts his arm around her and hugs her boisterously, and she does the same back. They are more like two pups greeting each other than a couple: what was I thinking? The old man beams at them both.

'I knew I was letting him down,' Elsá says, 'but . . . well, when I got the call from the TV station to say I was in the heats of Sweden's Singer of the Year, I just had to go. You understand, right?' She looks at Björn.

'I can't believe it! That's brilliant! Of course!' He picks her up and hugs her, swinging her round. 'And how did it go?'

'I got to the finals!' she shrieks.

'Woo-hoo!' Björn hugs her again. 'Tell me, what did you sing?'

'The songs from here, of course. The *yoik*; the songs in my heart.'

He smiles and nods. 'Of course. You sang from your heart.' He seems choked.

'The songs we grew up with, that Pappa taught us.' She beams at the old man.

'I'm so proud of you, telling the world where you came from and who you are,' Björn says.

'Me too,' his father agrees in a weak voice, and Björn puts his arm around him and sits him down, pulling the blanket around him again with a mix of joy and pain in his eyes, clearly shocked by the old man's frailty.

He looks at me and all I can do is try and offer silent support. Then his father says something to him in Sami, and they all laugh.

'He says he's glad I've shaved off the beard, but that I could still do with a shower and a sauna,' he explains. 'How about it?' he asks me, and the stars in my stomach come out once more.

The wood-burning stove throws out its glorious heat. The candles on the table flicker cheerfully, throwing up a warm orange glow onto the wooden walls. Björn helps in the kitchen, and we all lay the table. Elsá even lends me a charger to charge my phone, so I know I'm back in the real world, back in from the cold. My cheeks glow with the heat and the beer I've drunk. I look at Björn, so happy and contented with his friends and family, laughing, cooking and toasting old friends and new. He raises his glass and stares at me, and I feel my insides stirring like a storm building; faster and faster come the flurries of snow, swirling round and round.

We eat a fantastic dinner of wonderfully seasoned and spiced reindeer meatballs in thick, rich gravy, with buttery, creamy mashed potatoes and, of course, tart lingonberry jam on the side. Then there is cake, soft syrupy Swedish saffron cake, with warm glögg, like mulled wine.

'Björn steeps the saffron in his own vodka, giving it a special flavour,' Egel's mother tells me. They all beam, and a niggle suddenly scratches at the back of my mind.

'No point in having a chef in the family if you don't get fabulous food,' says Elsá, grinning at her brother.

A chef? I think. Maybe that's how he knows Daniel; how he knows the inscription in the recipe book . . . That's where I've heard about the vodka, I realise. The recipe book! Why hasn't he mentioned anything about this before? I frown and look at him. He tilts his head back at me, as if asking what the problem is.

But before I can ask him about it, Elsá produces a hand-held drum and a beater and begins to sing, joining in with the drum as she does. It's haunting, beautiful; it sounds like the wind in the tall snow-covered pine trees and reminds me of being in the forest. It makes me feel a sense of freedom.

'I must check on the herd,' Björn says when Elsá finally takes a break and sips at her glögg. His father attempts to stand, clearly wanting to accompany his son to see the reindeer, and Björn takes him by the elbow for support.

'More cake?' asks Egel's mother.

'I'll get some beers,' says Egel, standing and heading to the kitchen.

'And more vodka,' Björn's sister calls, still playing gently on her drum.

'And logs,' says Egel's father.

'I can do logs!' I jump up, wanting to feel helpful.

'Are you sure?' Egel's father looks surprised.

'Yes, it's the least I can do,' I say.

I pull on my boots and my coat and my hat, and suddenly wonder how I'll feel when I'm home and all I have to do is flick a switch to turn on the heating. I don't think I'll appreciate it half as much.

Outside, it's got colder, much colder. It's snowing harder and the wind is whipping round my ears. I turn back to look at the yellow house with its white window frames and snow-covered roof. The chimney is pumping out smoke merrily. Candles fill the windows with soft orange light. I walk towards the wood store and pick up the axe. I can hear Björn and his father crunching slowly through the snow. The old man is so small and dark compared with Björn's muscular blondness, but the love between them is unmistakable as he leans on his son's arm for support. I can hear the two of them talking and it seems to be becoming more intense, more serious. But I can't understand what they're saying, no matter how hard I try.

I think of my own family, the one I have shut out for so long and kept at arm's length when all they wanted to do was draw me in and hold me tight. I take a smiling selfie in the snow and send it to the family WhatsApp group. It actually sends! We have signal and wifi here! I'm back online. And the end of the journey, I realise again. Very soon I will be flying home, repacking and heading out to Australia. But once again my stomach refuses to do the excited happy dance I'm expecting.

I look up at the sky and a wisp of green drifts across the stars.

'It's said,' Björn's voice from behind me makes me jump, 'that the Vikings believed the aurora was the Valkyries' armour shining against the stars as they accompanied the dead warriors to Valhalla, where wounds are healed and health restored.'

I can see his breath against the cold air.

'Here, let me.' He goes to take the axe.

'No, it's fine. I can do it,' I say, putting a log up on the big stump. Is this it? Is this my Valhalla, where my wounds have been healed?

I swing the axe and the wood splits satisfyingly in two. I stand the log up and swing again. Again it splits, and Björn collects the pieces.

'Everything all right with your dad?' I ask, picking up another log.

He sighs. 'Yes, and no.'

'Oh.'

'He . . . he wants to sell the herd. He thinks it's time. He's happy in the retirement flat and doesn't think he has the stamina any more to be out with the herd all the time. I should've realised. I've left it too long to come back. I hadn't appreciated how . . . old he had become. It's quite a shock. I've been stupid. He needs to sell the farm to pay for the retirement flat too. The farm and the herd; he's decided to sell both.'

'So have you been away for a long time then?'

'Yes. I'm amazed Lucas even remembers me.' He looks at the dogs in the pen. Lucas stands on his hind legs and barks. 'But he does. I was determined to keep the line going when I got my first husky. Just like Sami people keep the herd going. When a son is born, he automatically gets a part of the herd.'

'So part of this herd is yours?'

He nods sadly. 'Which means he can't sell without my agreement. I thought that, with the herd back here, things would return to how they were. My father would come home. But you can't go back; life moves on whether we want it to or not.'

'Will you miss it, when you go again?'

'My roots are here. This is my home. This is what is inside me. When my parents met, my mother came here for the good terrain to run the huskies. People were very against their relationship, a Sami marrying a dog musher. They were an unlikely pair, but they loved each other and made their lives together at the farm. I lived and breathed the Sami way of life, but in school it was another matter. I stood out. Many kids said I wasn't true Sami. But my parents taught me that it's not where you've come from that matters; it's where you're going. And then my mother died when I was eighteen and suddenly nothing made any sense. Everyone was looking at me, pitying me. I had to get away. I just left, and went travelling. The worry I must have put my dad through!'

'But you came back?'

'I came back to Sweden eventually, but not here. This place still held too many memories for me.'

'And now?'

'It's where I feel most at home,' he says, and something cracks in his voice. 'It's where I left myself behind.'

I look at him, his face so close to mine. He knows exactly how I've been feeling. He knows how much it hurts to lose someone you love.

'So will you sell the herd?'

He looks up at the sky and lets out a big sigh. 'I don't know. I don't think I really have a choice. There's nothing for me here. Like you, I'll probably have to move on.'

'But if you had the choice . . . would you stay?'

He looks at me. 'If I had the choice? I'd . . .' His lips seem to be moving closer to mine.

'Where's the wood?' comes a call from the door of the house. 'Are you okay?'

'Coming!' shouts Björn, peeling away quickly and scooping up the logs. I do the same. He smiles at me and beckons me back into the warm.

'Here, give me your knife handle. Egel is going to put a blade on it for you.'

I hand it to him, still wrapped in the cloth.

Later that night, Elsá takes her father home on the snowmobile, and offers to come back and help Björn with the herd. But I tell her it's just one more day and I'll be fine. It suddenly feels important to finish what I started.

I'm shown to my own room, where I take time to look around as I get ready for bed. A family home. There are even framed photos on the chest of drawers. One of Egel and what looks to be Björn as young men, presumably before he went travelling. They're standing with the herd, antlers all around them, arms round each other's shoulders. I look at his young, clean-shaven face and smile. I put the picture back and get into bed.

It's a big wooden bed, so comfy I think I've fallen into a cloud. The covers are thick and I pull them up around my chin. It's the first time I've slept on my own since I left the hotel. I shut my eyes, but strangely, I can't sleep. Not like before, when I couldn't sleep because of how anxious I felt. Now it suddenly feels odd with Björn not there. I turn to the empty pillow where last night his head was lying. I remember the contours of his face up close when he was asleep. Something is scratching at the back of my brain. The photograph. His face now that the beard is so much shorter, showing off his cheekbones. It's like we've met before. But where? What is it about him that seems familiar?

I think about the meal tonight, the vodka-soaked saffron cake. And then that wonderful sauce he made to go with the reindeer loin that we ate in the Sami village. I must ask him about him and Daniel both being chefs. I can almost taste the lingonberries, and the memory scratching at the back of my mind suddenly erupts as I remember where I've heard about that sauce before, with that secret ingredient. Lingonberry vodka! I remember the sketches of the berries and a little bottle drawn in the margin. Daniel's lingonberry vodka, in Daniel's book.

Daniel is a chef. So is Björn. Björn uses lingonberry vodka and knows the inscription at the front of Daniel's book off by heart. Why on earth didn't I realise this earlier? How have I added two and two and made five? For an intelligent woman, I'm feeling incredibly stupid. Maybe it was the snow, the cold, the journey, the near-death experiences, but it's only now, seeing him relaxing with his family, seeing a different side to him, a really attractive one, that I get it.

I sit bolt upright in bed. Of course I know who he is!

Chapter Thirty-four

I creep down the hall, my heart thumping, hoping I've got the right room.

'I need to speak to you! Now!' I say in a forced whisper.

He comes out, hair standing on end, and we creep downstairs, where he guides me to the fire. He opens up the door of the woodburner and throws on another log, using a poker to shake the embers into life.

'I know who you are!' I hiss. 'I can't believe I've been this stupid!'

'Who am I? You tell me!' He turns to me still holding the poker.

'You're Daniel Nuhtte! The chef.'

'I tried to tell you I'm a chef. You've seen me cooking.'

'But you're *the* Daniel Nuhtte! I've had your bag all this time, and that means you've got mine.' I hold up the little case to him.

'Ah, well yes and no.'

'Where is it? Just give me my bag and I'll go.'

'You can't leave now. It's dark. The weather's getting worse. They say there's a storm on its way. We'll leave first thing in the morning.'

'I am not going anywhere with you. You lied to me!'

'I didn't lie, I just . . . didn't tell you the whole truth.'

I drop his bag and pull out the notebook. The letter I tucked inside it flutters to the floor, but he doesn't notice. 'This is the handwritten recipe book of a Michelin-starred chef,' I say, holding it out to him. 'I guess you'd better have it back. Oh, and sorry, there's a few pages missing from the back. You should have said something earlier, then I wouldn't have torn them out.' My words are laced with sarcasm and I know this isn't my finest hour, but I'm furious. Boiling with rage. I have told him everything about myself, and all this time he has kept this from me. I have been open with him because something about being here, with him, has made me think more clearly, open up. And all the time he was keeping his real identity from me. 'Here! Take it! And then you can tell me exactly where my bag is.'

'I told you, it's at the farm, Daniel Nuhtte's farm. My family farm. Yes, I'm Daniel Nuhtte. Actually, my name is Dánel, but Daniel was easier when I was travelling, but I am also Björn. That's what everyone here calls me. They have done since I was a child. It's my second name; like a nickname that my mother used. It means Bear, because I was bigger, taller than the other kids, with this wild hair. When I went travelling, I decided to use Daniel. It's like I'm two different people. In Stockholm and to everyone in the culinary world, I'm Daniel, but here, I'm just Björn. And this is where I am now. I've closed the restaurant, put it up for sale. I have a buyer. That's why I was in Stockholm, seeing my solicitor. Sorting out the final paperwork. I'd left the book behind, and he found it and gave it back to me. But I'd left it behind for a reason.'

I'm still holding it out to him; the letter is still ignored on the floor. I can hear what he's saying, but my breathing is short and I don't know what's real any more.

'Would you have come with me if I'd told you who I was?' he says. 'Look, I needed the help. You were there. You needed to go to the same place I was going to. It made sense. But I am sorry I didn't tell you the whole truth. Your bag is at the farm. I haven't touched it or opened it. I was in a rush when I left and I didn't check it. I didn't know I had the wrong one until I saw you with mine. I must have picked yours up from the overhead locker on the plane.'

That big mop of curly hair a few rows ahead of me on the flight; I remember it now.

'I said I'll take you to your bag, and I will. It's at the farm where we're taking the reindeer, just the other side of the hotel.'

'I'll meet you there first thing in the morning. I'm out of here. And you can take your book!' I thrust it at him.

He looks at it, then takes it. I drop my hand.

'I told you,' he says quietly, 'that part of my life is over,' and he tosses it on the fire then turns and walks away, back upstairs.

The flames lick up and around the book. I stare at it in horror. I can't bear to see all those memories, a whole life, destroyed in a spur-of-the-moment action. Without thinking, I grab the poker Björn used for the fire and flick the book out of the flames onto the stone hearth. It is smouldering and glowing. I pick it up with two fingers by a corner that hasn't been touched by the flames and carry it outside and drop it in the snow, where it sizzles and fizzes. Then I pick it up and look at the damage. The back cover is burnt through and the edges of the pages are scorched, but other than that, it's still intact.

I go back into the house and pick up the letter, tucking it inside the front cover. It's over. My Arctic journey is done. I leave first thing in the morning.

Chapter Thirty-five

'Halley, wait! What are you doing?'

'I told you. I'm leaving. It's morning. Just! I'm going.' I've stuffed all my belongings into my carrier bag and am about to leave. Björn is standing in the doorway. I thrust his case at him. 'We can't be that far from the town. You can bring my bag to the hotel when you get there.'

'Don't be ridiculous! You can't go off on your own. You have no idea how to get there.'

'Don't I?' I say, sounding more confident than I feel. 'I've got this far.'

'With my help. You're a liability on your own!'

'I was . . . but I'll be fine now. I can do this.' I look out on the snowy tundra. 'I just need to get the skis from the sled.'

'But I need a second pair of hands. I can't do this without . . . I can't do this on my own.'

'Call your sister, she'll come with you the rest of the way; she offered last night. Or Egel?'

'There's a storm coming in. I need to try and beat it. Please, Halley, just finish the journey with me.' He puts his hand on my shoulder.

I look straight ahead. I can't let him back into my thoughts.

He's not who I thought he was. He's Daniel, Michelin-starred chef. Not Björn.

I glance out at the darkening sky. He's right. I really don't think I can do this on my own. But I don't want to be here with him . . . Björn, or Daniel, or whoever he is.

'I just want to get my bag, deliver the rings and move on,' I tell him firmly.

'Because that's what you always do, keep moving on. One day you'll have to stop running, Halley.'

'What? You don't know anything about me!' I argue furiously. 'It's not running . . . I . . . it's . . .' My tongue ties with fury, and hot, angry tears fill my eyes.

'Here, you'll need this.' He hands me the knife he's made me. 'Egel put the blade in. You'll need it to keep out of trouble, to stay safe.'

'Thank you.' I can't stop myself adding, 'Whoever you are . . .' as I look into the face that has become so familiar, feeling I have once again lost someone I have come to care about. Björn is gone. This is Daniel, I tell myself. I should never have let myself get close to him.

'I'm just me. I'm not anyone different,' he says quietly, holding my stare. 'I told you, I've always been known as Björn here. There was no deceit. I just didn't tell you everything.'

'I asked if you were Daniel's brother.'

'I told you I wasn't, that I just grew up with him.' There's a pause. 'So you'll come with me?'

I hesitate. 'I think I should just go.'

'There you go again, running away, refusing to listen. God, you're stubborn!'

'Well at least I'm truthful!'

'I don't think so. You're the one who has been living a lie, lying to yourself as well as others. Don't worry, I'll get someone else to help me. You carry on running. That's what you do when the going gets tough!' He turns to walk out of the room.

What options do I have? Am I really going to leave him to get the herd home alone now, having come all this way? I suddenly think about Rocky, how stubborn *he* could be, how I had to pull him along. Maybe Björn was right that it was his way of asking for help. Am I being stubborn? Refusing to stop travelling, to listen to the people who are trying to help me?

'I'll come! Just don't speak to me, that's all.' I grab my bag.

'Deal,' he agrees, huffing.

We thank our lovely hosts, who fortunately don't seem to have heard our argument and seem none the wiser about our falling-out. They insist on us taking wooden poles with us, in case we need shelter on the way. The poles are long and cumbersome, but it's only one more day. I feel sad as we wave and say goodbye, knowing I'll never see these people again. This will just be another memory in my travel log. Egel and Björn hug like brothers before we set out on the final leg of our journey, the sky much darker, the wind much colder, the snow building and swirling. It may be the hardest part so far.

Chapter Thirty-six

The wind is biting cold. I can feel it in my bones and on my cheeks. My eyebrows are frozen like ice pops and my eyelashes are clumped together and heavy. My nose is so cold it hurts, throbbing with pain. I keep rubbing it but it doesn't seem to help.

The reindeer are travelling steadily through the building snow. We all have our heads down and are pushing forward slowly against the wind. The dogs are finding the snow harder and harder to run through, slowing them down too. The first hour passes in silence, the clicking of the reindeer's ankles the only sound apart from the constant forceful wind. There's an uneasy tension in the air, and it's not just the fact that we're not speaking. The weather seems to be worsening, the snow getting heavier, and I can hardly see Björn – or Daniel, or whatever I'm supposed to call him, not that that matters right now – just the fuzzy light from his head torch. The whiteness all around is starting to make me feel dizzy and disorientated. I don't know which direction we're travelling in or what might be in front of us. What if we hit a river again? I'm scared now – really scared. I don't want to die, I realise. I want to keep living. I want to do more things that make me feel alive, like riding downhill on a sled being pulled by a reindeer, eating freshly caught fish and making snow angels.

Suddenly the walkie-talkie crackles into life.

'Okay, we'll have to stop. We can't go on. It's going to be a white-out,' he says.

'What? Go back?' I turn to look in the direction we've come from but can't make out our tracks at all. Everything has been totally covered over.

'No, we can't go back. We'll have to sit it out.'

'What?' Crackle, hiss.

'We'll put the tent up. We have poles, thank God. The reindeer won't go far. They'll just wait it out.' Crackle hiss. 'We'll head into those trees.'

I can just make out where he is pointing. With effort, and me pushing it through the deep snow, Rocky gets the sled into the trees, where it lists and comes to a standstill. I unharness him and let him join the herd. Then, with the wind battering us, we try and erect the tent. It seems an impossible task, but Björn ties guy ropes to the trees, and eventually it's up. He goes back to the sled, grabs his axe and finds the makings of a fire.

'Get that going,' he instructs, handing me his flint. 'I'll see to the dogs.'

I quickly clear away the snow and lay up a fire, pulling out my knife and scoring the bark to light it.

'Come on, come on,' I'm saying out loud, my hands shaking with cold and fear as I try and create a spark from the flint. It's no good. In desperation, I pull out my little notebook and tear a corner off it, and another and another. I put the flint to them, and this time it lights the edges of the dry, crisp pages, my words going up in flames. I add moss on top, and curls of bark, and by the time the initial flames weaken and die, the fire is glowing. When Björn sticks his snow-covered head into the tent, there's a pot of pine tea on the go.

'We need to dig the dogs in deeper to keep them out of the snow.' He's out of breath.

I don't need asking twice. I pull on my hat and coat and gloves and, securing the tent door behind me, take the shovel he hands me.

Finally, with the dogs well protected, we practically fall back into the *lavvu*, the Lapp dogs coming with us to keep us warm. Inside, the fire has warmed it up and there's an orange glow welcoming us back in. Outside, I couldn't see my hand in front of my face.

'How long will we be here?' I ask.

'As long as it takes. It's going to get worse before it gets better.'

He unfolds a sleeping bag and wraps it around me.

'We have to keep warm, whatever happens.'

I feel more scared but strangely more alive than I have ever felt, but this time, I'm not reaching for my notebook. I can't. I've burnt most of it. This is about living, not documenting the events in my life to give them meaning.

'We'll be fine,' he reassures me, seeing the fear in my face. 'We just have to ride out the storm.'

I nod, my teeth chattering, but I am glad to be in the tent instead of outside in the white-out. The reindeer have moved in amongst the trees. I can hear them outside and find it strangely comforting. Then something hits the top of the tent with a thud.

'What's that?' The sound makes me jump.

'Just the snow falling from the trees where it's got too heavy. It's probably best we talk . . . to pass the time.'

I stare at him. A few hours ago, he was the last person on earth I wanted to talk to. I felt I'd bared my soul to this man and I didn't even know who he was. But now, well, there's no one I'd rather be stuck in a snowstorm with, I realise.

Another clump of snow lands on the tent, making me jump again.

'Tell me about your husband – Griff, isn't it?' he says.

'I don't want to talk about him.' I button up all over again. We fall into silence. Finally I ask the question that's been on my mind since last night. 'Why didn't you tell me who you were, who you really were?'

He sighs, a big long sigh. He seems to be gathering his thoughts and I don't say anything, just sit in the orange glow trying to gather mine too.

'I didn't want to be found. It seemed easier to pretend to be someone else,' he tosses some stray bark into the fire. 'I guess I was running away myself, again.'

'Again?'

'As I told you, after my mother died, I left here. I couldn't stand the looks, people talking about me . . . just as you must have felt after your husband died.' He looks at me with his pale blue eyes. He understands exactly how I've been feeling. And there was me thinking, what did he know? But maybe it was because he understood I found myself telling him about Griff.

'And it seemed easier to keep travelling. Did you travel when you were with Griff?'

'No. When we met, I helped him pick out a holiday for him and his mates from his barracks, an all-inclusive couple of weeks in the sun, the best I could find.'

The older of the two dogs lies across Björn's lap and he strokes it. The other is lying along my thigh.

'But you hadn't been there yourself?'

'No, I'd done a few trips, and Griff and I always wanted to do more. We had a bucket list we started together. He gave me the travel log for my birthday, just after our wedding and before he went on his last tour of duty. After that, he planned to leave the army and settle down. We'd enjoy our new house and all the wedding presents when he came home for good.'

Outside, the wind is whipping around the tent, billowing the sides of it, and the snow banks up the sides some more. One of the lanterns flickers. We both turn to look at it, but to our relief it comes back to life.

'When he was away, the travel brochures became my place of comfort. I'd imagine all the places we'd go together, reread the blurbs until I knew them inside out: the sights, the food we'd eat, the places we'd swim. I read them over and over again, keeping the dream alive.'

I look down and see that fat tears are dropping into my empty mug. Björn removes it from my hands and replaces it with more hot tea.

'We promised ourselves the trip of a lifetime when he got out and got home.'

The lights flicker again, as does the fire. I look into the flames.

'But we never made it.'

'And so you travel and write the descriptions and read them back to yourself, just like when he was in Afghanistan, keeping the dream alive.'

I nod. 'Or I did. Then I lost my book and . . . well, even though I have written a bit out here, it's been more about actually doing something rather than just being a bystander reporting everything. I've finally felt I'm living again. But I still can't help feeling guilty.'

He nods.

'The thing is,' I say in a strained voice, and I realise I've never really admitted this to myself, 'he asked me if he should go. He said if I didn't want him to, he wouldn't. One last tour . . .' I try and sip the tea but can't. 'And I let him go . . .' I stare into the fire, lost for words.

Finally, Björn speaks. 'I went travelling. France, Italy, Switzerland . . . started working in kitchens, moving on from job to job, not staying in one place too long. Like you, I wrote my experiences down, in my recipes, the smells and tastes of places. My mum gave me that book when I was younger and I took it with me.'

'So what does the inscription say?'

He swallows. 'It means, always remember what's in your heart, love and hugs, Mum.' He swallows again. 'Like I said, I filled it with dishes that I discovered, hoping I'd discover myself, I suppose.'

'And did you?'

'Eventually, after ten years, I returned to Sweden. But not here; to Stockholm. I'd worked in Michelin-starred restaurants and I had a backer who set me up in my first restaurant here. Then I set up on my own, with a team around me I trusted. I had a girlfriend at the time. She was my sous chef. We were a great team in the kitchen. Not always so great outside it! Luckily for us, we didn't spend much time out of the kitchen.' He tries to laugh.

Suddenly I remember the letter the woman at the restaurant gave me. It must be her. But I don't stop him in mid flow.

'Critics came to the restaurant, raved about the food, all inspired by my time in Europe. But the more the critics came, the more they wanted to criticise. I began to realise that the dishes weren't about me, they were about what I'd learnt from other people. There was nothing of me on the plate. I was tired, burnt out, but I couldn't stop working . . . like you couldn't stop travelling, I suppose. Because once we have to stand still and think, well, that's the hard part. Working out where we really are in life.'

Outside, the dogs bark and howl. I shiver.

'I couldn't stand the looks in the office after Griff died.' Our memories are like runners in a relay, handing over the baton, gathering pace with every leg. 'Everyone was really kind, but it was the "How are you today?" that I couldn't cope with. If I was having a good day, it reminded me, and if I was having a bad day, it made me worse.' I manage a little laugh, and so does he.

He reaches into his pocket. 'Here, something to keep out the cold.'

As I take the flask, his fingers brush mine, and I feel that frisson, that thrill, travelling right up through the middle of my body again. I sip. Lingonberry vodka. Its familiar flavour brings comfort.

'The night before I closed the restaurant, we'd had a good evening. We'd launched our new menu, to great feedback. We had a few drinks in the kitchen after service. I didn't drink. I was driving. Our young kitchen hand, however, had had more than she should.'

'More than *lagom*?' I say.

'More than *lagom*, more than enough.' He nods and smiles. 'She was young. Keen. Talented, even. I offered her a lift home. We were in good spirits. But when I arrived at her parents' house and pulled up, she leant in and tried to kiss me. I was surprised. Taken aback. Told her that was never going to happen. That I knew she admired me but this was very inappropriate. I told her she was good at her job but she shouldn't do anything like that again. The next morning, she was in the office with my sous chef, crying, saying I'd tried to kiss her the night before. It was horrific. Camilla said I should take some time off. So, you see, when you said I was hitting on you . . . well, I thought you knew. I thought it must have been in the press.'

I shake my head.

'Suddenly, everything I had worked for was unravelling. The critics were over-analysing the menu, pulling it apart. There was nowhere to hide. People were trying to bring me down at every corner. But this, this was unthinkable. Once the press got hold of the story, it would have been everywhere. I'd seen it happen before. Like vultures picking over your life. I didn't want that for my family. I couldn't disappoint my father. Not after everything he and my mum had done for me. They made me who I am. They didn't deserve that. So I came here. I came home. And it was then that I realised

I'd spent far too long building my career and not enough time looking after my family. So . . . I put the restaurant on the market. It sold within days. But now . . .' He breathes out heavily. 'But now I realise I left it too late. Dad's right. He can't look after the herd. I have to tell him that I agree to sell.'

'So that's why you didn't tell me who you really were when I met you on that first day,' I say, finally understanding.

'I didn't know you. You could have told the press where I was. Look, I know I did a bad thing. I needed help with the reindeer. The weather was too good to miss and you needed to get where I was going. I thought it was a simple swap. And then . . . well, I tried to tell you, but I didn't expect . . .' He trails off, staring at me, his blue eyes sending shooting stars off all around my stomach.

'What? Didn't expect what?' I'm hanging on his every word, wondering if he's going to say what I think he's going to say – that he didn't expect to start to like me, to care. Is this what I want to hear, that he cares?

'I didn't expect to . . .' He suddenly looks around and listens, his eyes narrowing. The herd are shifting outside. Then he relaxes and shakes his head. 'I just meant I didn't expect to meet someone like you.'

'What? A city girl out of her depth?'

'No,' he says softly. 'Someone with such determination and bravery. Someone who gets knocked down but gets right back up again. Someone as honest . . .'

He holds my gaze, and the orange glow from the fire lights up his face as a flame suddenly licks up the side of the logs. Inside I feel exactly the same, as if the flames in my stomach have suddenly burst into life.

At last he shrugs and looks down, picking at the reindeer rug beneath us, and just for a moment I wonder what it would be like to fall back into the soft skins here in front of the fire, in the lamplight. I'm suddenly feeling very attracted to this man I have come to know through his passion for his way of life here in the wilderness, but also through the pages of the book.

The wind outside suddenly whips at the sides of the tent, and a rush of panic surges through me. At least I think it's panic.

'It's fine,' he says, edging towards me. 'We're safe here. I promise. Nothing will happen.'

And I feel a strange mix of excitement and disappointment.

'So where will you go now?' I say to cover my burning cheeks. 'When you've delivered the reindeer.'

'I don't know. Maybe France, or perhaps further afield. Australia maybe.' He laughs. 'Where do you think? Recommend anywhere?'

'I'll let you know if I get there.' I look around. '*If*,' I repeat. 'The wedding is tomorrow. If I don't get the rings there, my boss will never forgive me. I won't have a job at all.'

'We'll get you there,' he says. 'Plenty of time. Like I told you, never . . .'

'. . . travel faster than your soul,' I finish, and we both smile and my insides dissolve.

I pass back the hip flask and our hands touch again. I wonder if he's feeling the same way I did, and as he looks at me over the flask, something tells me he is.

'So tell me, travel agent sales team manager . . . where

should I go next? Tell me about the places you've been.'

I go through all the places I've visited and some of the ones I haven't that are on my bucket list. The cities I'd like to see, the sights, the wonders of the world. Finally, when we have swapped travel stories, him telling me about the restaurants he's worked in and the extreme menus he's been part of creating, we both find ourselves smiling and laughing.

'About your book . . .' I say. 'The recipe one.'

'It's in the past for me, that part of my life. I don't need it any more.'

'No, but when I was at the restaurant, looking for you – well, for my bag – I met—'

'Shh . . .' He holds his finger up, and I don't need telling twice. The atmosphere inside the tent has changed. The warm glow and safe bubble we have been in seems to have evaporated. The animals outside are restless. The wind has died down and the snow seems to have eased up on the roof and sides of the tent too. He moves away from me. And suddenly I'm feeling out in the cold once more, and I realise quite how much I like being close to him.

Chapter Thirty-seven

All at once there's a cacophony of noise: squealing, barking, growling, gnashing and yelping.

'What's happening?' I jump up. Florá and Erik are on their feet too, and barking.

'Pass me the gun, quick!' Björn points. Again I don't need telling twice. He slips the gun from its cover, switches on his head torch and steps out of the *lavvu* just as there's another squeal and a howl of pain.

A shot rings out through the trees, and there's a thudding all around as snow falls from the heavily laden branches above us. Then silence. I don't move. There's a second shot, and once again the snow falls in heavy handfuls. I have no idea what's happened and can't seem to move to find out. I'm frozen to the spot.

Chapter Thirty-eight

'Halley! Halley?' I can hear Björn calling my name. It suddenly shifts me from my frozen position.

'Coming!' I pull my hat and gloves and coat from the overhead line. Outside, the snowstorm seems to have passed. The new snow is thick and deep, like a giant feather duvet. My legs disappear into it with every huge step I take. I make it round to the back of the *lavvu*. The herd are spread out, shifting this way and that nervously. And there, under a tree is Björn, his beloved Lucas cradled in his arms, the snow around him stained red with what looks like blood. Nearby is the dead body of one of the reindeer.

'Wolverine,' Björn says by way of explanation. 'Lucas was protecting his pack. It's what we do, isn't it? Try and be there for the ones we love, and feel useless if we're not.' He swallows. 'We need to cover the body.' He nods to the reindeer. 'Can you get a plastic sheet from the sled?'

He doesn't need to say any more. Once I've covered the dead animal with the plastic sheet, I turn to look at Björn and the dog in his arms. He shakes his head.

'I need to get him to a vet. There's one back in the village, where we came from.'

'What can I do? Phone someone? Your sister? Egel?'

He looks up at me, his blue eyes tired and blinking. 'There is something you can do.'

'Name it,' I say.

'Could you stay here, with the herd? Alone, without me?' He holds my gaze, knowing what he's asking of me. I take a deep breath.

'I can,' I say. And I really can.

I tell Björn to stay where he is whilst I get the dogs and the sled ready. I harness up the dogs and put on their booties, then lay a reindeer skin on the sled, having unloaded some of the provisions into the *lavvu* to make room for Lucas. I even make a flask of pine tea to keep him warm.

Slowly he stands and lifts his injured dog in his arms and carries him through the deep snow towards the sled. The dogs are eager to go but they know something is wrong. Their leader isn't there. He places Lucas carefully on the reindeer hide and pulls another hide over him.

'He's looked after me before now. It's my turn to look after him,' he says, and I nod.

'And the wolverine?' I ask shakily.

'Dead. In the woods,' he tells me.

'The reindeer . . . will we bury it?'

'No,' he says softly. 'We must respect the animal. For its life to have been worthwhile, we must respect it in death. We'll take the carcass back to the farm.'

I swallow and look up at the huge sky to stop my eyes watering. I can see the clouds finally moving out and the dark sky clearing. And I realise that's exactly how I'm feeling: like the clouds are finally parting and I'm seeing things properly. There are people and animals here that matter right now, that need me.

Björn stands on the back of the sled.

'Thank you, Halley, for everything.' He reaches out and touches my cheek. And more than anything right now I want to lean forward and kiss him and tell him to take care of himself and to come back to me safely.

'I will be back, I promise,' he says, as if reading my mind. But if I know anything now, it's that we can't make those promises; we can only hope. And I do hope as I watch the dogs and sled set off across the big white wilderness, getting smaller and smaller against the clearing sky, until I am finally alone. Well, me and a few hundred reindeer.

This is my *vargtimmen*, my Wolf-time, when I'm haunted by the fears that come with the long hours between nightfall and dawn. The time I hate most, when all my memories pile in. I need to keep moving to banish them, so I push back the door of the *lavvu* and stoke the fire. Despite it being cold, it's clear and still now, and I want to be able to see the herd as they mill around in the trees, just in case anything happens. I think about Björn and Lucas and hope they get there in time, and that they're safe and doing okay.

I'm missing Björn, and not just because I'm scared about what might be out there in the woods. I'm missing him being here next to me, like we were just before the attack. My thoughts jumble up like a tangled ball of wool and I have a feeling it's going to be a long night before I've untangled them all. I look out at the big sky that seems to reach all the way to another world. More and more stars pop out and the sky darkens, but it's not a threatening shade of black, more a beautiful dark inky blue. I take out what's left of my little notepad, and it feels like I'm doing it for the very last time.

Chapter Thirty-nine

Dear Griff, I write, leaning on the back of Björn's cookery book in my lap, drawing comfort from it, feeling him close to me. My hands are cold and it's hard to write small in gloves, but I only have one page left in my booklet. Still, it has to be right. I cross out the *Dear* and write *Dearest Griff* instead.

A noise behind me makes me jump, but it's just Rocky reaching into the branches of a nearby tree and pulling at the lichen there, bringing a great clump of snow with it, showering himself and making him look as if he's had a dusting of icing sugar.

What can I say about this trip? That it's been the trip of a lifetime? It's certainly been that . . . As I write, I think about my arrival at the Tallfors Hotel and meeting Lars. *I have to tell you about Lars. He is one of the most lovely people I have ever met. He's kind, funny, makes me laugh . . . a bit like you. But he's not you. No one will ever be you.* There will never be another Griff.

You would have loved this place, I continue. I write about the forest and my first day. How I was determined to push on; how I nearly lost the dogs; the ice road over the frozen lake, and the river. I look up at the sky and see that even more stars have appeared, like a child's painting liberally covered in bright silver glitter. Some people think the stars aren't really stars, but little holes in the sky so the ones we love can keep an eye on us. I try and work out where I've heard that, then smile as I remember: a cartoon sent to me by my sister.

I recall what Björn said as we looked at the stars in the Sami village: 'That's the thing when you go looking for something like the Northern Lights. You're so busy chasing what you'd like to have, you miss what's right under your nose.' I remember telling Pru's mother that we should make the most of love when we find it, and I also recall the guilt I felt afterwards. *I know now I have to stop running and hiding*, I write. *I can't feel guilty for being alive or for feeling again. I will never forget you. You are a part of me. But I need to stop just surviving and start living.*

It's really bright now with so many stars in the sky. I decide to do a check on the herd just to be sure. I switch on my head torch and pick up the other big torch. I put my hand to my little knife in its cover in my pocket, and look over at the gun that Björn has left with me. Then I put on my snow shoes and step out into the dark, silent forest.

The reindeer all seem settled, and I find the familiar sound of them snuffling in the snow comforting. It's just them and me. On my own. The one thing I've avoided doing for two whole years. But I know in my heart that no matter how hard I've tried to surround myself with people, that's exactly what I have been: on my own. I've pushed everyone away. I pull out my phone to see if I can text home. But there's no signal, otherwise Björn would have been in touch. I hope he's okay. I really couldn't bear the thought of anything happening to him.

I care, I realise. I really care. Am I about to be punished for finally falling for someone again? When I said I'd love Griff forever, does that mean I'm never to be allowed to love anyone else? What if Björn doesn't come back, like Griff? What if it happens again? I'm not sure I could bear it! I shouldn't have let him into my heart. That way I couldn't get hurt again.

I need something else to think about. I start counting the reindeer, in Swedish, grouping them in tens and then remembering the one we lost. Respect the animal, I hear Björn saying. Its life cannot have been in vain. Its purpose now is to feed and clothe us, to make sure that we survive and look after the rest of the herd. It's all about teamwork out here.

And Griff's life can't be in vain either. I can't let his memory be about the sadness his death has brought. 'I want to celebrate your life, not keep mourning it,' I say to the stars. 'I think you'd want me to be happy, not feel sad all the time.' I think about Lars, who made me laugh. 'You wanted me to be brave and that's what I thought I was doing, always on the move. But really being brave is this: allowing myself to stand still, to think about you, to think about how much I miss you . . . and to let you go.'

I walk back round to the opening of the *lavvu*, slip off my snow shoes and stoke the fire, then sit back down at the entrance overlooking the tundra spilling away in front of me and pick up my pen and paper. Big fat tears hit the page in front of me and make the ink run, but I don't care. No one is ever going to read this . . . no one is ever going to read any of what I've written. It was just part of the journey.

Thank you . . . thank you for being in my life, and thank you for the book that was my journey. Without it, I don't know what I would have done.

My writing is getting smaller and smaller. I pull off my gloves, despite the cold. I need to get these words out. But the book is nearly full. Will I get another one, I wonder, for my next journey? Am I going to make it to the wedding on time, so that Mansel Knott will trust me with the long-haul job? I still have bills to pay. I bite my lip. Or I could go for the job my sister has sent. Maybe that's what I'm meant to do now. Go home and put down roots. Sell up and move somewhere smaller, closer to the family, somewhere I could love again.

I look up again. The sky seems to be turning a lighter shade of blue, still scattered with sequin stars. A sky that has started to feel so familiar to me now. I remember how I felt when I got here, almost scared of its unknown expanse. But I'm not scared now. I look up at the stars and hope that Griff is looking down through those chinks of light in the dark curtain between us and knows I'm all right. I'm doing okay, Griff, I tell him; more than okay.

'The stars are always there, familiar and reassuring, ready to guide you,' Björn told me back in the Sami village. So . . . Björn. There is nothing else to do here but think. Yes, I couldn't stand him to start with, and yes, that's all changed. How do I feel? Would Griff be cross if I told him that I thought I could really like this guy . . . that maybe I've fallen in love with him, and that the thought of anything happening to him out there this evening is killing me? If only I could have a sign, ridiculous as it sounds, just to know that he approves, that he wants me to move on.

I reach the bottom of the page. *I will always love you, Griff. But I know I have to say goodbye*, I write, and sign it with as many kisses as I can squeeze in before I finally run out of space on the page. As I look up to stop any more tears falling, the sky suddenly changes and a ghost-like shaft of green light appears. Then just as quickly, it vanishes, and I wonder if I imagined it.

I wrap my sleeping bag around me and pull my gloves back on. The fire is lit but I don't want to shut the *lavvu* door yet. I want to keep looking out for signs. Florá and Erik snuggle into me, and I'm so grateful to have them here by my side, keeping me warm and keeping me company. I hold them both tight. I'm not sure what I'd do if another wolverine attacked the herd. I look at the gun. Yes, I do . . . I'd have a damn good try at saving them. Because out here, living for now, that's what's most important. I'm living in the present, not the past or the future, wondering where my next destination is going to be. On my own, in the middle of the Arctic wilderness! And actually, I realise, although I'm scared, I'm not running away any more.

Suddenly the green light on the horizon appears again, like it's popped up from its hiding place. As it dances across the sky like a soft green scarf caught on the wind, more shafts of green light appear, and then purple ones too. Before I know it, the sky is full of light, and I feel the delight of a child watching a magic show. I'm laughing, I realise, and crying at the same time. It's utterly beautiful. I look for my book to write it down, but the book is full. This is just for me to remember. Maybe Lars was right. Maybe there is such a thing as fate . . . a sign after all.

'Thank you,' I say out loud to Griff. 'Thank you for the time we had together, and for showing me that it's time to move on. That it's okay to fall in love.' I sniff and hug the dogs draped across my lap, sitting in the doorway of the tent surrounded by the herd. And although I'm alone, I think I may be happier than I have been for a very long time.

I don't intend to sleep. I want to sit and watch this night sky forever. It feels like a great big hug wrapping itself around me, and bizarrely, I don't feel scared any more. I feel very much alive; happy that I stopped writing and looked up, just like Björn told me to. I want to enjoy this, even though it feels like my last goodbye to Griff. My book is full. I've said all I can say to him, except . . . and I know now that he wants me to do this as I sit and watch the lights and say, 'And now, if you can, bring Björn back safely to me.' And the lights seem to shine even brighter than before, as if showing me the way ahead, and I hug the dogs tight and smile a watery smile up at the sky.

Chapter Forty

I wake feeling colder than I have ever felt before. My head hurts, my teeth chatter. Florá is licking my face. I've fallen asleep under the reindeer hides with the *lavvu* door open. I force myself to move, knowing I could be one step away from hypothermia. I should have shut the door! I turn and look at the fire. At least the embers are still glowing. I chuck on the last logs, my fingers crying out with cold, then scoop up some snow in the pot and put it on the fire. I need a hot drink, now! I need to get warm. I'm no good to these animals if I pass out from cold.

Digging deep inside myself, I pick up the axe and, with the reindeer skin wrapped around me, push out of the tent and into the deep snow. The wind is practically non-existent now. There's a stillness and a silence all around me. But I'm okay. I'm alive, and so are the reindeer, and I intend it to stay that way. I look for a branch and start to chop. When I run out of breath, I look up. A purple and pink glow is appearing on the skyline. It's dawn. Light is coming. I've done it! I've survived the night on my own, and now it's a new day and I can't help but smile through my frozen lips.

I take the logs to the fire, stoke it up and then make myself pine tea. With that inside me, along with some dried reindeer meat and Sami bread I've found in the supplies, and a bar of chocolate, I feel better. I feed the Lapp dogs and then look out on the tundra. It's still; there's no movement, no sign of Björn. The reindeer will start getting restless soon and want to move, and with no corral to keep them in, I'll have no option: I'll have to go with them and head for the farm. I'll probably only be able to contact Björn once I hit the town. If I can't get hold of him, at least I'll be able to send for help, and the sooner the better.

I begin to pack up the sled with the reindeer hides and sleeping bags, the cooking pot and finally the tent and the poles. As I load the final few things, I turn to look out over the tundra, but still there's no sign of Björn. I put the little notebook into my inside pocket for safety. But right now, I realise, I want Björn back safe more than anything. If I thought staying here and waiting for him would help, I would do it, for as long as it took. But I know I have to get help.

I call to the Lapp dogs, and thankfully, they respond. I have no real idea of how to get this herd moving in the right direction, but I know they do. 'Look, it's you and me,' I tell them. 'We need to get help. We need to find your master. We need to make sure he's safe and not lying out in the snow somewhere.' The knot of worry tightens in my stomach and my pine tea and chocolate threaten to make a reappearance.

I'm about to turn and move the reindeer on when suddenly Florá barks at me. And then I hear another bark, in the distance. Did I imagine it? Florá barks again and this time Erik joins in. I stand still and listen. There's nothing. Then, in the distance, against the pink and purple glow on the skyline, I see a tiny dot of light, with two others below it, like a head torch and two lights on the sled.

'It's Björn!' My heart suddenly leaps and does somersaults. 'It's him! He's come back!' And I could cry all over again.

I stand and watch the orange head torch as it gets closer. Bigger and bigger, brighter and brighter, like the sky behind him. Eventually I can see the dogs, running, panting, but still looking as if they're smiling. And finally I make out the outline of Björn himself, standing big and tall at the back of the sled, and in front of him, Lucas. He made it! They both made it! I stand and wave my arms, and he waves back, as pleased to see me, it seems, as I am to see him.

I have no idea how it happens, but as he brings the team to a halt and pulls on the brake, I find myself in his arms and kissing him like it's the most natural thing in the world, and as I pull away to see his beaming face, the last green wisp of the Northern Lights shimmies across the sky and disappears, like a final encore at a glorious gig, a magnificent performer leaving the stage. I smile as I watch it go.

'How is he?' I nod down at Lucas.

'He's okay. Stitched up and refusing to rest. But he needs to stay put to recover.' He looks at the dog, who looks right back at his master.

'It's the only way, Lucas,' I say, rubbing his head gently. 'Time is a great healer.'

'And what about you? How was your night?' Björn still has hold of my arms, and my lips are no longer frozen, but actually tingling as if they are on fire. In fact my whole body is feeling more alive and hotter than it has in a long time.

'It was . . . Actually, it was amazing!' My smile spreads even wider, if such a thing is possible.

He looks at me, a little confused, and tilts his head. 'Don't tell me, Lars came to your rescue!' he says, half joking, half unsure.

'No! It was just me. All night. And . . . it was okay. I had time to think, a lot.' I look down, trying to put my thoughts into words, and then back into his pale blue eyes.

'And?'

I take a deep breath. 'I was worried about you. I missed you. But not just because I was here on my own, in the middle of nowhere.' I throw my hands out. 'I think . . . no, I know, I'm ready to move on.'

'You're ready?' A smile lifts the corner of his mouth.

I smile back, and his eyes lock on mine, understanding everything I'm saying.

'In that case, we'd better get these reindeer back as fast as we can,' and he bends in to kiss me all over again.

Finally, we break apart, both smiling.

'Come on,' he says. 'Let's get this herd home and those rings delivered. There's a wedding today, and then I need to take you to bed – if that's what you want.'

'I do!' I breathe, and a million shooting stars rocket around inside my stomach.

He loads the covered reindeer carcass onto his sled while I climb back onto my own behind Rocky, the two of us beaming at each other, watching the herd then glancing back at each other, like two magnets being drawn together, back to home. So much so that I hardly notice that the herd isn't moving forward like they're supposed to. In fact, as I nearly topple from the sled as it comes to a grinding halt, they aren't going anywhere at all.

Chapter Forty-one

'What's going on?' I ask Björn in dismay.

'Oh no! Not now!' He throws his head back.

We both stare, turning this way and that, watching the reindeer, who have stopped walking and are dropping one by one to their knees.

'Come on, keep moving. Come on! Yah, hey!' Björn has put the brake on the sled, jumped off and tied it to a tree. He's now in amongst the herd, waving his hands. 'Yah, yah!'

'Björn, what's going on?' I call, spinning this way and that.

'They're lying down! The reindeer have decided to lie down!' He holds his head.

'But . . . What? No, they can't! Not now!' I start waving my arms too. 'Come on, let's go! I've got to get to the wedding!' But they don't budge. In fact, the more we move amongst the herd, the more they drop to the ground with what sounds like weary sighs.

'Please, it's just a little further.' I find myself pleading with them. 'It's really important I get to Björn's place and find my bag. There's a wedding today. Two people who really love each other are getting married. I need to get their wedding rings to them!' But the reindeer don't make eye contact with me. I look at Björn. He throws up his hands.

'Once they decide to lie down, there's no moving them until they're ready.' He shakes his head. 'They clearly feel they need to rest.'

'How long will that be for?'

He frowns, frustrated, and pushes up his shoulders. 'Can't tell. Could be hours, or even . . .' he looks like he daren't say it, 'days,' he finally finishes.

'No! This can't be happening! I have to get to the wedding at two o'clock. Please, Björn, do something.'

Björn surveys the resting reindeer herd. 'I'm sorry. There's nothing I can do. They won't budge.'

I look around. He's right. They're not going anywhere. What with the storm and then the attack, they're probably exhausted. I should be too, but actually I feel like I'm firing on all cylinders. I have to get to the hotel with the rings, finish the job. And then of course there's the promise of Björn's kiss. The blood surges round my body and I feel like I'm on fire.

'Now what am I going to do?'

'We could just sit it out, put the tent up again.' Björn grins, and my whole body screams 'Yes, please!' but I can't. I have to get to that wedding ceremony. I can't let them down. 'But I understand if you don't want to . . .'

Suddenly I realise that he's worrying his suggestion might be unwelcome.

'I want to do that more than anything,' I say, walking up to him and sliding my arm around his waist. 'But I have to deliver those rings. I can't stand in the way of someone else's happy-ever-after. I promised that nothing would stop them making their vows to each other for everyone to see.' I look up at him and he looks to the sky. 'I know what it feels like to find love. And when you do, you need to hang onto it as tight as you can. We're lucky if we get one chance at happiness in life, let alone a second . . .'

'Okay, let's make sure the path of true love runs smoothly,' he says with a resigned sigh.

'Oh, so now you do believe in finding true love?' I tease.

He smiles, a lopsided smile. 'Let's just say someone helped restore my faith in it,' and then he bends his head and kisses me all over again, and I wish it would go on forever.

Finally he pulls away.

'Come on, Cinderella, let's get you to the ball,' he says, reluctantly letting me go. 'You need to be there. And you need to make sure you still have a job,' he reminds me.

'But how?'

'Looks like I'm going to have to trust you,' he says and starts to walk towards the dogs. 'Think you can do this?'

I bite my lip, remembering how I nearly lost the dogs last time. I nod. 'I can do it. I promise.'

'On your own?'

I nod again.

'You're not scared?'

'I am. But being scared is what reminds us we're alive, right? It's part of the journey.' I find myself smiling. 'I can do it, Björn. Trust me.'

It seems both of us have come a long way from not trusting each other or even ourselves when we set out.

He sets up a smaller dog team while Lucas watches on, howling and baying to be allowed to go on the trip.

'No, you have to stay here and rest, like the reindeer,' Björn tells him, and strokes his head.

Finally the sled is ready.

'Do you have everything? Knife, lasso, torch?' He makes me check, and then explains how to get to the farm. It's not far from the hotel. I've come an awfully long way to get back to where I started, I think.

I step up nervously onto the back of the sled, behind my four-dog team.

'Look after my dogs!' Björn says with a smile, and then his expression becomes serious, 'and look after yourself!' He takes my face in his hands.

'I will,' I say, my breathing shallow, and he leans in and kisses me deeply, as if making sure I'll never forget him. And frankly, I don't think I ever will.

With my lips still tingling, I turn to go. 'And you'll be okay, you know where to go? If you have any problems . . .'

'I know. Just follow the brightest star, it'll get me home!' I smile and he shakes his head, smiling and steps back. I give him a final smile then turn back to the impatient dogs, release the brake and call, '*Hike, hike!*' and the team respond, pulling forward into the soft snow. I don't look back. I can't. I can only look forward. I have to do this on my own, and although I'm scared, I feel very much alive as we cut through the freshly fallen snow, like putting words onto a brand-new page of a book, starting a whole new chapter.

Chapter Forty-two

As day breaks and the sky fills with a lavender and salmon-pink sunrise, the farmhouse comes into view, just as Björn described it. It's red and white and nestled at the bottom of a slope, surrounded by tall snow-covered pines, where presumably the reindeer will graze. There's a corral and a handful of *lavvus* in amongst the tall trees. There's also a covered fire pit, right in the middle of the clearing, and dog pens to the other side of the house.

The snow is really thick here, piled up as if it's rolled off the hills behind and settled. It's hard work, but I don't care. I break into a wide smile and once more urge the dogs on for the last leg of the journey. At last we pull up by the front door, and I put the brakes on, then jump off the sled and tie the dogs up. I reach for the key, which is exactly where Björn said it would be. I have to kick and scoop away huge handfuls of snow in front of the door before I spot a snow shovel and clear a pathway. Then I put the key in and push open the door.

The first thing I notice is that it's not much warmer inside than out. The second thing is my case on the settee right in front of me. Finally, reunited! I fall on it and fling it open. There's my travel log in the front pocket, but more importantly, there are the rings in their velvet-lined box with the silver trim. I hold it to my chest for a moment and breathe a big sigh of relief. I've done it.

Before I leave to take the rings to their final destination, I light the fire, hoping it will warm the place up for when I get back. I close the door and take a final look around outside. I look at the corral behind the farmhouse, and the big covered fire pit, and the land that stretches up to the gentle slopes behind. An absolutely perfect spot for the reindeer, I think. I just hope Björn finds someone who wants the herd and this place together. It's . . . well, it's just perfect. Then I turn back to the dogs. I have a wedding to get to. Finally my work here is done.

Chapter Forty-three

'What? What do you mean, no wedding?' I am out of breath, clutching my knees as I try and drag in big cold breaths, having driven the dogs as fast as I could from the farm to the hotel. 'I've got the rings. Here!' I hold the little box high, one hand still grasping my knee.

'See for yourself.' Lars is pointing out of the glass conservatory at the back of the hotel. Slowly I straighten up. The room itself is lit with candles, but there is no music playing, just a stillness to it all. In front of the window, banked with snow, surrounded by candles in lanterns throwing out flickering orange light, Pru is crying quietly in Mika's arms.

'A landslide, after the storm.' Lars gestures to where the outside ice bar once stood, the igloo with green and purple lights, like a Northern Lights nightclub, where people could drink shots from ice glasses. Now it's just a pile of snow, with fallen poles and power cables sticking out of it. 'Thankfully, no one was in there,' he says. 'Everyone is safe.' He glances at the brides. 'If heartbroken.'

'But surely the wedding can go ahead?' I say. 'There must be a way.'

He raises his shoulders and shrugs sadly. 'Sometimes Cupid can be cruel,' and I'm wondering if he's talking about the wedding couple, or me and him, or the one that got away. 'Without power we cannot run the kitchen. We cannot serve the wedding meal. Such a shame when it has been planned with such meticulous detail and love.'

'But there must be something that can be done!' I say, not believing it could all have been in vain. 'Everyone that matters is here. That's what a wedding is all about. Telling people how you feel about each other.'

He slowly shrugs again. 'We will have to close the hotel altogether if we cannot get any power back. We don't have hot water or heating.'

'Well then, make fires. Do it the natural way. Fire is our best friend.' I can hear my own voice, but hardly recognise myself. Me, who only a week ago wouldn't have dreamt of not having central heating at the touch of a button, or being able to ping a microwave meal.

'Our chef cannot work like that. He's packed up his knives and gone back to civilisation, as he calls it.'

'Where?'

'Denmark. Everything runs like clockwork in Denmark, apparently.'

'But here . . . this place, it's about working with nature. Feeling alive!' I hear myself again. A week ago I would have loved the idea of Denmark. Who am I and where is the old Halley?

I look at the wedding couple.

'Please, Lars, there must be something that can be done.'

'Sometimes you just can't plan these things, no matter how hard you try.' He looks at me again, as if finally realising the truth of his words.

'I agree,' I say quietly. 'You might be right about fate, but I think sometimes fate has ideas for us other than the ones we actually want.' I smile, and he gives me a resigned smile in return.

'I hope so,' he says. 'My grandmother was never wrong.'

And I nod, hoping with all my heart that he's right and that he gets his wish. But sometimes we don't know what we're wishing for until we find it. And right now, I can't help but realise, I'm wishing I didn't have to leave. But this is it: wedding or no wedding, I've completed the job, and now my time here is done. I'm going to be leaving, and suddenly I'm going to miss snowy Lapland very, very much, and one person in particular.

I look down at the box in my hand. The least I can do is deliver it in person. As I walk towards the brides, Mika turns to look at me.

'You've probably heard, there isn't going to be a wedding any more,' she says, Pru still folded into her arms, gently sobbing.

I nod. 'I did hear. I'm so sorry. But just because there's no ceremony and no meal, it doesn't mean to say these rings are any less important. They have everything you wanted to say to each other on them. They were made with love, and that's what matters.' I hold the box out, and Pru raises her head. 'Love is what makes us who we are, no matter where life takes us,' I say, and then hug the pair of them. 'Enjoy it while you have it, and make the most of every day.'

'Thank you,' they both say, and Pru takes the box and opens it. She picks up one of the rings and looks at Mika.

'I love you,' she says, and slides the ring onto Mika's finger. Then Mika takes the other ring and looks at Pru.

'And I love you,' she says, putting the ring on.

'And you're quite right, that really is all that matters,' says a voice behind me. I spin round to see Pru's mother standing there. 'I realised it the night we sat under the stars by the fire at the Sami village. Finding love and being happy really is the most important thing. I'm sorry it's taken me so long to get my head around the idea. It's only when you lose love that you realise how special it is. Hang onto it tightly . . . and ignore the ones who don't agree!'

The two brides break into wide smiles. This may not have been the ceremony they were planning, but it's looking pretty much perfect to me.

I turn and move away from the family as they all hug each other. I have to get ready to leave. But before I do, I send a message to the office: *Delivery made*. Then I hold the phone to my lips for a moment, knowing that my time here is done.

I slip out the door while Lars is popping champagne and handing it round, and if he sees me leave, he knows that looking back isn't the answer. He keeps looking forward and I'm glad. I will always love Lars's optimism, his belief that something special is waiting for him just around the corner. Because he's right: you never know what is round the corner.

I rejoin the dogs and pat each of them and thank them for their patience. Then I untie them, release the brake and head back to Björn's cabin to return the dogs and to finally pick up my bag and leave.

* * *

313

Back at the farm, I put the dogs into the pen, check they have straw and water, give them some food I find in a store shed and thank them again. Then I go into the farmhouse, where the fire has warmed the place up nicely. I pull off my hat and gloves. There are some candles on the table and I light them and dot them around the room.

My phone pings into life. It's my travel documents from the office. My next job. I'm to take an antique typewriter to Los Angeles for a well-known screenwriter. Not Australia, Los Angeles! Number seven on our bucket list. Let's hope I don't lose that one and have to track it down. I smile to myself.

I look down at my travel log, but I don't open it. I slide my little booklet inside its pages, then raise it to my lips, close my eyes briefly and place a kiss on it before putting it back in my bag and zipping it up. Everything I needed to say is in there and safe. I don't need to reread it. It's part of my past, but it is in the past. Right now, I need to think about the future.

My phone pings again. It's Sara, my sister. A date for an interview for the job she sent me. It's on Monday, as soon as I get back. You'd think she'd have enough to do looking after her three boys without organising me as well. But I don't think any of my family will stop trying until they have me home and settled.

I stand and look out of the window, taking off my coat so I feel the warmth when I leave. Another of Björn's lessons. I pick up a soft blanket from the settee and pull it around me like a shawl. It smells of Björn. I breathe in deeply, then close my eyes again, remembering his kiss, and the promise in it. I can almost hear his voice too, as if he's really here. '*Hike, hike!*' he's shouting jubilantly.

I can see his smiling face with my eyes closed, standing proudly at the back of the dog team. I can see the wrinkles at the corners of his eyes, the freckles over his nose and cheeks. His face pink from the wind and sun, the stubble around his chin glistening with frosty flakes.

'*Hike!*' I hear again, and this time it seems even more real. And then a thundering noise, like . . . like a herd of running reindeer! My eyes ping open and there, coming over the hill, is the herd, and behind the herd is Björn. Alongside the sled comes a snowmobile driven by Elsá. She must have come out to meet him. She's smiling just as jubilantly as the herd start to spread out on the hillside of their new home, coming to a final rest, and on the back of the snowmobile is their dad, beaming widely too.

They stood up! I want to shout, and find myself jumping up and down with joy. The reindeer stood up! They're home! My stomach does somersaults, and shooting stars fly joyfully through me. We did it! The reindeer are home! I feel lit up, like all the joy has suddenly come rushing back into my life at once, and I dash to the door, step into my boots and run through the deep, thick snow towards Björn.

'You're home! You made it!' I beam, and I can't help myself, I hug him really tight as he brings the dogs to a standstill, not wanting to let him go. He pulls me close to him and stands me in front of him on the sled as he brings it round to the front of the house and towards the pens there to reunite the dogs with the others. Then we stand by the corral fence and watch the reindeer taking in their new surroundings.

Finally Björn goes to find them some feed, just to make them feel really at home, and his father helps pour it out, maybe for the last time, I think with a pang as the three of them pat the reindeer and look around with satisfied wide smiles. The three of them, a family, and there is just something about this place that feels like home.

Chapter Forty-four

I want to leave them chatting and patting the reindeer longer, but I really need to speak to Björn.

'So, did you get the rings there on time?' he asks, walking over to me with an empty feed sack hanging by his side.

I sigh. 'There isn't going to be a wedding. A landslide, from the storm, brought down the power cables. The chef has walked out. Look, I wouldn't ask unless it was important, but could you go and help? Cook for them so they can have their wedding?' I cling to a tiny bit of hope that this can still happen for them. 'It means so much to them to be here, together, showing the world how strong their love for each other is. Even Pru's mother has finally come round to the idea.'

Björn shakes his head. 'I'm sorry, no. I'm not going back into a kitchen. Besides, I promised to take you to bed as soon as I got here, remember?'

I swallow. I want that to happen so much. But tomorrow I'll be gone. My flights are arranged. I can't just sleep with him and leave. I can't let it mean nothing, because if I do sleep with him, it will mean everything. My head starts pounding. I can't think straight. I want this man. The first man I have felt anything for since Griff. But what good would come of me making love to him? I can't love a man I can't be with. We come from different worlds; worlds that keep changing.

'Hey! Come on! Don't look so down!' He puts his finger to my chin. I can feel his sister and father looking at us and I blush. Do they know what I'm thinking? I blush some more.

'I've had my itinerary through. I leave tomorrow. Los Angeles,' I state in a staccato voice.

He nods, saying nothing, and bites his lip, realising that I'm putting up my armour once more as I step back and drop my head.

'And I have a job interview. My sister applied for it for me. A job back home. Putting down some roots finally . . .' I trail off and there is silence between us, just the sound of the reindeer munching.

'And this couple,' he finally says, 'you want to help them celebrate their love for each other?'

I look up, optimism suddenly rising inside me. 'Yes.'

'Because you believe in true love, no matter how hard it is to be together?'

'Exactly!'

He looks at me, and I stop myself saying any more, and again we fall into silence.

'Okay, I'll buy your idea of true love,' he says.

'So you'll cook for them?' I ask tentatively.

'Yes, I'll cook for them.' He nods.

'Wait!' I run to the house as fast as is humanly possible in deep snow and reindeer-skin boots, and return out of breath with his recipe book.

'Here.' I hold it out to him. He frowns. 'Your book. The

one you threw on the fire. I saved it. You'll need it.'

He takes it from me. 'You saved it?' He looks at me in surprise.

I nod. 'Thought you might need it again when you came to your senses.'

He looks down at the singed corners of the book in his hand. God, I have come to love that face. I have come to love this man, I realise. But there can't be any future for us, can there? What I want more than anything is for him to find his way back to his passion, and if that means doing this, then I have to do this . . . I love him, but that also means I have to let him go.

He takes the corner of the book and opens it. The cuttings inside flutter and fly around in the wind. The brown envelope, tucked in there for safe keeping, slides to the soft snow.

'What's this?' He bends down.

'It's a letter. I tried giving it to you when I gave you the book. I mean, I'd've given it to you earlier if I'd known you were Daniel. But I didn't.' I stop gabbling. 'It's from Camilla, your . . . sous chef.'

'Okay.' He looks down at it.

'I said I'd deliver it to Daniel,' I say quietly.

He opens the letter and reads it. Then he lets out a long, slow sigh and looks out at the herd. His dad and sister are chopping wood, the sound of the axe in the background the sound of Björn's childhood.

'Do you want to read it?' He holds it out to me. I shake my head. It's not my letter. Besides, I don't speak Swedish.

'It says . . . it says that the girl who made the . . . accusation came to Camilla after I'd closed up the restaurant and put it

319

on the market and admitted she'd made it up. She was hurt. She'd apparently been in love with me for some time, searching me out, wanting to work in my kitchen. She told Camilla she'd tried to come on to me, took advantage of the moment. The day of the new menu.'

'So she didn't go to the press then?'

He shakes his head, holding the letter tightly in his hands.

'That's good news,' I tell him, bracing myself for what else is to come. The letter is from his ex. She wanted to find him. I know that he must take his second chance at love if that's what she's offering. I don't ask. He looks at me.

'She says there's a backer, wants to set up a new restaurant with me and her, the old team back together. Says she knows we can get the star back.' He looks up. I swallow hard.

'She wants you to go back? To Stockholm?' He nods. I take a deep breath. 'And will you go?'

It's Björn who takes a deep breath this time.

'Hey!' his father calls, carrying a big pile of logs unsteadily. Björn rushes forward to help him, putting the logs by the fire pit, under a big wooden pergola, like a cabin with no walls.

'What will you tell her?' I ask.

'Nothing yet.' He stuffs the letter in his back pocket and looks at his dad attempting to get more logs. 'We have a wedding feast to plan.' He smiles at me. And if I've learnt anything from this trip, it's to live in the moment and enjoy it while you can. It might be our last night together, but I'm determined to make the most of it.

'I'll come with you to the hotel. I can help in the kitchen.'

'Oh, I'm not going to cook there, not in a kitchen.'

My spirits plummet once more. This whole week has been

one long roller-coaster ride. The highs and lows, spinning me round so I don't know which way up my stomach is meant to be, but loving the experience – the ride of a lifetime – and not wanting it to stop.

'But you said . . .'

'I said I'll cook, but not in the kitchen. I don't need this any more.' He tosses the book to one side. 'I will cook here.' He holds his arms out to the covered fire pit and looks at me, amused. 'I'll cook for them here, under the stars, like nature intended. How food should be. Will that be okay?'

'That will be . . . perfect.' And I smile, because it really, really is.

Chapter Forty-five

At six o'clock on the dot, I am waiting with the brides by the front entrance of the hotel. Large candles line the path, and I'm hoping they keep their dresses well tucked in when they walk down it arm in arm to meet Björn.

'You both look beautiful,' I tell them. Tall, blonde Mika is all in white, with white fur trim, while curvaceous, red-headed Pru is in sumptuous deep red velvet to match her hair, nails and lipstick.

'This wouldn't be happening without you. Thank you,' she says.

Then I hear it, the sound of bells. We all stop talking and look in the direction from which it's coming.

'I've got ringing in my ears!' I hear Pru's nan say from behind us. 'Wonder if it was the sauna!'

The bells keep ringing, getting slowly louder, and now we can see the soft orange glow of lanterns coming closer. There, walking across the field from the direction of the farm, holding a lantern high, is Björn in full Sami outfit: blue poncho with bold trim, hat to match and reindeer boots. He's leading Rocky by the halter, pulling a sled with lanterns hanging off the sides and lined with reindeer skins. Behind him is Elsá, his sister, leading another reindeer and sled – a line of them, in fact, attached with lead reins, to take the guests to the farm – and bringing up the rear is their dad, sitting in a sleigh covered in a reindeer rug, and also in Sami traditional costume and a beautiful Four Winds hat. It is bright blue to match his tunic, with red braiding and red and yellow trim. He looks so resplendent and proud, it brings tears to my eyes. The lanterns are swinging gently with the rhythmic swaying of the sleds, casting an orange glow on the ground around them.

Björn is walking towards me, his smiling face lit up. My whole body feels like it's suddenly been set alight as he approaches me, his eyes on mine, and then he stops in front of us and smiles even wider. More than anything I want to kiss this man, just like we kissed out on the tundra. But I can't. Everything has changed now that Camilla, his ex, has asked him back, and I'm leaving tomorrow. He needs to find his way back to the kitchen, and by the looks of that letter, he's found it. I have to stop thinking about the fact that I can't have him. He needs to cook again. Just like he helped me find the light in my life, I have to help him find his, not complicate things for him.

'This is amazing,' says Pru. They stand and stare open-mouthed at the sled lined with reindeer skins to sit on, and the soft light from the lanterns. Snow begins to fall, tiny flakes dancing like fairies all around us in the lamplight.

'Ladies.' Björn holds out a hand and pulls back a reindeer skin for them to take a seat. They beam at each other, and with his help, guide each other into the fur-covered seats. Björn places a blanket over their legs, and then a fur, and tucks it in around them. 'And as it is your wedding day . . .'

He produces a flask and two mugs and pours out hot glögg, rich and spicy. 'Something to toast true love and to keep you warm on the way to your wedding feast.'

They raise a toast to each other and kiss lightly as the snowflakes fall around them, then they throw their heads back and laugh, happy, carefree laughs, because no matter what life throws at them, they have each other, they have found love and they are grabbing hold of it.

Björn pours out more wine, and his sister starts handing the cups to the other guests. I step forward and help too.

'Thank you,' mouth the happy couple, as the rest of the guests are seated in the sleds.

I choose to walk, and we set off back over the hill towards the farm, with me one side of Rocky and Björn on the other, where the brightest star in the sky is shining overhead. We see the farmhouse before we get to it, and I hear the brides catch their breath, as I do mine. There are lanterns all around the fire pit, and the pit itself glows orange. Little battery-operated fairy lights festoon the snow-covered roof of the outdoor gazebo, and lanterns hang from the corners of the roof too, throwing light onto the corral, where some of the frailer reindeer have been put to rest after their journey, including little Robbie. Behind the corral on the hillside, the rest of the herd look up, doe eyes gazing at us in greeting as we pull up by the fire pit.

Elsá, also wearing her bright blue traditional Sami dress, with a hat that covers her ears, and a red tartan shawl, serves up more drinks while Björn secures the reindeer then goes straight to the fire and starts cooking. The smells fill the lightly snowy night air. All the guests are wrapped up against the cold and are loving looking up at the big star-filled sky and over towards the lights of the town. Björn's dad and I unharness the reindeer and put down more feed for them in the corral, to thank them for their extra work today. I pat Rocky fondly on the behind.

'Can I feed one?' says Nan. I look at Björn's dad. He understands, and nods and beams and shows her how to hold her hand flat to let the reindeer eat the dried lichen from her palm.

I invite some more of the guests into the corral, and soon practically all the wedding party are there, stroking and feeding the little team of transport. We hang the lanterns from the sleighs around the corral and put the reindeer skins from the sleds onto the benches around the fire pit.

'You okay?' Björn takes hold of my wrist. 'You seem . . .' He doesn't finish his sentence. The fire pit is hot and I step away; he follows.

The fire spits and flares.

'Hold on, wait there.' He steps forward, a big leather glove on one hand, and with a pair of long-handled tongs turns the meat cooking there. He looks over at the herd and his dad with the guests, and then back at me.

I want to tell him exactly how I'm feeling, that everything has changed and I don't want to leave. But I can't. I can't tell him that. He has a chance to go back to Stockholm and put his life back together, and I can't ruin that for him just because I think I've fallen in love with him. I can't. I have to leave tomorrow, and he has a life to go back to. This is just a fantasy. I have to enjoy tonight. Tomorrow I'll be back at the airport, back in the city, where I'm at home. And this will be just another journey written down in my travel log. Except my travel log is full. Finished. That journey has ended. So now what?

I stand and watch as Björn serves up food hot off the fire, amid a blaze of flames and heavenly scented smoke. The hot, earthy mushroom soup that I have come to love, and creamy truffle and mushroom risotto to start. Then the best roast dinner ever, served with lingonberry sauce, jacket potatoes baked in foil in the embers, and deep red cabbage with lingonberries. There's also Arctic char, cooked over juniper leaves and served with mustard sauce and roasted onions; soft sautéed chanterelle mushrooms, seasoned with truffle, and deep-fried lichen served with Sami flatbreads and cloudberry jam and washed down with lingonberry vodka.

The guests sit around the fire pit, eating, drinking and chatting, talking about the week and the activities, the Lapp dogs and the huskies. Björn serves a wonderful apple and blueberry crumble, and a stack of toasted waffles with berries and ice cream and cups of creamy hot chocolate that we dip the waffles into. Then, as they finish their food to the sound of contented sighs and finger-licking, Elsá sits by the fire and begins to sing and play the drum, once again like the sound of the wind in the trees as the stars come out; and finally the Northern Lights slip and slide and dance across the sky to a chorus of oohs and ahs. And as the evening draws to a close, the big fire pit no longer keeping the cold night at bay, Lars takes the happy wedding party home in the minibus.

There is a final toast, from Pru's mother, who raises her glass slightly unsteadily as she stands by the fireside. 'Someone wiser than me told me that when you find true love, you should grab hold of it and cling onto it for dear life, because we never know what's round the corner. She was right. Here's to finding love and holding onto it with both hands,' she says, looking at Pru and Mika and smiling widely, her eyes sparkling as the soft white flakes of snow fall all around.

'*Skål*!' we all say, and raise our glasses. Over the rim of mine, I see Lars taking a final look at me and then dipping his head and walking away. I look at Björn, who looks back at me, and I walk over to wave the party off. As the minibus departs slowly, the tyres crunching over the snow, I turn back to see Elsá and Björn's Pappa wrapped up on the back of the snowmobile.

'Nice to meet you again, Halley,' Elsá says, and hugs me, as does her dad. 'I'm going to get Pappa back to the apartment and his central heating.' But Pappa doesn't look happy about leaving at all. In fact, he takes a sad look around.

'This place,' he says to Björn, 'is perfect. I wish I could stay here and look after the herd. But time just ran out on me. Let's speak tomorrow. Tell me what you've decided.' He's speaking in English, clearly for my benefit, and I didn't even know he could.

'Okay, Pappa,' and Björn wraps his father up in a great big bear hug, holding him so tightly I worry he'll suffocate him.

'I didn't realise your dad spoke English,' I say walking back to the fire pit once we've waved them off.

'My parents, and my grandparents before that, were guides, showing tourists our ways and how we lived. These *lavvus*,' he nods to the tents among the trees, 'were full of guests when my mother was alive. But since she died, Pappa stopped having guests here and so hasn't spoken English since. It was lovely to see him enjoying having people here again this evening.'

The snow is falling more heavily. Björn checks the dogs in their pens and the reindeer in the corral and out in the field. Then we head indoors, where the fire is still glowing in the woodburner and the heat welcomes us in like long-lost family. Björn is carrying the lanterns from the corral and puts them around the room. I step out of my boots and pull off my hat, scarf and gloves, my heart pounding like a drum against the wall of my chest. Finally it is just the two of us, and although it has been just the two of us all week, it now feels like a very different landscape.

Björn pours two vodkas and hands me one. His fingers touch mine as he does, sending an electric shock around my body.

'To us, and true love,' he smiles, his eyes crinkling at the corners where the sun from the trip has tanned his face. And I wish it could be, but I know it can't.

Chapter Forty-six

He steps forward to kiss me, but I turn away and look at the letter on the table, on top of his recipe book. He follows my gaze.

'The letter,' he says.

'Yes, the letter.' I take a sip of the vodka to steady my voice. 'You've read it. You can go back now, back to Stockholm, pick up where you left off. Start a new restaurant. Start again with Camilla.'

He stares right into my eyes, up close. 'What if I don't want to go back?' I feel the breath of every word.

'But your career, the chance to get your star back?'

'Why would I want to go back to get a star when I have all the stars I want right here?' He looks out at the big sky and then back at me. 'Sometimes what we want is right under our nose.'

We look at each other.

'And Camilla?'

He shakes his head. 'Camilla and I are over. We've spoken. I rang her and thanked her for the letter and for letting me know how things are for me back in the city. She's moved on. She asked me to join her in the new restaurant she's gone to. But . . . I'm not going back to her. We worked long hours in a kitchen, we fell into a routine. But when I needed her, she wasn't there, by my side.' His stare is burning into me. 'You never let me down when I needed you. I know what's important now.'

'What will you do?' There's a wobble in my voice that's excitement and anticipation too.

He shakes his head again. 'I don't know. Be a reindeer herder, I guess.'

'You could . . .' I bite my lip and look towards the window and the glowing embers of the fire pit as the snow falls all around it.

'Yes?' He narrows his eyes keenly.

'Well, this place.' I throw out a hand towards the fire pit and the hills behind the house. 'You love it. Tonight was amazing. You could set up here. Start over.'

He looks at me and frowns. 'Set up?'

'A restaurant. Here.'

'Here?' He laughs. 'Who would come?' Then he stops and looks at me. 'You're serious.'

A smile spreads across my face first, and then his.

'Build it and they will come!' We both laugh. Then he chews his bottom lip.

'You mean cooking like tonight, the way I grew up with. The way I love. Cooking with fire!' and his eyes light up like fiery flames themselves.

'Exactly!' I join in his growing enthusiasm for the idea. 'If people start to hear about it, they will come. I would.'

'Would you?'

'Yes,' I say quietly. 'I'll come back and visit. Maybe even set up a blog and write about it on my travels.'

'Or you could stop travelling, put down some roots.'

I think about the job my sister has applied for on my behalf. I could. I really think I could put down some roots now.

'And I could keep the herd,' he continues. 'Stay here. Listen to what my heart has been telling me ever since I arrived home.'

I don't say any more. I watch as he stands and looks out of the window at the snow falling, the lanterns lighting up his face as the ideas flood across it.

'Put on a daily menu, inspired by the seasons. And reindeer, the best around.'

'Respecting the animal,' I say.

'Respecting the animal,' he confirms, and smiles at me like I'm his star pupil.

'You could do it, Björn.' I join him by the window.

'I'm not going anywhere. I'm going to be right here. I'm not leaving. This is where I belong,' he says and he turns to look at me. Then his lips are on mine, and all my resolve disappears like melting snow, as we tumble, laugh and kiss our way up to the bedroom.

The next morning, in the pitch black, I'm woken by the sound of a snow plough clearing the driveway, followed by a car horn. Björn wakes sleepily and reaches for me as I grab hold of a blanket from the bed and look out of the window.

'What's going on?' He sits up.

'It's Lars!'

'Oh, not again!' He falls back into the big fat pillows with a thump.

'He's come to take me to the airport.' I gather my clothes from the bedroom floor and start to pull my socks on.

'Send him away,' Björn says with one arm over his eyes.

'I can't do that. I have a plane to catch.'

'Well . . .' he sits up and leans on one elbow, revealing his broad chest, 'you could just stay.'

I stop jumping around on one foot on the wooden floor. 'I . . . I can't. I have—'

'I know, a plane to catch. You said.'

The horn beeps again and Björn lies back down and turns away from me.

I look at him. He's right. I could just stay. Why don't I? What's stopping me?

'I'm staying here, Halley. You could stay here too. You could stop running. You just have to say the words. Tell me how you're feeling.'

I look away, trying to escape his gaze, and pull on my other sock. The idea is just . . . so terrifying. The idea of finally stopping travelling . . . stopping running.

'I have to go. It's what I do. It's my job.'

'No, it's what you do when you're scared of admitting how you feel.' He sits up fully, the blankets falling around his waist to reveal his taut stomach, and all I want to do is fall back into bed and kiss him all over again.

I want to tell him that I'm scared. I'm scared of falling in love again and scared of losing it all over again. He's right: I'm too scared to stand still.

The horn sounds again.

'Argh!' Björn launches a pillow at the window. I run to it and open it. The cold air hits me like a smack in the face.

'I'm coming!' I shout, and wave to Lars and the minibus packed with most of the wedding party on their way back to Stockholm and the UK. The dogs start to bark, disturbed by the noise and wondering if there will be a new adventure today. I haven't even had a chance to say goodbye to them.

'I have to go,' I tell Björn, pulling on clothes from my case, my old uniform of black jeans and roll-neck jumpers. I fold the clothes he lent me and put them on the end of the bed, as if leaving a precious memory behind. Then I pick up my bag and turn to run downstairs.

'Wait!' He throws back the covers and pulls on his trousers, his belt hanging loose. If he asked one more time, would I say yes? Go on, ask me, I think. But he just looks at me, and I turn back to the stairs and take them as quickly as the pounding of my heart.

I pull on my coat knowing that I don't want to hear the words, because I'd be too scared. I can't let history repeat itself, I can't let myself love someone again. I can't take the risk that they will leave me like my dad, abandoning my mum with two young children to bring up, then Griff. I can't let it happen a third time. I put my hands in my pockets and pull out the knife in its leather sheath. I look down at it and then up at him, standing bare-chested and barefoot on the lowest step of the stair. I offer the knife to him.

'Keep it,' he says. 'I made it for you, to keep you out of trouble, remember? Keep it with you always, to remind you not to be scared of living.' He gazes at me intently, holding the thick fur blanket to his chest.

I look down at the knife in my hand and think about how odd I would feel without it now. It has become a part of my life out here, but I'm not sure how much use it will be in my life back home. I can't imagine I'll be opening tins of beans with it, or trimming the edges of my little patch of lawn.

'Thank you.' My voice cracks. I'm shivering, and my hands are shaking as I try and put the knife in my coat pocket as clumsily as if it was a moving target. 'I have to go . . . I . . .' There are so many things I want to say to him. So many words that have been left unsaid, but I can't find any of them. Instead I grab my bag and head to the door.

'I got you something else.' He goes to the table and picks up what looks to be a book. 'It's made from reindeer hide. My sister makes them. I asked her to bring one for you last night.' He holds it out to me.

'Thank you.' Tears are welling in my eyes so I can barely see.

'With your old book being full . . . well, I thought you'd need a new one. You could write down all your travels.' He looks at me. 'Or even start a whole new chapter.'

We stare at each other, me through the tears that are filling my eyes like a lake about to burst its banks. The horn sounds again. My phone, finally charged, beeps telling me it's time to go.

'I know, you're on a schedule!' Björn throws up a hand and looks away.

I can't find the words. I turn and open the door and step outside. I don't look back. Isn't that what I've learnt on this trip? Don't look back, look to the future. Why then does it feel as if I'm moving in the wrong direction as I climb into the minibus, its heaters on full blast, and it pulls away from the farm and out onto the dark, snowy road, and overhead, like a handful of glitter, a burst of stars arcs and shoots across the sky.

Chapter Forty-seven

'*Fika*? You want *fika*?' asks the woman in the airport foyer as we come in out of the heavily falling snow. She has a small stall laid out with a big coffee flask and a tray of cakes, over which she is brandishing a pair of tongs.

'No thank you,' I say, making my way to the machine to check in, brushing the snowflakes from my hat and face.

'Oh bugger,' says a British voice next to me as a young woman drops her passport, all fingers and thumbs like me. I bend and pick it up and hand it to her, and recognise her immediately.

'Hey! You're Holly, from the night train. With Matty and Liv,' I say. 'How are you? Are you all here?'

'No, just me. Matty and Liv are back in the UK already. How about you? You were looking for a restaurant. Did you find it?'

'I did. I found the owner who I was looking for.' My mouth suddenly goes dry at the thought of the warm bed I've just left. 'And you? You were leaving someone behind. Did you . . . did you get in touch again?'

She looks down at her passport and boarding card.

'Actually, that's why I'm here. I came back to tell him how I felt. Like you said, holding onto love when you find it.'

'And?' My eyes open wide.

She shakes her head. 'It was a mistake. The hotel where he worked was closed up, and there was no one around. I couldn't even ring him: I deleted his number when I left. Looks like it wasn't meant to be after all. I'm going to work on the cruise liners, as a singer. They're looking for bar staff too. I just had this silly idea that he might want to come with me . . .' She trails off. 'But everything changes, doesn't it?'

'Yes,' I say slowly, 'everything changes.'

'If only I'd taken the chance when I had it.' She sniffs, and moves away from the machine.

'Wait! You said the hotel was shut. Not the Tallfors Hotel, was it?'

'Yes.' She blows her nose.

'It wasn't by any chance Lars that you were looking for, was it?'

'Yes!' She beams. 'But he's gone!' Her face falls again.

'No, he was just at a wedding.'

'He got married?'

'No, not his wedding, a guest's. It had to be moved because a landslide at the hotel wiped out all the power lines. You're not leaving without seeing him, are you?'

She nods. 'What if he doesn't want to know? I told him we were over before I left and that he should find some-body else. He's probably met someone by now. It was silly, but I . . . I saw a shooting star and thought of him. Thought he might be thinking of me. That we were supposed to be together. He said that you should wish on a shooting star every time you saw one and that fate had a plan for everyone, even when you least expected it.'

I think about Lars, nursing his broken heart, hoping that one day the love of his life would walk back in through the door.

'Oh, he'll want to know,' I say. So Lars's grandmother was right all along. There really is such a thing as fate.

'Lars!' I shout as I run out of the airport to where Lars has finished unloading all the cases and is about to leave. 'Lars! Fate has finally arrived!' and his face lights up like a thousand shooting stars when he sees who's right behind me, beaming back at him.

I leave Lars and Holly to their reunion, get some *fika* and sit down, waiting for my flight to be called to security. I pull out the new book Björn has given me and run my hand over the cover, then open it up and stare at the blank white pages, like snowy tundra, waiting for new adventures.

All around me it's busy and loud. So many people arriving and leaving, rushing here, there and everywhere, looking down at their phones, thinking they're living when really they're missing real life going on around them. I look out of the window. What I used to think made me feel safe is all of a sudden making me uncomfortable. I used to think this was where I fitted in, being around other busy people, rushing to get flights, keeping on the move. Airports were my favourite places. Now I just think it's noisy and crowded and I haven't even got to Stockholm yet. I'm not looking forward to it. In fact, I don't want to be there. I think about my house, the one I bought with Griff, the four-bedroom new-build on the housing estate, full of our hopes and dreams. And I think about Los Angeles.

I look down at the notepad and the clean fresh page again. Where do I begin?

This is the first day of the rest of my life . . . I go to write. But if this is the first day of the rest of my life, what has changed? What's different from the last book I filled?

Outside, it is just starting to get light. It's nearly 11 a.m. and it's dawn. The colours are amazing as they start to show themselves outside the tiny airport: baby blues and pinks behind the snowy clouds, reminding me of the morning after the night I spent alone. The night I finally said goodbye to Griff and knew he'd want me to stop running and be happy. Then suddenly there is a burst of orange on the skyline and the sun finally makes an appearance, bringing a whole new light, brilliant and bright.

'*Hej*!'

I look round from the window to see Lars and Holly standing in front of me. They are holding each other's hands tightly, as though they're scared that if they let go, they'll lose each other again.

'Lars is coming with me to see the cruise company and ask if we can travel together!' Holly beams, and he holds up a ticket.

'Look after each other!' I tell them.

'Oh Halley, I think it was you, you were the lucky star that brought me love after all!' Lars beams his happy smile, wider than I've ever seen it, if that's possible. 'Here, for you.' He holds out the keys to the minibus and unhooks something from them. 'I hope it brings you luck,' he says. 'My grandmother said it would.'

It's the bell that I broke on my first day, no longer with its handle, but attached to the keys with a ribbon.

'Thank you, Lars,' I say, choked, and tie it to my case. 'I won't lose my bag this time,' I say, smiling.

'I'll leave the keys at the information desk. Someone from the hotel will pick the minibus up later. They won't need it for a while, though, not until after they fix the power lines. The hotel is going to be closed for a few weeks at least.'

I watch as Lars and Holly head hand in hand to security, and wonder if they'll be able to unglue their hands and their lips long enough to get through. I glance down at the empty page in my book, and then close it again and instead look out to see the very edge of the orange sun pushing its way up over the horizon. I gaze at it, imprinting it in my mind, remembering to look up and see what's around me – right in front of me – instead of looking down. Then I slide the book into my case and touch the lucky silver bell there before heading towards security.

At the conveyor belt, I pull out my iPad and phone and slip out my earrings just in case. I slide off my chunky black boots and see bits of hay still hanging round the bottoms of my jeans from where I wore the reindeer-skin boots. It makes me smile. I look at the security frame, take a deep breath and go to step through.

Beep, beep! Beep, beep! it blares, making me jump, setting my senses flying. How did I ever find all this noise and bustle comforting?

'Raise your arms, please,' says the uniformed security officer. I do as I'm told, and the officer pats my arms and then my sides, before reaching into my pocket and pulling out my knife. She looks at me and lifts an eyebrow.

'My knife! In case I'm in trouble,' I tell her. 'It's made from reindeer antler. Did you know that every reindeer has its own antler pattern?' I ask, thinking about the herd, and realising that back with the herd and the dogs at the farm is exactly where I want to be right now. I take the knife from her hand and run my thumb over the carved handle.

'I'm sorry, you can't travel with that,' she says. 'You'll have to hand it over or put it in your hold luggage if you want to travel today.'

I look up from the knife. Suddenly everything seems really noisy and a bit blurred. In front of me I can see Lars and Holly beckoning to me. There's the gate. Once I go through, I'll be walking back to my old life, and more trips and journeys, more stories to go in my notebook. I can almost see my family waiting for me at home, wanting me to spend more time with them, and I want to spend time with them too, enjoy what I have in my life instead of running from it.

I look ahead to the departure lounge and my future and then I glance back at the queue forming behind me and remember the sun rising outside on a new day. I want to see the sun come up, I think. I want to see the day here, not from an aeroplane. I don't want to go back to my empty house and my fancy coffee machine. I want to make coffee over an open fire, boiled three times. I want to feed the reindeer; ride out with the dogs. I want to spend the day in bed with Björn. I want to spend every day with Björn, go to bed with him at night, wake up with him in the morning.

This is madness, but nothing like the madness that has had me travelling all over the world for the past two years.

This is a kind of madness that only comes along once in a lifetime, and I have to try it, even if I fail. I can't be scared of living any more. I have to tell him what I'm thinking. If I had told Griff I didn't want him to go, maybe life would have been different. If I leave here and don't tell Björn everything I feel about him, I'll lose him too. I can't let that happen.

'Actually, I don't want to travel today,' I hear myself saying to the security officer. 'In fact, I'm not sure I ever want to travel anywhere again.'

She looks at me a little taken aback.

I reach round her and grab my bag, my phone and iPad and my boots off the conveyor belt, and then back out through the security gate. Going backwards, yes, but finally in the right direction.

'Halley?' Pru is calling to me from the other side of security.

'I'm not coming. I'm not travelling any more! I'm staying here with an almost fanciable man, if he'll have me!' I say, and she whoops with laughter and claps, as do Mika and the other members of the wedding party, cheering me on.

'Good luck to ya, girl!' shouts Pru's nan.

'See, my grandmother is never wrong. It was fate for you to come here after all . . . Fate is out there for everyone, one day,' calls Lars, and I hope he's right.

I run out into the foyer, my boots and my knife still in my hand, and retrieve the keys from the information desk, telling them Lars has sent me and I'm returning the minibus to the hotel. And somehow, they believe me!

* * *

Having navigated the snowy roads with my thundering heart in my mouth, holding my breath as I pass big lorries, and gripping the steering wheel as I guide the minibus down the smaller lanes, I finally pull up at the red and white farmhouse in amongst the trees.

'Björn! Björn!' I jump out, but it's surprisingly quiet. No dogs barking. No Björn waiting to see if I would return. I run to the door and knock. The Lapp dogs are sitting in their kennel there, tails wagging, but there is no other sign of life.

'Björn!' I call again, and run round the house to the empty fire pit. A few of the reindeer raise their heads and look at me.

I'm too late! I've missed him. What if he's changed his mind about staying on here and opening the restaurant, his secret restaurant? What if he's gone to tell his sister and father that he's going to sell up after all, go back to Stockholm or start travelling again like me? I throw my hands up and shut my eyes, letting the little flakes of snow tickle my face. Wasn't it me who said you should grab love with both hands when it comes your way, and not let it go? And what did I do? I let it go . . . again! I let Griff go on that last tour of duty when he told me to say if I didn't want him to, and now, because I'm too scared of losing love again, I've gone and done exactly that. Lost it before we had even begun.

Then I hear it in the distance. The sound of '*Hike*, *hike*!'

I slowly open my eyes and look towards the skyline behind the house. And there, in front of the rising sun, is Björn and the dog team, coming over the brow of the hill, coming back to the farm.

I run up the hill as fast as I can in the deep snow, stumbling, falling and righting myself, as he travels downhill towards me.

'I thought you'd gone,' he says, finally reaching me, grabbing hold of my arm to steady me as I'm thigh deep in snow and barely able to move.

'I didn't know where you were,' I say, dragging in cold air as I try and catch my breath.

'I came to the airport after you.'

'You came to find me? You brought the dog sled team?'

'Quickest way! I came to ask if you'd come back, stay with me. But I was too late. Everyone was through security, in departures. I couldn't get through.'

'I thought you'd left, gone to tell your family you were going to sell after all.'

'I told you, I'm not going anywhere.' He puts an arm round my waist and pulls me onto the sled beside him. 'This is where I belong. This is my world and I plan to show it to people like you suggested. It's what's in my heart. There's only one thing missing: you. Do you think you could feel like that too, that you belong here?'

'I think I already do!'

He draws me to him and kisses me deeply, just as the sled starts to edge forward, nearly toppling us backwards into the snow.

'Whoa!' He pulls away and stands on the brake. 'I'm not losing any of you again. Especially not you!' He smiles at me and I look round at the sun coming up, a whole new day. 'Looks like they can't wait to get home,' he says. 'A bit like me!' He pulls me close to him and wraps his arms around me. 'Okay, *hike, hike,*' he calls to the team, and as they pull forward, an occasional reindeer raises its head, as if to welcome me home.

Epilogue

Hi! Sorry it's been so long since I've written. A lot has happened . . . I pause as I hold a pen to my lips, then put it down and carry on typing. Old habits die hard. *So here I am. A whole new chapter. No one could be more pleased to see the spring than me. Here on the farm there is huge excitement as most of the reindeer move back to their summer grazing in the mountain and the calves have started to be born. Robbie is like a jealous older sibling, intrigued by the new arrivals yet wanting all the attention. Rocky is now teaching him how to be a sled-pulling reindeer and he accompanies him on outings with our guests. Here's a picture.* I upload it from my phone.

And we have new arrivals of our own . . . *all my family are coming out to visit. They're staying in our* lavvus. *Testing them out for guests this winter. I'm not sure what my sister is going to make of that! But they're warm and cosy and great for taking in the sky at night. And the restaurant is going from strength to strength. Click here for this weekend's menu, but be quick, it's booking up fast.*

'Come on, we'll be late!' Björn sticks his head through the farmhouse front door, letting in a draught. I pick up my phone and press camera.

'Smile! It's for the blog.'

'How many new subscribers?'

'Another thirty overnight.'

'Not bad for someone who didn't want to show anyone what she was writing.'

I smile modestly. 'They love the pictures of Saturday night's secret supper. Loads of people want to know when the next one is. There's even a couple of reviewers who want to come.'

'Tell them they'll have to come as customers. I'm cooking for me now, not because of what I think reviewers want to eat.' He grins. 'Now come on!'

I look at the screen and sign off: *Until next time, love Halley, reindeer herder and part-time musher.* Then I take a deep breath, remembering how Björn persuaded me to set up a blog of my own and let the world see my words. But how could I not want to write about the life we have here? There's the reindeer that people come and visit, the dog sled team, and of course, every weekend, Björn cooks with fire as nature intended and people come from miles around to eat his food.

I press send.

'It's snowing!' I hear the voices before I see them. And when I do, I throw myself into their arms, into the heart of my family, as they emerge into the airport lobby. They're all here and it feels like Christmas at last.

'Of course it's snowing! You want to see some reindeer?'

'Yes!' My nephews jump up and down and my heart fills to have them all here with me, at home.

'Mum, this is Björn,' I say shyly.

And Mum seems lost for words and just hugs him instead.

'Come on then, let's get back and make a snowman!' And my nephews cheer again.

'Hey! How's your new house?' I ask the boys.

'We love it! We've got a room each!' they say.

'Thank you,' says my sister, kissing me on the cheek. 'The house is perfect. Just what we needed. I just wish you'd let us buy it from you instead of living there rent-free.'

'The house is yours,' I tell her. 'I'm having the paperwork drawn up. I want you to have it, enjoy it like Griff and I planned. A house full of kids! It's no use to me now.'

'But what if you want it back?' she says, worried.

'I told you, I have everything I need right here. I won't be going back.'

And we hug each other, knowing that no matter how far apart we are, we'll always be there for each other.

I check the computer when I get home and the boys are happily feeding the reindeer left behind in the corral with Pappa.

There's a message from Lars and Holly, on board their cruise liner, their home for the next six months, travelling life's path together wherever fate may take them. I smile and send them all our love. I look out of the window at my family making friends with my new family, the reindeer and the Lapp dogs bounding around.

Who knew that fate would bring me here? Lars's grandmother did for sure!

Acknowledgements

This idea came about some years ago, well, part of the idea. I wanted to write about husky racing. I knew nothing about it but was fascinated. I ended up going on a research trip with Katie Fforde to Aviemore in Scotland to experience it first-hand. It was a terrifying, yet laughter-filled trip for so many reasons. It was the start of our research road trips together and we have enjoyed so many since! We love travelling together. We sort out stories, life and laugh along the way. So my biggest thank you is to Katie for her faith in my writing, her encouragement and the wonderful fun we've had along the way. Thank you for coming with me on the journey!

I'd also like to thank the fantastic staff at Nutti Sámi Siida, Sámi eco adventures, in Jukkasjärvi, Sweden (www.nutti.se). This was one of our best research trips ever! We loved it there. If you ever want to experience the real Swedish Lapland, this is it. We stayed in a cabin in the woods, with just the trees and a herd of reindeer for company, and the two brilliant members of staff who looked after us, fed us, lit the sauna and accompanied us feeding the reindeer. We went out on a wildlife photography trip, raced reindeer, went on a snowmobile ride across a frozen lake and a husky ride through the forest. We sat on reindeer skins, beside blazing fires, in traditional *lavvus*, whilst all the time the snow fell like glitter around us. It was magical. If you want to see some of the videos we made there, have a look at my author Facebook page (www.facebook.com/JoThomasAuthor) to see Katie and me amongst the reindeer!

If you want to see reindeer in the UK head to the Cairngorm Reindeer Herd in Aviemore (www.cairngormreindeer.co.uk), Britain's only free ranging herd of reindeer and whose team were at the end of an email to answer questions I had about the reindeer and their migration habits. Thank you!

A huge thank-you to Jen Doyle at Headline for loving this idea and letting me write a romance, set out on the snowy tundra with a few hundred reindeer! To Siobhan Hooper who designed the beautiful cover. I just love it! And to all the rest of the team there.

As always, thank you to my fab agent David Headley at DHH Literary Agency for his support, encouragement and hard work.

And thank you to all my readers who get in touch on Facebook and Twitter to tell me they love my books. I love writing them! I hope you love this one too as much as I do.

Welcome to the world of

Jo Thomas

Hello all,

My name is Jo Thomas. If you've read my other books, you know you're in for a story about food and love, with a splash of sun, a dollop of fun stirred in and a cast of characters I hope you'll fall in love with. If you're new to my world, you're very welcome. I hope you're here to stay!

I was once at one of my favourite restaurants in Puglia, Southern Italy, where I wrote my second book *The Olive Branch*. The owner brought around a bottle of limoncello, a wonderful Italian lemon liquor, at the end of the meal with glasses for us all. As he pulled up a chair, he asked what kind of books I wrote. He didn't speak any English and I didn't speak much Italian, but I explained that my books were about food and love, because I have always felt that the two are intertwined. He told me that for him, life was all about the food that he and his family grew on the land, cooked in the kitchen and served on the table. He held out his arm to the olive grove surrounding us, gestured to the *forno* in the kitchen, where the burning wood was glowing orange and merrily pumping smoke out of the chimney, and slapped his hand down on the scrubbed, wooden table, *la tavola*. 'For the ones we love', he told me as he held his hand to his chest over his heart. And this is exactly the kind of book I like to write: about the food we grow to cook and put on the table for the ones we love. So, pull up a chair at my table.

You can find out more about me and my books and find out about my latest adventures at my website **www.jothomasauthor.com**, on Facebook **www.facebook.com/JoThomasAuthor** or on Twitter **@jo_thomas01**. Do get in touch, I'd love to hear from you.

Love Jo x

Q&A with Jo Thomas

What inspired you to start writing?
I've always loved telling stories, at dinner parties, recounting funny things that have happened to me, that sort of thing. But I never thought I could write. Until one day, I was working for Radio 2 and was making a series about people who had changed their lives. A man I was interviewing had given up his daily commute into London to retrain as a physiotherapist. He changed his life. He had a picture on his wall that asked what you would do if you could do anything and knew you wouldn't fail. He saw me looking at it and asked me what I'd do. Having interviewed the wonderful Jilly Cooper a few days earlier I said, 'Oh I'd be a writer,' and had no idea where that came from. Then when I finally had our three children and wanted a job I could do from the kitchen table I remembered his words and finally gave it try. Because every journey starts with the first step. What would you do if you could do anything and knew you wouldn't fail?

Where do your stories come from?
It's like walking into the pantry at home and wondering what I'm going to have for tea. I start with a food and a country I'd like to explore, that I'd like to taste if you like. I think once you discover the food of a place, it takes you by the hand and introduces you to the history, culture and people. It guides you round its city walls and is the very fabric of the community. So I start at the kitchen table. What are we eating and where did it come from? Because to me, the kitchen table is the heart of the home and where all of family life is played out.

Do you think visiting the places you write about is important?
Yes, I do. If you want to transport other people there, it's essential to be able to describe it. For me, it's often about the smell of a place. Smells are so important. But standing and taking in what you can see is important too. Like the colour of the soil, that's always a key detail to me. And how the place makes you feel.

What's the most extreme thing you've done in the aid of research?
Possibly reindeer racing, in a helmet, sitting on a sled, careering off down a track behind a bolting reindeer. I went on a research trip to Swedish Lapland with my friend, author Katie Fforde. We go on a lot of road trips together. But this was our best research trip yet. Thrilling and utterly invigorating. Or maybe it was the husky ride where we had a collision with another musher. Or maybe, riding over the ice road on a sled behind a snow mobile, listening for the cracks in the ice as it melted in places. It was amazing. The snow, the reindeer, the dogs, the feeling of being out in the wild. And that's where I set *A Winter Beneath the Stars*.

What's your most memorable holiday meal?
My 20th birthday. On the beach in the South of France. The sand between our toes, under an awning, beside a small kitchen and a storm picked up. The owners put down the sides of the awning and tied them together and told us to stay and carry on our meal. The storm did its worst, lashing the sides of the awing with wind and rain and thunder and lightning overhead as we ate, drank and laughed with the restaurant owners. It was a glorious birthday, and all the more special as it was the last one I spent with dear Dad.

Where are you going to next?
I'm just back from Sicily where I've been out visiting the citrus farms that grow all around Mount Etna. Did you know, you only get blood oranges from Sicily and it's the ash in the soil from Etna that makes them like that? The oranges there were just the best I have ever tasted, and I still find myself craving them now. The day we left the sun rose like a huge orange in the sky, as if leaving me with a permanent reminder of the fabulous citrus farms I'd found there.

Discover other books by

Jo Thomas

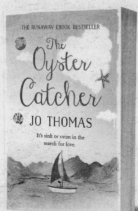

An irresistibly feel-good novel set on the charming coast of Ireland.

'A heart-warming tale full of Celtic charm, set against a beautiful landscape. What more could you wish for?' Ali McNamara

Can love bloom in the olive groves and vineyards of Italy?

'Romantic and funny, this is a great addition to any bookshelf!' *Sun*

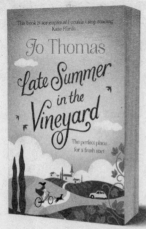

A gorgeous read filled with sunshine and wine in the South of France

'A fabulous French feast of fun' Milly Johnson

Let this novel transport you
straight to the breath-taking
mountains of Crete.

'Perfect escapist magic'
Good Housekeeping

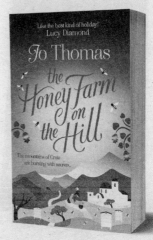

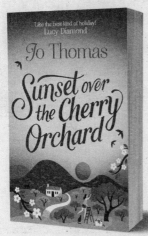

Escape to the sun-drenched
hills and cherry orchards of
southern Spain

'Warm, funny, romantic with
a terrific sense of place.
I loved it!'
Katie Fforde

Jo's novels are available in paperback, eBook and audio

Discover the novellas

An irresistible romance filled with love and laughter amongst the rolling green of the Kent countryside

A sparkling, feel-good short story set in the picturesque beauty of a Welsh costal village.

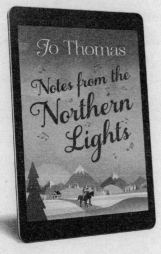

Dive into this gorgeous winter warmer, an irresistible winter tale set in Iceland that will melt the coldest of hearts...

Jo's novellas are available in eBook